PRAISE FOR T

'One of the most unusual and intense talents in the ...' Forshaw, *Independent*

'Spine-chilling and utterly unputdownable. Thomas Enger has created a masterpiece of intrigue, fast-paced action and suspense that is destined to become a Nordic Noir classic' Yrsa Sigurðardóttir

'Thomas Enger is one of the finest writers in the Nordic Noir genre, and this is his very best book yet. Outstanding' Ragnar Jónasson

'A gripping narrative that begs comparison to Stieg Larsson' *Bookpage*

'An intriguing new voice in crime' NJ Cooper

'Slick, compelling and taut, Thomas Enger combines layers of sophisticated mysteries with an intensely scarred hero embarked on a tragic quest. A dark and suspenseful blast of Nordic exposure' Chris Ewan

'*The Killing* took us by surprise, *The Bridge* was a good follow-up, but the political drama *Borgen* knocked spots off both. For readers who enjoy these Scandinavian imports, this novel is a treat ... the dialogue is sharp and snappy, and the characters seem to come alive in this sophisticated and suspenseful tale' Jessica Mann, *Literary Review*

'It has real strengths: the careful language, preserved in the fine translation, and its haunted journalist hero ... An intriguing series' *Guardian*

'From t[...] g emotional depths, [...] veReading

'Suspenseful, dark and gritty, this is a must-read' *Booklist*

'This promises to be a crime-fiction series worth watching' *Library Journal*

'Superbly compelling ... the characters leap right off the page, and the relationship between them is as twisted and complex as the story itself' Shotsmag

'Although the narration moves at scary speed, somehow the melancholy lingers and slows it down. If feels as if everything is just about to explode, and eventually it does in the shocking finale of the novel. For those who are as yet unfamiliar with the intense presence of Juul, I am sure that you will find elements of Jo Nesbø's fast-paced plots and brutal violence, touches of Karin Fossum's thoughtful questions on morality, and Jørn Lier Horst's portrayal of decent human beings caught in crime – all delivered in a gripping intriguing plot. Enger is an author to be treasured' Ewa Sherman, Crime Review

'Unexpected and surprising ... like a fire in the middle of a snowfall' *Panorama*

'I am always struck with the control of pace and plot that is a stand-out feature of his writing ... a real feel of storytelling in its purest form' Raven Crime Reads

'An excellent read ... fascinating' Journey of a Bookseller

'A fascinating addition to the Scandinavian Noir genre' Crimesquad

'It was stunning. It was patient, beautifully and precisely written, with a killer plot ... a really classy read' Louise Beech

'Satisfyingly tense and dark' *Sunday Times*

'It's clear the Henning Juul series has a large-scale plan and *Cursed* shows a great momentum, but it is the bombshell dropped in the very last sentence that carries his investigation one jaw-dropping step further and leaves you breathless for more' Crime Fiction Lover

'Thomas Enger writes with verve, colour and a pace that builds to a thrilling climax, cleverly and deftly weaving a complex of fictional elements into some uncomfortable details of his country's history. Highly recommended!' European Literature Network

'This is Nordic Noir at its best. Thomas grabs you by the throat with this one and I found the novel impossible to put down' Jacob Reviews Books

'A masterful depiction of what sits in the murky and sometimes frightening background of family lives' Ronnie Turner

'The vivid descriptions of Oslo and the surrounding landscapes are mesmerising; I felt that I could conjure clear images from the details given' The Quiet Knitter

'Gripping throughout … Thomas Enger is definitely a writer to watch out for. Remember the name!' Mrs Bloggs' Books

'Wonderfully written' P Turners' Book Blog

'The imagery created in this book, the descriptions of Oslo and the Norwegian landscape, the creation of individual character, are all brilliant … I could picture it all perfectly' Jen Med's Book Reviews

'With a tightly controlled plot, which is deeply moving at times, this is highly recommended' My Chestnut Reading Tree

'This book was all about surprises, from the subtle turns to the final shocking twist. It's certainly left me intrigued to read more' Off-the-Shelf Books

'An enjoyable thriller filled with suspense and surprises that will leave readers eager to read the fifth and final book in the series' The Norwegian American

'Waves of guilty, denial and anger wash around this suspenseful book' Blue Book Balloon.

'*Cursed* is a very well-written (and very well-translated) book in the best traditions of Nordic Noir. Thomas Enger is up there with the very best' TripFiction

'The tension kept mounting and mounting until things all came to a head in a spectacular conclusion. Then there was the very end, I'm talking about the last line ... Oh my God, did that throw me for a loop!' Novel Gossip

'A tightly written thriller that had me puzzling the clues throughout as the plot threads were untangled and then woven into place. An entertaining and suspenseful read' Never Imitate

'*Cursed* is dark and riveting, with a plot that zigs and zags through a twisting landscape of suspense, truth and lies. Brutal in places, but beautifully layered and plotted' Espresso Coco

'Brilliantly written and seamlessly translated' Have Books Will Read

'A gripping novel with strong characters. This complex backstory ... has had me buying Enger's previous volumes' The Crime Novel Reader

'The writing and story are gritty and hard hitting ... I thoroughly loved this book and I will definitely be going out to pick up the other Henning Juul books' Life of a Nerdish Mum

'Not since reading Stieg Larsson's *The Girl with the Dragon Tattoo* series have I felt so riveted by characters and plot … until now. And the ending … utter perfection!' It's Book Talk

'Enger has written a complicated, skillfully drawn story that rewards your close attention. This translation by Kari Dickson captures all the pared-back Nordic style of *The Bridge* or *The Killing*, combined with the most compelling chapter-end hooks I've encountered since reading *Harry Potter* to my children' Claire Thinking

'Thomas Enger's series reminds me why I love to read crime books. Its pacing is completely addictive, its characters are endearing and vivid, and it has that special something that makes me just plain happy to be reading. Scandinavian crime readers: Enger simply must be next on your reading list. Readers of any other kind of crime fiction: he should be your next read, too' Crime by the Book

'Enger's Norway is chilling … a crime-filled page-turner that doesn't disappoint' Words Shortlist

'A gripping thriller, plenty of twists and great characters to follow on the adventure. Dark, emotive and wonderfully written … kept this reader on the edge of his seat' Grab This Book

'Thomas Enger keeps you guessing right up to the end' Books, Life and Everything

'When I think of Nordic Noir, I think of cold climates, moody atmospheres, plots that are in equal measures dark and beautiful, books with the ability to capture, not only my interest but my heart too. After reading this book, in the above sentence, I can easily replace the phrase "Nordic Noir" with *Cursed* as this book encapsulated all that this genre is to me!' Keeper of Pages

'This book was exceptional. I am now adding more of Thomas Enger's books to my library' The Pages in Between

'Fantastic, believable characters … some you will love, some you will loathe. Beautifully atmospheric, completely gripping and full of intrigue … I can't wait for book five' DampPebbles

'Enger likes playing with language almost as much as he loves developing his characters, and there are times where he's clearly enjoying himself, but this never seems self-indulgent; indeed we readers are treated to fresh and vivid metaphor' Café Thinking

'For any fan of Nordic Noir Thomas Enger is a must-read' Liz Loves Books

'Thomas Enger teases the reader all the way along, revealing a little more with each chapter … This whip-smart shot of Nordic Noir is riveting and recommended reading' The Nut Press

'A tight, well-crafted read, skillfully translated by Kari Dickson … Through this tale Enger highlights beautifully how the echoes of the past are still heard in the present' Nordic Noir

'A complex, taught and thoroughly gripping read, Thomas Enger's *Cursed* is a first-rate, character-driven thriller that doesn't disappoint' Mumbling About…

'If this is Nordic Noir then I'm definitely a fan' The Belgian Reviewer

'With an oppressive atmosphere full of mystery and secrets, Thomas Enger has created a psychological thriller that will leave you stunned from the beginning till the end' Varietats

'The slow-burning tension soars in a deliciously addictive fashion. The dark tone paints a very atmospheric and gritty picture. *Cursed* also delivers one of my very biggest fictional temptations – a story where the secrets keep on unravelling' Book Drunk

'The end?! The last few lines? I needed to pick my jaw up off the floor. Please, Thomas Enger. Write quickly. My heart can't take it' Clues & Reviews

'Put simply, the more I read, the more I wanted to read' From First Page to Last

'From the stunning cover, to the atmospheric descriptions, all the way to that final page, I felt engaged and drawn into the story. The translation flowed well and I did not feel anything was lost. I've lately been savouring these dark, emotional Nordic Noirs and think it's due to the fact they have all come from the same fabulous publisher!' The Suspense Is Thrilling Me

'This is a thrilling crime read that is so multi-layered that – especially through the first, chilling opening pages – makes you wonder what really is going on, then it explodes in your hands … A powerful new Nordic crime writer' The Last Word Book Review

'Fast and furious, the type of book for which one chapter is never quite enough. And oh my God that bloody ending! Flipping amazing!' Emma the Little Book Worm

'With a captivating storyline, a couple of rather curious protagonists with their tragic history and some sharp and bleak writing, it is easy to whiz through *Cursed*' Northern Crime

'I may still be battered and bruised from this novel but, as I recover, it's a very satisfying' The Book Trail

'Craftily written and the translation is near perfect. The characters are fascinating with credible back stories. I can't wait to see the next book in this series!' Linda Strong

'This is one brilliantly constructed plot with various threads and layers that will keep you gripped right until the end' Novel Deelights

'There's a spell between those pages, and its power stems from the sophisticated writing style contrasting with the chilling and riveting crime it holds prisoner' Chocolate N Waffles

'A very enjoyable and satisfying read' Mrs Peabody Investigates

'The emotional roller-coaster is balanced out by the intricate criminal story and finely woven storyline. The book ends with a wee bit of a bookworm mousetrap by baiting the trap with a lovely morsel' Cheryl M-M's Book Blog

'The ending was a huge shock. I purposely covered the last paragraph with my hand so I didn't accidently see a name. And the name it revealed was one that had me aching for an immediate follow-up' Steph's Book Blog

'The plot is intricate, with several twists, the motive unusual and convincing, and the final scenes page-turning' Marsali Taylor, Promoting Crime

Killed

ABOUT THE AUTHOR

Thomas Enger is a former journalist. He made his debut with the crime novel *Burned* in 2010, which became an international sensation before publication. *Burned* is the first in a series of five books about the journalist Henning Juul, which delves into the depths of Oslo's underbelly, skewering the corridors of dirty politics and nailing the fast-moving world of 24-hour news. Rights to the series have been sold to 28 countries to date. In 2013 Enger published his first book for young adults, a dark fantasy thriller called *The Evil Legacy*, for which he won the U-prize (best book Young Adults). *Killer Instinct*, another YA suspense novel, was published in Norway in 2017. Rights have been sold to Germany and Iceland. Enger also composes music, and he lives in Oslo.

Follow him on Twitter @EngerThomas
on Facebook: *www.facebook.com/thomas.enger.77*
or visit: *thomasenger.net*

ABOUT THE TRANSLATOR

Kari Dickson grew up in Edinburgh, Scotland, but spent most of her summers in Norway with grandparents who couldn't speak English, so spoke Norwegian from an early age. She went on to read Scandinavian Studies at UCL. While working in theatre in London, she was asked to do literal translations of two Ibsen plays, which fuelled her interest in Norwegian literature and led to an MA in Translation at the University of Surrey. Having worked initially as a commercial translator, including some years at the central bank of Norway, she now concentrates solely on literature. Her portfolio includes literary fiction, crime, non-fiction and plays. Her translation of Roslund & Hellström's *Three Seconds* won the CWA International Dagger in 2011. Kari currently teaches Norwegian language, literature and translation in the Scandinavian Studies department at the University of Edinburgh.

Killed

THOMAS ENGER

Translated by Kari Dickson

**ORENDA
BOOKS**

Orenda Books
16 Carson Road
West Dulwich
London SE21 8HU
www.orendabooks.co.uk

First published in Norwegian as *Banesår* by Gyldendal, 2015
This edition published by Orenda Books, 2018
Copyright © Thomas Enger, 2015
English language translation copyright © Kari Dickson, 2017

ISBN 978-1-910633-99-1
eISBN 978-1-912374-00-7

This book has been translated with financial support from NORLA.

Typeset in Garamond by MacGuru Ltd
Printed and bound by CPI Group (UK) Ltd, Croydon CR0 4YY

For sales and distribution, please contact *info@orendabooks.co.uk*

Killed

Cast of Characters

HENNING JUUL – Reporter at *123news* who lost his son in a domestic fire in 2007. Scarred for life both physically and mentally he is now desperately trying to find those responsible for the fire.

JONAS JUUL KLEMETSEN – Henning's son. Died age six.

NORA KLEMETSEN – Henning's ex-wife and Jonas's mother. Works for the *Aftenposten* newspaper. Now in a relationship with Iver Gundersen and pregnant with his child.

IVER GUNDERSEN – Henning's closest colleague at *123news*. A reckless but clever reporter who has taken a special interest in Henning's case. Wants Henning's friendship and acknowledgment.

TRINE JUUL-OSMUNDSEN – Henning's estranged sister and former Secretary of Justice, who was photographed outside Henning's apartment on the night of the fire, as she was handing something over to Durim Redzepi.

DURIM REDZEPI – A gun-for-hire from Kosovo. Works for 'Daddy Longlegs' – a facilitator of criminal activity. Durim Redzepi is wanted for double murder in his home country.

TORE PULLI – Former gun-for-hire and latterly a highly successful real-estate broker in Oslo. Wrongfully sentenced to fourteen years in prison for a murder he didn't commit. Killed in prison. Henning Juul cleared his name post mortem, although Pulli was monitoring Henning's movements in the days leading up to the fire. Was married to Veronica Nansen.

VERONICA NANSEN – Former model who now runs a model agency. Discovered the photograph of Henning's sister among Tore's things.

ØRJAN MJØNES – Employed by 'Daddy Longlegs' to facilitate the murder of Tore Pulli. Currently in prison awaiting trial.

WILLIAM HELLBERG – Childhood friend of Tore Pulli. Lives in Tønsberg. Runs a very successful real-estate business, which has earned him millions. Grateful to both Henning and Nora as they recently managed to find his missing sister, Hedda, and get to the bottom of their aunt's murder in the late 1990s.

PREBEN MØRCK – Attorney-at-law. Long-time legal adviser to the Hellberg family.

CHARLIE HØISÆTHER – Tore Pulli's closest friend growing up. Had a falling out with Tore before Tore's arrest. Currently living in Natal, Brazil, where he makes a shady living laundering drug money and selling apartments to sun-seeking Norwegians.

RASMUS BJELLAND *aka* **ROGER BLYSTAD** – A carpenter who worked for Tore Pulli and Charlie Høisæther in the 1990s. Started to work for Charlie in Brazil as well, before vanishing off the face of the earth following a police operation where a number of thugs were arrested for money laundering. It was rumoured that Bjelland sold them out, trying to save his own skin.

BJARNE BROGELAND – Policeman. Henning Juul's friend from the small town of Kløfta.

ELLA SANDLAND – Bjarne Brogeland's closest colleague in the force.

PIA NØKLEBY – Assistant Chief of Police. Legally in charge of all of the investigations that take place in the Oslo police district.

ANN-MARI SARA – Forensics expert of Sami descent.

6TIERMES7 – Henning's secret online police source.

CHRISTINE JUUL – Henning and Trine's alcoholic mother. Suffers from Chronic Obstructive Pulmonary Disease. Widowed after her husband died, aged forty-four. It is believed he took his own life.

ALSO IN THIS BOOK

BODIL SVENKERUD – An old widow who lives in a posh neighbourhood in Oslo. Angry at Høisæther Real Estate for trying to force her to move.

ISABEL *aka* **CLÁUDIA ISABEL YPIRANGA** – Charlie Høisæther's girlfriend in Natal.

MARIANA DE LA ROSA – Rasmus Bjelland's wife. Deceased. Also the love of Charlie Høisæther's life.

FREDDY – Charlie Høisæther's driver and hired help.

HANSEMANN – A muscle-for-hire who works for Charlie Høisæther in Natal.

EDUARDO DE JESUS SILVA – A young Brazilian man who wants to work for Charlie.

LARS INDREHAUG – Ørjan Mjønes's defence attorney.

ANDREAS KJÆR – Policeman on call the night of the fire at Henning's apartment. Also Pia Nøkleby's lover.

HEIDI KJUS – Henning's boss at *123news*.

AGNES KLEMETSEN – Nora's mother.

JETON POCOLI – One of Durim Redzepi's friends and co-workers.

FLURIM AHMETAJ – Durim Redzepi's childhood friend from Kosovo, who also works with him in Oslo. Computer expert.

ANNE CECILIE HELLBERG – William Hellberg's wife. Works in a children's clothes shop in Tønsberg.

HELENE NÆSS – Rasmus Bjelland's love interest.

VANJA KVALHEIM – Rasmus Bjelland's mother.

Prologue

The body lying at Henning Juul's feet, in the bottom of the boat, was wrapped in two industrial rubbish bags. They had been pulled over at the head and the feet, and were sealed by several metres of silver-grey tape.

Henning tried not to think about the person inside. Instead he looked at the mist drifting in over the still, dark water – eerie wisps of white that seemed to reach out towards the shore. All he could hear were the oars breaking the surface and the drops of water that ran off the blades as the man in front of him lifted and lowered them. A pungent smell made Henning wonder if perhaps the lake had swallowed something old and rotten … and was struggling to digest it.

Henning liked water, but he didn't like forest lakes like this. They could hide anything – whatever his imagination might stretch to. And soon he would lie hidden here too…

The boat glided slowly over the water. Henning looked at the man in front of him, at his short, messy hair, the ripple of his arm muscles. Durim Redzepi had been hunting him for a long time. Now, finally, he would be able to finish the job he'd be given.

It had been a long and strenuous journey to get to this point. When Henning looked back at all the events that had unfolded, he knew that all of them had occurred because he had chosen to return to work two years after the fire in which his son Jonas was killed. By doing so – by investigating the Henriette Hagerup case – Henning had managed to turn the spotlight on his own scarred face. And Tore Pulli had been alerted to the fact that Henning was back in business as an investigative journalist.

Pulli, a former muscle-for-hire turned real-estate broker, was serving fourteen years in prison for a murder he didn't commit.

Desperate to clear his name, he had reached out to Henning, claiming to know the people responsible for Jonas's death. If Henning would help him, he had said, if Henning would find the real killer and clear Pulli's name, he would then disclose what he knew about the fire.

Of course he'd jumped at the chance, Henning mused. Why wouldn't he? But Pulli was killed in jail before Henning could meet his end of the bargain – and before Pulli had revealed the miserable secret he was harbouring. But the flood gates had been opened. What Henning had suspected all along had been correct: someone had set fire to his apartment. He was going to get to the bottom of it all, no matter what – without Pulli's help, and despite the fact that memory loss meant Henning couldn't recall the stories he had been following in the weeks leading up to that fateful day.

He'd worked with all the tunnel vision of a bereaved parent. Henning could see that now. He had finally managed to find an interview he had conducted in those weeks – with a carpenter who had been working for Charlie Høisæther, a friend of Pulli's in the Brazilian real-estate business. This carpenter – Rasmus Bjelland – had fled Brazil following a police operation that had led to the arrest of several hard-hitting Norwegian gang members, who were laundering their drug money through apartment businesses in the Brazilian seaside city of Natal. These thugs were convinced it was Bjelland who had provided the cops with key information about their operations, and a price was put on his head.

Henning managed to track the carpenter down, but in the interview Bjelland had maintained his innocence. Even now, Henning could clearly remember believing him. And that was one of the points at which his investigation changed. The carpenter also told Henning that if he dug a little deeper into Tore Pulli's past, he might just find out that he still had at least one foot in the criminal world. Go back to the 1990s, Bjelland told Henning, then you'll see what kind of transactions Pulli was involved in when he first started to make a name for himself in real estate.

The bit firmly between his teeth – the truth of his boy's death within reach, but still obscured – Henning was impelled to follow every lead, to rattle every cage, to put himself at risk. And he didn't regret one single moment of that investigation. When he discovered that Pulli had been sitting in a car outside Henning's apartment for three nights in a row before the day of the fatal fire, taking pictures and monitoring Henning's movements, he became certain that it was Pulli's business partners who were trying to prevent him from digging into the truth about Bjelland, the real-estate business in the Brazil, the drugs money and much, much more.

But it seemed these associates of Pulli would go to any lengths to silence anyone they thought might expose them. Not only was Pulli killed in prison, but a police report about Pulli's actions on the night of the fire had also been altered by someone with access to the classified records. And Durim Redzepi – the very man now sitting in front of Henning in the boat – had been hired to track Henning down and to end his life once and for all.

After narrowly dodging two attempts on his life, Henning continued his quest with ever greater intensity, knowing that time was working against him. He had been unable to give up, driven by memories and love for his dead son. He hung his head, putting together the pieces that had led him to this boat. Pulli's widow, Veronica Nansen, had supported his quest, and alerted him to another childhood friend of Pulli's, William Hellberg – also a highly successful real-estate broker. After Henning and his ex-wife Nora had managed to find William's missing sister Hedda, William, as a way of saying thank-you, disclosed that Pulli had broken Charlie Høisæther's jaw during a fight about an apartment in Natal, and that the two of them were no longer friends.

The details provided by Hellberg made Henning certain that Høisæther was the man behind it all – that there were secrets in his life so dark, deep and dangerous, he would stop at nothing to protect them, including killing his old friend and business partner, Pulli. Henning had even believed that his own sister, Trine, had been involved in this tragic story, as Tore Pulli had taken a photograph of her outside Henning's apartment on the night of the fire, handing something over to Durim Redzepi.

All of this felt like a lifetime ago, Henning thought to himself. But it had, in fact, all happened within the space of a short summer – just a few crazy weeks. And that was enough to bring him here. To his certain death.

During the last few hours everything had changed. And now, he was reconciled to his fate. He was convinced he could now die satisfied. His quest was over. He finally had the answers he'd been looking for.

None of them would bring Jonas back. None of them would take away the pain that lingered in his chest. Everything that meant anything to him belonged to the past now: the years he'd been a father; the years he'd been allowed to love Nora; the years she'd loved him.

Still, it was hard to let go, he thought, as the boat slid over the surface of the lake. He wondered if it would hurt. How it would all happen in the end.

No matter what, Henning told himself, *die silently. Die with dignity. Don't show him you're afraid.*

Redzepi took a few strokes with just one oar, the other resting, so the boat turned round. Then it stood still, the water lapping quietly at the prow. He pulled the oars in and got a hold of the body. He lifted it as though it weighed nothing, and threw it overboard like a bag of rubbish.

A heavy weight was attached to the body by a thick, rust-coloured rope. Redzepi dropped it into the water and the black plastic bundle immediately disappeared from sight.

Redzepi, businesslike and calm, then grabbed the rope coiled at his feet and started to tie a noose. He went to the back of the boat, pulled a grey concrete block from under a white tarpaulin, and put it down in front of him. There was a thick blue handle cast in the concrete. Redzepi fed the rope through it, then, without a single word, attached it to Henning's right ankle.

It all seemed so simple, so practical, and Henning wondered if he should put up a fight. But his shoulder still ached. How on earth was he going to overcome a man with a knife and a gun?

Redzepi lifted the concrete block over the edge of the boat and dropped it into the water. The dull splash broke the silence that covered the lake like a blanket. The rope vanished quickly into the depths, as though strong hands were pulling it from below. Then Redzepi put his feet on what was left of the coiled rope at the bottom of the boat and stood up.

'Your turn,' he said, as if they were playing some kind of game.

Henning tried to stand up, but his legs wouldn't do as they were told; he couldn't feel them, couldn't feel his feet in his shoes, the fabric of his trousers against his thighs.

'Come on. I haven't got all day,' said Redzepi, then casually pulled out a gun and pointed it at Henning. He made a 'get-up' gesture.

Henning nodded and tried to push himself up. He succeeded this time. But the sudden movement made the boat rock. Henning had to step forwards to regain his balance. He took a deep breath and looked up again.

It was hard to see anything. The mist had come down now, obscuring the shore. It had to be thirty metres or more to land.

He cocked his head, thinking he heard something – a splash or something moving in the water. But it was nothing. There were no cars approaching. No branches snapping in the forest. No shouts that might bring a different fate from the one that was now so unavoidable.

Henning put a foot on the edge of the boat and made sure he was steady, even though the vessel rocked a little again.

The surface of the water in front of him was glossy. A thick, cold oil slick. The rope pulled down into it like a fishing line, heavy with new catch.

He jumped.

He held his breath and as soon as he felt the cold water envelop him, he started to kick, trying to push his way up. But the weight was pulling him down. He mustered all the strength he could and kicked hard with his legs. They surprised him by doing what he wanted them to. He managed to slow his descent, then centimetre by centimetre he used his good arm to thrust his way back up. He broke the surface of the water with a gasp.

He blinked furiously and gulped down air, trying to orient himself as he paddled and kicked and thrashed with one arm, not sure that he'd be able to withstand the pull of the weight that was dragging him downwards.

Henning stretched his neck and tried to breathe at the same time.

Then he found himself looking at the boat. He saw Redzepi lift his gun and aim, and it dawned on him that this man didn't need to worry about blood or any traces of Henning anymore. In no more than a few seconds the muzzle of the gun would flash and Henning's head would explode.

He pictured Nora's smile, her beautiful face, the shine of her short hair. Her voice that made his body tingle. The warmth of her hands, how small they were.

He thought about Iver, and about Trine – about them playing in the water together at the cabin in Stavern, seeing who could hold their breath the longest.

And that was when he suddenly stopped kicking and let the water wrap round him like a shroud. He knew that no personal best time would help him now. That no one, nothing, could save him. And that he would rather die on his own terms.

That's why he closed his eyes and let himself slowly sink down into the cold, black nothingness.

1
January 1996

Had it not been for the snow, it would have been pitch dark. The cars were tightly parked along the edge of the pavement, and the buildings towered into the sky. The street lights had either been turned off or were not working.

If she hadn't lived there for over 50 years, Bodil Svenkerud might have been afraid – a lot went on after dark on the streets of Oslo these days.

But not in Eckersbergs gate.

She had never been afraid of anything there, and now she just wanted to get home and have a lovely cup of hot tea. It had been a long day.

Mrs Svenkerud urged her legs to keep moving on the soft snow. It was a disgrace that the roads and pavements weren't cleared sooner and more often; she had the feeling they always left her street until last. The slippery, dry powder snow had brought her more or less to a standstill.

That was why when she spotted a gap between two parked cars, she went out into the middle of the road – after all, it was her street – having checked both ways first. She saw a car coming slowly towards her, but it was still some distance away. She had time, she reckoned, before the car got close, and even though she could feel there was ice under the snow, it was still easier to walk in the tyre tracks.

Mrs Svenkerud pulled her fur coat tighter, looked up at the building that was in front of her on the right, where she had lived for so long. This was where they had had their wedding party in 1957 – they couldn't afford anything else. This was where they had had their children, and later played with their grandchildren, where life had raced by like a high-speed train. This was where the cancer cells had invaded Olav Sebastian's body and reduced him to a morose, sick shadow of the great man he'd once been, a man who'd engaged in local politics, who'd run eight kilometres three nights a week, even when he was over 70, and who'd loved going for walks in Frogner Park on Sundays, especially when pushing little Sofus in his pram. This was where he'd said his final goodbye one beautiful late summer day in 1992.

There were lights on in some of the windows up on the third floor. So they'd started already, the joiners, but she was not going to let anyone force her out. She most certainly was not!

That was what she'd told the young adviser in Oslo Council as well, the one who hadn't had time for her at first, but then had managed to squeeze in 15 minutes at the end of the day. The beautiful girl with dark hair – what was her name again? – had promised to take up her case as soon as she got to work in the morning. Were there no limits to how shameless people could be these days?

Mrs Svenkerud pressed on, and swung her arms to help her move faster. She was getting warm, and a thin layer of condensation had formed on the inside of her spectacles. She could just make out the crossing about 30 metres in front of her.

She looked back. The car was much closer now. Mrs Svenkerud tried to walk faster, but the snow was so loose and soft that it was hard to get a firm footing. She almost lost her balance, but fortunately managed to stay on her feet.

She looked round again. The car seemed to have speeded up. Surely the driver had seen her, with all the safety reflectors she was wearing?

She tried to wave at him, but the driver didn't slow down; in fact, he did the opposite, and that was when she realised the car was going to knock her down.

She made a last-ditch attempt to get out of the way, but the ice was deceptive and slippery under her winter boots, and she didn't manage to move before the car hit her side-on, throwing her up onto the bonnet. Her back was to the windscreen and she was forced up onto the roof, where she lay still for a brief second before the winter tyres bit into the ice as the wheels locked. She was thrown forward onto the bonnet again, and then rolled down onto the road, where she landed with her face in the soft, cold snow.

She couldn't move, though strangely enough, it didn't hurt; it was as though her whole body had been numbed. But she was bleeding from a cut on her forehead, and soon the whole side of her face was warm. The impact had also damaged one of the buttons on her hearing aid, and it was whining loudly, piercing her eardrum.

Mrs Svenkerud managed to haul herself up onto her knees. She felt the cold and damp seep through her trousers and long johns. She lifted her head and straightened her glasses, turned around and squinted at the car with its engine still running. She hadn't noticed until now, but in the beam from the headlights, she saw that big white flakes had started to fall again.

Why didn't the driver get out to help her?

The car reversed a few metres, then headed for her again. She couldn't get out of its way; she knew she wouldn't make it in time, even though the studded tyres were spinning on the ice and snow. Shouting wouldn't help. She braced herself for the pain, and when it came, it was intense and paralysing. The weight and speed of the car made her skid across the road until she stopped close to the kerb.

And there she lay, unable to move while cold, white kisses melted on her burning cheeks. The glass in her spectacles was smashed and she could barely see. Fortunately, the ringing in her ears stopped and was replaced by silence, bringing with it a diamond-like certainty.

She knew what this was about.

There was no doubt about it.

She only hoped that the bright, helpful girl at Oslo Council – what was her name again? – would realise as well. That she would hear about this, and do something.

Trine, Mrs Svenkerud remembered as the car headed towards her again.

The girl in the council offices was called Trine.

Trine Juul.

2

October 2009

The light seeped in through the white curtains and bathed the bed in a faint shimmer. The woman lying next to Charlie Høisæther turned slightly and breathed in sleepily through her nose.

'You're awake already?' she said in a drowsy voice, her face against the pillow.

'Mm,' he replied.

The light paled her cheeks as she curled up in a ball and pulled the thin duvet tighter. She stretched out a warm hand and found Charlie's soft belly.

'You always wake up so early,' she mumbled.

'Mm. You just go back to sleep.'

The curtains in front of the open window billowed in the wind that blew tirelessly off the Atlantic Ocean. The sound of the constant traffic rose all the way up to the fifteenth floor from the street below. Isabel opened her eyes, brown and dark. Charlie felt her look at him, more awake than before.

'You were so restless last night,' she said. 'Were you dreaming?'

He shook his head.

'What was it then?'

'Nothing. You just go back to sleep.'

The truth was that he'd barely slept at all. There was so much going on at the moment. Tore was dead, and that journalist kept phoning and leaving messages. 'Hi, I'd like to talk to you about Tore Pulli.' 'Hi, I'd like to arrange a time when I can talk to you.' 'Hi, would it be possible to have a few words about Rasmus Bjelland?'

No, it would not be possible.

Not at all.

And then there was the leisure complex they wanted to build, if only they could find the right place.

'But now that I'm awake,' Isabel said, and moved her hand, 'don't you think you should do something about it?'

She pressed her fingers a little harder against his stomach, just above the belly button, then moved down, but he barely reacted. Isabel pulled her hand back, turned onto her front and cupped her chin in her palms.

'Tired?' she asked affectionately.

'Just a bit,' Charlie said, grateful that she didn't make a drama out of it. Instead she snuck a hand over to his chest this time, stroked the hairs down, then up towards his neck, chin, gently tugged at the stubble there and ran a more curious finger over his scar.

'Don't,' he said, pulling his head back.

'Sorry.'

He pushed the duvet to one side and swung his feet down onto the cool, hard tiles on the floor, stood up and walked naked over to the window. Put his ear to his left shoulder, then the other to the right. There was a crack.

'I'm sorry,' she said again.

'It's fine. You just go back to sleep.'

He lit up a cigarette and went out onto the terrace, where he was greeted by a clear, blue sky. The floor tiles here were already warm and burned the soles of his feet. He leaned against the railings. The rare shower they'd had last night had dried up long ago. The smell of dusty asphalt and rubbish rose up from the street below.

Charlie took a drag on the cigarette and looked out over the shining, silver ocean. From a distance, it didn't look like the water was moving; it just lay there glittering, apparently smooth. Soon the beautiful wide beaches would start to fill up. Soon the local boys would meet to play football, filled with the dream of becoming the new Neymar or Pelé. People would buy chilled snowballs, chocolate and cigarettes, and lie dozing until the sun dipped down below the horizon again.

This was Natal.

Sun city.

The average temperature here was 28°C, with 300 days of sun a year. The town had previously been home to both Indians and French pirates, this town that he had helped to develop – certainly in terms of sun-seeking Norwegians.

It had all been a bit of an adventure, really, a dangerous one. They had played for high stakes, particularly in recent years. People had ended up in jail. Lives had been lost. But now things were back to where they'd been when they started in the late nineties. The way Tore wanted things to be.

Charlie looked over at the neighbouring terrace. The flat was still empty. A few dried leaves had been blown all the way up here to the fifteenth floor – he must remember to send someone round to sweep them away before the next viewing. He always felt a stab of guilt whenever he thought that they could have been neighbours, Tore and him, and that they could have stood each on their own side of the shoulder-high wall that divided the two terraces, with an ice-cold beer in their hands, looking out over the ocean while they reminisced about the good old days. When their bank accounts were filling up nicely and they partied practically every night.

But too much had happened between them. Things had been said and done that couldn't be undone. Tore should perhaps still have got the flat. At the end of the day, he'd earned it.

Charlie put a hand to his chin and felt the scar that Tore had given him, looked down at the street and sucked in some more nicotine. A man was out running, his bare chest already gleaming in the morning sun. Old cars, discoloured by sand and rust, sped by.

Charlie's eyes fixed on a dark Audi that was parked in the shade of a palm tree. The same car that had been in the same place every morning for the past few days. From up here it was impossible to tell if anyone was sitting inside. And it was always gone by the time

Charlie came down to start his day, but he decided he'd get Freddy to check it out.

Charlie stubbed his cigarette against the wall and flicked it out over the railing. He watched it fall, slowly, down towards the street until it was caught by a gust of wind and blown onto another terrace. He went into his enormous flat, where the walls were as naked as the woman in his bed, who raised herself up onto her elbows. The duvet still covered her stomach, slim hips and legs.

'Hi,' she said, and brushed a long curl of black hair from her eyes.

'Hi,' he said.

Charlie pulled on a pair of shorts and some sandals.

'What's up?' she asked.

'Nothing.'

'Are you sure? You're so … distant these days.'

'I'm going to make coffee,' he said. 'Do you want some?'

She pushed the duvet aside, revealing a suntanned body. Charlie didn't look at her, nor did he get an answer. A few moments later, he was in the kitchen.

'I wouldn't mind a cup of tea,' she called after him.

Charlie had met Isabel in the bar at Praia dos Artistas. She'd sent him stolen glances all evening, and when she later came over and said, in her broken Brazilian English, that she was a dancer and she'd like to show him what she could do – 'but preferably somewhere else' – he'd just assumed she was a prostitute.

But she was in fact looking for a job, and when she told him her name was Cláudia Isabel Ypiranga – 'but everyone calls me Isabel' – he'd turned and studied her dark skin, the Indian features, her long slender body. He'd seen the need in her eyes and wondered what poverty she'd suffered in the course of her barely 25 years, but most of all, he had seen who she looked like, and he'd felt a strange and rare need to be kind.

That was five months ago.

Now she danced at Senzuela six nights a week, and then came home to him.

To begin with, everything had been fine; for a while he'd even thought he might fall in love with her, but then one day he'd admitted to himself that she would never be Mariana. He'd been thinking of ending the relationship for a while, but hadn't managed to do it. He liked her, after all. Appreciated her company and gorgeous body, as long she didn't do anything stupid like get pregnant. He presumed he'd miss her if she wasn't there, and he liked the thought that he'd saved her from … well, something. He'd never really asked about her life up to that point, what she'd done. Perhaps he should.

Charlie took a cup of chai latte back into the bedroom. He'd made it just the way he knew she liked it.

'Thank you,' she said. 'You're so good to me.'

If only you knew, Charlie thought, as he pulled on a white t-shirt that stretched tight over his belly.

He noticed her watching him over the edge of the cup.

'So, what's happening today?' she asked in a bright, expectant voice.

Charlie took a deep breath which he released as a long sigh.

'Exactly the same as yesterday,' he replied.

∵

The dark Audi was gone when Charlie emerged onto the pavement. Instead, Freddy was standing there waiting in his usual jeans, t-shirt and light-brown linen blazer. Freddy was actually called Fred Are, and was from Oslo, but had taken his muscles and gun with him to Natal. Everyone in town knew he was on Charlie's payroll, so not someone you wanted to cross. And no one tried, largely because of the gun that was always in its holster underneath his jacket.

'I want you to post a man under that palm tree over there,' Charlie said and pointed. 'There's been a black Audi in that parking space for the past three nights.'

'Very good, boss.'

'I want the driver's name and who he's working for, if anyone.'

'Very good, boss.'

Charlie looked around. Then he got into Freddy's car, a Mercedes CLS Grand Edition, and they sped off through the streets. It was impossible for Freddy to stick to the speed limit – it was against his nature – but it didn't matter, because the police wouldn't dream of stopping them anyway.

'So, where are we going?' he asked.

'The club first,' Charlie said. 'And take an extra turn around the block before we get there.'

Freddy glanced over at him, but said nothing.

They drove through the town as it was starting to wake up. When they passed Juan's shop, someone came out carrying fruit, bread and drinks. A boy of around nine or ten had just got an inflatable killer whale and was tearing off the plastic packaging when his mother stopped him with a firm hand. They passed Pepe the fishmonger, on his small ancient moped that spewed out black clouds of exhaust, on his way to the harbour for the night's catch.

Charlie liked this time of day, when it hadn't quite started yet and the temperature was bearable. It was still possible to get things done when you were up early in Natal.

For the past few months, Charlie had been focused on drumming up funds for a new leisure centre where people could skate, bowl, play minigolf – everything under one roof. There would be restaurants and shops there too – it would be unlike anything else in Natal. A recreational oasis. Several investors had already said that they wanted to be part of the project, but Charlie hadn't found the right place yet. He had seen a few good possibilities in the past couple of weeks, but so far none of the owners had been willing to sell.

Charlie would continue to build residential complexes – it was clearly the best business in the area – but it was also smart to have more than one iron in the fire.

Ten minutes later, they stopped outside a fitness club. Freddy went in first and scouted the place, then gave Charlie a nod.

Charlie got out into the sunshine. Two women in their mid-thirties

walked slowly by. One of them turned to look at Charlie, then sa̶
something to her friend. Charlie automatically followed them with
his eyes, assessed their shoes, ankles, legs, behinds – trying to ascer-
tain if they'd bought their fuckability or if it was natural.

A curtain twitched on the other side of the street. Freddy stepped
out into the road and squared his shoulders. A car that was coming
towards them braked. Charlie didn't even look at the driver, just
carried on across the road and into the club. There he was met with
bass rhythms, sparkling mirrors and the thud of weights. Charlie
walked through the gym without looking at any of the people who
were there, and straight into the office – a small cupboard of around
eight square metres that was in desperate need of a revamp, but
Charlie didn't see the point. He liked the fact that there was paper
everywhere, that there were cracks in the walls – it reminded him
of the early days in Norway when he couldn't pay the bills, before
Høisæther Property found its feet and then sprouted wings.

The only thing that was a must was a top-end computer, and he
was more than happy with his latest procurement – the fastest iMac
model Apple had on the market. Charlie liked the contrast between
the stylish 27-inch screen and the shabby room.

'There's a flight landing from Amsterdam at 19:35 this evening,'
he told Freddy when he'd shut the door. 'I want you to collect one
of the passengers.'

Freddy smiled; he knew full well it wasn't the passenger that they
needed to get out of the airport, but rather the money that was glued
to his body.

'Shall I take Hansemann with me?'

'No.'

'But he's the one who usually takes care of customs. I…'

Charlie turned abruptly towards Freddy.

'I've got another job for Hansemann. You'll go alone.'

Freddy hesitated for a moment, then he nodded.

'Anything else you want me to do today, boss?'

Charlie sighed.

'There's the Audi.'

'Very good, boss. I'll get on to it right away.'

And a few minutes later, Charlie was alone in the office. He looked at the clock. Four o'clock in the morning in Norway. He wondered how everything was going at home, but it was too early to call Daddy Longlegs.

Charlie leaned back in the chair. Stared at the screen in front of him, which was currently black, saw his own reflection, the white hair, the blue eyes, the beard.

He'd been sitting here, exactly like this, when Mariana had come in for the first time.

'Hi,' she'd said. 'My name is Mariana de la Rosa. You need an assistant.'

'Do I?'

Charlie hadn't advertised for anyone at the time, but then he never did.

'Yes, you do,' she'd replied. 'Just looking round this office, I can see four things that need to be done immediately.'

'Right.'

He'd straightened up.

'First of all, you've got all your appointments written down there.'

She'd pointed to the diary that was lying open in front of him.

'No one uses them anymore.'

'Really?'

'I can put all that information on your computer, and then you'll get a message on your mobile phone 10 minutes before you have to leave.'

'Hm,' was his response, as he thought about it.

'You also need a system for your receipts. Invoices. They're all over the place. I can sort them out for you.'

Charlie had become increasingly curious about this tall, slim woman with jet-black hair and a slightly pointy chin – and not just because she had brown eyes that tempted him like an advert for caramel chocolate, but also because there was a resoluteness about her, she had opinions – and he realised she wasn't afraid to air them.

'You're a man who can't tidy up after himself,' she'd continued.

'Am I?'

She'd pointed at the two coffee cups on the table, both stained black. There was a plate by his mouse, with a scrunched-up baguette bag. An empty cigarette packet. An ashtray full to the rim with ash and stubs.

'I'm good at tidying.'

Then she'd stopped talking, and just stood there looking at him.

'But you're not very good at counting,' he'd pointed out.

'Sorry?'

'You said there were *four* things you could help me with.'

'Oh.'

Then she'd smiled for the first time and her whole face had changed, opened. This person whom he'd initially thought was quite hard and angular, now revealed a playful side.

'I forgot. Your t-shirt,' she said, pointed at what he was wearing. Charlie had looked down at his belly.

'You should keep a couple here in a drawer,' she said. 'In case…'

Then she stopped herself and lowered her eyes.

'Sorry,' she said. 'It's none of my business to…'

'Not at all,' Charlie assured her. 'You're right. Spaghetti sauce stains don't look good when you're meeting clients.'

She'd looked up at him again and flashed another smile.

She had started the following day, Mariana de la Rosa, and stayed with him for just over three years. Until she found love. Until she was killed. And even though Charlie hadn't attached the explosives to her car, he should have known what might happen.

And that was what haunted him at night.

3

Henning Juul stared at the screen in front of him, convinced that it couldn't be right. But when he checked the date and time again, there was no doubt: Trine, his own sister, had been outside the building where he lived only 10 minutes before Jonas died.

She had given something to Durim Redzepi – a man Henning was sure had tried to kill him at least twice, and who he now also believed was responsible for setting fire to his home. Then she'd driven off.

Henning understood why Veronica Nansen had insisted that he sit down before looking through the 213 photographs that her late husband, Tore Pulli, had taken in the three days before Jonas's death. It was hard to breathe and Henning felt hot all over.

He sat back and tried to think.

How the hell would Trine know a guy like Redzepi, who was wanted for a double murder in his own county? And what had she given to him?

'Are you OK?'

Veronica Nansen's voice was cautious, but warm.

'Stupid question, really,' she corrected herself. 'Is there anything I can do?'

Henning leaned forward and took a sip of water from the glass she'd put down in front of him.

'No,' he replied. 'Not sure that there is.'

He looked at the photograph of Trine again.

'What are you going to do?' Veronica asked, and put a hand on his shoulder. Henning used the arm of his shirt to wipe the sweat from his face.

'I don't know,' he said. At the same time, he thought about Trine, who was in the Bahamas right now, recuperating from the scandal that had forced her to step down as Minister of Justice.

'I've got a suggestion,' Veronica said, sitting up straight. 'Let's go through everything that you know and think you know. Anything you're not sure about.'

She closed the laptop.

'I'm sure you've done it a hundred times before, but let's go through it all again anyway. Maybe you'll get more out of it if you say it out loud to someone else.'

Henning had only ever discussed his case with two people before: Bjarne Brogeland and Iver Gundersen – one was a policeman and the other, Nora's boyfriend and a fellow journalist at *123News*. Iver, in particular, had tried to help him; Henning had even spent some nights on his sofa recently.

Henning didn't really want to involve anyone else, but Veronica had, after all, found bits and pieces in Tore's belongings that had proved to be leads that progressed Henning's investigation. And now she'd found photographs that went a long way to proving Trine's involvement in the whole thing. Veronica had also shown herself to be a good sounding board.

So Henning half turned towards her and said, 'I think it started with Rasmus Bjelland.'

For many years, Bjelland had worked as a carpenter for Charlie Høisæther, one of Tore's old friends and business contacts, first in Norway and then in Natal, Brazil, after Charlie moved there in 1996. Together they'd earned good money building apartment complexes for sun-worshipping Norwegians, but many of those who had bought themselves a pied-à-terre in Natal were known criminals.

Then, in 2007, a joint Norwegian-Brazilian police operation had resulted in a good number of them being arrested on charges of fraud and money laundering, and not long after, a rumour had started that it was Bjelland who had provided the police with the information that led to the arrests. A price was put on his head. Bjelland fled.

As a crime journalist, Henning had heard about the conflict, and after a lot of digging, he had finally managed to get hold of Bjelland and get an interview. In the interview, Bjelland had claimed that he was not an informer, and had tipped Henning off that Tore Pulli, who had previously been one of Norway's most notorious enforcers, but had since gone on to become a very successful property developer, still had close ties with people in the criminal world. Tore's existence as a law-abiding businessman was apparently a facade, and Bjelland was certain that he was responsible for the loss of a number of lives. Henning had, without much success, tried to get Bjelland to expand on this claim.

'Let me stop you right there,' Veronica said.

Henning, who had been sitting staring at the table in front of him as he spoke, looked over at her. The skin on her face had taken on a reddish hue.

'Basically, you're saying that Tore was still a criminal after he'd stopped being an enforcer? That he killed people?'

Henning held up his hands.

'That's what Bjelland claimed,' he said, 'not me.'

'I lived with him for five years,' Veronica snapped. 'I would have known if he was still breaking the law in some way.'

'Maybe, but if you look at the people around him, Veronica, the people he trained with, for example, there aren't many of them who would fall into the "mummy's blue-eyed boy" category. And is it really so hard to imagine that Tore may have been tempted to earn some extra money now and then? We both know that he had a gambling habit in the last years of his life.'

Veronica didn't answer, but sat back in her chair and crossed her arms. Henning could understand why she was so defensive. Tore had hung up his knuckle-dusters long before he met her, and had been very successful in the property market throughout the nineties and into the noughties. But he had also kept his gambling secret from her and he had not been 100 per cent honest about his past as an enforcer.

'I think that I'd started digging around, based on Bjelland's tip-off, just before the fire in my flat.'

She bristled.

'So you think Tore had something to do with the fire in your flat?'

There was an offended sting to her voice. Henning wasn't sure if it was due to him or her dead husband.

He shook his head and pointed at the computer.

'Why was he sitting in a car only a few metres away taking photographs then?' he asked. And before she could answer: 'I think maybe Tore had plans to do something, but then someone else beat him to it.'

'Who?'

Henning took a quick breath.

'Charlie Høisæther, possibly. Bjelland said that I had to go back to the nineties, that I had to look at Tore's acquisitions, and that if I dug around a bit, I would find plenty of dirt. I didn't actually uncover much at the time, but I did find out later that Tore did a number of deals with Charlie Høisæther around then, and that often the deals were done without the full details being reported to the Norwegian authorities. According to my source, they made an incredible amount of money for a while, and they were apparently without scruples.'

Veronica's eyes were guarded.

'Unscrupulous enough to take lives, you mean?'

Henning shrugged.

'I don't know. What I do know is that Tore and Charlie were not on talking terms for the last year that Tore was alive. Which could explain why they each had their own strategy for getting rid of me. Tore had one plan – he followed me to find out the best time to get me – whereas Charlie hired Durim Redzepi to do the job for him.'

'I'm a little confused, Henning – do you mean that Tore or Charlie, or even both, were scared that you might discover something serious about them? An unsolved murder, embezzlement, money laundering – what are you actually saying?'

'I don't know,' Henning said. 'For the moment, I'm just thinking out loud.'

'But why were you such a danger to them then?'

Henning had asked himself the same question many times in recent months. Veronica continued before he could say anything: 'Everyone knows that when a journalist is killed, the media gives it even more attention. There's more pressure on the police and they have to put in extra resources. It's an enormous risk to take, so I don't quite understand why they'd do that, if you didn't know anything.'

'Not yet, no. But I might find out.'

Veronica sighed.

The best thing, Henning thought, would be to talk to Rasmus Bjelland again, but no one had seen or heard of him for over two years now. It was quite possible that the death sentence he had hanging over him when Henning talked to him, had been fulfilled.

'But Bjelland worked closely with Charlie for years,' he said. 'Which might explain how he knew something about it.'

'But it doesn't explain why he would snitch on Tore?'

'No,' Henning said, picking up the glass of water again. 'But I've got a theory about that.'

He took a drink, turned a little, so his torso was facing her.

'I think Bjelland wanted revenge.'

Deep furrows appeared on Veronica's brow.

'Revenge?'

Henning nodded.

He let this lie while Veronica processed it herself.

'Why on earth would Bjelland want revenge on Tore?'

'I don't know yet,' Henning admitted. 'But just think about it,' he continued. 'Why would he say something like that to me otherwise? To be nice to me? To give me a scoop that would be printed in the paper?'

He saw no answer in Veronica's eyes.

'Bjelland and I had absolutely nothing to do with each other – he had no reason to tip me off about anything, certainly not something as big as that – unless there was a purpose. He wanted to make life difficult for Tore. Like I said, I don't know why, but can you think of any motive other than revenge?'

When she didn't answer, Henning carried on: 'Just because the papers have written that you're not an informant doesn't make it any more valid or true, and Bjelland was perfectly aware of that. He also knew what kind of people were after him, as he'd spent more than a decade with them in Brazil. So coming clean and being named and photographed in the paper was neither here nor there, they would be after him all the same.'

Henning took another sip of water.

'Which is why I think he had a completely different agenda. He wanted me to start a process that he hoped would end with your husband going to jail.'

Veronica shook her head.

'That sounds totally far-fetched to me,' she objected. 'As far as I know, they barely knew each other.'

'As far as I'm concerned, it would be even more far-fetched if they *didn't* know each other. Bjelland had worked closely with one of Tore's best friends for years. In the same business, even.'

Veronica squinted over at him, as though she still had problems accepting what she'd just been told.

A phone started to ring somewhere in the flat. She let it ring, and when it had stopped she said, 'Well, there's only one thing to do, then.'

Henning looked her.

'Find out what Tore and Charlie were so scared you might discover, and why Bjelland wanted revenge on Tore.'

Henning nodded.

'I know that Tore probably died because he was going to tell me what he knew about the fire…' Henning suddenly looked over at the laptop '…in my flat.'

He moved over and flipped up the computer screen. The picture of Trine appeared again.

'What is it?' Veronica asked.

Henning tried to gather all the disparate thoughts that were vying for his attention. Trine could actually have been involved in this in some way or another. That would then explain the warning that had been left on his door; she wouldn't want him, her own brother, to die. But then Tore was sitting outside in a car and took photographs of Trine meeting Durim Redzepi, photographs that went some considerable way to show that a cabinet minister had something to do with a fatal fire, and obviously had links with known criminals.

Henning shared his thoughts with Veronica.

'Just think about it,' he said. 'Tore was desperate to get out of prison, so desperate that he contacted me and said that he would give me information about the fire in my flat, if I could only help clear his name. But even if Tore had still been alive, he would never have told me about a murder that he and Charlie were involved in, because then he might end up with *another* sentence. And that would just be stupid.'

Veronica nodded, her eyes encouraged him to continue his line of thought.

'But this,' he said, pointing at the screen, 'this is something else. Potentially compromising information about Trine and very relevant information for me. *This* is what Tore wanted to share with me.'

Henning wondered for a moment if that was perhaps why Tore had been killed, but what did the photographs actually prove? That Trine had spoken to a criminal on the street, and that she'd given him ... something? Trine could easily have talked her way out of it if a newspaper had got hold of the pictures. But the idea that Trine might be involved in such a cunning murder as the liquidation of Tore while in Oslo Prison – it was simply too incredible for him to believe.

But the photographs showed that Trine had been outside Henning's flat only 10 minutes before it went up in flames, and the fact that she had anything to do with a person like Durim Redzepi was, in itself, suspect. The question was whether she had any dealings with Charlie Høisæther as well.

Henning sat back in the sofa.

'When is she coming home?' Veronica asked.

'In three days' time,' Henning replied quietly.

'Well, I have an idea what you might be doing on that day then,' she said.

Henning balled his fists and said, 'So do I.'

4

Three days later

There was nothing to beat this feeling, Iver Gundersen thought. Knowing he was about to make a breakthrough, that he, and no one else, had managed to find a way into the case.

And it wasn't just any old case, either.

That was why he'd left as soon as he'd woken up in Nora's flat. He was itching to discuss his findings with Henning, and had sent him a text message to see if he was up, asking if he could come to his flat as soon as possible. Iver even offered to pick him up.

The answer pinged in moments later.

On my way to the airport. Later today?

Airport? Iver thought. What was he doing there?

He replied OK, but he was disappointed.

Not long after, there was another ping.

What's new?

Iver thought about what to answer.

Too long to explain by text. Tell you later.

Henning said OK.

In the meantime, thought Iver, he could go through it all again and try to be his own devil's advocate – a demanding, but necessary procedure for anyone who wanted to blow the lid on something. He had to be 100 per cent certain.

Iver pulled out behind a bus and noticed that he needed petrol. Not surprising really, he'd practically been living in his car recently.

He tried to slow his breathing. He thought about Henning, and about Nora.

It had been an odd few months.

He'd never meant to fall in love with her, but her vulnerability after Jonas's death had made Nora irresistibly beautiful, and he'd almost felt it was his mission to make her smile again.

Deep down, Iver had kind of hoped that Henning wouldn't come back to work, but then he did, one day in late spring, and Iver wasn't sure which one of them felt most uncomfortable. The first case – the stoning of a film student, Henriette Hagerup, in a tent at Ekebergs-letta – had not helped much either, as Henning had worked out who the killer was and then given Iver all his information.

Iver couldn't understand why, to begin with, but gradually it dawned on him that Henning was actually protecting himself; he'd known that it was a scoop and would lead to a lot of media attention. And Henning wasn't interested in that, not then and not ever.

At first, Iver had loved the furore, but it didn't take long before he felt pretty ambivalent about it all. Every time Henriette Hagerup's name was mentioned, Iver thought about who actually deserved all the praise. The fact that Henning was the only person who knew didn't make it any easier. Which is why Iver had tried to return the favour. He had thrown himself into Henning's own mystery and the puzzle of Jonas's death, with the goal of finding the vital detail, the piece that made everything fit together.

Now he thought he might have done just that.

Iver parked the car a couple of blocks away from his own building, then hurried back to the flat. It was just gone half past nine when he opened the door and threw the keys down on the hat shelf.

There was something odd about the flat. And it took a few moments before he realised what it was.

It was completely dark.

He never closed the curtains, not completely.

And then he heard sounds from the living room. The TV was on. Had he forgotten to turn it off before he went to Nora's late last night?

Iver went into the kitchen and then into the living room, where the TV screen flickered, washing the ceiling and walls with colour.

The curtains were drawn in there too. *What the…?* He suddenly got the feeling that something was very wrong.

And then the living room light was switched on.

Iver stopped in his tracks.

There was a man sitting in the chair.

'And here he is,' the man said, in Swedish.

Iver stood as though glued to the floor, his mouth half open. He quickly looked around. There was a man sitting on the sofa. He had a gun on his lap.

'Who…?' Iver started. The words got stuck in his parched throat. 'Who are you?' he managed to say, and coughed. 'What are you doing here?'

'You took your time,' the man in the Stressless said. 'We were getting bored of waiting, weren't we, Jeton?'

The man who was talking to Iver looked at the screen for a few seconds before turning off the TV and slamming the remote control down on the table. Iver started at the sudden loud noise. It was then he saw that the man was wearing gloves. That there was a rope on the table. That the table had been cleared of all paper.

Iver swallowed. Considered whether he should try turning on his heel and legging it, but the man's gun and the way he was holding it made him stay put.

'What do you want?'

The two men got up at the same time.

'We want to know how much you know and who you've told.'

The man who was talking took a step closer. He was small, with thin, unkempt hair on his head, but all the more on his chest, which was bursting over the neckline of his black hoodie. He was compact, strong; Iver could see the muscles on his chest rippling. And he wondered why neither of them had bothered to hide their faces. How they had got in? What they were going to do with the rope?

'What are you talking about?'

Iver tried to be nonchalant, but could hear that he wasn't doing it very well, that his voice was trembling. He looked over at the windows. Were any of them open? Could he throw himself out? It was a long way down and the ground was covered in asphalt.

The second man grabbed the rope on the table.

'Do you see what I've done in here?' the first man asked, and looked up at the ceiling. Iver followed his eyes. At first glance he didn't notice anything unusual.

Then he spotted it.

The hook.

The man produced a knife.

'I saw this once, in a film,' he explained. 'I like films. Do you like films, Gundersen?'

He looked questioningly at Iver, who wasn't able to answer.

'I've never tried it myself, but do you know what happens if you start to bleed, from the neck, for example, when you're hanging upside down?'

The man put the blade of the knife to his own neck.

Iver swallowed again. Thought about how he could get out.

'It depends on the wound, of course, how deep the cut is, but if you cut the main artery here...'

He pointed to one of the two arteries on his neck.

'...just enough to start bleeding...'

He paused again.

'...it takes about half an hour to die.'

Iver noticed that the man talking also had a gun in his jacket pocket. You're going to have to be smart here, he said to himself, or it's not going to be good.

'I don't understand what it is that you want,' he stammered. 'I don't know anything, I haven't...'

'Shh,' the man interrupted. 'Enough.'

He shook his head and took a step closer.

'We'll find out what you know, whether you want us to or not. It's only a matter of time.'

Then he smiled – a flashing, Machiavellian smile – and shook a watch free from under his sleeve. He looked at his friend again, and said, 'What do you reckon, Jeton – do you think it will take more than half an hour?'

5

The air in the cabin was cold and dry – it almost felt like the air conditioning onboard the Norwegian flight from Frankfurt was set at *frost*, not *spa*, but that was perhaps also because Trine had spent the past couple of weeks in the Bahamas, far from the chilly, autumnal capital of Norway.

And it had been a truly fantastic fortnight. Just her, on her own, with an arsenal of e-books and a sunbed that she didn't have to get up at five in the morning to bag. She'd needed to think about something other than the reason she'd been forced to step down as Minister of Justice. She'd been accused, falsely, of sexually harassing a younger, male politician, which had left her drained of energy, and being in a place where no one knew who she was had allowed her to forget, certainly for shorter periods, how awful it had all been, how painful it had been – especially the conversation she'd had to have with Pål Fredrik the same evening that she'd publicly announced she was stepping down.

Trine hoped that no journalists would be waiting when she landed. She hoped that something else had caught their attention in the fortnight she'd been away, but she was sure they hadn't forgotten her.

Trine looked at the watch Pål Fredrik had given her before she left for work on her first day as a cabinet minister. Half an hour until landing. That alone was enough to make her heart beat faster.

She wondered what Pål Fredrik thought now that he'd had two weeks to digest the fact that she'd had an abortion without consulting him – after they'd said publicly that they wanted to have children. The question was whether he'd be able to live with her betrayal.

They had texted each other every day, but that was all, and then only about this and that – unimportant matters: she didn't even know if he would come to collect her at the airport, if he had the time – even though it was a Sunday. If he would *take* the time. He was probably out on a long bike ride, Trine guessed. He might never forgive her.

The PA system crackled. The co-pilot informed them that they would soon be starting their descent to Oslo Gardermoen airport and that everyone should return to their seats and fasten their seatbelts. Trine thought about what she would do when she got home. There might be a communications agency or three that would welcome a woman with her network, but she actually wouldn't mind doing nothing for the next few months. Take the time she needed to muster her strength until she was hungry for work again.

There were no text messages waiting for her when they landed, about 30 minutes behind schedule. She was disappointed when she got off the plane. Her legs were swollen and her shoes were tight. She kept her eyes to the ground as she walked.

She bought four bottles of Amarone in the duty-free shop and a big bag of marshmallow bears. Fortunately, she didn't have to wait long before her suitcase came and she could go through customs.

Once she was out in the arrivals hall, she looked up and, to her immense relief, saw no microphones or cameras, but nor did she see Pål Fredrik.

Maybe it was over between them, she thought. This was the proof – he hadn't even come to collect…

Trine stopped.

She saw a face in the crowd that she had certainly not expected to see. Not here.

But there he was.

Henning.

And he was looking straight at her.

6

Henning had to stop himself from running over to her.

She stood there, the shock and fear apparent in her eyes, the same look as when he'd found her in the cabin at Stavern when she was hiding from the press. Then she'd more or less chased him away, but things were different now. He knew why she was so frightened.

Over the past few days, Henning had tried to find explanations as to why Trine might have had dealings with a professional killer, what motives she might have had, and he had only come up with one.

Money.

The property market had been lucrative for a long time and if Trine had worked on the legal issues involved in the transfer of property, as she had done in the nineties, she might have been a good ally to have. Henning hadn't managed to find out how much she was worth, but if she had received financial rewards for her services, she would presumably have been smart enough to hide the money somewhere.

Henning pushed the strap of his bag further onto his shoulder and took a controlled step towards his sister; they'd got on so well when they were little, but now he'd barely spoken to her since their father died. All around them, people were shouting and waving to the new arrivals. Some had Norwegian flags and flowers with them. Others were weeping with joy.

Henning stopped about a metre from her, but said nothing. Just stared at her.

'Henning,' Trine stammered. 'What are you doing here?'

He was fizzing inside; he wanted to put his hands round her throat and squeeze. Instead, he indicated that they should leave the crowd. Reluctantly, she followed him.

When they were some distance from the throng, he stopped and turned towards her. Stared at her again. And as he did so, he pulled out a photograph from his inside pocket and held it up.

'This was taken on the eleventh of September 2007,' he said in a shaky voice. 'Ten minutes before my son died.'

Henning could see Jonas's quiet, dead face as he lay beside him on the cobblestones in the back yard, after they'd jumped from the balcony on the second floor. The railings had been so slippery and Henning hadn't been able to see anything; only minutes before he'd jumped through a wall of flames that had blocked the door to Jonas's bedroom, and the flames that set his hair on fire and melted the skin on his face.

Trine screwed up her eyes and looked closely at the photograph, which showed her a few metres behind Durim Redzepi; she was clearly saying, or shouting, something to him.

'What did you give to the man who set fire to my flat?' Henning asked.

He noticed her hands first, how they almost lost their grip on the suitcase, her handbag, the duty-free bag – then he saw it in her eyes, the film that seemed to fall before they rolled back into her head.

Then she fell towards him.

Henning only just managed to grab her arms before she fell to the floor. It was purely reflex – he wouldn't have minded if she'd hit her head – but everybody knew Trine's face. The fact that the first thing she did on her return from a holiday was to faint, was guaranteed to make the headlines. And he didn't want that.

Henning saw a bench a few metres away and dragged her over, sat her down and then sat down himself. He took off his courier bag, struggling to keep her upright. And it was with some discomfort that he rested her head on his shoulder.

A thousand emotions were churning inside him and he didn't know if he'd be able to stop the anger that was about to boil over. But then, what could he do? What should he do?

In an attempt to control the situation, he put his arm round her and hid her face as best he could with his jacket, as though she was a drunk girlfriend who needed to be shielded from public humiliation. One of the service staff came over to Henning with Trine's suitcase, bag and duty-free shopping, and asked if everything was alright.

'Yes, thanks,' Henning said. 'She just didn't eat enough on the flight.'

'Would she perhaps like a glass of water?'

'A glass of water would be good, thanks.'

The man put the luggage down next to Trine and hurried off. He was soon back with a plastic cup filled to the rim.

'Thank you,' Henning said.

'We have a room you could use if she needs to lie down for a bit?'

'Thank you, we'll be fine,' Henning said. 'It's happened before,' he added.

The man disappeared with an understanding smile. Henning dipped his fingers in the water and flicked a few drops onto her face, aiming for the eyes. He did this several times and soon enough he felt her stirring and could hear that her breathing was faster.

Then she moved her head.

When Trine opened her eyes, she started and pushed herself away from him as fast as she could. She blinked several times, as though waking from a long, deep sleep. Henning had no intention of waiting until she was ready for his questions.

'Answer me,' he demanded.

Trine jumped at the sound of his voice. Looked around again.

'What were you doing outside my flat just before it went up in flames?' he asked.

Trine was about to say something, but then stopped herself. Her lips quivered. Her eyes filled with tears and she blinked furiously and looked the other way. For a short moment Henning was frightened that she might vomit or faint again, but it was simply that she was crying so hard.

It took a while before she managed to pull herself together.

'They…' she sobbed. 'They said they weren't going to do anything. I didn't know that they … that that would happen.'

Henning just looked at her, the images of Jonas passing before his inner eye.

'What do you mean?' he said with gritted teeth.

'They threatened me,' she sniffed. 'Said they'd tell…'

The sobbing got the better of her again. People walked back and forth in front of them, but Henning was now in a force field where no one else existed. Trine was crying so violently that she was shaking and it took a long time before she calmed down.

'They promised me that nothing would happen to you,' she stammered. 'They were only going to frighten you, I had no idea that…'

She looked away and shed some more tears.

'I had no idea that they were going to set fire to your flat, Henning,' she continued. 'And that … Jonas was there as well, that…'

Trine took a deep breath and sobbed at the same time.

'You have to believe me,' she said. 'I didn't know that Jonas was going to be there.'

'But he was,' Henning said, bitterly.

The tears spilled out of her eyes once more.

For the first time since she came round, she dared to look at him. Her eyes were puffy, red, wet.

'Can we go somewhere else and…'

'No,' Henning said, harshly.

She nodded and looked down, dried her face with her hands. Then she picked up her handbag and got out a packet of Kleenex.

'I'll tell you everything,' she said. 'Everything that happened. But don't interrupt me. OK?'

7

No matter what she'd done the day before, no matter what the season, Nora Klemetsen woke up at seven o'clock every morning. This Sunday had been no exception, and the day had started so well, it was a morning that made her feel that perhaps, finally, she was on her way to being a whole person again.

She hadn't woken up and immediately thought of Jonas, as she usually did. She hadn't wandered around the flat looking for his snow globe, and she hadn't put her hands on her stomach and thought that it was wrong to be pregnant again.

Instead she had gone out into the kitchen, turned on the oven, thought about the rolls she was going to warm up, the scrambled eggs she was going to make, the slices of bacon she was going to fry and take in to Iver before he dragged himself out of bed. She'd made the coffee, picked up the morning paper and then sat there savouring the joy of a Sunday without any plans other than relaxing, eating good food and watching films on TV in which nothing really happens.

But then Iver had come out to the kitchen, much earlier than he normally would, wearing only his underpants, his shoulder-length hair pointing in every direction, as he slid his thumb up and down the screen of his mobile phone.

'I have to go,' he'd said.

Nora looked at him, astonished.

'Go?'

'Yes, I … just have … and I have to get hold of Henning, and…'

'Henning? Why do you need to get hold of Henning this early in the morning? And on a Sunday as well?'

He hadn't looked at her, but he'd answered, 'It's just some things…'

Nora should have noticed the evening before. When he eventually arrived, much later than planned, he had that distant look in his eyes that he always got when he had something on his mind, when a case had taken hold of him and he wondered how he could solve it, which sources to contact, what angle he should take. But when she asked him what was up, he replied, 'Nothing really, just something.'

As though that would explain everything.

It was Iverish for 'I can't, and don't want to say anything about it to you', and when he had repeated this vague and immensely irritating phrase that morning, she had felt it in her very core, the air seeping out of her body, as though she were a shrinking balloon. It had made her realise and understand what Sundays would be like in the years to come, as Sundays had often been when she was married to Henning.

Then Iver had turned around and thrown on his clothes, which were lying over the end of the sofa where he'd left them the night before; he hadn't even had a cup of coffee or given her a kiss on the cheek before he rushed out of Nora's flat and called over his shoulder. 'I'll ring you later on today.'

Then all was quiet.

After Jonas had died, Nora had done everything she could to block out the silence, because that was when the thoughts came, and the images, of the little boy with the flyaway fair hair. Iver, with all his energy and humour, had pulled her out of herself, away from the walls that seemed to be papered with Jonas's face, no matter where she was.

And then she'd discovered she was pregnant, without having ever really thought about it or known how deep her feelings for Iver actually were. She knew that they were miles apart in many ways – Iver was the very definition of messy, he couldn't even shut cupboard doors. He put his own interests and needs before anything else, something that the intensity of his work in the past few days had shown, and Nora had realised that Iver was not particularly well suited to being a father.

But she had decided to give it a chance. She owed that much to the child that was growing inside her. She owed that much to herself, she just needed to find a way to live with him. And that was why she put on her jacket and shoes, scarf and hat, and went out. If she wasn't going to enjoy a Sunday with Iver, she could at least try to enjoy it with someone else, or on her own.

She tried to get hold of Lise, but she was away at the cabin with her husband and children. Cecilie had taken the children to a waterworld somewhere in Asker. Nora rang her mother as well, but she was out walking with a friend. So in the end, Nora ordered a salad at Sagene Lunsjbar, but found that eating on her own was boring and sad, so she'd only eaten half before she quickly exited into the chilly afternoon.

October was a good time to be outdoors; so much happened as autumn turned to winter. The colours were less vibrant, but when the sun broke through the clouds, they seemed to quicken and crackle – as though they relished this brief memory of summer. She liked to feel the cool autumn air against her skin. She liked to watch the ducks seeking out food, to see dogs bounding around in parks, chasing balls and sticks. Enjoyed having enough time to follow a thought for more than a second. It was at times like this that the sight of an old couple could make her cry, and when good ideas for new articles might pop up unexpectedly.

When Nora had been walking for about an hour, with no real plan, she realised that she actually wasn't that far from Fagerborg. So she decided to take the 10-minute detour to see if Iver was at home. She might even catch a glimpse of what was so important that he had to work on a Sunday.

Outside his building it smelt of wet city and grass that was about to surrender. The building was five storeys high, and the clouds that lay like a lid over Oslo made the facade look grey and sad, not white and well kept. A single flower box hung from one of the balconies. The remains of something that had once been red were now a dull pink and most definitely dead, and the stalks were bent to the side

– as though trying to defend themselves against the wind and winter months to come.

Nora had her own key, but she didn't need it; the door to the back yard was standing open and when she stepped inside, she realised why. Someone was obviously moving and there was a constant stream of lamps, bags, holdalls and suitcases. Nora gave the removal men – obviously a group of friends – a sympathetic smile. She could see the sweat on their faces.

The last time Nora was pregnant, she had suffered symphysis pubis dysfunction, or SPD, at quite an early stage, and as she walked up the stairs to Iver's flat, she felt that it may well happen again, the pain in her pelvis expressing itself with every step. She cursed her body, which was increasingly unreliable, and dreaded the months ahead.

Nora stopped outside Iver's front door and listened. She couldn't hear him. Heard nothing. She put the key in the lock and turned it.

But the door was already open.

She pulled the key out again.

The kitchen was darker than usual and she realised that the curtains were drawn. She couldn't hear any movement, no one quickly getting up from a chair, filled with guilt, throwing down the remote control, no quick steps across the floor.

She went into the kitchen. The unmistakable smell of stale cigarette smoke drifted towards her, but there was another smell too. Something she couldn't place.

'Iver?' she called.

She didn't get an answer. This made her take a few steps towards the living room. She pushed open the living room door and stopped in her tracks.

Dropped her keys.

Dropped her handbag.

Then let out a scream.

8

Bjarne Brogeland sat down at one of the two monitors that showed live images of what was going on in one of the interview rooms. As it was a Sunday, the chances were that he would be in the control room alone.

Bjarne studied the man sitting on one of the chairs, squeezing the muscles of his forearms, apparently unfazed by what was about to happen. But then they'd been through the same procedure a few times in the past weeks. Ørjan Mjønes was not willing to say a word about who'd paid him to kill Tore Pulli when Pulli was serving a 14-year sentence, or why. It was only when he was asked innocuous questions that he deigned to open his mouth. What he was called, where he came from, his mother and father's names, uncles and aunts – which football team he supported. It didn't help when they got a so-called expert to question him.

But Henning had given them some new information, which Ella Sandland, the police force's *femme fatale*, was now going to put to Mjønes. Bjarne was curious to see what he would say.

Sandland pushed open the door and walked in. Every time Bjarne saw her, he felt a surge through his body. Her short, blonde hair was always perfectly styled with a side parting; she was carefully made up, with high cheekbones and an amazing, well-trained body. When Bjarne stood opposite her, it took considerable effort not to show, very visibly, just how attractive he found her – and he knew that he'd failed on several occasions.

She nodded to Mjønes and to his lawyer. Lars Indrehaug gave a theatrical sigh.

'So you managed to find us,' he said.

Indrehaug had long, thin, greasy hair. The skin hung loose around his chin and he had obvious warts on both his cheeks. Bjarne had never got on particularly well with Indrehaug, but nor did he aspire to.

'My apologies,' Sandland said. 'I got a phone call.'

'On a Sunday?' Indrehaug queried.

Sandland raised an eyebrow, wasn't at all perturbed by the lawyer's attempt to rattle her.

'Doesn't your phone ever ring on a Sunday?' she parried.

Bjarne smiled.

Sandland ignored him, sat down on a chair in the small grey interview room, her papers resting on her lap. They sat in a triangle. Mjønes was still looking at his arms, as though nothing in the world could interest him more. Bjarne could see that Mjønes would have a certain appeal to the opposite sex. He was just shy of two metres tall, with caramel-coloured skin and fair hair pulled back in a ponytail. He was wearing jeans and a t-shirt that was so white that it looked like it had come straight from the shop.

'What are we going to talk about today?' Indrehaug asked. 'Whether my client likes green or black bananas?'

'We're going to talk about Daddy Longlegs,' Sandland said, crossing her legs, keeping a hand on her papers. Bjarne kept his eyes fixed on Mjønes as the name was mentioned, and even though Mjønes pretended it meant nothing to him, there was a faint twitch in his face. Bjarne saw it, even on the monitor.

'That wouldn't surprise me in the slightest,' Indrehaug said.

'Do you know who Daddy Longlegs is?'

Sandland addressed this to the lawyer as well as Mjønes.

Indrehaug laughed.

'I think most people know what a daddy longlegs is. Honestly, Ms Sandland, you can't seriously mean that...'

'Daddy Longlegs gives work to people like your client – contract killers and enforcers. Daddy Longlegs is his nickname, and not many know his real identity. But your client does.'

There was silence. Bjarne kept his eyes on the screen, waiting.

'What makes you say that?' the lawyer asked eventually.

Sandland didn't answer straightaway.

Bjarne studied Mjønes, waiting for him to look up. When he finally did, it was with an obstinate 'I-don't-know-what-you're-talk-ing-about' face.

Mjønes had lost weight, Bjarne noted. But then he'd been in custody for a while now, and it was never easy to get used to the walls, routines, the absence of everything familiar. Even the hardest nuts broke at some point, it was simply a question of how long it would take. They had more than enough circumstantial evidence against Mjønes. He would be sentenced to fourteen or fifteen years, at least. He would probably serve eight to ten years, which was a decent amount, but still a bloody long time.

'Does the name Preben Mørck,' Sandland said slowly, keeping an eye on the other two, 'mean anything to you?'

Mjønes stopped squeezing his muscles. Then, seconds later, started again. Bjarne moved closer to the monitor. Saw Sandland hold up the photograph that lay on top of the papers she had with her.

'He looks like this,' she said, showing it to them.

It took some time before Mjønes even raised his eyes to look at it.

'He's been the Hellberg family's lawyer for many years, even though they are in Tønsberg and he's based in Oslo.'

'Never seen him before,' Mjønes said, and lowered his head.

Bjarne watched him carefully.

'If we get evidence against him, Ørjan, we'll bring him in. And then we'll question him about you and Tore Pulli. Do you think he'll be equally unwilling to say anything?'

Mjønes didn't answer.

'Lawyers love to talk,' Sandland said, and glanced over at Indrehaug – the lawyer scowled at her. 'He'll talk, Ørjan. And I happen to know that you two already know each other.'

Mjønes lifted his head again. It looked like he was about to give a sarcastic 'yeah, right', but the words never passed his lips.

'Killing someone as infamous as Tore Pulli in Oslo Prison is not the kind of job you'd give to someone you've never worked with before.'

Bjarne studied his face for the slightest reaction.

'You've done jobs for him previously, haven't you?'

Mjønes didn't answer.

'If Daddy Longlegs is smart,' Sandland continued, 'he'll cooperate with us and tell us what he knows – about what he's done himself and what those around him have done. And then we're back to square one, Ørjan. In this room. You, me and your lawyer.'

Sandland paused a while before carrying on.

'You'd make it easier for yourself if you started to cooperate.'

Mjønes gave a quiet snort.

'Tell us who Daddy Longlegs works for,' Sandland persisted. 'Tell us who else was involved in the Tore Pulli murder.'

Sandland had put her fingers together in a triangle. Indrehaug looked over at his client, who refused to look back.

'You've previously had a good deal of contact with the Kosovo-Albanians here in town,' she continued. 'Were they involved in this as well?'

Mjønes moved his hands from his lower arms to his biceps. Bjarne was sitting tight, waiting for the response when the door behind him opened. He turned and saw Martin Furuseth, the police laywer on duty, come in. And there was something about the plump man's serious, heavy face – his eyebrows seemed to be even more knitted than usual – that made Bjarne stand up.

'I need you to go to Fagerborg,' Furuseth said. 'Immediately.'

9

Trine dried more tears and blew her nose, crumpled up the tissue and looked around for a bin. She spotted one by a pillar and went over to throw it away. Her legs would scarcely carry her and she still felt dizzy.

On the way back, she looked at her brother.

He must have gone through hell, she thought. Being unable to save your only child, and then to have to live with it afterwards. And even though she'd known he was searching for answers, she'd never even contemplated that he might discover her role in it all, let alone get hold of photographs that proved it.

Trine sat down an arm's length from him. She wanted to say something, but couldn't decide how to say it. It was best not to look at him, she decided, better just to tell her story and pretend he wasn't there.

'You may already know this,' she started, and cleared her throat, 'but in the nineties I was working for Oslo Council. As a legal adviser in local administration.'

She could hardly hear her own voice. She tried to put into words the memories she'd fought to suppress.

'I was young and inexperienced at the time,' she continued, 'and I took the job because I thought that...'

'Get to the point.'

The edge in his voice made her jump.

'I'm trying,' Trine said, squaring her shoulders and exhaling slowly.

Then she carried on: 'One winter afternoon, I think it was 1996, an old woman came to my office. Bodil Svenkerud.' Trine said her name slowly, and shook her head. 'She wanted to hand in a written complaint. She'd lived in the same council flat in Oslo for most of her life, and it said in her contract that she would have a fixed rent until 2020 or thereabouts, I can't remember exactly.'

Trine put her hands together.

'But then, in the nineties, the council sold some of its properties, including the building where Bodil Svenkerud lived, to private investors. The new owner took over responsibility for the tenants and even though Mrs Svenkerud had an old contract she could put on the table, it didn't help much – the new owner tried to squeeze her out by putting up the rent by several hundred per cent.'

Trine took another deep breath.

'They wanted her to move so they could do up the flats and resell them, but Mrs Svenkerud was having none of it. So she came to me, and said that if I couldn't help her, she'd go to the papers.'

Trine's mouth was dry. She asked for the cup of water that Henning held in his hand. He passed it to her reluctantly.

She took a few sips before she continued.

'But because she'd come to me so late in the day,' she said, and dried her upper lip, 'I told her that I would look at her case first thing in the morning. Which I intended to do, but…'

Trine looked around. No one seemed to be paying any attention to them.

'Early the next morning,' she continued, in an even quieter voice, 'the phone rang in my office.'

She looked around again.

'It was a man who wanted to know if an old lady had been to see me the day before.'

Trine looked straight at Henning as she spoke. 'I hesitated, but eventually said yes. The man then asked me to look at page four of *Aftenposten*.' She shook her head again. 'God, I even remember which page it was.'

Trine lowered her eyes and put the plastic cup down on the bench. She needed a few moments to pull herself together.

'It said that an old woman had been run over the evening before and had died as a result of her injuries.'

Trine met Henning's eyes, which were increasingly intense. She took another Kleenex from the packet and wiped her nose, then balled the tissue in her hand.

'The man asked if I'd received anything from Bodil Svenkerud the day before. He even called me by my name, and seemed to know all sorts of things about me, where I lived, which floor, what my boyfriend at the time was called.'

Trine let her eyes wander again, before continuing.

'I was terrified. Sat there shaking, with the receiver in my hand. The man asked if anyone else had seen the complaint, but only I had. So he told me to shred it and not give it another thought.'

Trine crushed the paper tissue.

'I wish I'd been stronger,' she said, 'but I couldn't think what else to do, I just stammered yes. So…'

Trine looked up at her brother.

'When the man had hung up, I did what he'd told me to do – I shredded the complaint and tried not to think about it anymore.' It took a few moments before she carried on. 'The police took the case seriously, naturally enough; a hit-and-run in poshest Frogner was not exactly an everyday occurrence, and when they'd pieced together her final movements, they of course turned up at the office.'

She lowered her eyes again.

'I was convinced they would see that I was lying, but I told them that Svenkerud had wanted to complain about council services in her part of town, and that she was probably just an old lady who needed someone to talk to after her husband had died.' She shook her head. 'I didn't know I had it in me, to lie like that, but I managed and the police bought my explanation, and that was that.'

She wiped her nose again.

'I stopped working for the council not long after. And the years passed. I tried not to think about what had happened.' She gave a heavy sigh. 'Then I was appointed as Minister of Justice. I was always afraid that the past would catch up with me, and sure enough – after

I'd joined the cabinet at the start of September, I was reminded of what had happened to Bodil Svenkerud.'

'In what way?' Henning asked.

Trine took a deep breath. Waited a moment, before saying, 'I got another phone call, this time from a man who wondered if I remembered what had happened to the old lady who'd come to see me one winter's day when I was working for the council.'

Trine fought hard to hold back the tears.

'I asked who was calling, but the man wouldn't answer.' She looked directly at Henning. 'Instead he told me that I had a bothersome brother.'

Henning raised an eyebrow. Trine shook her head once more and dried a tear.

'I tried to tell the man there wasn't a lot I could do about *that*, but then he played a recording of me talking to the man who called the morning after Bodil Svenkerud died. And there it was, word for word, everything he'd said and everything I'd agreed to, I even confirmed that I was called Trine Juul.'

She stopped and sighed, and then continued in almost a whisper. 'This put me in a very difficult situation. The man said he was considering giving the recording to one of the newspapers. If he did, then I would be implicated in an unsolved murder. I'd given in to threats. My career, my life, would be ruined. I asked what he wanted,' Trine said, shaking her head, 'and that's when he said, "We want you to do something for us."'

She paused before carrying on.

'He said they needed to get into your flat.'

Henning stared at her, wide-eyed.

'And I knew that Mum had a key…'

It was Henning's turn to shake his head.

'I didn't know what to do, Henning,' she added, swiftly, in a louder voice. 'The man promised that nothing would happen to you. They just wanted to give you a scare, they said, to make you stop poking around in whatever it was you were doing.'

Henning stood up.

'And so I went up to Mum's later on that day, got the key to your flat and gave it to the man in that photograph you showed me. That's all, I promise.'

Henning said nothing. Just carried on shaking his head.

'If you look closely at the photograph, you'll see I'm shouting something at him. I shouted that he had to promise that nothing would happen to you.'

Henning started to pace up and down, rubbing his head with one hand.

'I promise, Henning,' Trine sobbed. 'What happened to Jonas was never supposed to happen. I promise.'

Henning's hand moved from his head to his face, from his forehead, down over his nose, mouth, then up and down again, and when he started to come towards her, Trine was frightened for a moment that he was going to hit her, so she pulled even further back on the bench. But instead he stopped in front of her and said in a shaken voice: 'The company that bought the building where Mrs Svenkerud lived, what company was it?'

Trine looked down.

'I…' she whispered.

'What company was it?' he repeated, coming a step closer and grabbing her arms.

'I don't know,' she said. 'I can't remember.'

'What street was it, then?'

Trine thought. For a long time. Then she looked up at him and said, 'I can't remember that either, I'm sorry, Henning.'

Frustrated that she couldn't, or wouldn't, tell him what he wanted to know, Henning let go of her.

And walked away.

10

Henning half ran, half walked. There was a sharp pain in his hip where they'd put in several pins following his fall from the second-floor balcony a couple of years back, but he pushed himself on. He bought a ticket for the airport express and hurried down the escalators onto the platform. A train was there waiting, and a minute after he'd boarded, the silver serpent, with its carbon steel axles, snaked towards Oslo at a speed of nearly 160 kilometres an hour.

As cars and fields and forests sped by, he thought about Trine and what she'd told him. Her explanation was plausible enough. She'd been a pawn in someone else's game, and he had a feeling that Tore Pulli and Charlie Høisæther were involved in some way. He decided to get hold of everything he could find on the Svenkerud case as soon as he got home.

But there was one thing he had to do first.

∴

Assistant Chief of Police Pia Nøkleby lived in a side street off Uelands gate. All the local drug addicts and alcoholics gathered on the corner outside the Tranen pub, by the traffic lights at Alexander Kiellands plass. Henning had never been to her flat before, he'd met her most recently in a café close to where she lived, after he'd discovered that a report in the police investigation system, Indicia, had been modified via her user profile.

The report was about Tore Pulli's movements in Markveien on the evening that Jonas had died, but Henning didn't think it was Nøkleby herself who had made the changes. The way she'd answered his questions gave him no reason to believe she was lying to him. She clearly had no idea what he was talking about.

In other words, someone else had done it.

Henning asked the taxi driver to drop him off in Elias Blix' gate, a stone's throw from the street where she lived. He didn't know if Nøkleby would be at home – police folk often worked at the weekend as well – but if he didn't catch her there, he'd go down to the police headquarters.

Henning's pulse was still racing when he rang the bell. On the other side of the street, an old woman was pushing her rollator in front of her. There were no cars here, but he could hear the traffic on Uelands gate. A helicopter that didn't seem to be moving was making a racket above him. The wind whistled through the leaves on some branches nearby.

It took about 30 seconds before he heard rustling on the intercom.

'Hello?'

Her voice was rusty, as though she'd just woken up from a deep sleep.

'Hi, it's Henning,' he said. 'Henning Juul. I need to talk to you.'

There was silence.

'Can I come up?' he asked.

'Now?'

'Yes.'

A long silence, then: 'I'd rather come down. Be with you in two ticks.'

It was already dark and the streets were wet. A taxi was approaching. Henning looked the other way, and heard it stop. The door opened and a woman got out. She said thank you and goodbye. The taxi reversed out of the street and disappeared.

Henning heard footsteps on the stairs and peered through the window in the door. Pia Nøkleby was coming towards him, but he barely recognised her. Her hair was normally short and tidy, but now it was untidy and standing on end. Her face was bare of any make up, which was unusual, and when she came out onto the step, she wrapped her slightly oversized jacket around her.

'Hi. How are things?' she asked with a concern in her voice that surprised him.

Henning shrugged.

'I've been better,' he said, and pushed the strap of his bag further onto his shoulder. 'How about you?'

'What are you doing here?' she asked.

He noticed her eyes.

'Bad timing?' he asked.

'Kind of,' she said. 'Why did you come here?'

'Indicia,' he started.

She looked up.

'You want to talk about Indicia? Now?'

'I've spoken to Bjarne,' Henning continued. 'He said that you knew that someone had used your username and password to get into Indicia and remove information about what Tore Pulli was doing outside my building on 11 September 2007. The night I lost my son.'

Nøkleby opened her mouth a fraction, as though she was about to say something, but nothing came out.

'Bjarne said you'd asked how I knew about it,' Henning said. He was quick to hold up his hands. 'And don't worry, I'm not here as a journalist. I just need your help.'

She pulled her jacket even tighter.

'For what?'

'I need to find out what it said in that report and who edited it. I know it wasn't you, but it has to be someone who could somehow get hold of your username and password.'

Henning was more and more certain that there was something in the report that would explain why Tore had been killed, or who was behind it.

Nøkleby sighed.

'Henning, I've no idea wha—'

'Well, I happen to think you do.' He paused before continuing. 'It has to be someone you know well, and I'm not necessarily thinking about the people at work – I'm sure they don't hang over your shoulder every time you go onto Indicia. I think maybe someone you meet outside work; here, for example. I'm sure you bring a work computer home sometimes.'

He indicated her building. Nøkleby looked at him and then looked down.

'Think carefully,' Henning asked her. 'It might be someone you trust. I know nothing about your private life, so maybe you have or had a partner…'

'My private life has nothing to do with you.'

She lifted her head and glared at him.

'No, no, I know. But please, Pia, help me if you can. I need to get to the bottom of this and, to be honest, I think you need to know who's used your name as well.'

A nearby garage door opened. The noise made him jump. A car rolled out. Henning turned his back to it.

'I don't know if Bjarne's said anything,' he carried on, when the car had passed. 'But I've got a couple of guys on my back who're pretty worried about what I might discover. If I manage to stay alive, that is.'

Nøkleby looked at him.

Henning saw something change in her eyes. It was a fear on his behalf, but not as he'd expected. It was more like a mixture of sympathy and horror.

'What is it?' he asked.

'You've not heard, have you?' she said.

He took a step closer, and said, 'Heard what?'

11

Durim Redzepi liked driving cars and he particularly liked this road. Not much traffic, lots of bends. He loved feeling the g-force on the bends, not knowing if he could keep the car on the road, but there were quite a few police around out here, so it was probably best to take it easy. Especially now.

Redzepi had never met Daddy Longlegs before and he wasn't quite sure what to think, really, about both the man and their imminent meeting. Up until now they had communicated via a phone box and pay-as-you-go mobile phone, but suddenly it appeared that they had to meet face to face, and as soon as possible. And Daddy Longlegs didn't want to say why.

So Redzepi had suggested that they meet at the cabin where he'd been living since spring, one that Daddy Longlegs had organised for him. At least he was familiar with his surroundings there. He had control. Given the job they'd done this morning, there was a slim possibility that he wanted him out of the way for good, so he didn't have to pay him, and so that there were no loose ends. But then he would have had the same plan for Jeton Pocoli, and Redzepi had let him off at the Colosseum Cinema half an hour ago. From there, his friend from Kosovo would go home to his flat in Tøyen and wait for the next phone call.

Redzepi took off from the main road, onto the forest track, where the grass and gravel crunched merrily under the tyres. He always drove slowly here, allowing the deep tracks to guide him until he turned left at the T-junction, with the small stream on his right. He liked to see it twisting between the trees, to hear the chuckling sound. Sometimes he walked beside the water and wondered if there were any fish in it.

Redzepi drove on, over an old, narrow stone bridge and up the small hill to where the red cabin looked proudly out over the forest.

It was more than big enough for his needs. Two bedrooms, living room, kitchen. He didn't have hot water, and there was only an outdoor toilet, but he was used to poor conditions from Kosovo. And it was fine to wash in the lake, which was only a few cone throws away. He even had a rowing boat on the shore that he sometimes used to fish for pike and perch.

And it was so quiet there.

What he loved most about the cabin and the forest were the days when he had the time to take a cup of coffee out with him in the morning and sit on the dirty white plastic chair, while he rolled two or three cigarettes and just enjoyed waking up gradually. It always reminded him of Izbica, where he had done the same as often as the weather permitted. If he really listened, he could almost hear Jaroslav's tractor, Mika's pigs, the cows in the field on the other side of the road that ran through the village, where everything was slow, all year round, where someone was always repairing something.

It hadn't been easy to find peace after he'd fled Kosovo. Stockholm had been too big. Oslo too small and polluted.

But in the forest, he could breathe.

When he stopped and got out of the car, he drew the fresh air deep into his lungs. It was so different from the air in Mitrovica, the hellish lead dust from the Trepca mines. That was the main reason why he'd taken Svetlana and Doruntina away from there; he didn't want his daughter growing up in such a polluted environment.

Izbica had been perfect. Good, friendly and helpful neighbours, clean, fresh air, enough to do in the garden and fields. They sold the potatoes they grew locally, sometimes even giving them away to friends who needed them. They'd receive something in return another time. Life had been good there.

Until that night in March 1999.

The soldiers who had forced their way into the village were wearing dark uniforms; some of them had balaclavas on, others had camouflage paint on their faces. Redzepi and many of the men, those who were in the Kosovo Liberation Army, escaped to the mountains because they knew the soldiers would show no mercy. But they hadn't reckoned on those soldiers making quick work of the old men who stayed behind. Some of the women and children were killed as well, shot with machine guns, quite simply executed.

When Redzepi came back down from the mountains three days later, he couldn't find his girls. He went to look on his own, taking only the bare minimum of food and drink, plus a gun and some ammunition. He searched everywhere, got more and more desperate, as he tried to picture where they might have walked or run, where they could have hidden.

But he didn't find them.

Tired and hungry, he got to Velika Hoca, a village in the municipality of Orahovac, just over a week later. There he more or less stumbled over two Serbian soldiers sitting guard. Redzepi didn't know whether they'd taken part in the massacre at Izbica or not, it didn't matter; he marched straight up to them and shot them. Eye for an eye, tooth for a tooth.

But someone in the village saw him, and he had to run deep into the forest, further and further away from Izbica, and from Svetlana and Doruntina. Even though it was winter, he hid in the forest. He didn't get much sleep. Or food. When he finally managed to make it to the capital, Pristina, 76 kilometres from Velika Hoca, there wasn't much left of him, but he found his way to the house where his brother Jetmir lived.

Jetmir and he had never got on that well, and at first his brother didn't want to take him in, nor did he want to help him. In the end, he agreed to lend him enough money to flee the country. Flurim Ahmetaj, a friend from Mitrovica, had escaped to Stockholm and Redzepi followed him, and stayed with his friend for the first few weeks.

Ahmetaj was good at anything to do with computers, and had some contacts in the Stockholm underworld who paid him well for his services. That was how Redzepi got involved. First as a favour to Ahmetaj, because his friends needed a driver for a robbery one night and then later, when they realised he was both trustworthy and not afraid to get blood on his hands, they recruited him for other, more dangerous jobs. It was good, quick money.

And it wasn't far to Norway, which was where he'd met Ørjan Mjønes, a man who plied him – and the others – with work. Every time they'd done a job, they went back to Sweden to lie low for a while; the reverse if they'd done a job in Sweden. Redzepi sent part of what he earned back to his brother, who in turn paid for people to keep looking for his girls.

And he was still waiting for an answer.

Of course he knew they might possibly be buried, like so many others, in a mass grave that had not yet been discovered. But he would never give up. Every evening before he fell asleep, he thought about them, about where they were and what they were doing. How they would look when he met them again.

∵

Three-quarters of an hour passed before Redzepi heard a car pull up beside his. He went over to the kitchen window and saw a tall man get out of a car that looked like it cost a fortune. The man was wearing a suit and a dark overcoat, and he had a briefcase in his hand. The remains of the afternoon light seemed to focus on the man's shoes, making them gleam.

Redzepi went out onto the step to wait for Daddy Longlegs.

'You're late,' he said.

'Apologies,' Daddy Longlegs said. 'It's been a rather hectic day, mainly thanks to you.' He smiled.

'Did anyone see you?'

'Difficult to say.'

Redzepi welcomed him in with a nod. Daddy Longlegs rubbed his hands together as he entered and looked around. He nodded to himself. Redzepi realised from his expression that Daddy Longlegs was used to something more upmarket than pine walls and red-checked curtains. The tall man walked over to the kitchen counter, picked up a glass that was standing on a tea towel, and held it up towards the light before filling it from the tap. When he'd emptied the glass, he put it down and said, 'Gundersen. Did you get anything out of him?'

Redzepi shook his head before answering. 'But I don't think he'd managed to tell Juul anything yet. They were going to meet later on today.'

Daddy Longlegs nodded slowly and put his briefcase down on the kitchen counter, opened it with two synchronised clicks and handed Redzepi some papers and a photograph. Redzepi looked at a man with a strong jaw, muscular neck and cropped hair. The skin on his face was flushed red. There were palm trees in the background.

'Is that the chippy?' Redzepi asked.

Daddy Longlegs nodded.

'The photograph is a few years old, so he may of course look a little different now.'

Redzepi mentally stored the carpenter's face and tried to imagine what he might look like now. People who went into hiding often changed their appearance. If they had short hair, they let it grow, and if they had long hair, they generally cut it short. They often dyed it as well. There was also a lot of other things you could do with your appearance. Put on weight, or the opposite. Redzepi tried to picture all permutations, but closely the area around the eyes in particular. That seldom changed.

'Everything ready for the funeral?' Daddy Longlegs asked.

'It is.'

'Good. There's a bonus waiting for you if it all goes according to plan. You need the money, don't you? It's been a while since you sent anything back to your brother.'

Redzepi looked up from the photograph and instead studied the man in front of him. It took a moment before he actually understood what Daddy Longlegs had just said.

'Yes. I know about your girls too, Redz,' Daddy Longlegs said. 'They're called Svetlana and Doruntina, aren't they?'

Redzepi was initially glued to the spot, but then he threw down the papers and grabbed Daddy Longlegs by his coat and pushed him up against the kitchen cupboard.

'What do you know about my family?'

'I know why you're doing this,' Daddy Longlegs said, unperturbed. 'You're looking for them.'

'What do you know about my girls?'

'I know all I need to know.'

Redzepi pushed him up even harder against the cupboard. Daddy Longlegs rolled his eyes, as though he was already bored of this game.

'I never do business with anyone without knowing as much as I can about them first,' he said. 'That shouldn't surprise you.'

'Tell me what you know about Svetlana and Doruntina. Now.'

Redzepi's voice quivered.

Daddy Longlegs smacked his lips. 'That's not the way it works, Redz. Could you…'

He made a gesture – he wanted him to let go – but Redzepi pushed him further up the cupboard.

Daddy Longlegs let out a theatrical sigh.

'I've got some information that you might be interested in, and yes – it's about your family. But if I'm going to give you that information, you're going to give me what I need first. There's no reason why this shouldn't be win-win for both of us.'

Redzepi gave no sign of letting go. Daddy Longlegs looked like he found the whole thing rather tedious.

Suddenly, Redzepi let go.

Daddy Longlegs' shoes rapped on the wooden floor. He puffed and straightened his coat. Then he smiled again, pointed to the papers lying on the floor and indicated that Redzepi should pick them up. While he did this, Daddy Longlegs filled another glass of water and produced a pillbox from the inner pocket of his coat. He took out two pills and swallowed them with water.

'Angina pectoris,' he said, and removed a drop of water from his lower lip with his tongue. 'I had an aunt who once thought it was called Vagina pectoris. It's true.'

He laughed.

'But it does actually sound like a sexual disease,' he finished, laughing at his own joke.

'It's a lot to do, all at the same time,' Redzepi said. 'There's Juul as well.'

Daddy Longlegs was done with laughing.

'Yes, it is,' he said, all at once serious. 'But you'll manage. Keep your focus in the days ahead, Redz. Do what you have to, and then I'll tell you what I know about your girls.'

12

Even though her work was calling, Pia Nøkleby took her time walking up to the fourth floor, past smells of food, and the rubbish bags and shoes that were standing outside doors on the stairs.

She thought about Henning, about the look in his eyes, increasingly distant, before he sat down on the pavement with his knees drawn up. He hadn't cared about the damp air or the wet ground.

Nøkleby had used Henning's phone to call for a taxi, but when the car drove off, she wasn't sure that he'd asked the driver to go to the police headquarters as she had requested. She didn't like what she had seen in his eyes just before he left. That rage that seemed to spark inside.

But he'd planted an idea that made her push the door shut with extra force when she was finally inside. She took her shoes off slowly, as though she needed more time to do what she had to do. She placed them beside the slightly larger trainers that had a temporary place in the hall, hung up her jacket and walked calmly into the living room.

'You were a long time,' he said. 'Who was that?'

He was sitting on the sofa smoking a cigarette as he always did after they'd had sex. As though he belonged there. Sometimes he had a cup of coffee as well, but as a rule, after his cigarette he just showered and went home or to work, leaving her feeling like a harbour he only visited when it suited him. Which was more or less the case.

Pia Nøkleby had known Andreas Kjær for four years, since they'd ended up sitting next to each other at a work Christmas dinner. They'd got on so well, and conversation had been easy. He'd made her laugh. At the time, she hadn't laughed properly with a man for as long as she could remember.

Nothing had happened that evening, not by a long shot, but because he was a team leader in the Control Centre, they would meet every now and then. They continued to get on well and this developed into stolen glances over food or coffee. Sometimes she found him at night as well, in her dreams, and then one Friday evening they bumped into each other in town, and at the end of the night, she asked him in what was a very direct way for her, if he was going the same way. She'd already seen the answer in his hungry eyes, and the fact that he was married with two children was simply not part of the equation at that point in time. Things took their course.

Pia's previous relationship had ended in arguments, and clothes and shared memories being thrown out, and she had not been ready for commitment, only intimacy. She had initially suppressed any thought of morals and allowed herself to be swept along. And goodness, things were still fine; he was a good and considerate lover – rough and ready if she asked for it – but he never stayed the night. What had been exhilarating and exciting at first had gradually become habit.

She had started to think about ending the relationship. It would fizzle out naturally at some point; she knew that Andreas was not the type to leave his wife and kids, but every time she had made a decision to say something, they ended up in bed.

She liked herself less and less. She'd never dreamed she would be someone with a lover. A married one, at that. If her mother only knew…

'It was Henning,' she said, and looked at him. 'Henning Juul.'

Andreas Kjær straightened up. He was more alert, guarded. He stubbed out his cigarette, quickly and vigorously. The horrible feeling that she'd had on the way up to the flat was reinforced.

'You know him, don't you?'

'I've heard of him, yes,' Kjær said, picking up his lighter from the table. 'What did he want? Why did he come here?'

Pia Nøkleby studied him.

'He wanted to talk to me about something,' she said.

Kjær lit another cigarette, then threw the lighter down on the table.

'About what?'

'Why do you ask?'

'Well,' he said, and blew smoke out into the room. 'I mean, it's a bit odd, isn't it, to come to your house like that?'

Pia Nøkleby didn't answer. There was a moment's silence.

'He came because someone got into Indicia with my username and password. And changed a report.'

'Really?'

He looked up at her, but couldn't hold it for long. Took another couple of quick drags on his cigarette instead.

'What kind of report?'

'A specific incident on Markveien on 11 September 2007,' Pia Nøkleby said. 'The night Juul lost his son.'

She looked straight at him.

For a long time, without saying anything.

'It certainly wasn't me,' she swiftly followed up. 'But I've given some consideration to who it might have been.'

Kjær looked up at her from the sofa.

'And what exactly do you mean by that?'

'What I mean, Andreas, is that I wonder if this,' she pointed from him to herself and back again, 'has perhaps been about more than just a fuck.'

He stood up.

'What are you saying, Pia?'

Andreas was a lot taller than her. Stronger, too. Still, she took a step towards him and said: 'You are the only one who's seen me log into Indicia here.'

He snorted.

'You can't honestly suspect *me* of...' He stopped and rolled his eyes.

Pia Nøkleby had dealt with enough liars in her time – she could recognise an amateur over-reaction when she saw one. So she just smiled and watched him shift his weight from one foot to the other, take another drag on his cigarette as he glared back at her, affronted. But he couldn't do it, and it didn't take long before he turned away and went over to the window. He stood there smoking, as he pretended to look out at the town.

'Why did you steal my password?' she asked.

He started to turn, but then stopped.

'Was it to incriminate *me*?' she asked.

'You? No, I…'

A few seconds passed. He turned and went over to the coffee table, where he stubbed out his cigarette in the ashtray, then he carried on into the bedroom and returned with his mobile phone. He took out the battery and SIM card and put them down on the bookshelf. He took her phone and did the same.

When he'd finished, he stood with one hand on the bookshelf, as though he needed something to hold on to.

He didn't look at her when he said, 'They threatened me.'

She could barely hear him.

'Who are "they"?'

'I don't know,' he said.

'How did they threaten you?'

He took a moment before continuing.

'First they rang,' he said. 'Wanted me to give them access to Indicia. I would get good money, they said, but I refused, of course. Then they said they knew where I lived and things like that, and what my kids were called. What the dog was called.'

He shook his head and looked up at her momentarily, as though to reassure himself she was still there. And when he continued, his voice was even quieter.

'Then one day, they cut the dog's throat and left him on the veranda, so my kids would find him. They said next time it would be one of us if I didn't help them. So I … did what they asked me to. I knew that you had access to Indicia, and…'

'Why did they need to get into Indicia?'

Pia Nøkleby could hear how hard her voice had become. Cold.

As though she was at work. She realised that it wasn't easy for him to talk about it, but she didn't give a damn.

'Andreas, listen to me. I've just found out about your role in all this, and if I was smart, I would go straight to my superiors and tell them everything, about you and the people who've threatened you. But then I would also have to admit that I've known there's been a certain security risk for a while now, without having mentioned it. In the best case scenario, you would lose your job, and in the worst, I would too. But whatever the case, we're talking about major changes, and even though no one is served by this becoming public knowledge, there's a real possibility that your wife would find out about what's been going on for the past six months. And I'm guessing you're not too keen for that to happen.'

Kjær's head seemed to have sunk down between his shoulders.

Pia Nøkleby continued: 'I would rather keep my job, too, and believe it or not, I have no interest in this affecting your family. So, as I see it, we – or that's to say you, really – only have one choice left.' She waited until he looked up at her. 'Talk to Henning.'

Kjær was about to come up with some kind of protest, but she spoke before he could.

'Tell him what you know about these people. If we're lucky, he won't write anything about our blunders.'

Kjær closed his eyes, as though he hoped the nightmare would be over when he opened them again.

'I'm going to have to go to work now,' Pia Nøkleby said, with a heavy sigh. 'Do you know why?'

She didn't wait for him to meet her eyes.

'Because Henning's closest colleague was killed a few hours ago.'

Kjær opened his eyes and lifted his chin.

'It's too early to say whether the murder has anything to do with Henning, but it may well do. Henning hasn't been staying in his own flat recently, because someone is after him.'

'So you think it's safe for me to talk to him?'

'I think it's time to stop hiding, Andreas. It's time to start pulling your weight. Seriously. People are being killed.'

'Yes, and I'm trying to stop that happening to anyone in my family. Or me.'

Pia Nøkleby looked at him with increasing scorn. Even though it was easy enough to understand that he'd been thinking of his children all this time, he'd still put her in an impossibly difficult position. He had betrayed her and she would never forgive him. And she felt that it was actually quite a good thing that they'd got to this point.

'I'm going to have a shower,' she said. 'And when I get out, Andreas, I'd like to hear that you've grown some balls.'

13

Trine closed her eyes.

Only now, as she was transported silently towards Oslo – long after Henning had left – occasionally feeling the rhythm of the wheels on the tracks and junctions, did she realise how exhausted and sleepy she was. She leaned her head in towards the window and tried to imagine that the world would somehow be different when she woke up. But the fields were still flying past half a minute later – cold, wet expanses that rolled towards the hills and mountains far away on the horizon. Everything was as it had been, except it was all different now.

She wasn't afraid for herself, but she was scared about what might happen to Henning if he continued his hunt.

You should help him, Trine said to herself. God knows, she owed him. But how? What could she do when faced with people who wouldn't bat an eyelid at killing?

The train swept past Kløfta, where Trine and Henning had grown up. The knowledge of what had happened in the house in Gjerdrumsveien, in Henning's bedroom, made her shut her eyes again; she tried to block out the images that sometimes came to her, especially at night, but her father's frightened eyes would not be blinked away. Or the sound of his bare feet as he crossed the floor when he'd pulled on his trousers, the careful knock on her door so as not to wake anyone else, the quiet in the house the next day. What happened later.

Trine had told Pål Fredrik about her father. Perhaps she should tell him about Jonas as well, now that it was all out, and Bodil Sven-kerud. But she couldn't make up her mind, not even when she got off the train at Skøyen and took a taxi home to Ullern. Pål Fredrik opened the door for her and pulled her into his arms as soon as she'd put down her things.

'Hello, my love,' he said, quietly.

'Hello,' she replied, suddenly on the verge of tears.

'How are you?'

She pressed herself against him, didn't want him to see her tears. She mumbled something about being fine, a good trip, but that it was better to be home again.

'How about you?'

'I'm fine,' he said, and she heard in his voice what lay beneath the words. Security. A home. The tears welled up again, and she had to force them back.

'Did you see Henning?' he asked, shortly after.

Trine pulled back abruptly and looked up at her husband, and then it dawned on her why Pål Fredrik had not come to meet her.

'Yes,' she said, and relaxed into his arms again.

'How did it go?'

She didn't answer, just held him as close as she could.

After what happened to Jonas, Trine had thought about taking her own life. She just wanted everything to disappear – the realisation of what she'd done, the pain she'd inflicted on others. But Pål Fredrik had managed to pick her up, as she now felt confident he would do again. 'What would you like to do, now that you're going to be the Minister of Justice?' he'd asked before she started the job. 'What are you passionate about?'

And Trine had thought about Jonas, decided that she would fight for children to grow up in a safe environment. 'Children's rights,' she'd said, and that was what had pulled her from the quagmire, the thought that she might be able to make a difference. And she'd managed to do a lot; she'd opened more children's safe houses around the country and she'd gone to work with a sense of purpose and the desire to do something every day. But she'd avoided anything that might remind her of Henning. And the past.

To begin with, it was fine; Henning was off sick, and for a long time no one was certain he'd ever go back. When he did return to work again, she just avoided *123News*, knowing that she couldn't bear to see his byline photo, with all the scars. But obviously it was difficult to avoid him completely and it didn't take long before he was part of the news scene again, both as a witness in the Henriette Hagerup case and as the leading reporter when Tore Pulli was murdered. And when Trine herself was caught in the media crossfire, he was the only journalist who tried to help her.

There was so much she wished she'd done differently. It might even be too late. She had the feeling she would never see him again, and so would never be able to repay him.

But now at least he knew the truth.

Even though she hadn't dared tell him everything.

14

The city rushed towards him and then slipped by outside the taxi window. Colours and people, rain and umbrellas, street lights competing with an ever-darkening sky. The radio was on, but Henning wasn't listening.

He had his bag on his knees and was clutching his phone, which he had turned off before he met Trine. Reluctantly he turned it on, even though he knew there would be a deluge of text messages and missed calls.

Bjarne Brogeland answered the phone as soon as Henning called, but he didn't say anything, just breathed heavily over the static on the line.

'Condolences,' he said, eventually. 'I know you worked closely together.'

'Are you there?' Henning asked. 'At the scene?'

'Yes, I…'

'I have to get into his flat,' Henning said. 'See the place.'

'Henning, you can't…'

'Can you meet me outside? I'm on my way there now.'

Bjarne sighed.

'They're still going over the flat, Henning. I can't just take an outsider in. You know that.'

Henning moved the phone into the other hand.

'It would be easier for me to tell if there's anything unusual,' he said. 'I'm the one who's been there the most in the past week or so.'

'That may well be,' Bjarne said. 'Anyway, regardless of whether I can get you in or not, we still have to wait until forensics are finished.'

Henning looked out of the window again.

'They might move things, take something away…'

'They won't,' Bjarne said.

'You never know. You can't guarantee that, can you?'

Neither of them said anything for a moment. Henning felt the taxi driver looking at him in the rear-view mirror, but he didn't look up.

'Iver texted me earlier on today,' he said, after a while. 'He wanted to show me something.'

'What?'

'I don't know. We agreed that I'd go round this evening, when I'd...'

A few more moments' silence.

'Does it have anything ... to do with your case, do you think?'

'I don't know.'

Bjarne asked Henning to wait a moment. Someone asked the policeman something; Henning could hear the mumbling in the background.

Iver had been killed in the middle of the day, on a Sunday. Someone obviously thought it was worth the risk. Iver must have found something, and it must be something to do with Henning's search, he was sure of it.

What the hell could it be?

Henning knew that Iver had been concentrating on Rasmus Bjelland recently. It might be something about him. Maybe Iver had managed to track him down, get something out of him. Henning had to try to find Bjelland himself, to establish what kind of relationship he'd had with Tore Pulli, why he'd wanted to get his revenge, and if it had anything to do with everything else that had happened.

'Would it perhaps not be better to meet at the police station?' Bjarne asked, when he came back. 'Then we can talk things through properly.'

Henning shook his head.

'I can't face the main station right now, Bjarne. Arild Gjerstad and all the others. Just can't do it.'

'You don't have to have anything to do with them,' Bjarne said. 'You can just talk to me.'

'Meet me at Iver's then, we can talk there.'

Bjarne sighed.

'I'll be more useful at Iver's than in the main station, you know that, Bjarne. Help me get into the flat, then we can go through it together. I have to find out what he was going to show me.'

The car stopped at some traffic lights. The engine automatically switched off, and there was silence. Henning could hear Bjarne breathing at the other end.

'OK then,' he said eventually. 'I'll meet you outside.'

.:.

Henning asked the driver to stop a block away from Iver's flat. He needed some air. Needed to walk, needed to think. Out of the car, he lifted his face to the drizzle that slowly washed the salt from his cheeks.

Iver was dead.

Gone. Him too.

Henning wanted to call Nora, but she would hardly want to talk to him, not now, perhaps never again. He had ruined her life, first by not being the husband he could and should have been, then by not waking in time to save Jonas. It was his fault that the wrong kind of people were after him, it was his fault that Iver had been caught in the crossfire, and even if Henning managed to find them and get them put away, Nora would never get back what she'd lost. Every time they met, every conversation they had, would be a reminder.

His phone rang. It was Bjarne.

'I can see you,' he said. 'Wait there.'

Henning ended the call and did as he was told. Soon he saw Bjarne striding past ten or twelve journalists, all of whom tried to talk to him. He dismissed them with a wave and angry shake of the head, and hurried towards Henning.

Bjarne held out his hand when he got there.

'It's just so awful,' he said.

Henning shook his hand, but said nothing. They stood in silence for a few seconds, neither of them bothered by the cold drops of rain.

'Chaos over there,' Bjarne said, and nodded towards the journalists. 'Stick close behind me and don't say anything.'

I wouldn't dream of it, Henning thought.

'OK,' Bjarne said.

A row of police cars was parked just outside the cordon. In addition to the journalists, a crowd of curious onlookers had gathered. Henning kept his eyes to the ground as they got closer, hoped that no one would notice him, but too late; he heard someone call his name. Henning didn't answer. Bjarne guided him past the two officers guarding the cordon.

'Why is Juul going in with you?' The question went unanswered. Instead, Bjarne muttered something to one of the police officers. Henning concentrated on Bjarne's feet and his own. Sounds came and went through his head, loud, uncomfortable.

They passed through the archway into the back courtyard. A forensic technician was coming in the opposite direction. Bjarne said hello; his voice was like a sound file played at slow speed, deep and gruff.

Henning trudged up the stairs, without looking at anyone. Before they went into Iver's flat, Bjarne turned towards him.

'Iver's not here,' he said. 'But there are still some remains. Wait a moment and let me see if…'

'It'll be fine,' Henning said.

'I don't know how wise it is for you to see…'

'It'll be fine,' Henning said again.

Bjarne looked at him for a few seconds.

'OK,' he said.

Then he pushed open the door.

Henning felt his heart thumping, faster and harder. He stepped into Iver's flat and took his time to look around. Shoes, jackets, bottles by the cupboard. The open bathroom door, the light inside.

The kitchen ahead of them, frying pan on the cooker, the smell of egg and bacon lingered. Plate by the sink, glasses in the washing-up bowl.

They were barely through the door when a voice from the living room said, 'Whoa-whoa-whoa, what are you doing, Bjarne?'

The sharp voice belonged to a petite, compact woman, whose accent suggested she came from the north of Norway. She emerged with her hands up to stop him. Henning looked at her. It wasn't hard to guess she was from forensics.

'You can't take a civvy in here. Not now.'

'He might be able to help,' Bjarne explained. 'He's been here before. In the past few days.'

'Yes, but...'

'He'll be able to see if anything's out of place in a way that we can't,' Bjarne interjected. 'I promise you, Sara, we'll be out of your way in a couple of minutes.'

She didn't respond, just stood there glaring at them.

'Thank you,' Bjarne said, taking it as silent assent. 'I owe you one.'

Henning turned towards the front door, looked at the row of shoes, the hooks on the wall, the coats and jackets, a clothes hanger. He turned slowly round and lifted his eyes towards the living-room door, took a step forwards, looked at the clothes on the floor, the wires, a beer can, newspapers, the coal and ash in the fireplace.

There was blood on the floor. Dark red. Henning had thought he'd be able to resist looking at it, but the colour was so deep, that he stood there staring until his vision was blurred by saltiness. It was as though there was a magnet in the deep red blood that kept drawing his eyes back.

He looked up. Saw the hook on the ceiling.

'Is that where he was hanging?'

Bjarne exchanged glances with the technician. Henning looked from one to the other.

'There's bits of fabric up there,' he said. 'And so much blood in one place...'

Neither Bjarne nor the technician answered, but he didn't need any confirmation. That meant there must have been at least two people involved. One person would never have managed to hoist Iver up by himself.

'Can you see anything … unusual in here?' Bjarne asked.

Henning studied the room. Saw a candlestick on the windowsill with no wax on it. A vase of something that looked like dry twigs. Book with the front cover facing down, two remote controls, another beside the telly. The small sideboard under the TV was closed. A blanket had been flung on the sofa. A lamp was on.

He stopped when he got to the coffee table.

'If Iver was working on anything,' he said, and felt acutely how hard it was to say his name out loud, 'he used to spread his papers out all over that table there.' He pointed. 'But there's nothing there. No paper. No printouts.'

'Do you think the people who did this took any papers with them?'

Henning nodded.

'It's certainly possible,' he said, quietly.

'Sara, do you know if anyone has taken stuff from the table?'

She frowned at him, then shook her head.

They stood there, all three of them looking around.

'I've seen enough,' Henning said. 'Get me out of here.'

They went out into the kitchen. Henning turned around again. Looked at the blood, at the rest of Iver's flat. The police had presumably started to map his final movements, but he wondered if he could work that out on his own, without having to ask Bjarne.

Henning looked up on the hat shelf in the hall, where Iver usually left his car keys. Bjarne's phone started to ring, and he answered and opened the front door at the same time.

Henning looked around again quickly; there was no one else in the hall. He reached up and managed to take Iver's keys in the nick of time, just before Bjarne turned round and held the door open for him.

'Are you coming?' he asked.

Henning nodded and left the flat.

15

'Stop,' Charlie Høisæther said. 'Stop, *now*.'

Freddy pulled into the pavement and stopped.

'What is it?' he asked.

'Wait here.'

'Shouldn't I…'

'Just wait here,' Charlie repeated, as he got out of the car. He looked in both directions and then ran across the road into the gallery. A bell tinkled above him as he entered the air-conditioned premises. Even that short dash across the road had made Charlie sweat. The cool air was refreshing.

'Hello,' said the owner, a short man with a dark comb-over. He came towards Charlie, the palms of his hands pressed together. 'A pleasure to see you, sir. How can I help you?'

'That painting there,' Charlie said and pointed at the large canvas that was in the window. 'Who painted it?'

'Ah, *A mulher da minha vida*,' he exclaimed with delight. 'Roberto Souza. He's from Castelo Branco.'

Charlie took a step closer.

'It's in Portugal,' the owner enthused.

'Can you take it down?' Charlie asked.

The man looked questioningly at him. 'You mean… now?'

'Yes, now. Out here.'

Charlie pointed to the wall in front of them.

'I'm interested in buying it,' he added.

'Ah, yes, of course. But let me just get my assistant. One moment, please.'

The gallery owner called out a name and some instructions in his own language, and soon another equally short man appeared. They looked like twins, the same height, the same features, the same small, pointy chin. Not without difficulty, they managed to climb into the window and take down the painting. They then propped it up against the wall, as Charlie had asked them to.

The painting was of a woman in profile, with long, jet-black hair, against the golden-red sunlight of early evening. She was on a beach, staring longingly out to sea. Her hair fell beyond the edge of the painting, where two hands were just visible under the black locks. She was wearing a white dress.

'The painting is 77 by 53 centimetres,' the owner told him. 'The same as the Mona Lisa.'

'How much does it cost?' Charlie asked.

'34,500 reais.'

'Can you deliver it to my home?'

The two men sent each other a speedy and thrilled look, then turned back to Charlie.

'I'll pay extra if you can deliver it today,' he said.

'Of course, sir,' the owner said eagerly. 'We'll arrange that.'

Charlie went over to the till and put his credit card down on the counter. The owner was promptly beside him, the sweat breaking on his brow from the last few minutes of exertion.

'Roberto Souza is a very talented painter,' he said.

'I'm sure he is, but I just want this one.'

'Of course. One moment.'

Charlie turned back to look at the painting.

It was perfect.

She was perfect.

∵

When the doorbell rang a couple of hours later, Charlie was sitting on a bar stool in the kitchen, reading the Norwegian papers on his mobile phone.

Isabel called from the living room: 'Who is it?'

Charlie didn't answer, just went over to the intercom on the wall beside the door.

'Yes?'

'Delivery for Mr ... um, Mr ... um...'

'Fifteenth floor.'

Charlie stood by the door and waited for the lift to ping open. He said hello to the two men who carried the painting in. Their shoes immediately left marks on the floor tiles.

'Where do you want it?'

'The living room,' Charlie said.

He showed them in. Isabel was sitting reading a fashion magazine when they came in. She stood up and looked at them with round, curious eyes.

'Over there,' Charlie said, pointing at a bare white wall behind the dining table. The men did as they were told.

'What have you bought?' Isabel asked.

Charlie sent her a long look.

'Is it a painting?' she asked.

'Mm-hm.'

The large rectangle was packed in bubble wrap and paper.

'Shall we hang it on the wall for you?' the men asked.

'Just leave it there, thanks,' Charlie said, pointing at the floor.

'OK.'

Charlie gave them each one hundred reais. The men bowed their heads in thanks and quickly retreated. Charlie locked the door behind them and ran back into the living room.

'How exciting,' Isabel said.

Charlie removed the paper and bubble wrap with care.

And there she was.

A mulher da minha vida.

'Oh,' Isabel said dreamily, 'how...'

She put an arm round him from behind, pulled him to her.

'So...'

Charlie just stood there, looking at the hair, the beach, the sand, the sunset.

'Is it…?'

Charlie wasn't listening.

'I mean … she doesn't have my curls, but…'

Should he say something?

No, that would nasty.

And then Isabel kissed him on the neck and slid her hands down over his chest muscles, stomach and then lowered herself down on to her knees in front of him. He looked at her – *A mulher da minha vida* – 'Woman of my life'. *Love of my life*. He could swear he could even smell her.

16

Bjarne spoke into his phone on the way down the stairs, but hung up as soon as they came out into the courtyard. The rain was heavier, splashing on the cobbles.

'Could you drive me to *123News*?' Henning shouted over the steady hiss of the rain.

Bjarne looked at him for a long time, then at his shoulder bag.

'You're not thinking of working now, are you?' Bjarne asked loudly.

'No,' Henning said. 'I just want to be there.'

Bjarne gave an understanding nod.

'Of course.'

They went out onto the street, into the chaos and cordons, and tightly packed journalists under umbrellas, ready to attack. But Henning didn't look at them, didn't listen to the questions they shouted at him and Bjarne, and instead concentrated on the reflection from the streetlamps on the dark, wet asphalt.

'Have you found any evidence?' Henning asked, when they got into the car. Bjarne put the heat on full blast. The windscreen wipers went back and forth briskly.

Bjarne looked over at him.

'I can't say anything about that at the moment, Henning. Certainly not to you; you can't start your own investigation.'

'And you think I'll just accept that?'

'Henning, I…' Bjarne searched for words.

Henning sighed.

'Fine,' he said. 'I'll find other ways.'

He knew that Bjarne was only trying to protect him. But there was no way he was going to leave the police to investigate Iver's death alone. The question was how he would get hold of the information if

Bjarne wasn't willing to supply it. Henning's secret online source in the police, *6tiermes7*, had not been active for some time now.

Bjarne drove slowly and made no unexpected manoeuvres in the traffic. The police radio peeped every now and then, but Bjarne had turned down the volume. Henning leaned his head against the window, felt it banging against the glass. Outside the window, the buildings and dark streets passed by. The cars and buses sprayed water over the pavements and pedestrians made themselves as small as they could beneath their umbrellas.

'Where are you going to stay tonight?' Bjarne asked.

Henning thought about Veronica Nansen, who he assumed would be happy to open her home to him if he asked, but he didn't want to expose her to any more danger.

'Don't know,' he replied.

Bjarne held his gaze for so long that the car almost mounted onto the kerb. He realised this just in time and managed to pull back into the road. Henning grabbed the handle above the door.

Soon they turned into Urtegata, where *123News* had its offices. Bjarne stopped in front of big, black iron gates. Let the engine run.

'You'll have to come down to the main station tomorrow,' he said. 'For questioning. In a more formal setting. If Gundersen's death has anything to do with you, then it won't be just Sandland and me who want to know what you've discovered.'

Henning considered this. With dread.

'Nora,' he said, as he opened the door. 'You'll keep an eye her, won't you?'

'Of course,' Bjarne said.

'OK.' Henning got out. 'Thanks for the lift.'

∵

Henning didn't have his staff card with him, so he had to ring the bell and wait for someone to come down. He didn't recognise the girl who eventually appeared, but she seemed to know who he was.

'Come in, Henning,' she said. 'Everyone's up on the second floor.'

He went up the stairs behind her, even though it made his hips ache. Henning hadn't been into the office for two weeks; he'd managed to persuade the home news editor, Heidi Kjus, to give him two weeks' unpaid leave so he could focus fully on finding Jonas' killer. On the way up to the second floor, he wondered how the other journalists would react to his presence. Everyone knew about his complicated relationship with Iver: they were friends, but with Nora in the middle too.

The girl in front of him pushed the door open and went into the offices. It was so quiet in there. The only person to be seen when he rounded the corner by the coffee machine was the man sitting alone at the front desk.

'We're all in the big meeting room,' the girl told him.

Henning heard hushed voices, a glass or cup being put down on the table. He stopped outside because he couldn't face going in. But Heidi Kjus spotted him through the open door, jumped up from her chair and came out.

She looked even thinner than before, if that was possible, but was, as always, dressed like a lawyer, in a smart skirt, shirt and jacket – all in the same dark blue. And she was, as always, extravagantly made up, but the usual stiffness in her face, that middle-management look, had been replaced by a softer expression. A welcome change, Henning thought. It was good to know that Heidi could be human too. But he could see that she hadn't shed any tears, as several other colleagues clearly had.

'Hello Henning,' she said, and stopped in front of him. Then she took another step closer and put her arms around him. It felt strange to be hugged by a person he'd argued with so often, but he hugged her back all the same. What surprised him even more was discovering that he felt like bursting into tears.

'I tried to ring you,' she said quietly into his ear.

They let go of each other.

'Right, I've been … at the scene of the crime,' he said.

'I heard. How...'

She stopped herself and looked away briefly.

'I take it you're covering the case?' Henning said.

'Yes, but it's fairly low key at the moment; not many people can face it. Or deal with it, for that matter. So, it's mainly Norwegian News Agency information.'

Henning nodded.

'We've just had a small ceremony,' she continued. 'Sture said a few words. He's written the obituary as well. You should read it. It's good.'

Henning nodded.

'Have the police been here?' he asked.

'Yes,' Heidi said, then walked past him. 'They took his hard drive and all his papers and notepads.'

Henning hadn't expected anything less, but had hoped all the same that he might get a look at Iver's notes first. He followed her over to the empty desk. A single lit candle cast a shiny golden sheen on the black screen.

Heidi took a deep breath.

'It's so...' She shook her head and turned her face away.

'What did they ask about? The police, that is.'

Heidi turned to look at him again.

'The usual, I guess. What he was working on, if he'd been anywhere in particular before the weekend, if he'd written anything recently that might have upset someone.'

She shrugged.

'And had he?' Henning asked.

Heidi shook her head.

'He was in Tønsberg with you last week, and then he was in hospital for a few days with...' She stopped.

Henning thought about Nora again. About how she must feel right now.

They stood there looking at the candle for a while. The silence was broken by a telephone ringing. It took a couple of seconds before Henning realised it was his.

He took it out of his pocket.

'I have to take this,' he said, then retreated a few steps.

'OK. I'll go back in to the others for the moment. It would nice if you came in too, Henning.'

He didn't answer, just nodded and waited until she'd left. Then he answered and put the phone to his ear.

'Ah, there you are, at last,' Pia Nøkleby said. 'I was starting to get worried.'

'What's up?' Henning asked.

'I've got something for you,' she said.

She told him about her relationship with Andreas Kjær and that he had confessed, shortly after Henning had left.

'He's agreed to meet you tomorrow morning,' she said. 'Do you know where Skar is?'

Henning thought quickly.

'At the end of Maridalen, is that right?' he said.

'Yes. Start walking towards Øyungen, and he'll find you along the path. He's going for a run tomorrow morning around ten o'clock.'

'OK. Great. Thank you.'

'I want you to call me afterwards so we can discuss what to do next.'

Henning thought about it.

'OK,' he said again.

'I sincerely hope that you won't write anything about this, Henning. I'm trying to protect myself here, as well as Andreas. Not to mention the force. The man on the street has to trust the police.'

Henning was far beyond the point where he was thinking about journalism.

'Don't worry, absolutely not,' he said. 'Speak tomorrow then.'

17

It hurt to lift her hands to her face to wipe away the tears. It hurt to pull the blanket tighter round her. It hurt to hear the sound of her own breathing.

Everything hurt.

To blink. Swallow. The slightest turn of her head.

What hurt least was to squeeze and shake Jonas's snow globe. To see the snowflakes swirl around and slowly fall to the bottom again.

Nora dreaded the night, when everything was quiet around her. She knew that Iver would find her in the dark, that she would try everything possible to block him out, to avoid thinking about his blood-smeared face, the pool of blood underneath him, but she couldn't.

She wondered if he'd thought about her before he died, or the child, or if everything had been consumed by trying to understand why he had to die. The dread. The pain.

The kettle in the kitchen hissed more and more furiously. Drawers were opened and closed, cupboard doors opened and closed. Agnes Klemetsen, Nora's mother, got into the car as soon as she heard what had happened. She had pushed her way through all the people outside the police cordon, and found Nora sitting on a bench behind Iver's building, with a trauma-management expert beside her. The woman, who was around Agnes's age, had looked up and immediately realised who she was, and without a word being said, Agnes had sat down and pulled Nora to her and stroked her hair.

Nora shook the snow globe a little and held it up to her nose.

Once upon a time it had smelled of Jonas.

She leaned her head against the back of the sofa and closed her eyes tight. Reflected on how bad she'd been at making a real home and building something permanent. How hard she'd tried by keeping things just so. How little she had actually achieved.

Curtains and silver polish, cushions that weren't lying as they should, toys that should be put in plastic boxes at the end of the day, jackets that should be hung up, cupboard doors that should be closed, shoes that should be stamped clean of snow before going indoors...

Nora knew that she had got all this from her mother, and more, but what the hell was the point? What the hell had it given her? None of it meant anything when she had no one to do it for.

Henning. Jonas.

Iver.

Loss. Grief. Pining. Only brief glimpses of happiness. How was she going to carry on now, how would she ever find joy in anything after this...

There was a click in the kitchen and the hissing stopped. Nora heard her mother pour the hot water into a teapot.

'Goodness.'

Nora opened her eyes again and looked towards the kitchen. She heard a magnet being put back onto the fridge again.

'You haven't shown me this.'

Her mother came out into the living room with a small photograph in her hand. Nora looked at her.

'You haven't been here since I got pregnant, Mum.'

A soft smile slipped over her mother's lips, and she tilted her head.

'How wonderful. Is it a boy or a girl? I've never understood how they can tell from a picture like this.'

'Don't know, Mum.'

'Don't you want to know?'

'Mum...'

Her mother studied the photograph for a little longer, then disappeared out into the kitchen again. She soon returned with a tray of clinking cups and a steaming pot of tea. She put the tray down and set a cup in front of Nora.

'Here,' she said.

Nora forced herself to sit up. The thought of putting anything in her mouth right now made her stomach churn. Her lips and throat were dry and her tongue felt alien.

'Drink,' her mother said. 'You need some fluids.'

Her mother tried to smile. She sprinkled some sugar into her tea and stirred it. The spoon chimed against the porcelain. She put the spoon down and helped herself to a Ritz biscuit. Then she sat back and looked around.

Nora knew what was going on in her head. She was evaluating what was needed, if there was anything she could paint or sew, anything she could get rid of or improve. Agnes Klemetsen was a person who could not sit still for very long, who could never enjoy sitting against a wall feeling the warmth of the early spring sun. She always had to be doing something. And now Nora would be her mother's project, she knew that, and she didn't know if she could handle it.

She'd done something to her hair since the last time they'd met, Nora thought. Dyed it a darker brown. It was cut short, into the neck, full and wavy. She had more wrinkles on her face, more folds in her skin.

It struck Nora that she didn't know much about her mother anymore, that several years had passed without them having a proper conversation. There had somehow never been time. Or – they hadn't been good enough at making the time.

After Jonas died, there wasn't room for much else, unless it was work-related, and her parents hadn't exactly beaten a path to her door. They'd kept a distance, said they were there if she needed any help. They didn't want to fuss.

'How's Dad?' Nora asked.

'Well, you know,' her mother said, then waited a beat. 'Your father's fine. He's started to play golf.'

'Has he?'

'Yes, now that he's retired, you know, he needs something to do.'

'Mm.'

A dog barked outside. A car drove by. The city carried on.

'Has anyone else called?'

Her mother's voice was soft and warm again.

'Cecilie,' Nora replied. 'And Lise.'

'Oh lovely.' Her mother was pleased. 'How are they? I haven't seen them in a hundred years.'

'Well…'

Nora thought about her friends, who were probably sitting on the sofa right now as well, as they usually did, wrapped up in a blanket, surrounded by their families. Everything was as it should be for them. In place.

It made Nora cry again – it started with a sob when she drew breath and then just grew and grew. She was so angry, so fucking furious with Iver, with Henning, with herself, with life and the world.

Her mother got up and hurried out to the kitchen. A moment later she returned with a kitchen roll and tore off a few sheets. Then she sat down quietly beside her daughter and dried her tears.

18

When Henning entered the meeting room, everybody stopped talking.

They all looked at him.

He felt the urge to say something, to break the silence, but no words came out. Instead, Rikke Ringheim, the head of the gossip pages, came over and gave him a hug. Knut Hammerstad from the foreign desk followed. Some of his male colleagues offered their hands.

Henning found himself a chair and sat down. There was coffee and water, cups and glasses on the table. The newspapers that usually spilled over the table had been removed. Everyone sat with lowered eyes. Several were crying openly.

Henning found it hard to believe how much warmth and peace he felt simply from being with them. And he thought to himself how lucky he was to work with such a great team. That it was good to have someone to sit with, in silence.

Later that evening, Henning sat down at his own desk, beside Iver's, and stared at the candle that was still burning. Until very recently, he hadn't been able to cope with flames, but now he watched the orangey-yellow flickering light until everything else fell out of focus. He closed his eyes and pondered what Iver must have discovered, something that was so important he had to die.

Henning took his PC out of his bag and checked the *123News* front page. The first eight posts were about Iver's murder, most of them taken from the Norwegian News Agency. One of the posts had a black frame round it. The headlines included 'Killed in his own home'. In the obituary, the editor-in-chief, Sture Skipsrud, spoke of

Iver's charisma, his warm character, the positive energy and fun that he brought with him wherever he went. The Henriette Hagerup case from earlier that year was cited as the highlight of his career.

Several leading news celebrities had condemned the killing, and articles had been written about other journalists who had suffered a similar fate. The reports about the actual investigation didn't say much, and Henning understood why. For both technical and tactical reasons, the police were, as yet, sparing with any information.

Henning checked his emails in case Iver had sent him anything before he was killed. As expected, there were countless emails waiting for him, but nothing from Iver.

You have to find out what he discovered, Henning told himself. If it had anything to do with Rasmus Bjelland.

But first he looked up everything he could find about Bodil Svenkerud's death. Trine's story had been at the back of his mind all day, behind the shock, behind the anger. The old lady had been knocked down and killed on Eckerbergs gate in Oslo's posh west end in January 1996, and the case had never been solved. However, it didn't take long for Henning to find something that confirmed his suspicions about Tore Pulli and Charlie Høisæther.

The building where Mrs Svenkerud lived had been acquired by Høisæther Property in autumn 1995, and then been sold on for a considerably higher sum to Pulli Property not long after Svenkerud's death. Henning had heard that the friends often agreed an under-the-table price for acquisitions and sales like this, but then registered another. The buyer, most frequently Pulli, also conned the banks into providing more capital than he strictly needed, and the extra money was used for other investments and to finance his increasingly extravagant lifestyle.

Mrs Svenkerud had got in their way.

So they'd made sure the obstacle was removed.

If that was the case, it would explain how Bjelland knew about the death. According to Iver, Bjelland and Charlie stopped working together, certainly in Norway, in 1996.

Henning logged into FireCracker 2.0, a chat program that his secret source in Oslo Police, *6tiermes7*, had designed especially for their highly confidential two-way communication. Henning didn't know the identity of his source, but after communicating back and forth for many years now, he'd concluded that he or she could hardly be much older than 40, primarily because of their computer skills, but also because of the words they used – it was the language of a young person. The fact that *6tiermes7* had given him the handle *MakkaPakka* also indicated that the source was familiar with recent children's TV shows.

Henning had never looked into it any more than that. It was part of the unspoken pact; he would never ask who his source was, and they would never meet face to face. *6tiermes7* fed Henning with information from the various investigations that he or she had access to, and Henning made sure he used the information judiciously. This teamwork had led to a good number of headlines over the years.

However, it was a while since Henning had had any contact with his source, even though he'd tried regularly to get in touch. He decided to stay logged on to FireCracker 2.0 for the rest of the evening, if that's what it took.

Almost everyone else had gone home when finally there was a ding-dong from his computer, like someone ringing a bell. Henning closed all the other windows, keeping only FireCracker 2.0 open.

6tiermes7: *I hoped you'd be in touch this evening. My condolences.*
MakkaPakka: *Thanks. Long time no see.*
6tiermes7: *Been extremely busy recently. How's it going with you?*

Every time *6tiermes* sent a new message, Henning's computer sang out ding-dong, so he turned the volume down.

MakkaPakka: *I'm working on a few things.*
6tiermes7: *That's not what I meant.*

Henning took a deep breath and looked over at Iver's empty desk again.

MakkaPakka: *It's hard to take it in, that he's dead. And hard to believe it's not my fault.*

Henning explained that Iver had been helping him with a few things recently, and that he'd saved Henning's life when someone tried to knock him down on Seilduksgaten.

MakkaPakka: *They might have found out that Iver was helping me. Or at least suspected.*
6tiermes7: *Maybe, but you'll never know the answer. Best not to waste time and energy blaming yourself. Gundersen was an adult. He knew what he was doing.*
MakkaPakka: *And he wasn't always careful. Just waded straight in. Was beaten up not long ago because he didn't go easy.*

A man came into the office. Henning guessed he was in charge of the nightshift.

6tiermes7: *If you're interested, I've got a couple of things from the investigation.*
MakkaPakka: *Very.*
6tiemers7: *Gundersen's PC and mobile weren't found in the flat.*

Henning raised his eyebrows.

6tiermes7: *Either the people who did it wanted to check them – mails, log files, folders, etc. – or they wanted to delete the content. Probably both. But we're working against the clock here.*
MakkaPakka: *How do you mean?*
6tiermes7: *Apple and Google aren't keen to give us access to people's private accounts, even when they're dead, so it might take a while.*

Henning swore under his breath.

6tiermes7: *No doubt all the data will have been deleted by the time we get our hands on his computer. It's easy enough to remove documents from all the servers.*

Henning looked up and saw the night-shift guy talking to the girl who was sitting at the newsdesk. They gave each other a hug. There was another muffled ping.

6tiermes7: *But I heard that you've also got someone after you. Any idea who? Or why?*
MakkaPakka: *Yes and no. But I'm pretty sure that the attempts on my life, Iver's death and maybe even Tore Pulli's death, have something to do with Rasmus Bjelland. And no one knows where he is. Either he's dead or he's got another identity and is living somewhere else.*
6tiermes7: *That's certainly a possibility.*

Henning drank some water from the glass.

6tiermes7: *So what are you going to do now? You said you were working on something…*
MakkaPakka: *I've got a meeting tomorrow that I hope might give some answers, and then I'd thought of going down to see William Hellberg in Tønsberg. He was the one who told me that Charlie Høisæther and Tore Pulli had fallen out. He might know more. Maybe even something that might lead to Bjelland.*
6tiermes7: *I'll try to log on tomorrow evening as well, around the same time. Might have more to tell about the investigation by then.*
MakkaPakka: *Thanks.*
6tiermes7: *OK. Going to log out now. Stay healthy.*
MakkaPakka: *You too.*

'Hey.'

A voice rang out over the general noise in the shop.

Just keep looking straight ahead, Roger Blystad thought. He's not shouting at you, not at Bunnpris on a Sunday evening. He carried on looking for the coffee he needed for the morning. Couldn't start the day without coffee.

'Fancy meeting you here.'

The voice had come closer. Blystad turned his head a fraction, saw some feet very definitely coming towards him.

Shit.

'I'd recognise that face anywhere.'

What the fuck was he going to say? What the hell was he going to do?

'It's been a long time.'

Blystad lifted his chin and turned round to face the smiling man who had stopped half a metre in front of him.

It was Alfred.

Or The Shower, as they'd called him in high school, because he always stood right in front of you when he was talking to you, so it was impossible to avoid the spray of his spit.

What the hell was he doing in Brandbu?

'Jeez, man, how's it going?'

Alfred held out his hand.

'Hello Alfred,' Blystad said. 'Alright, thanks.'

They shook hands.

Alfred had close-set eyes, a round, boyish face, and messy hair that stood out in all directions. It must be at least twenty years since they'd last seen each other at school, and the main difference was that he'd put on about thirteen kilos in the meantime.

'What are you doing here?' Blystad asked, even though the answer seemed obvious. Alfred was wearing an Oslo Taxi uniform.

'Got a long fare from Oslo,' he said. 'Just popped in to get something to eat before heading back. And you? D'you live out this way then?'

He'd thought a lot about what he should say if he bumped into anyone from the past. And the answer he had come up with was: as little as possible. He'd say that he didn't have much time and had to be going. But if Alfred was anything like he had been back then, that would just make things worse. Not only did he stand right up in your face when he spoke to you, he talked incessantly, and fired constant questions. A real gossipmonger.

'And Brandbu, eh – wife and kids, the works, eh?'

Blystad pictured the photographs of the car his wife had been sitting in. What was left of it. What was left of her.

He blinked furiously a few times.

'No, just me,' he replied.

'What're you up to then?'

'Well, between jobs, you might say.'

Alfred nudged him hard on the shoulder.

'Have to say, you're in good shape. You were always a litttle podgy at school, I remember, but you're looking bloody fit now.'

'Yes, I … work out.'

And it was true. He didn't know how many miles he had done on the treadmill in the basement.

'Great to see you again,' Alfred said.

Blystad had to stop himself from wiping off the shower of spittle that landed on his cheek.

'Have you signed up for the reunion, eh?'

Blystad looked into his round face.

'Reunion?'

'Yeah, think an invitation was sent to everyone. Don't have

anything to do with the organisation, but it's next month. Or the one after, can't remember. Would be great, man, if you came. Fucking hell, twenty years!'

Blystad tried to smile, but realised he was failing.

'Seriously, did you not get an email, eh?'

Blystad wasn't sure what to answer. A woman went past with two bags of nappies in her hands. He followed her with his eyes. Felt hot and bothered.

'There's a Facebook group for people who went to our school,' Alfred prattled on. 'Are you on Facebook, eh?'

Blystad shook his head.

Alfred snapped his fingers.

'Tell you what, give me your address and I'll make sure you get an invite.'

Blystad didn't answer. It was hard to breathe.

'I'm a bit busy actually,' he said, abruptly. 'It's getting late, I have to get home.'

He stepped back, then stood and took a measure of Alfred.

Alfred stepped forward and nudged him again, this time in the side.

'Well, good to see you again anyway.'

Blystad smiled briefly; he wasn't sure if Alfred could tell how desperate he was to get away, as quickly as possible.

'See you again.'

He lifted a hand, then turned and walked away, picking up speed. He felt Alfred's eyes on his neck, like two laser beams. When Blystad turned into the next aisle, he stopped, leaned against the shelves and squeezed his eyes shut.

What the fuck was he going to do?

Should he ask Alfred to keep quiet and not say that they'd met?

He might not mention it to anyone. Why would he? But then there was the fucking reunion. Hundreds of old pupils would be there, all reminiscing, and then that old gossip, The Shower, would say guess who I met at Brandbu…

Blystad knew what it meant.

He had to move.

Again.

∴

He always had a rucksack ready in the bedroom at home, packed with everything he needed. Money, passport, clothes, light and practical tools, dehydrated food that didn't take much space, water, a basic first-aid kit. He got the rucksack out of the cupboard, checked that everything was there and nothing was out of date. It was all good.

Damn Alfred, he thought.

Damn Facebook and damn the fucking reunion. He didn't want to move, not again; he'd kind of settled in Brandbu, even though his life was monotonous and boring. He didn't do much more than sleep, watch TV, play on the computer, and go to the shop. And work out, of course.

He occasionally took on a job or two, but only for something to do and to earn a bit of extra money, but more often than not he said no, as there was always a microscopic chance that he might bump into someone he knew.

Norway was far too small. He should have gone to the USA and disappeared in some enormous city, but then he'd have to start all over again in a new country. At least here at home he knew how things worked, the social code, the culture. And he'd always liked Norway, Norwegian milk, the newspapers and TV programmes. And he wanted to be near his mum, as she was alone with the cat and all those demanding patients at the Majorstua Clinic in Oslo.

Blystad went down into the basement and started the treadmill, ran for three-quarters of an hour, even though it was late, while he listened to AC/DC and thought about what he should do. By the time he stopped, he'd decided to wait and see and keep an eye on the situation. He didn't need to move immediately. After all, it was some time until the reunion. It wasn't likely that Alfred would meet anyone and tell them before then.

So he took a long shower, made up some sandwiches, then sat down at the kitchen table and opened his PC. It had become a habit – since Tore Pulli was killed – to check the news in the online papers before he went to bed. He always started with *VG* and the first headline he saw was that a journalist had been killed in his own home.

Blystad clicked on the report and took a bite of his sandwich. He stopped chewing as soon as he saw a photograph of the dead journalist further down.

But … it was…

Iver Gundersen.

Blystad didn't register his own gasp. Nothing was said about how Gundersen had been killed, but Blystad opened his emails straightaway. He hadn't used his computer since the morning. He'd been playing *Call of Duty* all day. He checked to see if he'd received any new emails.

He hadn't.

All the same. Gundersen was dead.

Him too.

Blystad sat back and thought about what it might mean, and whether he should say anything to the police. But then again, what would he say?

Gundersen had been given strict instructions to delete any correspondence between them, not to print anything out, and to make sure that the emails were wiped from any servers and hard disks.

Had he done that?

Could he be *sure* that Gundersen had done that?

Blystad went to all the online newspapers he knew, to see if there were any more details. The police were still examining Gundersen's flat for clues. They hadn't finished questioning the neighbours and potential witnesses, and there would be a press conference the following morning. But for the moment, there was nothing more to be found.

Blystad thought about his wife, the escape he'd planned for her that she never had the chance to try. He'd told her to trust him and that had killed her. Henning Juul had also taken him on his word and look what happened to him.

And now Iver Gundersen.

Blystad took a deep breath, then released it through his mouth.

What the fuck was he going to do?

20

Isabel was wearing nothing more than the tiniest of bikini briefs and a scarf – a scarf that she would pull round her neck, torso and over her nipples. Sometimes she pulled it back and forth between her legs as well – to whoops and wolf whistles from the audience. Her dark curls were sleek, as though she'd taken a dip and then laid in the sun for ten minutes.

She really was a talent, Charlie Høisæther thought. She had the audience in the palm of her hand, with her seductive eyes and sensual moves. She was elegant and sexy, and used the whole stage; she wrapped herself round the pole with ease and grace, showing off the muscles in her stomach and arms. Made it look effortless.

The pumping rhythms reminded Charlie of Oslo, of Odeon.

And Tore.

In the past few weeks, Charlie had been trying to remember when they first met, how they'd become friends. But he couldn't, he couldn't remember the sequence in which things had happened. He just knew that his entire childhood and youth, his life here today, was pervaded by Tore.

Perhaps the strongest memory he had of Tore was the evening that Tore's parents were killed in a car crash, and he'd knocked on Charlie's window late that night. They'd sat in his room all night, talking and listening to music. Tore had wept on and off – the first and only time Charlie had seen him cry. Perhaps that's why this memory had stuck for so long. Because he was the one Tore had come to. Not William, nor any of their other friends. He and Tore were most alike, the two of them understood each other.

For a few moments, Charlie had forgotten the show and music, but then suddenly he felt the scarf round his neck. Above him, Isabel got closer, bent down towards him, pulled the scarf to the left and right until his neck burned, then drew his face in towards her and kissed him on the cheek. Charlie knew that the audience at Senzuela, which was 95 per cent men, was jealous of him.

He finished his drink, turned round to look at the audience with a cat-that-got-the-cream expression on his face, which produced a few cheers. She took the scarf back onto the stage and finished the dance, but didn't get many tips. The men were too scared to give her much when Charlie was there. So he took out 200 reais and tucked it in her bikini, but when she was about to thank him with another kiss on the cheek, he stopped her, held her firmly by the neck, under all her curls.

'Never do that again,' he said brutally.

Then he let her go and went to the back of the club where Freddy was waiting for him, standing tall and broad.

'Did everything go well at the airport?' Charlie asked over his shoulder, as he moved towards the exit.

'Yep,' Freddy replied. 'The plane was delayed, but everything went fine at customs.'

'How much did he have with him?'

'Just over 20,000 euros.'

A quarter of an apartment, Charlie mused. That wasn't much. A good thing the deliveries were frequent.

'Has Daddy Longlegs called?'

'No,' Freddy said.

Charlie swore to himself. He'd read what had happened in Norway, but the details in the online papers were scant.

As soon as they were out on the street, Charlie lit a cigarette. A car sailed by, close to the pavement in front of him. It made him look up and over to the other side of the street. A black Audi had stopped there, motor running. There were two men in the car. Charlie nodded to Freddy, who immediately knew what he was thinking.

Freddy dodged the passing cars and crossed over to the other side of the road, putting a hand to his inner pocket as he approached.

As he was about to rap on the car window, the Audi sped off, tyres screeching. Freddy was left standing in a cloud of exhaust.

And the car was gone.

Moments later, Freddy was back with Charlie.

'I got the registration number.'

Charlie took a draw on his cigarette as he looked to see if the car was coming back.

'Do you think that's the one that's been outside your building recently?'

'Don't know,' he said. 'Looked the same. Same colour and model.'

He didn't like it, that was for sure. God knows, he had plenty of potential enemies in the area. And knowing what was going on at home in Norway at the moment, who knows what might happen.

'I'll find out who they are,' Freddy said.

Charlie continued to stare down the road. The car was nowhere to be seen.

'There's a party at Hassan's in B Block later,' Freddy said. 'Do you want to check it out?'

Charlie shook his head.

'Going in again?'

Freddy nodded towards the strip club.

'No,' Charlie said, and threw the cigarette butt down on the ground, but didn't step on it. 'Take me home. I've had enough of whores for one night.'

21

Henning thought about Iver, the fact that they'd left him to hang there and bleed to death.

It bore all the hallmarks of torture; someone had tried to get information out of him. His flat had been ransacked, which also indicated that whoever was responsible had been looking for physical evidence as well. Notes, printouts – presumably that was why they had taken Iver's mobile phone and computer.

Henning thought about what he'd asked Iver to do no more than a week ago: to try and find out more about Rasmus Bjelland, in particular, about his relationship with Tore Pulli and Charlie Høisæther. Henning had done some research on Bjelland himself in advance of interviewing him in 2007, and remembered that carpenter Bjelland and his Brazilian wife had fled Norway and started out for themselves in the property development business down there in Natal, Brazil, with Bjelland working as Charlie's carpenter. But then one of Bjelland's business associates had been shot when he went to look at a potential site. And even though the man still had cash on him when he was found, the local police had concluded that he'd been the victim of a robbery.

Brazil was a country of corruption and crime, and it wasn't entirely unthinkable that someone in the business didn't like the fact that Bjelland and his wife had also set up store – especially as Bjelland had been accused of supplying the police with information as part of their 2007 Norwegian-Brazilian operation. It was widely rumoured that what Bjelland told the police had led to a lot of people being arrested, charged and then sentenced.

His wife might be of interest.

Mariana, wasn't that her name?

Bjelland hadn't told him much about her, except that he'd had to leave her, or rather: send her away to a secret address. Presumably that meant she would be just as hard to find as Bjelland himself, but Henning decided to give it a try all the same.

He opened a new window and typed 'Mariana+Bjelland+Natal'. Got hits for a hotel in Hordaland, an Italian language school and a horoscope for celebrities who had Saturn in Aquarius. He found some Brazilian sites as well, but nothing that was relevant. Google asked if he meant Marianne.

He tried just Mariana+Natal. Found the Facebook profile of a woman called Mariana Natal, photographs of what looked like a town getting ready for fiesta, a website that claimed to give the precise distance from KwaZuluNatal to Ilha Mariana.

Henning sighed.

His thoughts went back to Charlie Høisæther and the fact that Bjelland had worked for him. He did a search for Høisæther as well, used his proper name Charles and then typed in Natal and Mariana. The first hit made him sit up and move closer to the screen.

It was an article from a local paper in the Natal region. Henning couldn't understand the text, but judging from the pictures, it was about the development of a new residential complex. Charlie was standing smiling in front of a digger. There were several other people around him, including a Mariana de la Rosa. She was standing in the background with a file in her hand and a hard plastic helmet on her head. If she didn't actually work for Charlie, she certainly knew him.

This was the woman Bjelland had married, Henning reasoned, and then googled her name. Found a woman with exactly the same name, who had a Twitter account. She was also on Facebook, but she was from Monterrey. It was, Henning discovered, a very common name and he started to lose hope. If Mariana de la Rosa didn't want to be found, or if Rasmus Bjelland had hidden her away, she would probably keep a low profile, just like her husband.

Henning worked his way through the first thirty hits, but found no one with any likeness to the woman who was photographed with Charlie. Not until he clicked on to a news website and saw a report about a woman who had died in a car explosion not far from Alto do Rodrigues on 16 June 2007. The woman was called Mariana de la Rosa and there was a small square photograph of her further down the page.

It was her.

So Mariana de la Rosa was dead.

Henning Google-translated the article, and even though a lot of the text made no sense in Norwegian, there was little doubt about the essence of the story: Mariana's car had blown up because someone had wanted it to. The police went as far as to say the explosion was caused by a bomb.

Henning remembered the sadness in Bjelland's eyes when he spoke about her. Henning had originally thought it was because he missed her, because she was on the other side of the world and it would be a long time before they saw each other again, but now he understood.

Mariana de la Rosa was killed not long before Bjelland left Brazil himself. A threat to Bjelland could equally be a threat to his wife, or both of them. And the fact that they'd taken her out had given him the incentive to flee.

Henning realised his thoughts were running wild, so he sat back and tried to get them into some kind of order. He thought about what Bjelland's motive for telling him about Tore Pulli's involvement in the nineties murder might be, and wondered if perhaps he had now found it.

What if it was Tore's fault that Mariana was killed?

What if Tore had spread the rumour that Bjelland was an informer?

Then we're talking about a serious motive, Henning thought enthusiastically. And somebody had clearly given the police valuable information prior to their massive operation in May 2007, which had resulted in so many people being arrested. But it wasn't Bjelland. Henning believed him.

What if it had been Tore?

What if he'd tried to lay the blame on Bjelland afterwards?

Henning checked the time. It was late, but if he knew Veronica Nansen, she would still be up. He decided to ring her.

'Hi,' she said when she answered the phone, clearing her throat at the same time. Henning heard her sit up on the white leather sofa. 'I'm so glad you called,' she said. 'I've been worried about you. I heard what happened to your colleague. I'm so sorry.'

'Thank you,' Henning said.

'How are you?' she asked before he could start on his questions.

'It…' He straightened his shoulders. 'I'm fine,' he said. 'There's something I want to talk to you about. Is this a good time? Had you gone to bed?'

'No, no. I was just sitting here watching a bad film. What is it? Do you need somewhere to stay?'

'No, I…'

Henning wondered how best to say it.

'I've found something,' he said, and spent the next few minutes telling her about Rasmus Bjelland's wife. He then shared his most recent theories and ideas with Veronica.

The fact that Tore might have started a false rumour about someone, and that his rumour might have led to a woman being killed, didn't seem to make her angry or sad. Perhaps she'd just learned to accept that Tore had a criminal past and was still a criminal when they married, Henning thought.

'But he must have had his reasons for doing it,' Henning said. 'Which could indicate that he had a more active role in Natal than we've previously thought. And that he was still working with Charlie in some way or another.'

That wasn't hard for Henning to imagine; Tore had lied to Veronica before, and it was perfectly feasible that the two former best friends still had a kind of criminal partnership.

He shared his line of thought with her.

'Tore might have given the police information,' he carried on. 'So that Charlie's competitors – of which there were quite a few by then – would get into trouble or disappear altogether.'

It made sense, especially as Tore had struggled with debt for a few years. And who was best placed to take the blame afterwards?

Rasmus Bjelland.

A man who had branched out on his own and was not affected by the police operation in 2007. A man who knew a lot about Charlie's business – and therefore possibly also Tore's – after working with him in Brazil for years. He was a danger to them.

'Charlie's offices were also searched by the police,' Henning told her, 'but that might just have been a scam. Charlie had been in Natal for years, and he may well have strategically popped a few thousand real notes in important police pockets. Anyway, he was never charged with anything.'

'But it sounds a bit foolhardy all the same,' Veronica said.

'What?'

'Putting the blame on Bjelland. It could have backfired.'

'Exactly. And that's what Charlie's so scared of now. He doesn't want the truth to come out about the scam in Brazil, because then a lot of people would come after him. Thugs who got arrested in 2007.'

'And yet…'

It was obvious she was thinking about something.

'What?'

Henning kept an eye on the night manager, who didn't seem to be paying any attention to the conversation.

'And yet, it would be pretty smart too, if you think about it. Charlie had a clear playing field again in Natal as a result. If Bjelland was killed as well, as was obviously the plan, then all their problems would be solved. The scapegoat – the man they'd said had informed on those involved in the scam – would be gone.'

Henning nodded. It was fair point.

'The question is how to prove it,' she said.

'Yes,' Henning replied. 'Charlie would never admit anything, and no one knows where Bjelland is.'

But, Henning thought, Iver must have found *something*. The
people who'd killed him were looking for something, and had taken
something with them, not just his mobile and PC. It had to be something concrete that he could find too.

There was a short pause, but it wasn't awkward or embarrassing.
Henning liked talking to Veronica. Her voice, and the silences they
allowed to grow between them, had a calming effect on him.

'If it really was a matter of revenge on Bjelland's part,' she said,
'why didn't he just tell you that? Why didn't he say: "It wasn't me who
was the informer, it was Tore"?'

'Maybe he didn't have enough hard evidence,' Henning suggested.
'But if he knew, and was 100 per cent certain that Tore had been
involved in the murder of Bodil Svenkerud in 1996, then he might
at least try to get him done for that. Perhaps not blood revenge, but
a kind of justice, all the same – if only I managed to do my part.'

Henning could tell she was thinking about his answer.

At the same time, it was strange, Henning thought, that Tore and
Charlie should go to such drastic measures to make him stop digging
into an old murder case, when, at the time, he didn't even know it
was a murder case, let alone who the victim was. All he'd known at
that time was that Bjelland wanted him to dig about to find out
more. Even though he did suffer from memory loss from his fall from
the second-floor balcony on the evening that Jonas died, it seemed
unlikely that he'd come across any sensitive information about Tore
or Charlie so soon after the interview with Bjelland. Poking around
in old property sales and acquisitions took forever, and he would
have to have worked on other things at *123News* as well. At the point
he'd still been a long way from putting two and two together...

So, the measures Tore and Charlie took before 11 September 2007
must have been about something other than the murder of Bodil
Svenkerud.

Henning stood up.

Of course.

If Tore and Charlie had arranged for all the competition in Natal to disappear, if they had been informers and then laid the blame on Bjelland – if the truth were to ever get out, who would be the target of any revenge?

The thoughts were coming fast and hard and got him so worked up that he started to pace back and forth. He told Veronica what he was thinking.

'This isn't about an old murder case,' he said. 'Certainly not in the first instance. It's about now, about the fear of revenge from some of the hardcore gangs that were targeted in the 2007 police operation.'

It was a case of fire-fighting.

Tore and Charlie were scared of getting caught out, Henning thought. They were afraid that Bjelland had put two and two together and that he'd told Henning about his suspicions. So they got nervous when Henning started to ask questions. Which was why Tore had been keeping an eye on him, and why Charlie took a more physical approach ... the fire.

And who was left, now that Tore was dead?

Henning had long suspected Charlie, but for the wrong reasons. This made sense.

Charlie was still in Brazil, and he was trying to make all his problems vanish. In the course of the fifteen years that he'd been there, he'd worked on one residential development after another; he'd managed projects worth hundreds of millions, so Henning had no reason to doubt Charlie's financial clout. He could easily have paid for people to fix things for him in Norway – cover up what needed covering. Stop Henning's investigations. After all the arrests, he was as good as alone in Natal, and business appeared to be booming.

'But there's a lot of people who might feel the need for revenge if the truth got out,' Henning said. 'And that's why Charlie was so keen to hide it, which must also be why Iver was killed.'

It was all theory and speculation; he somehow had to verify or disqualify it all, and the only way to do that was to find Bjelland. If he was still alive.

'I think it sounds like you're onto something,' Veronica said.

'So do I,' was Henning's response.

'Just be careful, whatever you do.'

Henning smiled.

'I'll do my best.'

They finished the conversation and he turned back to Iver's desk. The police would definitely have gone through the call log on his mobile phone, but Iver wasn't exactly known for making phone calls; he preferred to talk to people face to face and to ask them things they didn't expect; to catch them unawares.

He must have spoken to someone who knew what he was onto. Maybe he'd even uncovered it all.

I have to get hold of Nora, Henning thought, whether she likes it or not. Iver might have told her, or she might know something without realising its relevance. But it was late. It could wait until morning to call. The police would also want to talk to her, which made Henning think about the grilling he'd have to go through the next day as well.

He had to delay it for as long as possible.

Henning went back to his desk and sat down, thought about what he could do to expose Charlie, if his line of thought was right. It wasn't just a matter of going to Brazil, even though that might be necessary at some point.

One step at a time, he told himself.

The following morning he was going to meet Andreas Kjær and hopefully he would then know what kind of information had been removed from the Indicia report about Tore, the evening Jonas died. It might prove to be important.

Henning looked over at the candle that was still burning down on the desk beside him. It reminded him that his time was steadily running out.

22

When he eventually got out of bed, far too early, Roger Blystad wasn't sure that he'd slept at all. But the light was forcing its way into the bedroom and it sounded like a family of birds had built a nest right outside his window.

He'd been lying there for a while thinking.

About Iver Gundersen.

About what he should do.

He'd come to the conclusion that the best thing would be to leave and start anew elsewhere. Lie as low as possible. But it was quite an effort to move and he couldn't face starting right away. And he should at least have a cup of coffee before making such momentous decisions.

When he got out into the kitchen he discovered that meeting Alfred had in fact made him forget why he'd gone to the shop in the first place. He had to have a cup of coffee, so he got dressed, and looked out of the kitchen window. There was no one outside. He looked around again when he got out onto the front step before hurrying over to the car.

Nothing out of the ordinary.

The big building on the other side of the road – a former adult education college – was still empty. As was the house beside it, which was why he had chosen to live right here. Brandbu was the perfect place to lie low. It was somewhere you drove past, rather than visited, and it wasn't on one of the main roads. Blystad was renting the house, fully furnished, from an old man who couldn't look after it anymore, but who didn't want to sell it yet as he still hoped that one of his children or grandchildren might want to live there.

It was perfect for Blystad; the old man was still the registered owner, and his name didn't appear in any register, as the contract was only between the two of them.

Blystad drove down to the shop, bought some coffee and picked up that day's edition of *Aftenposten*. While he waited for the coffee to brew, he sat at the kitchen table reading the paper.

As expected, the murder of Iver Gundersen was given a lot of attention. He flicked quickly to page three, but couldn't see anything there or on the next couple of pages that he hadn't read in the online papers the night before.

When the coffee was ready, he poured himself a large cup. He then read the paper from cover to cover, largely because he wanted to think about something else and to put off, for as long as possible, all that he had to do if he was going to move. But a name in the obituaries made him freeze, the cup halfway to his mouth.

Our beloved, wonderful sister
Our dearest sister-in-law and aunt
VANJA KVALHEIM
Born 31 December 1951
Passed away suddenly today
Oslo, 9 October 2009
You were deeply loved,
Our loss will be great.

Anne-Marit
Helmer
Brith
Lars
Beate
Olav
The rest of the family
The funeral will be held at Grorud Church
16 October
There will be no reception after the service.

Blystad sat there staring at the words, the names.

Put down his cup.

No, he said to himself. This isn't happening. This isn't fucking happening. Not her.

But there was no doubt that it was her. There they all were: Anne-Marit, Lars, Helmer and Beate. Brith and Olav.

What the hell had happened?

He went to the *180.no* directory enquiries website and typed in his uncle Lars's name. While he waited for an answer, he wondered briefly if he should perhaps not use his own phone, but then he looked at the notice again and told himself he didn't have time to go out and look for a phone box. It can't be true, he thought over and over again. That she's dead.

'Hello, Lars speaking.'

Blystad hesitated before saying hello. It occurred to him that it was quite early in the morning.

'It's…' He couldn't say his name; his throat was dry. He tried again, but the same thing happened.

Blystad heard a sigh at the other end.

'And now you call.'

Blystad still couldn't speak. He could only think of his mother, his dead mother, that he hadn't been there when it happened. The last time they'd emailed each other she hadn't said anything about being ill, she'd just told him about the journalist who had wanted to get in touch, and who had now been killed.

'Yes,' he finally managed to pull himself together. 'I just saw the notice about Mum in the paper.'

It hurt even more to say it out loud. It took all he had to stop himself from crying.

'How … did she die?' he asked.

Uncle Lars sighed.

'We're not quite sure yet,' he replied. 'But it seems most likely that it was a heart attack. She died very suddenly in the afternoon, just after she got home from work.'

Blystad swallowed a sob.

'So there's nothing suspicious about it?' he said, once he'd regained control of his voice.

'Suspicious? Why do you ask? Why on earth would there be?'

'Oh, I don't know,' Blystad said. 'I just thought…' He couldn't finish the sentence. 'Forget it,' he said, and sniffed.

They sat there listening to each other breathing for a few moments.

'Where are you?' Uncle Lars asked. 'Will you be coming to the funeral?'

He thought about it. He should, but he shook his head.

'No,' he said. 'I can't.'

Uncle Lars snorted.

Then he hung up.

Blystad sat with the receiver in his hand. 'Heart attack.' 'Died very suddenly in the afternoon, just after she got home from work.'

His mother was only fifty-seven years old. She had at least another twenty or twenty-five to go, that was certainly what he'd assumed. And he would definitely have sorted out his life by then. It had never occurred to him that she might die before.

But now she was gone.

Blystad put the phone back down on the kitchen table and buried his head in his hands.

23

Henning woke with a start and quickly sat up. It took a few moments before he realised that he was still in the *123News* office and that it was morning. A TV was on by the main desk, but only the night manager and Henning were there.

He couldn't remember lying down, and it felt like he'd spent the night with his head in a vice. He blinked hard in an attempt to shock-start his eyes, and moved his head from side to side to stretch his neck. Looked over at Iver's desk. The candle had burned right down. All that was left was an empty workplace.

Henning looked around, spotted a box of candles on a table further in. He stood up, went to get another candle, which he then put in the candlestick and lit with his zippo lighter. He stood there for a few minutes, before going to the coffee machine and pressing a button. While he waited the thirty seconds or so that it took to get a cup of coffee, he glanced bleary-eyed over at the front desk, where the night manager looked just as beat as he did.

'Morning,' Henning said, blowing on his coffee as he went back to his desk. 'Has anything happened overnight?'

The man – Henning didn't know what he was called – looked up from the screen.

'The police have just announced that they're looking for two men who were seen in the area close to Iver's flat yesterday morning,' he said.

Henning immediately felt more awake.

'Have they given any descriptions?'

'Yes.'

The man clicked on the screen a few times before starting to read what was written there. The screen reflected like a shiny skin on his glasses.

'Both are around 1.7 metres tall, they were dressed in dark clothes and looked like they might be of Eastern European descent. One of them was wearing a hoodie. The police have asked that they contact them as soon as possible.'

The man continued to read, but Henning's concentration drifted. He remembered what Durim Redzepi looked like, and the description fitted him to a tee. It seemed reasonable enough that he'd had someone with him, as no one would have managed to hang Iver from the hook and winch him up alone.

Henning remembered the first attempt on his own life, when Iver had managed to push him out of the path of the white car that was driving straight at him.

There had been two people in the car then too.

Mapping Iver's final movements had become a priority, Henning thought. He had to find out who Iver had been in touch with.

Henning thanked the manager for the update and wondered if he should go and get Iver's car – if he could find it. There was a chance that the police had discovered that Iver had a car and perhaps already managed to locate it and bring it in for examination.

The clock on the wall showed that it was just before seven. According to Pia Nøkleby, Andreas Kjær was going to be out running around ten. That meant that Henning would have to leave soon, before the office started to fill up – he didn't feel like chatting to anyone, and anyway, he wanted to get to Iver's car before the police found it and towed it away.

He finished his coffee, went out onto the street where he hailed a cab and gave Gørbitz gate 3 as the address. The police cordons had been removed, but there was still a police car outside Iver's block.

Iver had had a special relationship with his car, an old wreck that he'd owned for about fifteen years. It was a Toyota, but Henning wasn't sure of the model, only that it was red and rusty. However, it was easy to spot down one of the side streets.

He opened the door and got in, but before he put the key in the ignition, he sat there and sniffed the air. It smelt mostly of cigarettes, but also a trace of something sweet.

It smelled like Iver.

Suddenly it felt wrong to be sitting in his car. This was where Iver had sat while searching for the same answers Henning was looking for now. Too many people had been hurt because of all this. Because of him.

He turned the key and started the engine. It was still a few hours until ten o'clock. He decided to go to a café for some breakfast. It was going to be a long day.

∴

Maridalen was a long, thin valley, with lots of trees and forest, so the colours were beautiful on an autumn Monday. Henning had, on a few occasions, taken Nora and Jonas out there for a walk; he'd made sandwiches and juice, in an attempt to continue a tradition that he'd experienced as a boy – long walks in the country, Trine and him on the path, asking lots of questions.

But Jonas was a child who quickly lost heart, and felt imaginary pains in an arm or a leg, so it was seldom enjoyable. That, Henning thought, was the main reason they hadn't done it more often. If he was to be perfectly honest, however, he had to admit that, all too often, he'd used work as an excuse to leave Nora alone with Jonas at the weekend.

Henning drove as far as he could into Maridalen on asphalt, and stopped at the big, open parking place by Skar. He stepped out into the autumn day; the clouds were wispy grey with the odd patch of white, and were starting to gather ominously above the trees. Henning did up the zip on his jacket and looked at his watch. It was just before ten.

There were four other cars in the car park, but Henning had no idea if one of them belonged to Andreas Kjær, so he started to walk.

To begin with, he followed the wide cycle track that went up to the river, and soon the fast-flowing, burbling water appeared to his right. Henning had expected to meet someone running or on a bike, or perhaps see a tent on the shores of the lake, but he saw no one, and his only companion was the river.

Henning looked from side to side, turned around, looking in every direction, and realised that he had walked almost the full two and a half kilometres from Skar to Øyungen Lake without any sign of Kjær. The big lake opened out in front of him, with camping sites and shelters along the shore, and a dam to stop too much water flowing down towards the city.

But no Andreas Kjær.

Just when he felt it had all been a waste of time, he heard footsteps behind him. He spun round.

The policeman looked different from when he'd last seen him, largely because it was now daylight – it had been dark in the entrance to the building on Fossveien. Henning had gone to Andreas Kjær's home to ask him a few questions about the night of the fire, the night a report was made about Pulli sitting in a car outside Henning's home. But Kjær hadn't been home. So Henning had talked with Kjær's kids and learned that someone had recently killed their dog. Put it on the veranda for the kids to find. It was obvious to Henning then that pressure had been put on Andreas Kjær to stay quiet about something. And when Andreas Kjær had turned up, it was clear he wanted Henning to stop digging.

The man who had thrown Henning up against the wall that evening and told him to stay away from him and his family, now scoured the shore with eyes that looked as though they hadn't seen much sleep for a while.

'Should we go over there?' Kjær asked, pointing to the dam.

'Why not?' Henning said.

Kjær was wearing running clothes, black trousers and a sky-blue jacket that rustled as he walked.

'Have you got your phone with you?' he asked.

'I left it in the car,' Henning told him.

They walked down a gentle slope. The dam rose up a couple of metres to their left, perfect for anyone with a sense of adventure and balance to walk along. As they got closer to the sluices, the thunder of fast-moving water increased.

They stopped in the middle of a wooden bridge. The water poured over the edge of the dam in an arc that cleared them by several metres. Kjær got a packet of cigarettes out from his jacket pocket and lit one with a lighter that he then returned to a trouser pocket. He scoured the surroundings before taking a step forwards and leaning against the side of the bridge.

'What's your deal with Pia?' he asked.

Henning watched the water thundering down below them, then carry on to a quieter stretch as the river headed towards the city. He positioned himself closer to Kjær.

'I know what's at stake for you both,' he said. 'I've promised not to write about anything you tell me, on the condition that you tell me everything.'

The policeman gave him a disconsolate look.

'I don't really have much to tell.'

'You changed the Indicia report about Tore Pulli from 11 September 2007, the evening I lost my son.'

Kjær shook his head. 'Not exactly,' he said.

Henning turned towards him.

'What do you mean?'

'I didn't change anything.'

The muscles in Kjær's face tensed.

Henning waited for him to continue.

'You know that they threatened me. My family. They wanted access to Indicia.'

'Yes.'

Kjær sighed.

'The bloke who called spoke Swedish with an Eastern European accent. I don't know his name. After they'd killed the dog, I agreed to meet him one evening, and I managed to sneak a laptop out from the station, one that I knew had Indicia installed.'

Kjær took a last draw on his cigarette and then threw it into the water. He scrutinised the trees along the river as though he expected someone unwelcome to jump out at any moment.

'We agreed that I would get a room at the Scandic Hotel out in Asker, and that I would wait there for five knocks on the door. Which I did. And I opened the door to two men who looked more or less the same. Quite short, strong. They both had guns. They were both wearing hoodies.'

Henning thought about the two men that the police wanted to talk to in connection with Iver's murder. Kjær's description was almost the same.

'I'd managed to get Pia's username and password, and I'd already logged on to Indicia when we sat down. The man who spoke Swedish took over the computer, while the other one made sure that I couldn't see what they were doing on the screen.'

Henning listened carefully to every word Kjær said.

'But I did manage to see that he went into a report and that there wasn't much written there, maybe five or six lines, only I couldn't see what it said.'

Again, Kjær looked around. There was no one nearby.

'So I don't know what he deleted.'

Henning considered what he'd said.

'Do you think you'd recognise them if you saw a picture of them?' Kjær took his time.

'Possibly,' he said. 'I don't know. Let's put it this way: I tried to have as little eye contact with them as possible.'

Henning thought about the report after the fire in his flat, which concluded that the cause of the fire was unknown. The cursory, routine police investigation had found nothing, and by the time Henning had felt strong enough to start asking questions himself, the Indicia report, the details, had been changed.

'When was this?'

'You mean when did it happen?'

'Mm.'

Kjær squinted up to the left.

'Now, when was it, let me think. Some weeks ago, maybe? Maybe more.'

Some weeks.

So that meant the information hadn't been considered dangerous or incriminating until two years after the report was written. About the time that Henning had finally reached a point when he thought he had no choice but to examine the circumstances of his son's death. About the time that Tore Pulli had been killed, and about the time that Henning himself had had two attempts on his life. Which meant that the information in itself was worth the risk of threatening a policeman and all that that entailed, and that it was urgent.

They stood together, looking around for a few moments. Henning remembered the patrol car Kjær had sent to Markveien that evening, where Pulli was sitting, monitoring Henning's movements. He also knew that the police had checked Pulli's car and knowing who Pulli was, and wondering why he was sitting in the same place, several nights in a row, thought it necessary to report the fact.

'Was there any spoken communication between you and the patrol officer who wrote the report about Pulli being on Markveien those few evenings?' he asked.

Kjær shook his head.

'But then I didn't ask for any particular feedback. If there had been anything important, I would have heard about it.'

'So the fact that my flat went up in flames ten minutes later wasn't important enough? You didn't think that there might be a connection?'

Kjær looked at Henning.

'Fires happen all the time in this town, Juul. You have no idea how many callouts we get, every day, every night, and as a rule it's just someone who's forgotten to turn off the hotplate. It would be easy enough to miss it, especially as it's not the force's primary responsibility.'

But it was shoddy police work, all the same, Henning thought, not to check Indicia for any details that had been reported that evening. That should be standard procedure.

They were both silent for a few moments.

'Is there anything else you'd like to know?' Kjær then asked.

Henning thought about it.

'Just one thing,' he said. 'You said that he deleted something.'

Kjær wrinkled his nose.

'Just now. You said you didn't know what he'd deleted. How do you know that he deleted something? How do you know that he didn't just change the details instead?'

'Well…'

The policeman shifted his weight.

'I just assumed he'd deleted something because…'

He seemed to think about it.

'I heard the keyboard. You can hear the difference between someone writing something and someone deleting something. Or moving up and down through the text with arrows, for that matter.'

Henning considered this claim, and agreed that he was probably right.

'And you were sitting beside him when he was doing this. How long did it take?'

Kjær shook his head.

All of a sudden, he looked more alert.

'When I think about it, it was actually really quick. Just a few taps on the keyboard, I'm guessing the arrow keys, and then a firm, decisive click. As though something was being deleted. And that was that. They got up and left.'

Henning thought through what Kjær had just said. No more than a few taps. What could be so important that it had to be removed, and yet it didn't take more than a moment to delete?

The answer was simple.

A name.

Tore Pulli had not been alone in the car that evening.

24

Twenty-five minutes after Andreas Kjær had continued his run, Henning got into Iver's car, sweaty and tired. He didn't start the car straightaway, but instead rested his hands on the wheel and took some deep breaths. He removed his mobile phone from the glove compartment and saw that Bjarne had called, and that he'd sent him a text message as well.

Booked an interrogation room for two pm. Good if you could come a bit before. BB

Henning looked at his watch. Nearly half past eleven. Going to Tønsberg and back would take about three and half hours, probably even longer, but he would rather do that than hang around killing time at the police headquarters.

So Henning didn't answer the text. Then, just as he was about to put his key in the ignition, something caught his attention. Iver's car was full of rubbish – old newspapers, half-empty bottles, coins and squashed cigarette packets – and on top of some old parking tickets in the mid-console lay a business card that made Henning very curious indeed.

Preben Mørck. The lawyer.

The man Henning suspected was Daddy Longlegs.

When had Iver got that?

Henning checked the parking tickets under the card. One of them prompted him to start the car and head towards the centre of Oslo. Tønsberg would have to wait for the moment.

∴

Preben Mørk's office was no more than a stone's throw from the

Oslo Courthouse, and when Henning arrived, the lawyer was not around. His secretary – a woman with long dark hair who was sitting straight-backed like a priestess – told him that Mørck would probably be back in about fifteen minutes. He'd gone out to meet a client, she said, and had called only minutes ago to say he would be a little delayed.

'I don't think he has time to speak to you today,' she continued. 'His schedule is…'

'Not to worry,' Henning interrupted, 'I just have a quick question for him, then I'll leave.'

The secretary scowled at him, but Henning turned away before she made any further attempt to get rid of him.

Preben Mørck was lawyer to the wealthy Hellberg family from Tønsberg, and Henning had met him there briefly, when suspicion fell on the mother of the family, Unni Hellberg. There was evidence to indicate that she had orchestrated the death of her sister-in-law, Ellen, sixteen years earlier, and that she had contracted Tore Pulli to carry out the murder.

Henning thought it highly unlikely that a woman like Unni, who hardly frequented the criminal underworld, would have contacted Tore Pulli herself. She had presumably used a middleman, someone she knew and trusted, who in turn knew who to contact.

The family lawyer, for example, whom she'd known for years.

And Tore was a childhood friend of Unni's son, William, as was Charlie Høisæther. So it was more than likely that Mørck, who had spent a lot of time with the family over the years, knew both Tore and Charlie.

Henning approached the secretary again.

'How does it work?' he asked when he got to the reception desk. 'Do you make a note of everyone who comes to see Mørck?'

'You mean some kind of log?'

'Mm.'

She shook her head.

'We're only a small firm, and as you saw for yourself, there's no reception downstairs. So, if you're wondering if I know who's been here, well, I've got Mørck's diary. Most people who come actually have an appointment.'

Henning ignored the thinly veiled criticism. Instead he looked over at a small stack of business cards on the desk. He picked one up and studied the gilt lettering that said Preben Mørck, Lawyer.

'Well, if I wanted to know who was here on Friday, could you tell me?'

He put the card down again and gave her the most charming smile he could muster.

'In principle, yes, but I'm afraid I can't.'

'That's a shame. Perhaps you could tell me then if someone like me came by on Friday? Who didn't have an appointment?'

The secretary hesitated before saying, 'I wasn't here on Friday.'

'That's a shame too.'

Just then, the door opened and Henning smiled broadly at the lawyer who walked in. He stopped in his tracks as soon as he saw Henning. Preben Mørck was wearing a full-length coat, with a navy blue scarf round his neck, which he hung up on the coat stand. He put his briefcase down and placed his coat on a hanger.

'Hello, Mr Mørck,' Henning said, while wondering at the same time if this could really be Daddy Longlegs, who gave jobs to people like Ørjan Mjønes and Durim Redzepi? This tall man, who looked utterly harmless? In fact, he didn't even look like a lawyer, more like a man who hated wearing suits, and didn't fit the one he was wearing. The jacket was a few sizes too big, and his thin arms seemed to drown in the sleeves.

'My secretary has undoubtedly already told you that I don't have time to…'

'Yes, she has,' Henning said. 'I'll leave right away. I just wanted to ask one quick question, if that's OK. Maybe two.'

He smiled as disarmingly as he could. Mørck took a deep breath.

'Be quick then, I've got a teleconference in…' he looked at the clock.

'Four minutes,' his secretary piped up behind Henning.

Mørck picked up his briefcase again and then stood about a metre away from Henning.

'So, how can I help you?'

Henning studied him for a moment. Is he alarmed to see me? Nervous? Nothing in his eyes or demeanour gave anything away. Mørck just stood there, waiting for his questions.

'You've no doubt heard that a colleague of mine was killed yesterday,' Henning said. 'Iver Gundersen?'

'Yes, of course,' Mørck replied. 'Terrible business. My condolences.'

'Thank you. I just wondered if you'd ever met him personally?'

Mørck didn't answer straightaway.

'If I'd met Iver Gundersen?'

'Yes.'

He thought about it.

'Very possibly. After all, he's – sorry, was – a journalist. Why?'

'Has he ever been *here*?'

Henning indicated the office. Again, Mørck took a moment to think.

'Why do you ask?'

'Well, has he or hasn't he?'

'No,' Mørck said. 'Not that I can remember.'

Henning studied his face.

'OK,' he said. 'That's it. No more questions.'

'Really?'

The lawyer laughed.

'Journalists seldom run out of questions, Juul, so is that really all you wanted to know? And what does that mean, the day after your colleague was killed?'

'Nothing at all, Mørck, I was just curious. I know that he came to see someone around here on Friday, and that he parked just up the street, but that of course doesn't mean it was you he came to see. Thank you for taking the time. You better make sure you don't miss your conference call now.'

Henning smiled, turned and headed to the door.

'Bye,' he said. 'See you again, no doubt.'

He closed the door behind him, but didn't go down the stairs to the street. Instead he pulled out the ticket he'd found in Iver's car, from the same car park where he'd parked only half an hour ago, which showed that Iver had been there only last Friday. And Mørck's business card had been on top of all the rubbish in Iver's car – and the card looked just as new as the one he'd just seen in the office.

Iver was here on Friday, Henning thought. Everything seemed to point to that.

So why hadn't Preben Mørck admitted it?

And what was Iver doing here?

25

Bjarne called again just as Henning drove out of the Hanekleiv Tunnel on the road to Tønsberg. He pulled into the inside lane behind a silver Nissan Primera and picked up his phone.

'Where are you?' Bjarne asked. 'Sounds like you're in a car.'

'Yes,' Henning said. 'I … I'm going to meet someone.'

'Right. And who would that be?'

'I'm going to see if I can get hold of William Hellberg.'

There was silence for a beat.

'But he lives in Tønsberg.'

Henning didn't answer.

'Did you not see the message I sent you earlier on today?' Bjarne asked, his tone more aggressive.

'Yes, but I was already on my way,' Henning lied. 'Can we not do it later in the afternoon? Four-ish or thereabouts?'

Bjarne sighed.

Henning could hear from the background noise that the policeman was in the office. He heard a mouse click.

'I'll see if we can delay a bit,' Bjarne said. 'But get back as soon as you can. I'm not the only one waiting for you here.'

'I'll do my best,' Henning said. 'How's the investigation going? Have the two guys you wanted to speak to come forward?'

'No.'

'One of them sounds like Durim Redzepi,' Henning said. 'Do you remember I told you about him?'

There was another silence.

'He's one of the people we're checking up on, of course,' Bjarne said.

Lies, Henning thought, but he didn't confront him with it.

'I have to go now,' he said. 'I'm nearly in Tønsberg.'

'OK. Come back as soon as you can then.'
'Will do.'

∴

William Hellberg lived in a highly desirable area on an island close
to Tønsberg, where each house was bigger and grander than the next.
Hellberg's large black SUV took up the greater part of the cobbled
driveway in front of the house where he lived. Henning parked
beside a manicured hedge and rang the bell.

A thin woman in her thirties opened the door. Her lips were dry,
her eyes were swollen and she was wearing no make-up.

'Hi,' Henning said, and introduced himself. 'Is William at home?'

She tilted her head and looked up at him.

'What's it about?' she asked.

'It's about a case I'm working on,' Henning said. 'I work for
123News. I dropped by William's office in Tønsberg and they said he
was working from home today.'

'What case?'

Henning wondered for a moment if she was Hellberg's personal
secretary, but then he noticed the diamond ring on her finger and
the fact that she wasn't exactly wearing office clothes – jeans, a white
top and grey woollen cardigan.

It was Hellberg's wife.

'It involves a few things,' Henning said. 'Including a murder.'

The colour drained from the woman's cheeks.

'Murder?' she said, and pulled the cardigan tighter. 'What on
earth would William have to do with that?'

'Nothing,' Henning assured her quickly. 'But he does know some
of the people who might be involved. From a while back … in his
past.'

The woman nodded slowly, studying him.

'Did you say your name was Juul?'

'Mm.'

'One moment, I'll see if he's got time to talk to you.'

The woman pushed the door to, without closing it, and disappeared into the house. Henning took a step back. The well-maintained lawn around the house still looked remarkably green and summery although the scattering of leaves showed it was definitely autumn. And the house gleamed white, even though it was a grey day. The driveway looked like it'd just been swept, and a moped was parked next to the garage. Presumably it belonged to the son.

It took a few minutes before the woman returned.

'Please, come inside and wait,' she said in a rather thin voice. 'He's on the phone.'

'Great. Thank you,' Henning said, as he followed her inside.

Hellberg's wife showed him into the living room, where he sat down on a generous sofa and placed his arms on the wide leather armrests. It made him feel he was lording it up, so he folded his hands on his lap instead.

'Nice house,' he commented.

'Thank you,' she said.

'Lived here long?'

She paused before answering: 'Six years.'

She moved a tablet that was lying on the sofa and put it down on a small table in the corner, by an armchair that looked like it might be an expensive antique.

'Would you like a cup of coffee while you wait?' she asked, without looking at him.

'Yes please, I'd love one.'

The unnamed woman swiftly disappeared into the kitchen. A couple of minutes later she came back with a cup and saucer that she put down on the table in front of him, the porcelain clinking. Her hands were shaking.

'I've had a little too much coffee today,' she said, apologetically. 'It always makes my hands…'

She gave them a little shake and tried to smile. The colour that had drained from her face a little while ago had still not returned.

She looked ill, Henning thought, and for a second he felt slightly guilty to have barged in like this.

He took a sip of coffee.

'It's tempting to drink too much coffee when it tastes this good,' he said, and smiled. 'Are you also working from home today?'

'No, I'm not working,' she said. 'I only work on Thursdays and Saturdays.'

Henning nodded.

'Where do you work?'

'In a children's clothes shop in Tønsberg. I need ... something to do as well.'

The woman gave another cautious smile.

Henning could well imagine it. The Hellberg family was very wealthy, so even though she probably didn't need any extra income, it no doubt helped her self-esteem to contribute a little. Polishing the family silver must be pretty boring in the long run.

She pushed her shoulders back ever so slightly when her husband came into the room. Henning turned to greet William Hellberg, who came towards him with his hand out and a smile.

'Henning,' he said. 'How nice to see you again. What are you doing down here?'

It was less than a week since they'd last spoken, at the hospital in Tønsberg, after Henning and Iver had found William Hellberg's missing sister, mainly thanks to Nora. The gratitude and friendliness that Hellberg had shown Henning then did not appear to have waned.

'Hello,' Henning said, standing up.

They shook hands.

'Sorry to disturb you at home,' he said.

'I'm the one who should apologise for making you wait so long,' Hellberg said. 'How are you?'

Henning gave a fleeting thought to Iver, but tried not to show it.

'Not too bad, thanks. And you?'

'Well ... yes, I'm fine, thank you.'

Hellberg glanced over at his wife.

'The past few weeks have been rather demanding, what with Mother and … well, all the rest,' he said. 'Which is why I'm working from home today. There's so much going on in the office at the moment. Though it has started to quieten down now.'

'Of course.'

They looked at each other for a few seconds, then Hellberg stepped past him.

'Anne Cecilie, could you maybe get me a cup of coffee too?'

Hellberg gave his best salesman smile as he watched his wife go into the kitchen without a word. He sat down opposite Henning.

'So,' Hellberg said, the leather sofa squeaking under him. 'What brings you to Tønsberg again, Henning? Are you looking for somewhere to live?'

Henning shook his head.

'I'm here because of your lawyer,' he said. 'Among other things.'

Hellberg's salesman smile disappeared, and he frowned.

'Preben?'

Henning nodded.

The sound of a coffee machine could be heard from the kitchen.

'And why's that?' Hellberg said.

Henning didn't answer his question, and instead posed his own: 'How well do you know him?'

Hellberg looked surprised, then laughed a little.

'I know Preben very well, of course. He's been the family lawyer for many, many years. Why do you ask?'

Hellberg gave him a searching look. On his way to Tønsberg, Henning had wondered about how far he should go. He was taking a chance by airing his suspicions, based on nothing but speculation, but then again, he didn't have much time, and none of his potential sources were overly friendly.

So he shared his theory with Hellberg, namely that Mørck had been Unni Hellberg's contact with Tore Pulli in connection with the Ellen Hellberg murder, and it was very likely that he was also the middleman for several other criminals in Oslo.

When Henning had finished, Hellberg shook his head and said, 'That's an absurd theory, Henning. I know Preben to be a good man through and through. And I find it hard to believe that he would be involved in anything like that.'

A moment later, Hellberg's wife came back into the living room with a cup of fresh coffee. The cup was bigger and thicker than his, and didn't have a saucer, but she held it with both hands. She gave it to Hellberg without looking at either of them. Her hands were no longer shaking.

'Thank you, darling.'

He smiled up at her. Anne Cecilie Hellberg retreated again, and William followed her with his eyes.

'But then,' Henning started, as soon as they were alone, 'do you know of anyone else who your mother could have trusted in that situation?'

Hellberg took a sip of coffee.

'No, but…' He shook his head. 'But it still sounds utterly far-fetched.' Hellberg met Henning's eye. 'Have you told your theory to the police?'

There was an aggressive edge to his voice now.

'No,' Henning said. 'Not yet.'

He took a sip of coffee, and looked at Hellberg. The man wore a suit, even at home. He was running a hand over one side of his head, pressing his shoulder-length, slicked-back hair even more neatly into place. He got up and paced back and forth.

Henning wondered if he should mention Iver's possible visit to Preben Mørck, but decided against it. Instead he moved the conversation onto a different track.

'The last time we met, Hellberg, we talked a bit about Tore and Charlie, and the fact that they'd fallen out over a flat in Natal.'

Hellberg was apparently still lost in his own thoughts.

'Sorry?'

Henning repeated what he'd just said.

'Yes, yes, I remember that.'

'Can you tell me anything about them?'

Hellberg frowned. 'About Tore and Charlie?'

He took a few steps back towards Henning and sat down on the sofa again.

'I'm trying to get a better understanding of their relationship,' Henning explained. 'How serious the conflict might be. I know that they did a lot together and that they'd done some deals that were not entirely legal, but … do you know if Tore was involved in Charlie's business in Natal as well?'

Hellberg looked up at him.

'How would that work?'

Henning shrugged. 'I don't know.'

Hellberg shook his head

'I very much doubt it. Tore certainly never said anything about it to me.'

Both were silent. Hellberg took some careful sips of coffee, and Henning wondered how to further the conversation.

'So Tore beat Charlie up at some point, because of the flat we were talking about, and they had no contact after that, until Tore was killed?'

'Not as far as I know, no,' Hellberg said.

'But I don't get it,' Henning said. 'Was that all?'

Hellberg didn't seem to understand his question.

'Let me put it another way … I've been thinking about this,' Henning said. 'And I can't quite believe that the argument they had was only about a flat.'

Hellberg held up the palms of his hands as if to say, I have no idea.

'I haven't spoken to Charlie for a long time,' he said. 'So I don't know.'

'But surely they'd disagreed or argued about other things before? Had Tore never thumped him before?'

'No, I don't think I ever heard either say anything bad about the other,' Hellberg said, with a faint smile. 'And even if Charlie could be a complete bastard when he was younger, he would never have dared cross Tore.'

Henning put down his cup.

'Tell me more,' he urged Hellberg. 'What were they like when they were young?'

Hellberg breathed in and gazed up to the left. Then smiled.

'Tore was naturally the centre of attention,' he said. 'Wherever we went. He was incredibly charismatic. The women…'

Hellberg's smile broadened. Then he shook his head.

'Tore was a classic leader, took up a lot of space. And people listened to him. If there was any disagreement about where we should go or what we should do, Tore decided and we did what we were told.'

He paused for thought.

'I imagine it can't have been easy for Charlie, always to be overruled and steamrollered. But you should ask him yourself.'

'I've tried to get hold of him,' Henning said. 'He doesn't answer his phone.'

Hellberg shrugged.

Charlie might like being the one who has the final say, Henning thought. The one with power. And at the time, Tore was struggling with money and debt and Charlie's pockets were full. But that still didn't explain why Tore had floored him. Veronica knew nothing about it either. She'd never met Charlie.

Henning asked Hellberg if there was anything else he could tell him about his two friends.

'No, I'm not sure that there is,' he said.

Henning waited a moment, in case more memories resurfaced. Then he finished his coffee and stood up.

'I won't take up any more of your time then,' he said. 'But if you do think of anything in relation to what we've talked about, I'd really appreciate it if you got in touch.'

Hellberg stood up as well. His face was thoughtful.

'There's no point in going any further with your Preben theory, I'm sure of that. He's solid.'

'Perhaps,' Henning said. 'But if you do think of anything, anything at all, it's easiest to get hold of me by email.'

Henning didn't want to give out his mobile number unless it was strictly necessary.

'Right you are.'

Hellberg gestured for Henning to go first. He put on his shoes in the hall and then turned towards Hellberg.

'Thank you for the coffee. Sorry to bother you again.'

They shook hands.

'My pleasure,' Hellberg said. 'It really was no bother at all.'

Henning turned back and opened the door, then walked out into the day: the clouds were higher, and the sharp light hurt his eyes.

Hellberg followed him out onto the step.

'Let me know if you ever consider moving down here, and I'll sort out a good house for you.'

Henning looked over his shoulder at Hellberg, and saw that the smile was back on his face.

'I'll certainly do that,' he said.

26

On the way back to Oslo, Henning thought about what Hellberg would do now, if he would challenge his lawyer straightway, or if he would choose not to.

Henning guessed it would be the latter.

It was just a theory, and regardless of whether it was true or not, it was dynamite enough to destroy the trust that had been built up over the years, perhaps even a friendship. And there had been too many scandals in the Hellberg family recently. Henning found it hard to believe that William Hellberg would want to create even more fuss without substantial proof.

Henning checked his mobile phone and saw that Bjarne had booked a room for four o'clock. That meant that he had plenty of time, even if there were traffic jams and delays on the way into the capital. He didn't make any effort to get back faster, and instead looked around at the fields that stretched out on either side of the road as he drove. He saw some smoke snaking up from a chimney in the distance. It made him think of winter, which was fast approaching: the worst time of year in Norway, when darkness forced people indoors and curtains were drawn.

He wondered if he would be here when the snow came.

Or if the people who had killed Iver would get him as well. They'd already tried a couple of times.

Henning had never dwelled on the idea of his own death before Jonas was born, but when he became a father, all that changed. And he thought about it every day. He didn't want to die.

Yet death wasn't as frightening anymore. He'd even found himself longing for it, a way to find peace. He thought about what he would do if he survived the next few days and weeks. If he would stay in

Oslo, if he could cope with being near to Nora and watching the child grow up. If he would continue to work as a journalist.

As he passed the toll booths at Fornebu, a thought struck him. He was sitting in Iver's car, a car that Iver had obviously used a fair bit recently. And even though it was an old model, it still had an electronic pass that registered every time the car went through the tolls. Henning made a mental note to mention it to Bjarne when they met. There was no way of knowing whether it would tell them anything other than that Iver had been out and about in Oslo, but it was worth checking.

∵

Nora was lying on the sofa, half dozing, when the doorbell rang. The loud noise made her start and she sat up and looked around.

She'd been lying there all night.

And all day.

She hadn't dared go to bed, scared that she would still be able to smell Iver on the sheet or pillow, scared that she might find a sock or a t-shirt that was his. The book on his bedside table – *The House of the Mosque* by Kader Abdolah – was a book she'd given him. She knew that the very sight of it would make her cry, and she couldn't bear it. She'd cried enough.

She pushed back the blanket, put her feet down on the floor, and shuffled her way slowly to the intercom out in the hall.

'Hello?'

'Hello, it's Bjarne Brogeland.'

The police.

No, she couldn't face that now.

'Can I come up?' he asked.

Nora didn't answer.

'It'll only take a couple of minutes,' he added.

Nora sighed and put a hand to her forehead, which suddenly felt very hot. She moved her hand to her hip, which had gained some extra padding in recent weeks. She pressed the button, and listened to the buzz at the other end.

'Thank you.'

Nora put the receiver back in its cradle and stood there waiting for twenty seconds until there was another ring. She pressed the button again, then opened the door, leaving it ajar. She would normally have panicked and looked around to make sure the flat was presentable, but her mother had done nothing but tidy before she left for work.

There was a gentle knock on the door, then Bjarne opened it and came in. He gave her a grave nod and said hello.

'Hi,' Nora replied.

Bjarne closed the door behind him and stood there looking at her. Nora couldn't deal with his concern, so she pushed herself away from the wall and went into the living room. She heard Bjarne take off his shoes in the hall and then follow her in.

'How are you?' he asked.

She didn't answer.

'Sorry,' he said. 'Stupid question.'

They sat down on either side of the coffee table.

'Have you noticed the officers that are watching you?' he asked.

'No.'

'Good,' he said and smiled. 'That means they're doing their job.'

He pulled a notebook out of his jacket pocket.

'I have to ask you some questions about Iver. I hope that's alright.'

Bjarne's voice was so soft and warm that it had her on the verge of tears.

She nodded.

'Yesterday,' Bjarne said. 'Iver was here with you in the morning, wasn't he? But he went back to his flat pretty early, is that right?'

She nodded.

'Did he say what he was going to do?'

She shook her head.

'Only that he had to work.'

'Do you know what he was working on?'

She shook her head.

'And you didn't ask?'

'Yes, I did, but he didn't tell me.'

Nora heard how hard her voice was when she said that.

'He didn't mention it the evening before, or anything else in the past few days?'

She shook her head again.

'But he was very distracted, so I realised he was busy with something. Something big enough for him to want to work on a Sunday morning.'

Bjarne scribbled a few words down in his notebook.

'But otherwise, there was nothing about his behaviour that might indicate he was in trouble or having problems?'

Nora shook her head.

'He didn't seem to be frightened or anxious?'

'No.'

Just thinking about a normal day, an evening like any other together with Iver, made Nora's stomach start to knot. She straightened up and tried not to think about the fact that she'd gone to bed only half an hour after he'd arrived, partly because she was nauseous and tired, but mainly because he was so much later than he'd said he would be.

'It's possible…'

The reservation in Bjarne's voice made her look up.

'…that Iver was working with Henning on something,' Bjarne said. 'In connection with the fire in his flat.'

The thought had been lurking just below the surface since she found Iver, but she hadn't allowed herself to think about it, not until now. She felt a surge of anger through her body, so powerful that she couldn't say anything.

'He didn't mention anything to you?'

She immediately shook her head.

'Did he talk about Henning at all?'

She knew what she wanted to say, but it was none of Bjarne's business that Iver seemed to be more concerned about Henning than her.

'Have you spoken to Henning since…?'

Nora shook her head again, then a long silence ensued.

Bjarne leaned in towards the table.

'What about Rasmus Bjelland … Did Iver ever mention that name?'

She looked up at him again.

'Who's that?' she asked.

'A joiner,' Bjarne replied. 'That's to say, he certainly used to be one.'

'What about him?'

'I don't know,' Bjarne said, and tried to smile. He looked at his notebook and the few words he'd written down.

Did this Bjelland man have anything to do with Iver's murder, Nora wondered. Or the fire at Henning's flat?

'It's just a name that's cropped up,' Bjarne said. 'Needn't mean anything at all. But you've never heard of him?'

'No.'

A heavy silence filled the flat for the next thirty seconds.

Until Bjarne's telephone started to ring.

27

Henning was glad to find a free parking space on the street below police headquarters. The stop-start drive into the centre had worn him out, so he was grateful that he didn't have far to walk.

He looked at his watch. Five minutes to four. He locked Iver's car and was hurrying towards the zebra crossing when he noticed a car crawling next to the pavement. The sun was reflecting on the windscreen, but Henning could see that there were two men inside. The window on the passenger side was open. When Henning saw an arm reach out, he at first assumed that the man in the passenger seat wanted to ask him for directions or something. Then he saw the gun, and it was pointing straight at him, and he understood what was about to happen.

The man holding the weapon was called Durim Redzepi, and he was an experienced killer – perhaps the one who killed Iver – and now he'd found Henning too. Henning quickly looked around for somewhere to hide, something to grab and use as a weapon or protection, but no, it was at least five metres to the nearest car or barrier; there was nowhere to hide, no one nearby to help him.

A moment later he felt a sharp stab in his chest, a force strong enough to spin him halfway round, before a second projectile grazed his ear.

But Henning didn't register anything more, as he was already falling backwards.

Downwards.

Towards the ground.

∵

The sudden acceleration pressed Durim Redzepi back against the seat, but he managed to poke his head out of the window and look back. He caught a glimpse of Henning Juul lying on the pavement.

He wasn't moving.

He hadn't fired the best shots and the distance was greater than it should have been. But there wasn't time; there were cars behind them and Juul would have suspected something if the car had been just waiting by the pavement. The question was how good his aim had been.

He had *definitely* hit him though. He was sure of that.

Jeton Pocoli pressed the pedal to the floor and it wasn't long before the police station disappeared behind them. They jumped the lights at Schweigaards gate and tore on towards Tøyen, past the prison, then up to Carl Berners plass.

'Is there anyone behind us?' Pocoli shouted.

'Don't think so,' Redzepi said. 'Stop driving so fast.'

Pocoli slowed down, they merged with the traffic, and then had to stop at a red light by the Munch Museum. They both kept a vigilant eye on the side mirrors. Soon they heard the sirens.

'Drive up towards Økern,' Redzepi said, clutching his gun.

Pocoli did as he was told; as soon as the lights changed to green, they roared up the hill, past the public baths on the left. And then very quickly they were surrounded by trees.

'We have to dump the car,' Pocoli said.

Redzepi nodded, but his thoughts were elsewhere. Juul had seen him. Just before he fired, their eyes had met. So it was more important than ever that they'd succeeded this time.

28

'What d'you say, Mister High? Nice, eh? Good?'

Charlie Høisæther looked at himself in the mirror. The white suit fitted neatly around the shoulders, arms and legs – just as it should. The shirt underneath – also white – was stiff and smooth, elegant.

'No, no, no,' Mariana had said the last time he tried on a similar outfit. 'You look like a snowman. OK, so you're Norwegian – we can see that – but you need something that compliments your beautiful eyes. A blue shirt, for example, and a grey suit.'

Charlie was, of course, perfectly aware that his eyes were blue, but he hadn't known that she'd noticed them, or liked them. And later, when he'd changed into something else, she'd come right up to him, pulled down the shirt sleeves so they peeped out from under the sleeves of his jacket, and her tiny fingers had stroked his skin – then she'd taken a step back and studied him.

'Perfect.'

He hadn't been sure if she was talking about the suit or him, but he'd thought a lot about it later. Whatever the case, he'd bought two suits and shirts in the colours that Mariana had chosen, and he had bought her a dress, too, as a kind of bonus.

But there was no Mariana to help him now, no assistant who knew what was needed before he knew it himself. And when he'd stood on the beach after her wedding to Bjelland some years later, he'd felt something he'd never felt before. Not for any woman.

The feeling that he'd done something wrong.

That he'd made a mistake.

That he'd not grabbed the opportunity before it was too late. The chance to have Mariana for himself. To make her his wife instead of Bjelland's.

And when she'd come over to him and thanked him for the gift and his 'blessing' – that he was fine with the fact that they'd started up in the same business – she'd seen it in his eyes. She knew him so well after working with him for three years, she knew her and Bjelland being in the same business wasn't the problem. Her now being Bjelland's wife was. Deep down, she knew he loved her. And when, a few seconds later, she gave him a hug, her hair had brushed his neck, light as a feather, and her skin had smelled of lavender, of the sea, and a different future, without him. One that he now realised he yearned for.

The wedding party had carried on through the night and late into the morning. But Charlie had gone home early. He'd sat on another beach and gazed out over the ocean with the scent of lavender in his nose. And when he heard, several months later, that she was dead, he'd wept for the first time that he could remember. He'd been angry. He'd felt the need to take out his anger on someone. Which was why he'd taken a rare trip home to Norway, which was why he'd argued with Tore.

Again.

They had, for a while, disagreed about money, but when Tore had asked him again if there was anything that would make him change his mind about the damned flat, Charlie had replied, in an invincible rush of cocaine, that he might consider it, if Tore would give him a night with Veronica.

He hadn't meant it, not really, and even though they'd shared women before, he should have known that those days were long gone, and that the rules were different when it came to Veronica. The next thing he remembered was waking up with a jaw that was broken in the same precise way that had become so famous when Tore worked as an enforcer that the staff at Ullevål Hospital had named it after him.

'What d'you say, Mr High?'

The question jolted him out of his memories. He rubbed the scar on his chin and looked at himself in the mirror.

'I need something darker,' he said. 'I look like a snowman in this shit.'

∴

Mister High.

Charlie had liked the nickname to begin with. There was humour in it, as no one in Brazil managed to pronounce Høisæther, and it said something about who he was and how far he'd got in the years that he'd lived in Natal. But it had other connotations that he liked less and less, that he was high on drugs – as if he needed to do that anymore. Charlie had had his last line of coke at the Odeon the evening that Tore broke his jaw.

Freddy was sitting in the Mercedes, when Charlie was done with his shopping.

'That went well then, boss?' he asked. 'Looks like you've got two, or even three, suits?'

'Two,' Charlie replied. 'Only two this time.'

He got into the car and they drove off. The car's suspension worked hard on the uneven, cobbled road, but soon enough they reached a smoother surface.

'So, what's happening tonight, boss? Senzuela?'

'No,' Charlie said. 'Drive me home.'

Ten minutes later they were outside Sports Park, where Charlie had his penthouse. He looked over at the palm trees on the other side of the road, where the dark Audi had been parked in the past few days – the car that had sped off outside Senzuela the evening before. Charlie hadn't seen it this morning. The car didn't belong to any of his competitors in the area, but according to Freddy and the police it had been reported stolen a couple of weeks ago.

Charlie didn't like it.

Something was brewing.

29

There was a wailing sound.

Something pressed, pushed. Him?

Henning wandered in and out of a fog that seemed to be alive. His chest was gurgling. His head ringing. It was night, no, day – or evening; every time he opened his eyes, the light changed. He felt nothing, realised that he was being lifted out of a flashing blue car, down onto the ground. The wheels rattled as someone pushed him into a building and along a corridor where long yellow and white arrows flashed above him. He tried to lift his hands. Couldn't. Tried to swallow. But it only left a dry metallic taste in his mouth.

He was turned over – it felt like floating. He was cold, could hear voices around him, urgent voices that spoke in some sort of code that he couldn't understand. They went down what must be another corridor, through a door, into a room where the light was even brighter.

Then he lost all consciousness.

Didn't even notice that everything went dark.

∵

When Henning came to, he realised where he was. He was in hospital. He couldn't feel any pain, not in his arms or legs. For a moment he was scared that he'd been paralysed, but then he managed to move a finger, then an arm. Pulled it out from under the covers and lifted it ever so slightly.

So this was what it felt like to be shot.

A nurse opened the door and smiled; he wasn't even sure it if was a man or a woman, he just saw a white figure moving. He or she said something that Henning didn't catch. He heard a tap being turned on. The nurse's smell reminded him of something, but he couldn't remember what.

He closed his eyes.

Durim Redzepi had tried to kill him. Again.

Henning attempted to push himself up, but he had no strength in his right arm. He tried with the other, only just managing to lift his upper body, and ended up lying on his side.

'No, no, no, you mustn't do that,' the nurse said. 'Lie down again.'

Henning didn't lie down. He focused on the nurse who came over to him. It was a woman. Long brown hair in a ponytail. About thirty. Kind eyes.

She helped him to settle back down.

'You were incredibly lucky,' she said. 'The bullet went in here,' she pointed to a spot just below her collarbone, 'and out the other side.'

Lucky, Henning thought. Yes, perhaps.

'There's a major artery just below the collarbone, the subclavian artery. If you'd been hit there, well…'

Then it could well have been a fatal wound, Henning thought.

She gently moved his leg.

'We opened the wound and cleaned it, gave you a tetanus injection, so you won't be able to move your arm much for a while. It'll be very stiff, because of the bleeding in your shoulder joint. You will gradually regain feeling, but we've put your arm in a sling in the meantime. And we've given you some morphine for the pain.'

That explains the drowsiness, Henning thought.

'Where am I?' he asked.

'Ullevål Hospital,' the nurse replied.

'Is there anyone from the police here?'

'There's an officer just outside the door.'

The nurse then turned around and sailed out of the room. Henning felt dizzy again and let his head sink into the pillow. He closed his eyes and immediately went back to sleep.

30

Whenever he went to a hospital, Bjarne Brogeland thought of Alisha, his daughter, and the woman who had given birth to her. The labour had lasted for 42 hours, and the strain and blood loss had left Anita looking like a wan, worn-out heroin addict. It had taken her a long time to recover.

Henning's room was at the end of the corridor on the third floor, and Bjarne showed his ID to the officer sitting outside, before rapping on the door three times and going in.

Henning barely opened his eyes when Bjarne sat down by the bed. Bjarne looked at him for a long time and then shook his head.

'I've known a few people in my time who had guardian angels,' he said. 'But you really take the biscuit. Have you been speaking to someone up there?'

He pointed to the ceiling.

'The next floor up?' Henning asked, coughing. He blinked furiously. 'No, I haven't done much other than lie here.'

Bjarne laughed.

Then was promptly serious again.

'Have you spoken to anyone since you were admitted?'

'Anyone in the same uniform as you, you mean?'

Bjarne confirmed this with a nod.

Henning gave a slight shake of the head.

'It was Durim Redzepi who shot me,' he said.

His voice drawled. He sounded drowsy.

'Are you sure?'

Henning nodded slowly.

'He's not been caught then?' he asked.

'No one's been arrested,' Bjarne said, shaking his head. 'We found the car in flames at Etterstad, not long after. But no Redzepi.'

'There was someone else in the car too,' Henning said. 'A driver.'

'Did you get a look at him?'

Henning shook his head.

'Bet it's buzzing on the fifth floor right now. First Iver, then me.'

Bjarne didn't answer.

'Has the media got wind of the fact it was me who was shot?'

'Don't think so. Not yet, anyway.'

Henning nodded slowly again.

They were both silent for a while.

'I can't stay here,' Henning said.

Bjarne had guessed Henning might say this.

'There are so many entrances to a hospital this size,' Henning continued.

'Yes, but we're keeping a close eye on you, obviously.'

'So, one officer out in the corridor – that's your definition of keeping a close eye?'

Bjarne lowered his head.

'I can't stay here,' Henning said again. 'I've got too much to do.'

Bjarne gave him a stern look.

'*You* are not going to do anything at all. Not now, and not when you're better. You have to let us deal with this now. Someone is trying very hard to kill you, Henning. You need protection.'

'You can start by getting me out of here.'

Henning's speech was faster and more determined now.

'You know you can't even stand up.'

'I can if I have to.'

Bjarne shook his head and said nothing. He knew how stubborn Henning could be.

He took a deep breath.

'I'll go and make some phone calls,' he said. 'But there's someone else here who wants to speak to you.'

'Oh right,' Henning said. 'Who is it?'

Bjarne walked over to the door, opened it and waved to someone. Opened the door a little wider.

∴

When Henning saw her face in the doorway, drawn and pale, but beautiful, he immediately tried to push himself up in the bed, but didn't manage. He sank back down onto the mattress.

Nora took a few hesitant steps into the room. She brushed the hair from her eyes, then came towards him.

There was so much Henning wanted to say – that was perhaps why no words came out. He followed her with his eyes as she sat down on the chair where Bjarne had been sitting, keeping her distance at first, but then moving the chair closer.

Neither of them said anything, they just looked at each other.

'I'll be back shortly,' Bjarne said, and closed the door behind him. There was silence in the room. Tears streamed from Nora's eyes, and she rummaged in her bag for a handkerchief.

'I want to thump you,' she said, and put her bag down on the floor.

Her voice was tense, quiet – as if there was something holding back the words.

'Thump away,' Henning said. 'Just don't hit me here.'

He pointed to his shoulder and attempted to smile, but his lips were split and dry, so he ran his tongue over them. But instead of carrying out her threat, Nora held a hand out to him.

He took it, held it.

Cold, sweaty. Small.

Once upon a time, they'd held hands everywhere, all the time. It had felt so strange to begin with; he didn't like public displays of affection, and found weddings and kissing in front of other people awkward.

But after a while it became natural. As did the distance that gradually crept in later, the daily routines that never quite worked, not once Jonas had come into the world. Their hands never sought each other out, because they were always full of something else – food, a rucksack, nappies, a pram, post – everything became so trivial and they didn't have time to see each other, to look after each other.

And they drifted apart.

Henning and Nora were separated when Jonas died. It was Nora's week to have him, but because she wasn't feeling well, she'd phoned Henning and asked if he could collect Jonas from school and have him for the night. She didn't want him to catch anything. A decision that was so full of love had changed their lives forever, and he knew that Nora would carry it with her for as long as she lived.

'How do you feel?' she asked.

'Awful. How about you?'

'Me?'

She let go of his hand and wiped her nose. Gave a fleeting, albeit sad smile.

'How am I? Well, actually…' she said, as though she hadn't thought about it for a while. 'I don't have the words to describe how I feel.'

Henning said nothing.

'They'll keep you in here for a few days, no doubt,' she said, after a pause.

Henning was about to say 'I can't', but gave a quick nod instead. He noticed her cheeks were slightly plumper than when they last met.

'Iver was a good man,' Henning said.

It felt odd to say it out loud.

'However strange it sounds, well … we actually became quite good friends.'

Nora's head sunk down to her chest.

'He talked about you a lot,' she said.

'Did he?'

She nodded and dried a new tear.

'He really looked up to you. As a journalist.'

Nora stood up and turned away. She sniffed and quickly put a hand to her face. Henning tried to push himself up in the bed again, and this time managed. He half sat up, holding his weight on his left elbow.

She turned back. Another Nora was standing in front of him now. She was angry, more determined.

'I've tried to think if there was anything about Iver's behaviour in those last few days that might explain what happened. If he said anything in passing. But…'

She shrugged and opened her hands.

'I can't think of anything. Iver's dead, and you're lying here half dead.'

She waved her hand at him.

Henning didn't like what he saw in her eyes.

'So,' she said, coming towards him. 'What can we do to stop all this?'

Henning shook his head.

'You don't need to do anything.'

'I knew you'd say that.'

Her voice was hard and angry.

'Yes, with good reason,' Henning replied. 'There's no way you're getting involved in all this as well.'

She stopped right by the bed.

'So you don't think I'm involved enough already?'

'You know what I mean.'

Henning looked at her.

'You're pregnant, Nora,' he said, trying to control the volume of his voice. 'The risk is too high. These people don't think twice about killing. And I can guarantee that they're interested in you, as you were Iver's girlfriend and my ex. So the best thing you can do, is to lie low, and wait and see if I manage to…'

'Right, that's so bloody typical,' she snapped. 'No one can sort this out except you.'

Henning took a deep breath.

'I don't want to argue with you, Nora. You and I can't work together on this. I would never forgive myself if anything happened to you. It was enough with J—'

Henning looked away, but he could feel Nora's eyes on him all the same. A moment later Bjarne came in through the door with a steaming cup in his hand.

'Hi,' he said.

Neither Nora nor Henning answered. Bjarne registered the loaded atmosphere and kept quiet.

'It's too dangerous, Nora,' Henning said eventually. 'Do me a favour. Stay away. Keep out of the way until this is over.'

Nora just stared at him, for a long time, then she picked up her bag from the floor and put it over her shoulder. She marched towards the door, and said to Bjarne as she passed: 'I'll be waiting outside.'

Bjarne and Henning said nothing until she'd banged the door closed behind her.

'Make sure she stays out of this,' Henning said.

Bjarne gave a faint smile.

Henning knew that Nora could be just as stubborn as he could when she wanted to be.

'Just look after her,' he said, and realised he was tired. 'Now more than ever.'

Bjarne nodded.

'We will.'

31

Their retreat had been long and time consuming, and only now that they were back at Flurim Ahmetaj's place, did Durim Redzepi finally feel safe. But he was far from relaxed. He paced back and forth in the living room, still clutching a gun in his hand.

'Brother, can't you just sit down for a moment?' Ahmetaj asked.

Redzepi shook her head.

'You're making *me* stressed as well,' Ahmetaj added.

'I can't help it.'

Ahmetaj was sitting in front of two big computer screens. Redzepi had never really understood what he did and how he did it, but his good friend from Metrovica was invaluable when it came to data, cameras and surveillance. And that would definitely come in handy over the next few days.

His phone rang.

Redzepi didn't recognise the number, but he guessed it might be Daddy Longlegs.

'Hello?' he said, with a kind of sigh.

'Juul is in Ullevål Hospital,' Daddy Longlegs said. 'You'll have to go there and…'

Redzepi closed his eyes and blocked out the rest of the sentence. He shook his head.

'I can't just walk in and…'

'I don't care how you do it, as long as you do it – and preferably before he talks to the police.'

'Juul saw me,' he protested. 'He knows what I look like. I'm no good to anybody if they arrest me. And we've got the funeral tomorrow so I can't…'

Redzepi was interrupted by an exasperated sigh at the other end.

'We shouldn't be talking about this on the phone,' Daddy Long-legs said. 'But you'll just have to find a solution, and fast. You were given a job, and it's not finished yet. Call me on this number from another phone when you've got something to tell me, and it better be good news.'

He hung up.

Redzepi swore again and threw the phone down onto Ahtmetaj's sofa.

'I can tell that went well,' Ahmetaj remarked.

Redzepi didn't answer. Carried on pacing back and forth.

What the fuck was he going to do?

He looked over Ahmetaj's shoulder. There were live pictures on the screens from each of the cameras they'd set up in the graveyard. Each screen was divided into four squares. Eight cameras in total. He took a step closer.

'Henning Juul's got an ex-wife, hasn't he?'

'Yep.'

Redzepi thought it all through again. Neither he nor Jeton Pecoli should venture outdoors right now. He pointed to Ahmetaj's screens.

'Do you have any more of those?'

Ahmetaj understood that he was talking about cameras.

'No, but I could get some. How many do you need?'

'Two, three. And I need someone who's good at getting into peo-ple's houses. If you can do that for me, I'll make you rich.'

Ahmetaj smiled.

'Now you're talking my language, brother.'

∴

Trine wandered around the living room as she checked the news-papers on her mobile phone. None of them had anything new to report. Not even *TV2 News Channel*, which she had on in the back-ground, could tell her anything she didn't already know.

The journalist who had been shot had not been named yet, but

Trine was terrified that it was Henning. They said on the news that the journalist would live, but how serious were the injuries?

Trine found the telephone number for Ullevål Hospital and dialled – asked to be put through to intensive care. After a long wait, she heard a woman breathing heavily into the phone, and then spit out: 'Intensive care.'

'Hi,' Trine said, hesitantly. 'I'm calling to … ask if my brother was admitted earlier on today?'

'What's his name?'

'Henning Juul,' Trine said.

There was a moment's silence.

'And you are…?'

'Trine,' she said, and wondered briefly if she should give her surname, that she might get help then, but she didn't. 'My name's Trine,' she repeated. 'I'm his sister.'

There was another long silence.

'He was admitted at 16:04,' the woman at the other end said, finally.

So her fears had been right.

She closed her eyes and swallowed a sob.

'Can you tell me … how he is?' she asked, when she'd pulled herself together.

'I'm sorry,' the woman said, 'the patient has to name you as family before I can give you any information. And I'm afraid he hasn't.'

No, Trine thought. Of course he hasn't.

'I can go and ask if he'd like to talk to you?'

'No,' was Trine's prompt reply. 'No need. I just…'

She stopped herself.

'Sorry?'

The woman's voice was softer now.

'It's nothing. Maybe you could say…'

Trine changed her mind.

'Forget it. Thank you for your help.'

Trine hung up and sat down on the sofa, wrapped herself in the blanket, thought long and hard. Then she got up and started to walk around the room again.

Eventually she had an idea.

She wondered how much money she had in her account. It didn't really matter – if she was short, she could always ask Pål Fredrik for help. She tapped on the speed dial for Katarina Hatlem, her former head of communications at the Ministry of Justice and Public Security.

'Trine?'

Katarina's voice rose as she said the name, as though she was surprised to get the phone call, but was also a bit wary.

'Hi,' Trine said.

There was a pregnant pause.

'How are you?' Katarina asked.

'I'm fine,' Trine said. 'But I have a problem, and I wondered if you might be able to help me.'

32

Henning was not prepared for how unsteady he would be when he got out of bed and took his first few steps. It felt like the morphine and blood loss had knocked everything off balance. And his arm was also stiff and couldn't be moved.

He put one foot in front of the other. The doctor who had come by only half an hour ago said it was a matter of time – he would soon be able to go to the toilet, eat, shower and dress on his own. The pain would also ease, the doctor assured him, even though that seemed unlikely to Henning at that moment.

Henning sat down again and took some deep breaths.

There was a knock on the door. Bjarne popped his head round.

'There you are,' he said. 'Are you ready?'

'Depends on how you look at it.'

Bjarne smiled.

Henning could see through the window that it was dark outside. He wondered if it was late afternoon, evening or night.

'We're the only ones that know about this, right?'

Bjarne chuckled softly.

'What do you think – that I'd sacrifice my job to get you out of here, without clearing it with my bosses first?'

Henning looked at him.

'There was no other way of doing it,' Bjarne said. 'And relax, hardly anyone knows where we're going. Anything else you want to know before we go?'

Henning raised his good hand to his face to wipe away the sweat. Then he took a deep breath and said, 'Right. I'm ready.'

He stood up again, took a step, stopped. The walls were dancing in front of him.

'Do you want me to hold your arm or support you in any way?'

Henning scowled at him.

'You look a little groggy, that's all,' Bjarne said. 'It's OK to ask for help, you know.'

'That's exactly what I'm doing.'

'A bit *more* help then,' Bjarne said, and smiled.

Henning didn't answer.

The policeman looked around.

'Did you have a jacket with you?'

'I did,' Henning said, 'but I think they had to cut it off, and must have thrown it way.'

'Anything else we can wrap round you? A blanket or something? It's pretty cold out.'

Henning shook his head.

'I'm so warm that...'

'Yes, yes, and it doesn't hurt anywhere,' Bjarne teased. 'I'm sure it won't matter if you get a cold as well.'

Henning ignored him and took another step. It was more control led, even though he felt like he was on board a tiny boat on a vast ocean.

'You OK?' Bjarne asked. 'Should I get a wheelchair?'

'It'll be fine,' Henning said. 'I need to take my keys.'

'I've got them,' Bjarne said.

Henning nodded and breathed steadily, trying to stop the images that undulated and spun in front of him.

'Medicine?'

Henning hadn't noticed that Bjarne was holding a plastic bag, which he lifted and shook. You could hear the pills rattle in their bottles. It sounded like it was coming from inside Henning's head.

'You're going to turn into one hell of an addict.'

'Mm,' Henning responded.

Bjarne walked to the door and opened it for him.

'Come on then, Rocky. Let's get ready to rumble.'

∴

They left the hospital via a spiral staircase at the back of the building. The effort made him sweat, so it was good to get out into the cold evening air.

'Where are we going?' Henning asked, when they were sitting in Bjarne's car.

'To a safe house we sometimes use when we need to look after someone. The owner is in Spain at this time of year. You'll be safe there.'

'Spain,' Henning said. 'That sounds nice.'

Bjarne drove carefully, making sure to avoid as many of the potholes in the road as he could. Henning tried to straighten up in the passenger seat. The movement made him grimace, so he tried to turn his mind to anything other than the pulsing pain in his shoulder.

When they'd been driving for a few minutes, Bjarne's phone started to ring. He picked it up, checked the number, and then put it down again.

Henning glanced over at him.

'Just work,' Bjarne said. 'Nothing that can't wait.'

Henning must have fallen asleep, because when he opened his eyes again, they were there. The street was called Tennisveien. There was a big hall nearby with cars parked outside.

Henning tried to get out by himself, but couldn't do it. Bjarne hurried round to the other side of the car and helped him out.

'Careful,' Henning said.

His arm hit the door as he got out, and a sharp pain shot through him. He stood swaying for a while as he gritted his teeth. Took a few small steps, which made the world spin. The windows of the house were like mirrors, and he was glad he didn't see himself. He wanted to have a bath, but it would probably be a while before he could do that.

Bjarne supported him up the small slope and then let him go when he was steady again. Fumbled for the keys and unlocked the door.

Bjarne went in, deactivated the alarm and turned on the lights.

Henning managed to get in by supporting himself on the door. He kicked off his shoes in the hallway and looked around.

It was a fantastic house.

Clean, white surfaces. He could see into a large kitchen that led into the living room, with a fireplace in the corner, TV, dining table. Stairs up to the next floor.

'The bedroom is upstairs,' Bjarne said.

Henning nodded, and headed towards the stairs. He could manage as long as he held onto the banister. Upstairs there was a TV den with a door into another room. The room was small, but big enough for Henning and it had everything he needed – a window, a bed, a desk and a small TV mounted on the wall.

'I'll just go down and make a couple of phone calls,' Bjarne said. 'Shout if you need anything.'

'There is one thing,' Henning said.

Bjarne turned to look at him.

'What's that?'

'Do you know any Samis? Are there any Samis who work for the police?'

Bjarne frowned.

'Samis? As in the Sami people – the Laplanders?' He looked at Henning with puzzled eyes. 'You're joking?'

'No.'

'You want to know if I know any Samis?'

'Yes, I do.'

'Why do you ask?'

'Because I want to know.'

Bjarne looked at him perplexed.

'I know one,' he said, eventually. 'A girl – or rather, a woman.'

'Who is she?'

Bjarne continued to study him.

'She's called Ann-Mari Sara,' he said. 'A forensic technician from the crime investigation service who's been seconded to us for a while. We met her briefly at Iver Gundersen's flat. Why do you ask?'

Henning thought about it. He remembered Sara, of course.

'No particular reason,' he said.

Bjarne burst out laughing.

'No, right,' he said. 'And there's a virgin with three children living just down the street.'

Henning sighed. He would have gladly told Bjarne what he was thinking, as he'd helped him so much, but he couldn't say anything. Not yet.

'Thanks,' was all he said. 'For everything. You're a good man, Bjarne.'

'Tell that to the taxman.'

Bjarne smiled and went downstairs. Soon all was quiet around Henning. He breathed deeply and relished the feeling of being alone, without having to fear that someone might burst in through the door at any moment.

He sat down on the bed. His head was still spinning. He needed more painkillers, couldn't think with all that pulsing and thudding, so he got two tablets out from the bag that Bjarne had brought with him. There were a couple of bottles of water in the bag as well and, not without difficulty, Henning managed to unscrew the lid from one. He swallowed the tablets, turned on the TV and read about himself in the captions on the screen, even though he was as yet unnamed. Assistant Chief of Police Pia Nøkleby said that there would be a press conference later on that evening.

Henning relived the moment when he saw the mouth of Redzepi's gun, the sting in his chest. He was tired, so he lay down. His shoulder felt like it would explode, but he closed his eyes, saw the colours on the inside of his eyelids churning, round and round and round. A peace fell over him and then once again, darkness.

33

That evening, Roger Blystad did something he hadn't done for a long time. He went down to Brandbu and found a seat in the Sandbeck pub.

A football game was being broadcast on a large TV screen, so he sat as far away from it as he could, but it was impossible to avoid the noise. The pub was fairly empty, and it didn't take long before he was half cut. At regular intervals, the barman came over and replaced the empty glass he had turning in his hands with a full one, as he thought about his mother and her funeral the next day.

When his grandfather died in the late eighties, Blystad had been in Amsterdam setting up a drugs delivery to Norway. His mother had phoned late in the evening to say that the cancer had finally got the better of the tough old man.

Blystad had sat in silence for a long time after, thinking about what a fine man his grandfather had been. Then he felt the need to walk, to find a bar that was still open and to raise a glass to him. So he'd ended up sitting in Café Pollux, and had a couple of beers. It was a fine farewell, even though he was hundreds of kilometres away.

Which was why he'd wanted to have a couple of beers in honour of his mum now. But once he'd sat down, he'd found it hard to stop at two.

It did cross his mind how stupid it was to sit there in the open when what he should really be doing was getting ready to leave. To drive far away from Brandbu as quickly as possible. But it was liberating and it felt good not to give a damn. He liked the feeling of living on the edge, not quite being in control.

But he would be stupid if he didn't do anything. He'd met Alfred in the supermarket. Iver Gundersen was dead. And now his mum was gone too.

How many more warning lights did he need?

It was half-time in the match, and an advert blared out over the loudspeakers. The glasses and bottles twinkled in the mirror behind the bar. A man was sitting on a stool in front of the taps, both hands round his glass. It looked like he was searching for the meaning of life in the froth. Blystad heard the odd burst of laughter, but no conversation he could follow.

A baby was crying on TV. And again, he thought about his mother. She had cried a lot. Every Christmas Eve, when that boys' choir sang on TV, her eyes welled up, but he always got the feeling it wasn't related to the music.

He sat there drinking until everything was blurred. Perhaps that's why he didn't hear the voice at first, which belonged to a woman who was trying to get his attention. It was only when he saw something waving in front of his eyes that he raised his head a touch, and looked straight into a face that he recognised, but couldn't place.

'It *is* you,' she said, and smiled.

Blystad blinked a couple of times.

'You do recognise me, don't you?'

Her smile was teasing.

'Of course,' he said, rifling through his memory.

'Helene,' she said. 'You came to my house a few months ago – changed the weatherboard cladding on the south wall?'

Blystad clicked his fingers.

'That's it,' he said, and tightened his grip on the glass. 'Sorry, I…'

'Ach,' she said, poo-pooing it, 'I'm used to no one paying attention to me.'

She pretended to cry, which made him smile. And God, it was good to smile. Helene revealed her uneven teeth. But he liked the fact they were wonky, and that it looked like she smoked. She was wearing an almond-coloured Stetson, a short jacket and tight trousers.

He actually liked pretty much everything about her.

'Are you here on your own?' she asked.

'Yes, I…' He looked down.

'I'm here with some girls,' she said. 'We haven't seen each other in a hundred years, but all they're talking about is their kids.' She rolled her eyes. 'So just say if you'd like a little company.'

He glanced up at her, saw the look in her eyes. He remembered how chatty she'd been. He'd thought then that she was lonely, recalled the painful gratitude when he'd said yes to a cup of coffee after he'd finished the work.

She lived alone, had presumably done so for a while – Blystad hadn't noticed any men's shoes in the hall. The whole house had felt like a hangover from the seventies, something she'd inherited. Helene herself could hardly be more than thirty-five. But there was something cheerful about her. Her face made him think of the sun.

'I … don't think so,' he said. 'Not today.'

It sounded like a rejection, and in a way it was. But still she stood there.

'You look sad,' she said, gently. 'Like you could do with a bit of comforting.'

Again, the underlying invitation. Another time, Blystad thought. Any other day. But right now, he wanted to be alone.

'Well, let me know if you change your mind. We're sitting just over there.'

She smiled, he raised his glass to her, and she swung her hips as she sashayed back across the room to her friends. Blystad sent her a sheepish smile before buying another beer and settling down to meditate on his mother.

It was a few months since he'd seen her. At the opera house at midday on the fourth of August. He'd found her down by the water. She'd given him a big hug and started to cry straightaway – as she always did. Blystad had chuckled in her ear and told her she mustn't do that. 'I know,' she said. 'But I can't help it.'

They'd sat there for several hours; she'd taken a picnic with her for both of them. And then she'd shed a few more tears when he said he had to go. They'd agreed when and where to meet again: Frogner Park at midday on the twelfth of December, so it would be easy to remember. They only had minimal contact via email.

I have to give her a proper send-off, Blystad thought. He couldn't go to the funeral itself, but he had to be there. See her. The coffin. Be near her one last time. Lay some flowers on her grave.

And he realised then how sick and tired he was of being on the run. Sick and tired of keeping a low profile, not engaging with people. Like Helene. Girls in cowboy hats. He didn't actually like Stetsons, not on men or women, but she'd worn it with a teasing smile. As though she was perfectly aware that it didn't suit her, and that was the whole point. She'd made him smile. He could count on one hand the number of people who had done that in the past two years.

It would have been nice not to care about a thing, he thought. Just to live, be, not worry about the consequences. Maybe he should just say 'here I am' and see what happened – he immediately stopped that thought experiment. It would not end well.

He had to think of something.

He couldn't live like this any longer.

34

Charlie Høisæther was in the bath, alone, when the phone rang. He half expected it to be Isabel calling to say she was sorry that she'd been so difficult before she went to work – it was just that she wanted to do more than dance at Senzuela, now that everyone knew she was his girlfriend. 'I'm tired of disrespecting myself,' she'd said, 'and surely it's not good for your business having a girlfriend who's an exotic dancer.'

'Well, then maybe I shouldn't,' he'd replied, and later regretted it. Isabel had started to cry and then ran out of the flat.

But it wasn't Isabel on the other end, it was Freddy. Charlie sat up in the tub and let the water run off his arm and hands before he put the phone to his ear and said, 'Talk.'

'You wanted to know who was driving the stolen Audi that's been parked outside your apartment recently,' Freddy said. His voice sounded miles away. 'Well, the driver's sitting on a chair in front of me right now. He's a bit out of it as Hansemann gave him a bump on the head. We can carry on having fun, if you like, but I thought maybe you'd have some questions you'd like to ask yourself?'

Charlie stood up. The bathroom mirror clouded over, but he could still see the outline of his well-rounded paunch. He got out of the bath and opened the door out into the hall.

'Pick me up in 10 minutes. Hansemann can keep an eye on him in the meantime.'

'OK, boss.'

∴

As usual, Freddy sped through the streets and it didn't take long before they stopped outside a half-finished building to which Charlie had managed to get keys. The previous owner had had plans for a shopping centre, but then went bankrupt before the project was complete. Charlie didn't know what he wanted to do with the site yet – it was far too small for his leisure complex – so while he bided his time for the right idea to come along, the place was perfect whenever they needed to talk privately to someone, one on one. The closest neighbours were well out of earshot.

Charlie and Freddy walked down the spiral driveway that should have led to the shopping centre's underground car park. The road was not surfaced, so they kicked up a dust cloud. There were a few lit bulbs down there, and ahead of them they saw a young man sitting on a chair with his hands tied behind his back. And behind him, a large, fair man with a goatee beard and huge tattoos on his arms. Hansemann was wearing a black, short-sleeved linen shirt and black linen trousers – clothes that would hide a splash of blood or two.

'Mister High, I swear…'

'Shh,' Charlie said, and walked slowly towards the young man, who couldn't be more than eighteen or nineteen. His skin was brown, childishly smooth and he was sweating. A thread of blood was trickling down from one nostril, and there was a large red patch in the middle of his forehead.

Quite literally, as Freddy had said.

'What's your name?' Charlie asked.

'Eduardo.'

The fear in his voice made him sound feeble.

'What else, Eduardo?'

He tried to straighten up.

'Eduardo de Jesus Silva.'

'Where are you from? Nazareth?' Charlie asked.

Freddy and Hansemann laughed, even though Charlie had used the same joke before.

'I'm from Natal,' the boy said, in broken English.

'How old are you, Eduardo?'

'Nineteen.'

'And do you want to be twenty?'

He nodded quickly.

Situations like this were always easier with young people, Charlie thought. A few simple threats were often enough for them to find out all they needed to know.

'So, tell me, who do you work for? Is it someone in Norway?'

Eduardo shook his head.

'I don't work for anyone.'

Freddy took a step closer, balled a fist and punched it against his other palm. Eduardo de Jesus Silva paid attention.

'Please, Mr High, I don't know what you...'

'You clearly know who I am.'

Eduardo nodded.

'Everyone knows who you are.'

'Who do you work for?'

'No one. I...'

'Why are you following me?'

'I...'

He looked away, at Freddy, and then turned to Hansemann, who put his great hands on the back of the chair and leaned forwards.

'I'm not following you,' he stuttered.

'What are you doing then?'

'I...'

He closed his eyes. A pearl of sweat ran down one of his cheeks. A few long seconds later, he said, 'I was dreaming.'

Charlie stood there and studied him. His eyes widened and the furrows in his brow deepened.

'My family's never had anything. My mum and sister clean other people's houses, rich people – some of them live where you do. That's how I heard about you. My dad, he doesn't even have a job, all he does is...'

Eduardo de Jesus Silva looked away for a moment.

'And you...' he continued. 'You've got it all. You live on the top, you … you've always got the best women, you never pay for your drinks…'

He took a deep breath.

'You've got it all,' he repeated. 'So when I say I was dreaming, I was dreaming that I was actually … well, that I was you. That I had everything you have.'

Charlie stared at him. *Nobody should dream about having his life*, he thought.

'Why did you drive off then outside Senzuela the other night?' he asked. 'When Freddy came over to talk to you?'

Eduardo looked up at Freddy.

'Look at him,' he said. 'He's a mountain. And everyone knows that he's dangerous.'

Freddy gave a crooked smile.

'So what you're saying is, you were scared?'

He lowered his head slightly, then nodded.

'He had his hand in his inner pocket,' Eduardo said. 'Everybody knows he carries a gun.'

Charlie nodded slowly. He felt an enormous relief; he had nothing to fear, except that Henning Juul was still alive.

'So, what am I going to do with you? I don't need scaredy cats.'

'Please, Mr High, just give me a chance, I know I can help you,' he pleaded.

'How?'

'I know the town,' was his quick and eager answer. 'I know people. I can do anything you ask me.'

Charlie looked at his slight body, his thin face. The wind could probably blow him over. A slap would break him.

'The car you're driving,' Charlie said. 'How did you steal it?'

Eduardo de Jesus Silva took another deep breath.

'A friend of mine knew where the owner used to park it. I broke into his house and stole the keys.'

'Without being caught?'

'I wouldn't be sitting here otherwise.'

Eduardo attempted a smile, but gave up as soon as he saw it had no effect. The first glimpse of cockiness, Charlie thought. He'd stolen a car exactly the same way in Norway when he was seventeen. He'd also dreamed of another life, a better life.

'I don't employ criminals,' he said, then turned around and started to walk away.

'Please, Mr High…'

But Charlie just carried on walking. Freddy followed.

'What do you want me to do with him, boss?' he asked, when he caught up with him. 'Shall we…'

Charlie lifted a hand as a sign that Freddy should stop talking. When they were out of earshot from the others, Charlie stopped and turned around.

'See if you can find something for him to do,' he said. 'Anything. Let's see what he's made of.'

Freddy stared at him. 'Are you sure, boss?'

Charlie thought about it.

'No,' he said. 'But do it, all the same.'

35

When Henning woke up, he lay there blinking for a while, until the ceiling came into focus and he remembered where he was.

He had no idea why this particular thought struck him now, so soon after he'd woken, but he realised that it was a while since he'd been to see his mum. Henning had stayed away after she'd more or less accused him of killing his own father; he'd contacted social services to make sure she got what she needed in terms of food, cigarettes and alcohol. But because she'd refused to say any more about her accusation – had given him no reason for saying what she'd said – he hadn't been able to bring himself to see again. Now he found himself wondering if she knew he'd been shot, if she'd heard it on the news or if someone had contacted her.

If she cared.

Slowly he levered himself up and put his feet on the floor, hobbled over to the table where the painkillers were, and took two. The wooden panelling on the walls in front of him seemed to move.

He caught sight of his reflection in the window. His face was drained of any colour. He had big circles under his eyes. It looked like he'd aged fifteen years in the course of the past two weeks.

'Keep going, just a little bit longer,' he said to his reflection.

Henning thought about *6tiermes7*.

Tiermes was one of several names for the Sami god of thunder, who, according to mythology, ruled over life and death, a god who could call on thunder, kill trolls, who could wreak revenge. Then he thought about who might know that he'd been called in for questioning at the main station at four o'clock, and who might have told Durim Redzepi and his driver. It seemed they'd been waiting for him.

One of the last things *6tiermes7* had written the evening before was that he or she would try to log on around the same time this evening. Henning looked at the clock on the TV screen, which was still on. About half an hour to wait. He swallowed another tablet, went over to the wardrobe and looked inside, found a dark-brown fleece and pulled it onto his good arm, then draped it over his shoulder and the sling and staggered into the TV room. He felt like he was drunk.

The house was silent.

'Bjarne?'

Henning stumbled a bit, trying to keep his balance while he waited for an answer. It didn't come. He took a couple of steps towards the stairs. Still no answer.

Henning concentrated hard, but could still only hear the faint humming of the fridge. The wood in the walls creaked, a sound that made Henning jump. He was used to similar noises from home, but the sound of timber moving always made him wonder, for a moment, if he was not alone.

He went down into the kitchen. There was a handwritten note on the table.

Had to go to work. Didn't want to wake you.
Help yourself to what's in the fridge.
Don't worry, you're safe.
BB

Henning looked out of the window. All he could see was a hedge, the neighbouring house with a light in one of the windows, stars in a dark sky. He checked to see if he had any money. Found two 200-kroner notes in his trouser pocket and put them on the island in the middle of the kitchen.

Where was his phone?

He couldn't remember if Bjarne had taken it with him. So instead, Henning used the house phone in the hall to call for a taxi. He asked them to send a car to Tennisveien as soon as possible.

Henning went back into the kitchen and gulped down a couple of glasses of water. He had to hold onto the counter in order not to fall over. He stood like this for six or seven minutes, then he ventured outside. The cold air made him realise how hot he was. He stumbled down to the garage. A taxi was parked outside the tennis hall. With great difficulty, Henning walked towards it and somehow managed to get into the back seat.

'Could you look up the address for Ann-Mari Sara for me, please?' Henning asked, as the car pulled out. The driver was middle-aged and Asian-looking, and he asked Henning to spell the name for him. As he did this, they passed a car with two people sitting in it. It happened so fast that Henning didn't see the faces, but he noticed that the engine was switched off.

'Ivan Bjørndals gate, is that right?' the driver asked.

'Don't know,' Henning said, and tried to turn round. 'But if there are no other addresses under the same name, that's where we're going.'

The driver typed the address into the GPS. The car behind them turned on its lights and pulled out.

'And if you could put your foot on it, that would be great,' Henning said.

The driver looked at Henning in the rear-view mirror and grinned.

Henning held tight and for a moment considered whether he should get the driver to call Bjarne. He turned around and saw that the car was behind them.

Was it Redzepi and his pal?

'I'll pay you extra if you can go a bit faster.'

The distance between the two cars increased. When they jumped a light, the car behind, a Lexus, had to stop, and then suddenly there were three cars between them.

They turned a corner and carried on at full speed, then turned into a bigger road, the driver still pushing the car over the speed limit. Henning felt certain that they'd managed to shake off the Lexus. He no longer felt the need to contact Bjarne.

Ten minutes later, they stopped in Ivan Bjørndals gate, to the east of the Aker River. Henning gave the driver a generous tip and got out. No other cars were moving on the street. He walked as fast as he could, but there was a slight delay between thought and movement, which made him unsteady. The brick buildings on either side of road seemed to loom larger in the dark. Henning noticed there were still plastic chairs and tables on the terraces. He saw lights in the windows.

The local greengrocer was open. A man came out carrying a blue plastic bag. Opposite, there was a restaurant with big windows. It looked warm and inviting, but there weren't many customers inside.

Henning stopped to draw breath, he blinked a few times, then walked on to number 17, where he looked for Ann-Mari Sara's bell. He pressed the button and waited, didn't get an answer. She might still be at work, he thought. So he crossed the street and went into a poorly lit park area, where he stood under a tree and waited. He couldn't do the fleece jacket up all the way, so it didn't offer much warmth and his thin trainers did little to protect his feet from the cold ground.

Henning was freezing by the time Ann-Mari Sara finally appeared. He recognised her from Iver's flat. She was small, with untidy hair and a quick step, as though she was always busy.

Henning moved out from the shadow and said, 'Hi Ann-Mari.'

She stopped and looked up at him with alarm in her eyes.

'Or should I perhaps call you by your internet name. *6tiermes7.*'

Sara tilted her head and squinted, as though she wondered whether she'd heard right or not.

'The Sami are generally proud of their roots,' Henning said. 'And you look like a woman who could have been born around 1967.'

She continued to look him square in the eye for a few seconds, then she glanced around and took a step closer.

'Did I not make it explicitly clear that we should never meet?'

'Yes. And that's suited me very well. Until now.'

'What does that mean?'

'You knew that I was going to Tønsberg today,' Henning said. 'And as you seem to have access to all kinds of information at headquarters, it would be easy enough for you to find out that I was coming in for questioning at four o'clock.'

Ann-Mari nodded pensively and he saw the corners of her mouth twitching.

'So you think I told someone. Who then came and shot you.'

Henning shrugged with his good shoulder.

She shook her head and pulled some keys out of her bag. She found the one she wanted, then walked towards the entrance. Suddenly she spun round.

'Henning, tell me, how long have we worked together?'

And before he could answer: 'How many cases have we drawn attention to? How many scoops have I given you?'

'Loads,' Henning said.

'And yet you're standing here, saying…' She tried to find the right words. 'That *I* am involved in trying to have someone killed?' She pointed her thumb to her own chest. 'And *you*, of all people?'

Henning didn't answer, just registered that he was feeling dizzy again. He had to squint in order to focus on her, and he saw a woman who looked like she wanted to punch him. Her eyes were glistening, and her cheeks were flushed.

'If that's what you truly believe, Henning, then you can go straight to hell.'

Ann-Mari Sara disappeared out of focus again.

'Then prove it,' Henning said, and struggled to see better.

'I don't need to prove anything.'

As she walked to the door, put her key in the lock, she shook her head and swore at him under her breath. Henning followed behind, and forgetting the state he was in, tried to go too fast; everything around him started to spin, and when he stopped abruptly, it was hard to keep his balance. As he fell to the ground, he saw the outline of a car a little further away, a car he recognised, that he had seen not long ago. He didn't have time to notice anything else before something warm pressed down over his eyes and everything went quiet.

36

Nora sat in the kitchen and tried to eat something. Not for her own sake – food was the last thing she wanted – but for the baby. The banana tasted like cardboard, the yoghurt like bad strawberries, but she managed to drink a glass of milk – calcium and vitamin D were important. She also managed to swallow a couple of seal oil capsules with some water.

It was evening and the flat felt even quieter and darker than usual. She suddenly realised that she missed her mother. They'd agreed that she would come tomorrow, as it might be late by the time Nora got back from the hospital and talking to the police. Agnes would have fussed about and stirred up a bit of life, if nothing else. Filled the walls with sounds.

Nora decided to light some candles, so she went into the living room where she thought she'd left the matches, but the box wasn't on the table.

She went back into the kitchen again and spotted the matchbox. On the counter.

She was sure she hadn't left it there.

Nora got the acute feeling that someone else was in the flat, at that very minute. She listened. No movement, no sound, nothing to indicate that another person was there. But the more she thought about it, the more certain she was. Someone had been in her flat while she'd been out most of the day.

And now that the thought had taken root, she noticed a few other things that weren't as they should be. One of the magnets on the fridge had been moved. She hadn't hung the ultrasound photo there, had she? It was normally beside the sushi menu, not under the fridge brand name. The newspapers weren't hanging over the edge of the counter, as they had been this morning.

Or was she imagining it?

They could have been looking for something, she thought, something they thought Iver had left here. But what could it be?

Nora went back to the living room, stopped and listened again. Nothing, no strange sounds. But still she went out into the hall and inspected the lock on the front door. There was nothing wrong with it.

But the umbrella.

It had been knocked over and was lying on the floor. When had she done that?

She blinked a couple of times. You're going mad, she said to herself. Go back into the living room, sit down, breathe, and go through it all again.

Nora obeyed her own instruction and sat down on the sofa, concentrated on her breathing. She remembered her mother had taken down the ultrasound picture, looked at it and then hung it back in a different place, she was pretty sure of that. And she could well have put the matches somewhere else without thinking about it. There was no need to panic.

And in any case, there were people down at street level keeping an eye on whoever went in and out of the building, and they would have noticed if anyone had broken into her flat.

But had they been there when she was out?

She looked at her watch. It was quarter past midnight. That didn't stop her from dialling Bjarne Brogeland's number and asking.

'No, they weren't there,' he said in a weary voice. 'They're working shifts and you were with me, after all, so…'

She heard a sharp intake of breath.

'Why do you ask?'

'Well, I…'

She thought about it. It was highly unlikely that the people who had killed Iver and shot Henning would risk breaking into her flat when all manner of people from the press and police were looking for them. And in any case, she knew nothing, she wasn't dangerous to them.

'Is everything alright?' Bjarne Brogeland asked, with more force in his voice.

'Yes, I … think so.'

'Think so? Why do you say that?'

Bjarne sounded suddenly more alert and slightly anxious.

'Well, it's just … I got the feeling that someone has been in my flat. But I'm sure it's nonsense.'

'Do you want me to come over and check? Or … should I send one of the officers up?'

'No, no,' she said. 'I'm sure it'll be fine. I'm probably just … a little frightened. Or paranoid, I don't know. I'll be fine. Sorry for calling you so late.'

Bjarne hesitated before saying, 'That's OK, I'm still at work.'

'Oh right. Is there … any progress?'

'We're working on several leads,' he said.

Vague, Nora thought, but then that's the sort of thing the police said when they had no hard facts.

'OK,' she said, eventually. 'Good night.'

'Good night. Try to get some sleep.'

'I will.'

They both hung up, and Nora took a deep breath, then leaned back in the sofa.

Put her hands on her stomach.

She hated to admit it, but the last ten minutes had really frightened her.

When Bjarne had come to the flat earlier in the day, he'd mentioned a carpenter called Rasmus Bjelland. Nora had planned to find out more about him, but should she really start digging around in something that had already got her partner killed? Weren't there more important things to think about in the time ahead?

Henning was right, she thought, as she stroked her belly. She had to stay away from it all. It was too dangerous for them both.

37

Roger Blystad drove back and forth, around and around. Couldn't bring himself to park the car and get out. Instead he stopped at a spot where he had a good view of the cemetery and could see the maybe thirty people, including the minister, who were gathered around a large mound of earth.

Blystad let out a sob.

He would have given anything to be standing there himself, singing, even though he never usually sang. To have shaken the minister's hand and been given an overdose of the words that always sounded so strange and impersonal. He could never bring himself to say them to other people who'd lost someone. He wondered who they all were and how they knew her − if they were neighbours or colleagues. Or maybe someone she'd gone to school with. No doubt people he'd never met before.

It was a strange thought, that other people he knew nothing about had also in some way been connected to the most important person in his life.

He drove around the block again. When he got back, the small crowd was moving away from the grave. The minister had finished. She was in the ground.

Blystad sobbed again.

He let the engine run as he watched them leaving the cemetery. He recognised Uncle Lars and some other family members. But no one else. Some people got into their cars, others stood around talking. One of them laughed. Blystad wanted to get out and hit him. Never mind, on with the show. Go back to work, back home and watch TV.

He put his foot on the accelerator and drove off.

∴

Durim Redzepi remembered how dark it had been in Vanja Kval-heim's flat the day she died. He remembered hearing her come up the stairs, fumbling outside the door, the key slowly slipping into the lock – as though she was completely exhausted by a full day's work at the Majorstua Clinic, and had no more energy left. The shock on her face when she'd come into the living room and seen the light from the TV reflecting on the ceiling, and then seen him and Jeton Pocoli sitting on the sofa.

'Do you seriously record *The Bold and the Beautiful*?' he'd asked.

It was a good opening line. Not threatening. But Mrs Kvalheim hadn't been able to say a word, she just stood there staring.

'How many episodes are there of this crap? 18,000?'

'W-who are you?'

'You don't even need to watch this shit to know what's going to happen.'

'W-what do you want?'

Redzepi had looked at the TV screen for a few seconds, before freezing the picture and throwing down the remote control. The sudden loud noise had frightened Mrs Kvalheim.

'But I think I know why. Look at that guy there.'

He'd taken a few steps towards her as he pointed at the screen. Stopped right in front of her.

'He's the spitting image of your son.'

And then she'd started to cry. Vanja Kvalheim had probably just realised why he hadn't bothered to cover his face. Why he was wearing gloves. Why they'd closed all the curtains. Why Jeton Pocoli just sat there looking at her.

'Where is he, Vanja?'

'Who?'

He'd laughed at this. So helpless.

'Please,' she said, 'I don't know where he is.'

And they had seen the tears in her eyes, her pleading face, watched when her knees buckled.

'What do you reckon, Jeton – does she or doesn't she know where the carpenter is?'

Jeton Pocoli had stood and taken a step towards her, then shrugged. Redzepi had produced a small box from his jacket pocket, opened it, taken out something that looked like a pin, which he kept in his hand. From the other pocket he'd taken out a small glass bottle that contained a clear liquid. It looked like water.

With great care, he'd slowly removed the lid.

'I've only used this on a cat,' he said. 'D'you remember, Jeton?'

Jeton Pocoli had nodded.

'It's really nothing much.'

'W-what do you mean?'

'But we do know it works on humans too.'

Her lips had started to quiver when he dipped the pin carefully into the clear liquid, and then held the point up to the light, so that a drop fell on the carpet.

'I believe you,' he'd said, finally. 'I really do believe you don't know where your son is.'

At the same time, he'd nodded to Jeton Pocoli, who took another step closer and grabbed her by the arms.

'But we're going to have to kill you anyway.'

It had been a good death, a simple one. It was how they should have killed Henning Juul as well. But hopefully there would be more opportunities.

He should really have stayed hidden away in the forest, now that he was wanted all over Norway, but they'd planned the operation for so long, and as he was in charge, he had to be there. It wasn't, however, such a good idea to be seen on the streets, but it was helpful to have Flurim Ahmetaj's friend working with them now. He'd been quick to say yes when they needed someone to break into Nora Klemetsen's flat the day before.

Redzepi kept his eyes on the monitor. The funeral was over. Flurim Ahmetaj turned on one of the wireless cameras they'd installed in a tree nearby, and he saw a man in a digger filling the grave.

Their plan had failed.

The carpenter hadn't shown up to say goodbye to his mother.

Daddy Longlegs would be furious.

Again.

Flurim Ahmetaj folded his hands behind his head. His friend was sitting beside him, his thigh muscles twitching, ready to jump out if necessary. Jeton Pocoli was hunched forwards, resting his elbows on his knees. The van reeked of sweat.

'How long do we have to sit here?' Pocoli asked, and looked at his watch.

'A bit longer,' Redzepi said.

'How long is a bit longer? I mean, he's obviously not coming.'

Redzepi sent him a dark look.

'We'll sit here until I say we're done sitting here. You got a problem with that?'

'Yeah, I don't like wasting time.'

'Who says that…?'

Ahmetaj straightened up. Tapped his finger on the screen in front of him.

Redzepi leaned closer.

And smiled.

∵

Blystad stopped at a petrol station just outside Oslo to fill the tank. The wind was sharp on his face, but he couldn't care less.

It felt wrong to leave without having seen her, without a proper farewell. He hadn't dared earlier, afraid that someone would be waiting for him. But he'd bought flowers – roses, his mother's favourite – and he'd got himself a new suit and shoes.

When he'd filled the tank, he sat in the car with his hands on the steering wheel.

You coward, he said to himself. Your entire life is a joke. The thought of her lying there in the ground, alone, without him even saying goodbye, was like a scratched record in the background of his mind.

He started the engine and turned around.

Accelerated.

Twenty minutes later he was back at the cemetery. The sky was still grey and heavy, but it wasn't raining. There were no cars left in the car park. No people around.

Blystad turned off the engine and took a deep breath, waited for a minute or so before he opened the door and got out. His new shoes were uncomfortable, like he had a plaster cast on his feet, and they clacked loudly as he walked on the asphalt and then crunched when it changed to gravel.

There was only an old man left in the cemetery, and it was not hard to see where she lay. Blystad walked over the grass between the gravestones, not looking at the names, the flowers, candles and lanterns round about.

He stopped in front of the grave, a mound of earth and a cross bearing the name Vanja Kvalheim. Blystad was glad that the grave-diggers had already filled the grave; he couldn't have coped with seeing the coffin. The flowers that were to be buried with her.

Blysted had expected it to hurt, but the pain was sharper and deeper than he'd imagined. His dry throat swelled and he found it hard to swallow. He sobbed, then looked around surreptitiously.

There was no one else there.

He approached the mound of earth and laid the roses by the white cross. Lowered his head and folded his hands. Somewhere in the distance a car door slammed. A chainsaw started up.

He felt like he should say something, but no words came.

Blystad didn't know how long he stood there, but it was a long time. The earth was dark and fine. And she was lying in the dark, gone forever.

Eventually he turned and went back to the car. He had felt a need for some time, but it was stronger now, perhaps stronger than ever before.

He couldn't, did not want to spend the night alone.

∴

Durim Rezepi kept his eyes on the monitors, with one hand round a small, thin microphone.

'He's nearly there,' he said. 'Is there traffic around you?'

'No,' was Jeton Pocoli's reply.

'Good. Get started. You've got plenty of time, but make it quick all the same. And get the registration number.'

'Got it.'

Redzepi watched the man's heavy steps. Flurim Ahmetaj moved closer, switched to another camera that showed the carpenter from an angle that caught him face on. Suddenly the sun broke through the cloud and illuminated him. The grass around him lit up. The carpenter had one hand in his pocket. He was looking around.

There was a crackle on the communication system.

'The package has been delivered,' Pocoli said.

'Good.'

'I put a tracker on the car and his overcoat; he hadn't taken his mobile with him, so I put one on that too.'

'Even better. Now, move it.'

Redzepi looked back at the monitor. The man stopped in front of his mother's grave. A pile of earth. It was tempting to kill him right there, lay him out on top, but it would be too risky. And would require an aim that none of them was capable of achieving. It was too far and the risk that there would be witnesses was high.

Redzepi jumped when the back door of the van opened. Jeton Pocoli got in and sat down, took out his earpieces.

'Here,' he said, and handed over a piece of paper with two letters and five numbers written on it. 'The registration number.'

Redzepi handed the piece of paper to Ahmetaj.

'An address would be good,' he said, 'in case we lose him.'

'We won't lose him.'

Ahmetaj took the number. Redzepi continued to watch the

carpenter's movements while he waited, and thought about Henning Juul.

They had shot him too soon.

They hadn't waited for the prime moment.

This time they would get it right.

They would take this man out at close range. When he least expected it.

38

Given the occasion, it didn't seem appropriate to drive fast, but the car rattled and shook all the same. Roger Blystad's only toolbox knocked against something in the back – the nail gun, perhaps – and the noise provided a kind of companionship.

He neither knew nor cared how long the journey back to Brandbu had taken; it was as though his hands on the wheel and feet on the pedals had a will of their own. Before he knew it her house appeared in the distance, and it was only then that he really registered where he was.

As he drove into the residential area, a boy on a bike followed him with his eyes. There was house after house, rows and rows of them. Gardens, and hedge and garages with gravel driveways. Even though it was autumn, the colours around him had a summery feel. Green and fresh; in some gardens the branches on the apple trees were heavy with overripe fruit. It was a quiet afternoon.

Should he go on?

He released the brake, let the car move on until he was outside her house. He stopped. The brakes complained. Even then, Blystad still wondered if he should turn around. But he turned off the engine and got out.

No, you really shouldn't, he said to himself. She'll think you're mad.

He looked up at the house.

Helene was standing in the window, looking straight at him.

Roger Blystad thought: You can't turn back now, it's too late. To begin with, she was clearly surprised to see him there. Then slowly a smile appeared on her lips. Even at a distance, he could see that they were soft and red. She opened the window, stuck her head out.

'Well, hello,' she said. 'Where are you going?'

He had no answer. He was there to see her. Her.

'Did you take a wrong turn or something?'

'No, I…'

She was nearly hanging out the window. And Blystad thought: just one push from behind by an ill-intended hand and she would topple out, into the bushes below. The thought, the image, made him smile.

'Hang on, I'll come down.'

She straightened up and closed the window. Blystad stayed where he was and looked around. Wiped his hands on his trousers. Put them in his pockets and stepped back.

Then the door opened.

Helene came out, without the Stetson this time, in wellies, track-suit bottoms, a tunic and a jacket on top. She had her hair in a ponytail.

He took a step towards her, stopped, ran his hand through his hair. This was a bloody stupid idea, he told himself, but her smile had him captivated.

'Wow, you're looking smart,' she said, as she came towards him. 'But why did I say smart? I should perhaps have said handsome. Because you're looking very handsome.'

She grinned.

'Has someone died, or something?'

Blystad was about to say something, but stopped, his lips parted. She must have seen his expression, his mouth that locked, because she rushed towards him, her hand to her mouth. 'Oh my god,' she said. 'I'm so sorry, I didn't mean to…'

She stopped herself.

'I'm always putting my foot in it,' she said, looking at him with sympathy. 'I'm sorry.'

'Not to worry.'

She bit a nail as she gazed at him in silence for a few moments. Blystad didn't know what to do with his hands.

'Was it … someone close, family … or a friend…?'

'My mum,' Blystad said.

She opened her mouth again. 'Oh Roger.'

'I'm fine.'

'Sorry. That was so stupid of me.'

'It's fine. Really.'

Helene just stood looking at him. Blystad felt he should say something, but he couldn't. His mind was stuck on his mother and the fact that he was somewhere he shouldn't be. He wasn't used to talking to people anymore.

'Were you … close?' she asked, after a while.

He nodded.

'Well…'

He couldn't sort out his words, his memories. All that he wanted to say, but couldn't.

'Yes, yes, we were.'

'Would you like to come in and have a cup of coffee?'

He looked around again. Saw a curtain twitch in the neighbour's house.

'Thank you, that would be nice,' he replied eventually, and smiled again.

Helene smiled back, then turned around and started to walk towards to the house.

'I've got some food left from lunch as well, if you'd like it.'

'No, thanks, I'm … not hungry.'

He followed her in. Everything felt awkward. For two years, he'd run from shadow to shadow, only allowing himself minimal contact, only meeting and greeting the odd client. He knew the people at the sawmill, of course, but really only to say hello. They sometimes had a quick chat over the counter, but never anything personal.

He took off his shoes, even though she said it didn't matter. It felt good to get them off, but his socks were a bit clammy. He hoped they wouldn't leave a mark on the newly cleaned floor, prayed his feet didn't smell. But all he could detect was a hint of floor soap. It reminded him of his mother. She was always cleaning, and the house was scoured from top to bottom every Friday, so she could relax over the weekend.

He went into the kitchen behind Helene.

'Sit yourself down,' she said.

It felt like an age since he'd sat in exactly the same place, after he'd finished replacing the timber panels on her south-facing wall.

'I should perhaps offer you something stronger than coffee, but…'

Blystad looked up at her. Was there a subtext to her suggestion? An invitation?

'Thanks, but no,' he said. 'I don't drink much these days.'

'I thought maybe a dram for your mum. Do you have far to go? Of course, I know you live in Brandbu.'

'Yes,' he said. 'I do.'

There was enough coffee for two in the pot. She reached up on her toes to get a cup down from one of the top cupboards. Her tunic slid up and he caught a glimpse of her skin, her waist. In the light that shone through the kitchen window, it was the same colour as the beaches in Natal.

'So tell me about it,' he said.

She turned to look at him.

'What?'

'You said you were always putting your foot in it. Give me an example.'

She smiled teasingly, and took her time.

'No, I don't want to.'

'Please. I could do with a laugh.'

She poured the coffee. Shook her head, still smiling, and leaned back against the counter. It looked like she was weighing up the pros and cons.

'I was at one of those water parks once,' she said, and pushed herself away from the counter, lifted a hand and brushed her fringe to one side. 'You see real women's bodies there. And when you start looking, you realise there're so many variations – I'm sure you men do it too.'

Blystad couldn't remember the last time he'd been in a shower room, probably back in the early nineties, if he thought about it. He thought about all the muscles and tattoos he'd seen there, hardly the norm for the male population, but nodded all the same.

'Anyway, I was standing in the shower beside a little girl, she was maybe three or four, and she didn't want to get wet, no matter what, and she was howling. And her mother, she was, well … pretty big. So I said to the little girl: why don't you just hide under Mummy's tummy? It was only after I'd said it that I realised she wasn't actually pregnant.'

Blystad threw back his head and roared with laughter, and Helene giggled sheepishly. It was the first time he'd heard her laugh, restrained, as though she didn't dare let go.

'You can imagine the look I got from the mother,' she said, with a big smile.

Blystad had to wipe his eyes.

'That's a good one,' he said.

Their laughter subsided, but she continued to smile. And he sat, happy to be on the receiving end, helpless, like some idiot who'd never seen a woman smile at him before. But it melted his heart, the block of ice that had lain frozen in his chest for so long.

'Not easy to talk your way out of *that*.'

'No, I made a quick exit to the pool, I can tell you.'

Blystad chuckled. Then the moment passed and he drank some more coffee. Helene leaned back against the counter, but looked at him over the rim of her cup, he could see her blue eyes, the long lashes, the neat brows.

'What about you?' she asked. 'Have you ever made a fool of yourself?'

'Me?'

He smiled and started to laugh again.

'I never put a foot wrong.'

It was her turn to laugh.

'Never?'

And again, he noticed the suggestive undertone; it wasn't really a question, there was something challenging about her voice, as if she wanted him to do something bad.

'No, I mean, I've thanked people for gifts they haven't given me, that sort of thing.'

'Ah,' she said, 'that doesn't count.'

'No,' he agreed. 'Maybe not.'

There was a short silence. Helene continued to watch him over the rim of her cup.

'Can you bear to talk about her?'

He lifted his head, abruptly, felt his stomach burning at the very thought. Then he lowered his eyes, didn't quite know where to begin. But he took a deep breath, and started at the beginning, how his parents met – on the boat to Denmark, in the queue to pay for food and a glass of wine, how they started talking and neither of them wanted to go back to the people they were with, that they kept sending each other looks across the tables. And when they then bumped into each other by the meat counter, in a shop in Fredrik-shavn, they both felt it was fate. They agreed to meet when they got back to Oslo.

'But my dad was the sort who could never sit still,' Blystad said. 'He was always on his way somewhere else. Even after he and my mother got together and had me and…'

He changed his mind.

'Mum was left on her own with me when I was four. He couldn't stand it anymore. And I've never seen him since.'

'Not even at the funeral?'

'No, I…'

He just shook his head.

'I think he went to sea, or something like that. He's probably dead as well.'

Helena nodded quietly.

'So you've got no one left?'

Her voice was tender and sad. His chest tightened.

He shook his head.

'But you must have some friends who can look after you?'

But that was the problem. Friends.

'No, I … not so many of those either, really.'

Helene put her cup down carefully and came towards him with slow, deliberate steps. And when she leaned in towards him and kissed him on the mouth, he let it happen, he let her take control, allowed himself to be led, and when they made love a little later, it was fast and furious; she wrapped herself round him and pulled him down towards her. It was strange to feel a woman's hands on his body again after so long.

Afterwards, he lay looking at her as she rested beside him.

'So,' he said. 'Tell me your story now.'

She turned towards him, her neck and cheeks still flushed. Her hair all over the place. Beautiful.

'Just when we were having such a nice time?'

She tried to laugh it off, but he wasn't willing to let her get away with it.

'You haven't told me anything about you,' she tried.

'I've told you about my mum.'

'Yes, but you're not your mum.'

'No, but I've already told you things I don't normally talk about. That way I'm still on top, and you've some way to go.'

She smiled. Blystad could see that she was going to say something crude, but she refrained. Instead, she looked up at the ceiling and asked, 'You don't happen to have a cigarette, do you?'

'Yeah, I…'

Blystad started to get out of bed.

'I haven't smoked for four years,' she said.

He stopped and turned to her.

'Then you're not going to start again now.'

'I want a cigarette, Roger. Now.'

'Helene, I…'

It was her turn to sit up.

'Please, Roger. Just do it. OK?'

He could see she was on the verge of tears, so he went out into the hall and got the cigarettes from his jacket pocket and the lighter from his trousers. He lit two cigarettes and handed one to her.

Blystad was still naked, but it didn't feel awkward or embarrassing. She took the cigarette, put it between her lips and closed her eyes. She coughed a little before she took the first puff. And then another.

'Aah,' she said, blowing the smoke out slowly. 'I'd forgotten how good it was.'

She tapped herself on the forehead.

'Why use the past tense when it's something I'm experiencing now.'

'It *is* good,' Blystad said, and took a drag himself.

'But I think one's enough,' she said, and sucked in more nicotine. 'I'm starting to get a head rush already.'

She let out a little laugh.

Blystad crept down under the duvet again, turned over onto his side and looked at her, and the long ash tip on the cigarette that would soon fall.

There was an empty Coke can on the bedside table. She reached out for it and used it as an ashtray.

'I used to smoke in bed,' she said, putting the can down between them. But it wasn't the can that Blystad was looking at. Nor the cigarette, nor her eyes.

But her arm.

He hadn't thought about the fact that she wanted to keep the tunic on, but at some point the button on the sleeve had become undone, revealing her lower arm. All the scars. A puckered spider's web.

Helene noticed him looking at it, pulled down the sleeve and put her arm under the duvet.

'We don't need to talk about it,' he said. 'We don't need to talk about anything you don't want to.'

She lay down again and stared at the ceiling, motionless, as though she'd found what she was looking for up there. After a few seconds, she took another drag on the cigarette.

'What else are you called, besides Helene?'

'Don't you remember?' she said, with some indignation. Blystad wasn't sure whether she was joking or not.

'You just gave me your first name when you called about the job,' he said.

'Oh right,' she said, and continued to stare blindly at the ceiling. 'Næss, my surname is Næss.'

'Helene Næss,' Blystad said. 'Well, do you know what, Helene Næss?'

He waited until she'd turned to look at him.

'My name isn't really Roger.'

39

Henning opened his eyes.

He blinked, but couldn't get the room into focus. There was something familiar about it though. Something about the colours. The size.

He lifted his head, still heavy after such a long deep sleep, and then it dawned on him that he was back in hospital. If it wasn't actually the same room as last time, it certainly looked remarkably similar. The table was the same caramel colour. The same strip lighting in the same rectangular box, which reminded him of an exceptionally long bread tin with two tubes in it. The walls were the same colour – eggshell. He saw a print of a pot plant on a round coffee table.

What the hell had happened?

How had he ended up here?

The most obvious answer would be that Ann-Mari Sara had driven him here or called the police. But she wouldn't have done that. The police would want to know why Henning had gone to her house on the day that he'd been shot, and she was hardly likely to want to do anything that might identify her as his secret source over the years. But the fact that he was awake and alive did seem to indicate that all his assumptions were wrong.

But how then had Redzepi found him?

Had someone else at the police station told him?

All these thoughts made Henning dizzy again, and he wondered what the doctors had given him. So he closed his eyes, and felt a heaviness pressing down on him.

::

The next time Henning opened his eyes, Bjarne was sitting on a chair beside his bed.

'Good morning,' Bjarne said. 'Or rather, good afternoon. It's half past five. In the evening.'

Bjarne gave a fleeting smile.

Henning took a moment to focus his eyes. He tried to pull himself up into a sitting position, but he'd forgotten that one arm was still in a sling. There was a stabbing pain in his shoulder and he managed to bite back a scream. His efforts made him sweat.

'How are you?' Bjarne asked.

'How long have I been here?'

Bjarne looked at his watch.

'About seventeen or eighteen hours.'

Henning stared at him.

That was a long time.

'I think they gave you some sleeping pills,' Bjarne said. 'They had to do something to stop you.'

He smiled again.

'What were you thinking? Going out the same day you'd been shot. That's asking for trouble.'

Henning blinked furiously. Was it the same day? He realised it was. Time had lost its importance. Only answers mattered to him now.

'I had to check something out,' he said.

'What?'

'Doesn't matter now. I got it sorted. Nothing important.'

Bjarne scowled at him for a few seconds.

'Do you know how you got here?'

Henning stalled, before shaking his head.

'You don't know?'

Bjarne looked at him, astonished.

'No,' Henning said. 'Do you?'

The policeman waited a moment before continuing.

'You were found outside A&E sitting, or rather, half lying, in a wheelchair.'

Ann-Mari Sara, Henning thought, as he cast about for something to say. Luckily, Bjarne didn't ask any more questions.

Henning wondered what he'd missed in the last eighteen hours, if Durim Redzepi and his mate had been arrested in the meantime.

He asked. Bjarne shook his head.

Neither of them said anything for a few moments.

'We found Iver Gundersen's car keys, Henning. In your trouser pocket.'

Henning lowered his eyes. He was still a bit groggy. Any movement took time.

'That wasn't very smart. I could arrest you for obstructing an investigation. There'd be no problem getting support for that at the station, let me tell you.'

Henning didn't say anything.

'Why did you take them?'

He thought about what he should say.

'I needed transport,' was his simple reply.

'And your own car wasn't working?'

Henning shook his head, uncertain whether the lie was visible in his face or not.

The door opened, and Ella Sandland – one of Bjarne's colleagues – came in. Her smile was terse when she said hello. Sandland was thin and sinewy in a masculine way, and her movements were also quite macho. She hooked her thumbs into her uniform belt.

Henning knew that Sandland was one of Bjarne's allies down at the headquarters, and that she was aware of his suspicions regarding Preben Mørck. So he told them about the meeting he'd had with the lawyer, the parking ticket he'd found in Iver's car, and the business card.

'It's undeniably odd that he should lie about Iver having been there,' Henning continued, spurred on by the fact that his head seemed to be working again. 'And another thing: of course Tore Pulli knew who gave him the contract to murder Ellen Hellberg in the nineties. That might be why they had to kill him – Mørck needed to make sure that Tore wouldn't snitch on him.'

Bjarne and Sandland looked at each other. Bjarne nodded to her.

'I got Ørjan Mjønes in for questioning a few days ago,' she said. 'As expected, he denied that Mørck had paid him to killed Pulli, but there was a reaction, albeit small, when I mentioned Mørck's name and held up a photograph.'

Daddy Longlegs and Mørck have to be the same person, Henning thought. But was it Mørck who was in the car beside Tore, the evening his flat went up in flames? Who had ensured his name was deleted from Indicia?

The probability was high, given that Mørck would certainly not want to be associated with Tore after Tore was killed. And yet Henning was unsure if Mørck could be anything other than a middleman, or if he had enough financial muscle to pay for a contract killing on his own.

Whatever the case, the question remained: how could Durim Redzepi know that Henning was going to be outside the police headquarters at four o'clock in the afternoon.

'William Hellberg described Mørck as solid,' Henning said. 'But that doesn't necessarily mean anything. If Mørck helped Hellberg's mother with the murder in the early nineties, he may have been leading a double life for years.'

'But we can't just call Mørck in for questioning,' Bjarne said. 'We have to have something on him first. Proof, something concrete, like Gundersen perhaps had. Mørck has been in the game a long time, he knows how to counter our questions if we're just fumbling in the dark.'

Henning moved slightly, and was racked again by pain.

'Sounds like you've got enough to do over the next few days,' Henning said and winced. 'What about me?'

'The doctor thought it would be best for you to stay here tonight,' Bjarne said. 'And I think that sounds sensible. We've got a man in here keeping watch, and another outside.'

Henning lay down again. He was, truth be told, utterly exhausted, but he knew that his mind would not be able to switch off. Not now, not when they were so close.

'What are *you* going to do?' he asked.

Sandland and Bjarne looked at each other.

'We're going to dig a bit deeper into Preben Mørck's life,' Bjarne said. 'See what we can find. But I wouldn't set your hopes too high, Henning; we've done some pretty thorough investigating already. He doesn't have a single blemish on his CV. People talk about him in glowing terms.'

'But there must be *something*,' Henning said. 'Iver found something. And we have to find it as well.'

Bjarne took a step closer to the bed and put a hand on his shoulder: 'We'll do all that we can.'

40

Later, after Roger Blystad had driven home, he regretted it. Not the few hours he'd spent in Helene's bed – that had been pure pleasure – but the fact that he'd exposed himself. He'd been quick to cover his tracks – hadn't said anything about Tore or Charlie, only that someone was after him and he didn't know if he was out of danger yet – which was why he'd taken on another identity and was lying low.

It was perhaps wrong, he thought, to have left so soon after, but he'd felt restless and uneasy, like a fire was burning under his feet, and he had to get away, go home so he could think about what he was going to do with the past, with the future.

With the present.

Perhaps it was time to forget the past. To stop running away from it.

'But if you'd like to meet again,' he'd said to Helene before he left, 'you'll have to carry on calling me Roger. So I don't get confused.'

She'd looked at him for a long time.

Maybe she just needed a shoulder to lean on as well, someone to give her a cigarette. She was glad, she said, that he'd been so open with her. And now Blystad wasn't sure if that was a good or a bad thing.

For the first time in ages, he felt like food, so he went by the shop on the way home and bought bread, cheese, fruit and vegetables. When he got home, he ate two slices of bread before sitting down in front of the TV and channel hopping a bit before settling on an athletics programme, and as he watched the people running, it dawned on him that he hadn't done any exercise for a few days.

So he changed into his running gear, went down into the basement and started the 45-minute treadmill programme, found the album he'd downloaded onto his phone that he liked listening to when he was training – the soundtrack to *Rocky IV*.

At his heaviest, Blystad had weighed 112 kilos, then one day he'd got out of the bath and been horrified by what the full-length mirror had so mercilessly shown him. He got himself a treadmill, started to record each session, kept a note of how many calories he ate and burned. His project was to lose weight. The target was 80 kilos, the same as he'd weighed when he started high school. He was only five kilos short of that now.

The cellar was spartan and dirty, with uneven walls, and plaster dust constantly falling everywhere. The floor was uneven too – it was amazing that he'd managed to find an area that was flat enough for the treadmill. But he liked it down there: it reminded him of Rocky when he was training for the Ivan Drago fight, with 'Training Montage' by Vince DiCola and Survivor's 'Eye of the Tiger' playing in the background. The rough, masculine cellar was inspiration in itself and always made him want to watch the film again.

He'd got to Robert Tepper's 'No Easy Way Out', when a shadow passed the cellar window. He looked up, alarmed, and saw another shadow stop by the front door. Blystad pressed the emergency stop button and jumped down from the treadmill.

Through the window he could see the men outside huddled together and talking, but he couldn't hear what they were saying. They were both dressed in black, one had a hoodie on, the other a denim jacket.

The man closest to the window put his hand inside his jacket and took out something that he then fiddled with; it looked like he might be turning it round and round.

Then he lowered his arm.

Blystad gasped.

From where he was standing in the basement, it was easy to see the gun and silencer, and he knew immediately that they had found him and what would happen.

What the hell was he going to do?

You have to get out and run for it, he told himself, somehow get the rucksack you've got ready for emergencies. The problem was that it was in one of the cupboards in the bedroom. Upstairs. There was no way out of the house other than through the door where the two men were now standing. They didn't ring the bell; instead Blystad heard the glass pane being smashed.

He looked around the room. Weights, too heavy to swing as fast and hard as he needed. Mats, medicine ball – nothing he could use as a weapon. He didn't even have the keys to the box room.

He tried to control his breathing, but it wasn't easy, his heart was hammering in his chest – as though it would jump out.

He couldn't remember if he'd turned the TV off or not, but it wouldn't be more than a few minutes, maybe even seconds, before they came down into the cellar. And what would he do then? He couldn't just stand there and wait for them to kill him.

The cellar window, he thought. He could climb up and slip out.

No.

It was too small and too narrow, it wouldn't work.

Blystad dialled the emergency services, and put his phone down on the treadmill. He didn't want to talk, it would give away his whereabouts to the men upstairs. They would see where he was calling from at the control centre, and then, when he didn't answer, they would send a patrol round to check. Wouldn't they?

But it would still take some time before they got there; Blystad didn't know where the nearest police station was, and how much time he had was questionable.

He put down the headset and looked around the room again. He had some rope he could use if necessary, but the others had a pistol. He needed something he could surprise them with, something that would quickly put them out of action.

Footsteps on the floor above. They were in the bedroom. Soon they'd find the door that led down to the basement.

Blystad left the room and went into another. He moved as lightly and silently as he could. Passed an ice pick, tested it. Far too heavy.

Garden hose. Too unwieldy. Tyres, buckets, piles of wood. Paint brushes. Paint tins.

How strong were they?

If he could only rid them of their guns, how good would they be at fighting?

Blystad hadn't fought with anyone since high school. To a certain extent, his stature had meant that people generally avoided confrontation. But he was fitter now than ever, so he might have an advantage.

He couldn't go up the stairs to turn off the light, because then they would hear him. There was no switch at the bottom of the stairs. But he had turned the light off in the room with the treadmill, so only the stairs were lit up.

A foot on the top step.

He tried to draw the air deep into his lungs, hold it for a while, and then exhale slowly, but couldn't do it. His heart was thumping too hard.

More footsteps. Just one set. For now.

He heard a sound.

Knew what it meant.

Blystad lifted the spade, ready to strike. Wiped the sweat from his face on his shoulder, making sure not to hit the wall with the spade.

Footsteps on the concrete.

Something loose crunched on the floor. More feet at the top of the stairs. Blystad knew he only had a couple of seconds, then there would be two men instead of one and when the gun appeared in front of him, like a long finger, he whacked the hand holding the gun with the spade with all his might.

The gun fell to the floor.

The man was surprised by the sudden attack and screamed with pain. Blystad didn't think about hitting him again, he threw the spade down and picked up the gun, pointing it blindly at the stairs, from where a short bald man came running towards him at full speed. Blystad didn't think, he just pulled the trigger, three shots in quick succession, and judging by the sudden splash of colour on the wall, he'd hit his mark. The man fell forwards and landed at Blystad's feet.

All of sudden, he felt something heavy bang his head, hard enough to make him see stars for a few seconds. He'd completely forgotten the first man in the chaos – but he saw him straight ahead through the fog and pointed the gun in his general direction, waving it around. He was about pull the trigger when he felt a hand clamp over his, which forced the muzzle of the gun upward, so when the shot was fired, plaster dust immediately sprinkled down from the ceiling. Some fell into his eyes. He blinked frantically to clear it at the same time as he tried to gauge the strength of the man who had hit him.

As the tears cleaned his eyes, his sight returned and he took another deep breath. He had the advantage of a few kilos over the other man and he managed to push him so far into the room with the treadmill that they hit the wall. The man groaned, but was not put off his stride, not by a long shot; he raised his knee and hit Blystad in the stomach, knocking the wind out of him. He dropped the gun and before he managed to straighten up, the man had bent down and picked it up.

Blystad threw himself at the man, and managed to grab hold of the gun just as he fired a shot – he felt a wave of air rush past his face, and bent his hand away from his body as more projectiles ripped into the walls around them. Their faces were only centimetres apart, and Blystad headbutted him, as hard as he could, twisted him round and pushed him over to the other wall. He butted his head again, hard enough to make the man crumple in his arms, and he used the opportunity to thump his hand against the wall several times until his visitor dropped the gun to the floor.

Then he pummelled his face and upper body, punching as fast and hard as he could, aiming for the man's nose, because he knew that the bone in the nose was easy to break; he felt and heard it crunch under his knuckles.

Finally the man sank to the floor.

Blystad stood with his hands on his knees, gasping for breath, but he knew he didn't have much time; he had to get out and away as fast as he could. He stood up again, wiped off the sweat and blood and plaster dust as best he could. His hands were shaking.

There wasn't time to think, and he saw his mobile phone flashing on the treadmill. He rushed over, saw that someone was calling and ignored it. He didn't want to talk to anyone in emergency services now, it was too late for that. Even though it was self-defence, he had killed someone. And he had a record that would not play in his favour.

Blystad ran out of the room, and stopped abruptly by the man who was lying there. He had a gun in his hand, but there was no doubt that he was dead. Blystad hardly dared look at him, but he did all the same – saw that one of the bullets had hit him in the chest, another a little further down. The third bullet had hit the wall.

A moment later he heard the man in the room behind him gasp. Blystad stepped over the body and ran up the stairs as fast as he could. He dashed into the bedroom, picked up the rucksack, knowing that it didn't matter what he left behind in the house, it would be impossible to hide his tracks anyway – so he just grabbed the most important things, car keys, credit cards, put on a pair of shoes by the door in the hall, pulled on a jacket and ran out of the house, where he was met by a welcome cold wind that stripped off a new layer of sweat that had formed on his skin.

He was just about to get in the car when the side mirror splintered.

The man he had knocked unconscious was standing in the doorway with a gun in his hand; he was obviously still groggy because he held on to the door frame when he fired another shot. The bullet flew over the top of Blystad's head. Then the man charged down the steps onto the gravel.

There was nowhere to hide, other than the car. And he wouldn't be protected there for long. All he had in the car were his tools. Lots of tools.

The heavy steps lurched closer over the gravel. His mobile phone started to ring. For a moment Blystad was completely paralysed, then all at once he did the first thing that popped into his head – he opened the boot and rummaged around.

The nail gun.

He couldn't remember if it was loaded or not, but he picked it up. In itself, the nail gun weighed nearly three kilos, and judging by the extra weight he guessed there were nails in it. Luckily he didn't need any plugs, cables or compressors; he simply switched it on and held it out towards the house, he didn't even aim, just fired away. He knew that a nail gun could spit out up to 60 nails a minute, so he just carried on. Blystad saw that he'd hit his target and that the man staggering towards him had been caught off guard. Soon he was lying on the ground screaming, holding his face with both hands. His gun beside him.

Blystad dropped the nail gun, hurried over to him, kicked the gun out of reach. One of the nails had hit the man in the eye. His phone continued to ring, but Blystad still didn't answer. Instead he turned and ran back towards the car with only one thought in his head.

To get away.

41

Durim Redzepi waited.

And waited.

It was supposed to be an easy job. Jeton Pocoli and Flurim Ahmetaj's friend, in and out. Two against one. Two experts against an unsuspecting idiot.

What the hell were they doing? How hard could it be?

Redzepi ran his fingers through his hair. Looked at Ahmetaj who was leaning back, totally calm, as if he didn't have a care in the world. For him, it was simply a matter of doing the job he'd been asked to do. Getting the money, moving on. They were on overtime now, and some, and he was bored.

Redzepi took his wallet out of his jacket pocket and opened it, took out the photograph of his girls. He'd done this so often the picture was in danger of wearing thin.

He'd called home the day before and spoken to his brother Jetmir, who didn't really want to talk to him, or that's what it felt like – he couldn't wait to put down the phone. Said that Mischa was screaming in the bedroom, but Redzepi couldn't hear a child crying.

Jetmir was just fed up, Redzepi thought. Fed up of him calling and nagging, only to get the same answer. 'No, Durim', with a sigh in his voice. 'We haven't found your girls.' And he knew what his brother was thinking.

But Jetmir didn't know what it was like to live with no answers. The pain had dulled over time, but the fire was still burning somewhere inside.

'Do you ever think about the people back home?' Redzepi asked.

Ahmetaj sent him a lazy look. Took his time.

'There's not much to think about.'

'What do you mean?'

'It's another life. They're there and I'm here.'

Redzepi nodded pensively.

'So you've never thought about going back?'

Ahmetaj shook his head.

'Why would I?'

'Well, I just thought ... like me, you've got no roots here. No family.'

Ahmetaj leaned back again and closed his eyes.

'I'm happy here,' he said. 'I don't need a family.'

There was silence, but Redzepi continued to think about Kosovo until there was a beep on the screen in front of Ahmetaj. They both sat up. There was movement on the GPS trackers.

All of them.

Redzepi looked at Ahmetaj.

'How can he be on the move now?'

He rang Jeton Pocoli. No answer. Tried Flurim's friend, with the same result.

'Shit,' he said to himself, and started the car. Put it into first gear. 'Where's he heading?'

'He'll be on the main street any minute now,' Ahmetaj said. 'Then we'll see.'

They stared at the monitor. Waited. A minute passed.

'Shit,' Ahmetaj said. 'He's coming this way.'

Redzepi thought hard. He looked at the gun lying beside him. He couldn't shoot a man through a car window, not when the car was moving. There was a food shop on the other side of the road. People might see them. See the car. Tip off the police.

'Here he comes,' Ahmetaj said, and pointed out the window. Redzepi followed the red car with his eyes. Saw the carpenter behind the wheel. Alone.

What the hell had happened?

Redzepi stared at him as he passed.

'Are you not going to follow him?' Ahmetaj asked, when the van Blystad was driving turned out onto the main road.

Redzepi shook his head.

'We've got him on GPS.'

Redzepi was more concerned about Jeton Pocoli and Flurim Ahmetaj's friend, as neither of them had answered the phone. It was obvious that they hadn't done the job.

Redzepi drove towards the residential area where he'd dropped them off only twenty minutes earlier. He stopped outside the red house and saw Jeton Pocoli lying on his back in the front yard, not moving.

'Keep an eye on where he's going,' Redzepi said, pointing to the monitor.

He got out and hurried over to his friend, who had dark stripes of blood running down both sides of his face.

'Get me away from here,' Pocoli begged. 'Get me to hospital. This is fucking agony.'

Redzepi looked away.

Thought about what might happen. A stint in hospital, questioning, the possibility of too much talk – everything. Too risky, no gain.

He picked up the gun that was lying beside Jeton Pocoli and remembered what Daddy Longlegs always said about critical situations. It was all about damage control.

Durim Redzepi put the gun to his friend's head.

And pulled the trigger.

∵

Roger Blystad couldn't slow down, even though he knew he was driving much faster than he should. The adrenaline was pumping through his veins. He looked at his knuckles, still bloody and raw from the fight.

He replayed what had happened over and over, hitting the guy with the spade, the gunshots, the man falling down the stairs, the fight that followed, and the bullets he'd dodged; it was like a film he couldn't stop. The worst thing was the open eyes, devoid of life. He now knew why they always closed dead people's eyes.

And the blood.

All the blood.

Blystad had seen a dead person before, but only from a distance, from the third floor in Eckersbergs gate. He had still never dreamt that it would feel like this, so intense, so juddering, so sickening.

And now? What was he going to do now? Where was he going to go?

The emergency control centre had rung him again, and when he was finally calm enough to answer, he told them that his three-year-old son had got hold of his phone and pushed the buttons. Blystad had done his best to assure the man on the other end that everything was fine.

He overtook a small car that was driving religiously at the speed limit, checked in the rear-view mirror, couldn't see anyone following him. There was no reason to either – the two men had come to his house. Easy enough, then, you would think, to kill him. There weren't likely to be more.

Or were there?

He hadn't seen a car outside, but they definitely hadn't got there on foot. His car was so big and heavy that it wouldn't be hard to catch up with it. He decided to dump it as soon as possible, but first he had to find somewhere safe.

But should he go to the police or not? The right thing to do would be to hand himself in.

But then again, he'd shot someone with a nail gun. He'd killed a man. He could of course plead self-defence, but did that guarantee that he'd walk free? Would he survive another spell in prison?

No, he thought, he would rather chance it on the run. And now he was driving to Oslo, the largest city in Norway. The easiest place to disappear. He would find somewhere out of the way to park, book into a cheap hotel, and then try to work out what to do next. Maybe head down to the continent. Take the train to Gothenburg and go east from there. There were plenty of options.

There was nothing for him in Norway. Mariana was dead. His mother was dead. Nothing left to fight for.

Or yes, thinking about it, perhaps there was.

Blystad struck the steering wheel. Wasn't it about time that he stayed in one place, confronted his problems, got rid of them once and for all? He was no longer the same man, not after he'd killed someone. He was done with being the victim who hid himself away. He'd fled too many times before.

It was time to start living again.

And he had an idea about what he could do, who he could talk to. It was two years since they'd last met, and he'd steered clear of him on purpose ever since. But now, he no longer had a choice.

42

Charlie Høisæther was in the middle of a takeaway supper – fried acarajé filled with onions and prawns – when the phone rang. He finished chewing what he had in his mouth, washed it down with a couple of swigs of beer, then popped the white earpieces in and turned the page in the newspaper.

'Talk,' he said.

'I think we've found a good place,' Freddy said.

Charlie scanned the headlines. He'd learned some Portuguese in the time that he'd lived in Natal, but he would never dare try to speak.

'For what?' he asked.

'For the leisure complex you want to build.'

Charlie grabbed the beer can again and emptied it.

'*We* have found a good place?'

'Yes, Eduardo and me.'

Eduardo, Charlie thought, the young lad.

'Were you asked to do that?' he said.

'No, but we have, all the same – that's OK, isn't it? You wanted somewhere. You've been looking for a good place for ages.'

Charlie turned to the next page.

'Where is it?'

'On Avenida Bernardo Vieria, not too far from Midway Mall.'

Charlie frowned.

'So, in the middle of town.'

'Yes, it's more likely then that punters will see it and come.'

Charlie would rather that the centre was away from the worst of the traffic, he wanted it to be a place where people went because they wanted to, not because they happened to drive past.

'Parking space?'

'Plenty of possibilities,' Freddy said. 'We might have to knock down a few buildings, but we can manage that.'

'We' again, Charlie noted.

'It was Eduardo's idea, in fact,' Freddy continued. 'There's a petrol station and car wash nearby where his dad used to work. And there's an electrical goods supplier in one of the buildings, and according to Eduardo, the owner wants to sell. Doesn't cost much either.'

Charlie scratched his head.

'So everything's going well with Eduardo then?'

'Very well. He's keen. Does everything I ask him to, and more.'

Freddy laughed briefly.

Charlie put the phone in the pocket of his shorts, got up from the white stool by the kitchen island and carried his plate and beer can over to the sink.

'Shall I come and pick you up?' Freddy asked.

'Give me fifteen minutes,' Charlie said.

∵

Twenty-five minutes later, he found himself out on the street, dressed in shorts, sandals and a white t-shirt. It was scorching hot and the cool air in Freddy's Mercedes was a pleasant reprieve.

'Where's Eduardo?' Charlie asked.

'He's waiting for us there,' Freddy said.

They passed low white houses, red- and green-painted shops, with shutters rolled down over the windows, and the usual tags and graffiti. Charlie had got used to the potholes in the road. They passed people on mopeds without helmets, who wove in and out between the cars, tooting their horns – a feature of Brazilian traffic culture that Freddy had quickly adopted after arriving here a couple of years ago.

Not long after, he parked on the right-hand side of the road by two girls in short dresses leaning against a wall outside a clothes shop.

'Is this it?' Charlie asked.

'Yep,' Freddy said, and got out.

Charlie followed him, but took time to assess the girls. They could both have danced at Senzuela, he thought. The shop next door looked pretty disused, and the corrugated iron looked like it hadn't been hosed down for years. There was an advert for a tyre manufacturer plastered on one of the doors.

Freddy walked over to a fence and then pointed towards an open area about the size of half a football pitch. The odd grass tussock burst out from the ground; there were some planks here and there, stones, and earth that looked coarse, grey and dry.

'What d'you think?' Freddy said, full of enthusiasm. 'It could work, couldn't it?'

'Where's Eduardo?'

'Inside,' Freddy said.

'I want to talk to him.'

Freddy sent Charlie a long look.

'OK.'

The girls outside the clothes shop had gone when Charlie and Freddy came back. Freddy opened a green metal door beside the shop and went down some stairs.

'Cars and bikes could park down here,' Freddy said, his voice bouncing off the walls. 'We'll just make an opening outside somewhere with a barrier and that kind of thing, then people can drive down here.'

Charlie didn't answer.

Soon they came into an area that resembled a car park. A big, open area, with load-bearing pillars and widely spaced bulbs that washed the dark walls with a yellowish-white light.

'Is the owner here as well?' Charlie asked.

'No, he's…'

Eduardo de Jesus Silva slipped out from behind one of the pillars. Charlie had expected the nineteen-year-old to grin and come towards him as though *he* were Jesus.

He didn't.

Instead, he had a serious expression on his face.

'Mister High,' he said. 'I'm so sorry.'

Then he heard a sound behind him – a sound he'd become very familiar with at close hand, over the past two years. The rustle of Freddy's holster as he drew his gun, the sound of metal against one of the rings he wore on his fingers.

Charlie turned slowly and stared straight down the barrel of a Glock 17.

'Freddy,' he said. 'What the fuck?'

Freddy held the gun to Charlie's head.

'There'll be nothing left of this place tomorrow,' he said. 'They're going to blow it to bits.'

He stared at Charlie with cold eyes.

'I don't know if there'll ever be an ice rink here.' He shrugged, showed the one palm that wasn't holding a gun. 'Maybe I'll build a gym complex instead.'

The other arm was absolutely straight, not a shake. No hesitation. No feeling.

He turned towards Eduardo de Jesus Silva, who was kicking the dust with the toe of his trainers.

'I'm sorry, Mister High,' he said. 'I didn't know.'

'What's he promised you?' Charlie asked.

But he already knew the answer. Money. Everything Eduardo had ever dreamed of. Enough money to look after his father. His mother and sister.

'I need someone who knows the city,' Freddy said. 'Someone who knows the people here. I'm sure Hansemann can help me a bit, but you know how valuable local knowledge is.'

Charlie turned back to him.

'So you're thinking of taking over – is that it?'

Freddy nodded.

'Just like that?'

'No,' Freddy said. 'I'm actually doing it for Daddy Longlegs. But it's a great opportunity for me too.'

Daddy Longlegs, Charlie thought.

No.

It wasn't him who'd arranged this.

'You can have…'

Charlie stopped; he knew there was nothing he could offer Freddy to not kill him. Given all the opportunities that would arise as a result, he would do well, no matter what.

'Let Isabel keep the apartment,' he said. 'She doesn't have anywhere else to go.'

Freddy seemed to consider this, but said nothing.

Charlie lowered his eyes, took a deep breath. Threw up his hands and said, 'Let's get it over with then.'

43

Daddy Longlegs was sitting at his desk in the office when his mobile phone rang. He saw the number on the display and grabbed the phone.

'Hello,' he said.

'It's all gone to hell,' Durim Redzepi shouted. 'The carpenter got away. We know where he is, but Jeton and Nikolai are dead.'

Daddy Longlegs closed his eyes and slowly shook his head. Redzepi's fuck-up quota was full, over full. It had not been the intention, two years ago, to give Henning Juul a warning. He was supposed to have died in the fire. But Redzepi had overheard a conversation that Ørjan Mjønes had had with Juul's sister, where he promised that they wouldn't harm him, that they just wanted to scare him. And Redzepi had thought Mjønes meant it.

He should never have given them another chance, Daddy Longlegs thought, before asking, 'Where are you?'

'On our way to Oslo,' Redzepi replied. 'We've got him on GPS.'

Daddy Longlegs rubbed his face with his available hand and sighed; he looked at the man sitting on the sofa with his hands folded.

'I don't want to hear another word from you until the job's done,' he said. 'Is that clear?'

There was silence.

'Is that clear?'

'Yes, yes.'

Daddy Longlegs hung up and threw the phone down onto the desk. He shook his head.

'Problems?' asked the man sitting on the sofa.

Daddy Longlegs nodded.

'The joiner's proved to be more resilient than we reckoned.'

'Soon only Juul will be left,' said the man on the sofa. 'And he knows nothing.'

Daddy Longlegs stood up and went over to a cupboard behind the desk, opened it and took out a bottle of Talisker. And two glasses, as well.

'Would you like some?' he asked over his shoulder.

The guest shook his head.

'I'm driving.'

Daddy Longlegs poured a glass and lifted it to his mouth, swallowed, and felt it burn down into his chest. He smacked his lips with pleasure and poured himself another dram.

'How are things down in Natal?' the man on the sofa asked. 'Charlie's been dealt with, hasn't he?'

'I got a phone call just before you came,' Daddy Longlegs said. 'Charlie is no longer a potential problem for us.'

Daddy Longlegs put the bottle back into the cupboard and closed it.

'That's good.'

He turned towards the sofa and froze when he saw a straight arm holding a gun, aimed at him. He heard a muffled sound and then everything fragmented; floor, ceiling, walls. He heard his glass of whisky shatter, then fell to the floor. He tried to breathe, but there was no air.

In his youth, when he had been on stage, Daddy Longlegs had always wanted a role in which he could die. He'd mused on what he would do, if he should die with his eyes open, if he should shake and cramp, if he should make any noises.

Now he knew that he shouldn't have done any of those things. He should just have lain there, waiting, until the curtain fell. Anything else was impossible.

∵

Durim Redzepi thumped the steering wheel.

'Fuck!'

Flurim Ahmetaj sat up in the seat behind him and leaned closer.

'What is it?'

Redzepi told him what had just happened and the order he'd been given. Ahmetaj shook his head and sat back.

'I'm out,' he said.

Redzepi caught his eye in the rear-view mirror.

'What d'you mean?'

'When we get to town, drop me somewhere near the main station. I'm out of here.'

'What? You can't just go now, Flurim!'

'I fucking well can. You should, too. Let Daddy Longlegs sort out his own problems. I'm fed up with it. Two of our friends are dead. It'd be crazy to stay in Oslo now, Durim. The police have issued a sketch of you, it'll only be hours before we're caught.'

Redzepi hit the wheel again and swore to himself. He knew that Ahmetaj was right. At the same time, he knew what he had to lose. If he did a runner now, he would never know what Daddy Longlegs had found out about Svetlana and Doruntina. And the man they'd been looking for and tried to kill, who'd managed to get away, was somewhere on the road ahead of them, and he was the reason that he'd had to kill Jeton Pocoli himself. His hands were pulsating as though they had their own mind, their own will. They were aching for revenge.

But one thing at a time.

'Is he far ahead of us?' Redzepi asked.

No response from the back seat. Redzepi looked at Ahmetaj in the mirror. He was staring out the car window at the passing fields, and appeared not to have heard Redzepi's question.

'So that's how it's going to be?' he asked.

'What?'

'You're not even going to help me while you are still in the car?'

'You're an idiot if you go through with this, Durim.'

'That's my problem, isn't it?'

Redzepi took one hand off the wheel and put it on the gun on the seat beside him.

'But, if I were you, I wouldn't do that,' Ahmetaj said, without looking at him. 'We know each other too well for that.'

Redzepi didn't move his hand from the gun.

Ahmetaj leaned forward again and looked at him.

'I don't know what you think you'll get from all of this, brother. Be smart. Get out while you still can. You can always come back later.'

Redzepi hesitated, before returning his hand to the steering wheel. Ahmetaj was right again. He just didn't like half-done jobs. And he liked giving up even less, especially when he was so close.

'At least let me have your PC,' he said, 'so I can follow the GPS trackers.'

Ahmetaj shook his head.

'I would never get it back. And you wouldn't know what to do with it anyway.'

Redzepi sighed.

Ahmetaj was right. For the third time.

44

The boxes from the sushi restaurant were on the floor, with the remains of wasabi, soya sauce and ginger. The sight of them made Nora think about Iver again; to begin with he'd been very sceptical about eating raw fish, but then he'd come to love it. Soon they would be laying him in the ground, and she hadn't even started to think about it.

She hadn't had time to miss him yet; she'd been paralysed by the thought that he was dead and that she'd never see him again. She'd rebuked herself for having thought ill of him only hours before he was killed. While it was in no way certain that they'd spend the rest of their lives together, she'd been prepared to give it a try. For the child's sake.

For her own sake.

Nora got up and went out into the hall. One of his jackets was hanging there, and she took it down off the hook. It was a corduroy jacket, worn at the elbows, and it smelled of him when she put it over her shoulders. It was far too big, but she put in on all the same.

How long had he had this jacket?

For years.

It had almost become a part of him; he always wore it when he went to work. Like it was his uniform.

Nora went back into the living room and emptied the jacket pockets. Not surprisingly, there was a lighter there. A half-empty packet of chewing gum. Some paper, a receipt?

She looked at it. It said 'Little & Light' along the top. Iver had bought something that cost 149 kroner; it didn't specify what. Nora felt to see if there was anything in the inner pocket. A small package that crackled.

The bag had the same logo on it – Little & Light – two capital Ls in old-fashioned writing, joined by the squiggly ampersand. She squeezed the package gently, felt something inside. She opened it.

Put her hand to her mouth.

And started to cry.

It was a baby hat. Size 52. White, soft and beautiful.

She thought about her child, who would never know its father. Who would never know how funny he could be, how warm and tender and loving.

Nora sat down on the sofa and pulled up her legs. She found Jonas's snow globe and held it in her other hand. So she had two things she could feel, and hold.

Soon the baby would start to kick, she thought. Soon a part of Iver would carry on living, as someone else. It was cold comfort, but right now she clung to anything that might help.

∴

Durim Redzepi was alone on the road.

In the forest.

He was alone, full stop.

Jeton Pocoli and Flurim Ahmetaj's friend were dead.

And Ahmetaj himself had gone back to Sweden, taking with him all the technology that might help Durim.

He had no one. Nothing.

Durim Redzepi parked by the cabin, but instead of going in, he stood outside and listened to the evening, to the falling night, to life around him. It had been a long time since his girls had disappeared.

Too long.

He was tired. Tired of hunting, waiting, hoping. Hoping for what?

A definitive answer. Something he could reconcile himself to, and move on. Wasn't that what they said he should do?

But he had actually got his answer already, didn't he? They

disappeared in 1999. What the fuck did he think happened? They were killed, just like all the others. Forget Daddy Longlegs, he told himself, he can't tell you anything you don't already know.

But then, there was always that hope.

That fucking hope.

He hadn't held onto it for so long only to give up now. He had to continue, to find the bastard carpenter and get rid of him.

And that meant that he had to think.

Redzepi thought best when he was moving, so whenever he had to come up with quick, smart solutions, he did something. He decided to tidy up a bit, start getting ready to move out. He was struck by how much stuff he'd managed to accumulate in the four months that he'd been living here. It was mainly things he might need for work – tools, rope and big, black binliners. Ammunition. Extra clothes. Rucksacks, suitcases. He would have to think about cleaning the place as well. That in itself would take hours. Certainly if he was to do it properly.

He got started, heated up some water, got out the ammonium chloride and soap, mops and rags.

What would the carpenter do now that he knows people are after him? he wondered.

He'll make a break for it, he concluded, disappear again. From what Daddy Longlegs had said, he'd been in hiding for over two years now, and done a damn good job of it too. He'd done it before, so he could do it again.

What would he have done himself?

He would have tackled the problem head on. He would have found out who was chasing him, and then *he* would have tracked *them* down.

Was the carpenter that kind of guy? Deep down? He'd obviously thought that attack was the best defence yesterday, and he was still alive. His strategy had been successful.

Dawn had started to break in the east by the time Durim Redzepi had finished cleaning. He was tired, had to sit down, and decided to check the news on his mobile before sleeping for a few hours. Then he would get into the car and drive to Sweden.

He saw that his mates had been found. The emergency services had sent out a patrol after someone had called from that address and then hung up. *Aftenposten* online said that the police were working with several leads, but couldn't give any information in light of the ongoing investigation.

Redzepi also read that a lawyer had been murdered in the capital. A reader had posted a link in the comments on one of the online papers, and written: 'Here is the victim.' Redzepi clicked on it, and froze with a bottle of water at his lips.

It was him.

Daddy Longlegs.

Was he … dead? How…?

There was no doubt. He was the one who'd come to see him that day, with a picture of the carpenter in his briefcase. But if Daddy Longlegs was dead, he thought – then I'll never know what happened to Svetlana and Doruntina.

He punched the table, then hid his face in his hands, and felt the hope drain out of him. Now he would never get the answers he'd been promised.

'Fuck this,' Redzepi said, and stood up.

He grabbed the car keys and walked out.

45

Henning was sitting up in the hospital bed, as he had been doing for most of the night.

As expected, he hadn't slept much, mainly because he'd been thinking about Durim Redzepi and how he could have known that Henning would be outside the main police station at four o'clock that afternoon. He'd been so preoccupied with Ann-Mari Sara and Mørck and other possibilities that he hadn't even thought of the most obvious answer. In other words, the person who knew with absolute certainty that the interview would take place at that time.

The man who had booked the interogation room.

Bjarne Brogeland.

Could he be colluding with the bad guys in some way or another?

Henning tried to go through everything that he'd done together with Bjarne in the past few weeks and months, all their telephone conversations and meetings since they first met at the police head-quarters. Was there anything about his body language?

No.

Henning was unable to convince himself. Not Bjarne.

All night, Henning had been aching to get hold of his mobile phone, so he could search on the internet to see if there were any possible connections between Bjarne and Mørck, but none of the officers watching him knew where it was. And they wouldn't lend him theirs. He just had to wait.

But he wasn't good at waiting, wasn't good at lying there doing nothing. He wanted to get up and move, to try and get hold of Ann-Mari Sara and find out what really happened after he blacked out. But she probably wouldn't want to talk to him now, not after the accusations he'd hurled at her. And he wouldn't blame her.

Bjarne came by just after breakfast, without Sandland this time. The policeman was lighter in his step than last time, and Henning wondered why. He looked for signs of nervousness or anything else that might indicate that Bjarne had interests other than the best for either Henning or the investigation. But he saw nothing.

Bjarne nodded to the officer in the corner, who stood up with tired legs.

'You won't believe what's happened,' Bjarne said, as he hurried over to the bed. Before Henning could respond, Bjarne had grabbed the remote control and pointed it at the television on the wall in front of Henning.

Henning studied Bjarne, who looked from the screen, to the remote control and back. He seemed just like he always did. He indicated that Henning should lift his head and look at the screen, at the teletext page he'd just switched to. Henning did as he was told.

'Lawyer shot and killed' it said in big letters.

Bjarne flicked onto another page. Henning squinted so he could read what was written there.

Prominent Lawyer Killed

A lawyer has been found dead in his office in central Oslo. The police said in a statement that he was probably shot late yesterday evening.

'It's too early to speculate about motives, but we are working through the victim's client list and current cases as fast as we can,' Assistant Chief of Police Pia Nøkleby told NTB.

The lawyer was found by one of the cleaners around midnight.

Read more on nrk.no.

'It's Preben Mørck,' Bjarne said, pointing at the screen with the remote control. Henning looked over at him in surprise.

'What did you say?'

'I've come straight from the scene,' Bjarne said.

Henning tried to work out what this meant. Yesterday evening he'd told Bjarne about his suspicions regarding Mørck, and then, only a few hours later, someone had shot and killed him.

Henning wasn't sure that he'd be able to hide his suspicions from Bjarne. If Mørck was Daddy Longlegs, and Henning was sure he was, then he would have valuable information about all the people he had helped over the years, and maybe even about their motives. Perhaps someone was frightened about what he might tell the police if he was questioned – if he was put under pressure.

'So he was shot?' Henning said, with some hesitation.

Bjarne nodded.

'Once in the head and twice in the chest. No room for doubt.'

Henning thought about Iver, who had apparently gone to see Mørck only days before he died. If what Henning knew of Iver was right, he would have asked questions that made Mørck's alarm bells ring. Possibly also those of whoever Mørck was working for.

But who did he work for?

'But that's not all that happened yesterday,' Bjarne said, and pressed the remote control again. Another news site appeared.

Henning read.

Double Murder in Brandbu

Two foreign nationals were found dead at a house just outside the centre of Brandbu in Oppland. According to a spokesperson from Gran and Lunner police, the deaths are being treated as suspicious, but no further details have been released.

A press conference will be held later on today.

'One of the victims was called Jeton Pocoli,' Bjarne said, clearly engaged. 'He's somehow linked to Durim Redzepi. A gun was found at the scene, and some bullet cases, and the grooves on the inside of the cases match those on the cases that were found where you were shot.'

Henning tried to process this new information.

'So Redzepi was there as well?'

'Well, it was certainly the same weapon as the one he fired at you,' Bjarne replied. 'We're trying to find the man who lived at the address where it happened. Apparently the owner is an old man, and he'd rented it out to a joiner.'

Henning turned away from the screen and stared at Bjarne.

A joiner.

'So, it's been quite a night, you might say.'

Bjarne was still keyed up.

But all Henning could focus on was what he'd just said.

'What was he called?'

'Who?'

'The joiner.'

'He's called…' Bjarne pulled a notebook from his jacket pocket. 'Roger Blystad.'

Henning tasted the name. Not such a big leap, in terms of phonetics, from Rasmus Bjelland. He'd thought, certainly guessed, for a long time, that Bjelland had changed his name.

'But you don't know where he is?'

Bjarne shook his head.

'We've put out a call to every district in the country that he's wanted for questioning, so it would be quite a feat if we didn't manage to find him.'

Henning tried to work out what could have happened. Someone who was connected to Durim Redzepi had been in Brandbu and had been killed…

'It could have been self-defence,' Henning said.

'The thought also struck me. And there are things to indicate that there was a fight in the cellar, where one of the bodies was found. Several shots had been fired, among other things.'

Henning thought some more.

'But there's still no sign of Redzepi?'

Bjarne shook his head.

'If I was him, I'd have left the country long ago. His face is in all the papers. He's obviously just a foot soldier. But foot soldiers don't like being arrested either.'

And now that Daddy Longlegs – his employer – was dead, there was certainly no reason for Redzepi to stay, Henning reasoned.

'Have you managed to reconstruct Iver's final movements?' he asked. 'Who he was in contact with, and the like?'

'We don't know,' said Bjarne.

'But what about where he'd been, then? His car, for example?'

'We're checking that, of course – I've been a bit busy with other things recently, so I'm not up to date on it right now.'

Henning wondered what 'other things' Bjarne was talking about.

'I have to get back to the station,' Bjarne said. 'You know how it is. Meetings, meetings, meetings.'

'Before you go,' Henning said. 'You don't happen to know where my mobile phone is?'

'No,' Bjarne said, and turned off the television. 'But give me two seconds, and I'll see if it's lying around here somewhere.'

'Great. Thanks.'

46

Roger Blystad checked the time. Nearly eight o'clock. The last time he'd looked it was ... nearly eight o'clock.

He sighed, lay down on the hotel bed and stared at the ceiling – his main pastime for the last twelve hours. The unfamiliar bed had not provided much sleep. At some point during the night, he had woken suddenly and sat up, certain that someone was in the room; he had even reached for a weapon he didn't have, and looked for the intruder. It was only some time after the imagined danger that he could breathe normally again.

Blystad closed his eyes.

He could feel the past 48 hours in his body. In any other circumstances, he would have been able to sleep without a problem, but now his mind wouldn't rest. The images were burned into his memory, and played on repeat to his inner eye.

Lots of people have lost their lives recently because of you, Blystad thought, and sat up. And, from what he'd read in the newspapers, it had been a close call for Henning Juul as well.

Blystad looked at the clock again, just after eight this time. Still no answer.

You can't stay here much longer, he said to himself.

He decided to give it another hour. Then he would have to leave.

∵

Bjarne came back into the room, and smiled as he waved with the telephone.

'I found it,' he said. 'It's been here since the last time. One of the nurses has even charged it for you. Talk about extra service!'

Bjarne came over to the bed and handed it to Henning. Henning studied Bjarne as he took it.

No.

Bjarne was still Bjarne.

There was a new scratch on the glass on his phone. Must have been when I lost consciousness, Henning thought, and heard Bjarne's phone ringing. Bjarne fished it out of his pocket and answered, at the same time moving away from Henning's bed.

Henning checked any missed calls and saw that Veronica had called four times, and Bjarne seven. Not many people knew his new number, so it wasn't so strange that there weren't more, but he had hoped that Nora might have rung.

Henning went into his email account and waited half a minute while the day's emails ticked in. The first four were advertising, but the fifth one startled him. He glanced over at Bjarne, who seemed to be fully focused on what the person on the other end was saying.

It said 'Rasmus Bjelland' under subject.

He opened the email.

From: roger.blystad@gmail.com
To: henning.juul@123news.no
Subject: Rasmus Bjelland

Hi Henning,
Something tells me we've got the same people after us. Can we meet again?
Answer as soon as you can. I'll be leaving soon.
Rasmus Bjelland

Roger Blystad, thought Henning. The carpenter. Who lived in the house where the two Kosovo-Albanians were killed yesterday.

He tried to write an answer, but it was slow work with only one functioning arm, and he didn't manage to press send before Bjarne came back.

'Is there anything else you need?'

Henning shook his head.

'You just stay here then and get better,' the policeman said. 'We can talk more later.'

Then he disappeared.

Henning finished the email to Bjelland, and waited for five minutes. Then he pulled the cord that switched on a green light outside his room, and waited for another minute for a nurse to come in.

Henning pushed himself off the bed.

The nurse asked, 'Do you need to go to the toilet again?'

'No,' Henning replied, feeling a little unsteady. He went over to the chair where his clothes were.

'I need a bit of help to put my clothes on.'

The police officer raised his drowsy eyes from the book he was reading.

'Why do you need to get dressed?' the nurse asked.

'Because I'm going out.'

The nurse hesitated. 'I'll have to talk to your doctor first.'

Henning shook his head and started to unbutton the hospital nightshirt.

'My shoulder hurts, but everything else is working. I don't have time to be here any longer.'

The officer put down his book and stood up.

'And no,' Henning said, turning towards him. 'You don't need to ask anyone if that's alright. I'm perfectly capable of deciding myself whether I stay here or not.'

The officer didn't answer, but got out his phone and left the room.

'We can't force you to stay, obviously,' the nurse said. 'But let me have a quick word with the doctor before you go, so we can be sure you don't do anything you'll regret.'

The nurse helped him to get dressed. It took some time.

Henning agreed to wait until both the nurse and officer had let their seniors know. The nurse was the first to come back. She gave him a nod and a smile.

Then the officer came back. He still had his mobile phone to his ear, as if he were in mid-conversation.

'Brogeland wants to know where you're going,' he said.

Yes, I bet he does, Henning thought.

'Tell him I'll call when I know myself,' he said.

Then he left.

47

The car radio was still on the Norwegian P4 channel, even though Durim Redzepi had crossed the Swedish border some time ago. Once every hour, the news reminded him of what had happened the night before, and each time he saw Jeton Pocoli's face twisted with pain. And every time, Redzepi had reached the conclusion that he couldn't have done anything else. It had been both compassionate and necessary.

He wondered if he'd managed to remove all trace of himself from the cabin. He'd started to rush towards the end because he just wanted to finish and go. Now that Daddy Longlegs was dead, the police would probably investigate every detail in his life, and as he was the one who'd organised the cabin for Redzepi in the spring, it was equally probable that they would come knocking.

But it didn't really matter if they found anything or not, he was never going back. Gothenburg was his first stop. He'd dump the car there and contact a friend who knew most of the Kosovo-Albanians in Scandinavia, find out if there was work elsewhere.

It was a good morning for driving. Clear and still. The road was dry. Redzepi was driving at just over the speed limit, but he knew that the speedometer was always on the high side. He was overtaking a semi-trailer on a long, gentle slope when his phone started to vibrate in the centre console.

Redzepi had thrown away the phone he'd been using for the past few days, and this was his old one, the one he'd used before Daddy Longlegs asked him to switch. Redzepi didn't recognise the number on the display, but so what – it could hardly be relevant to him now.

He pulled into the inside lane and tried to concentrate on the road and the traffic ahead, and he managed quite successfully for the next hundred metres or so.

But the phone wouldn't stop ringing.

Redzepi picked it up and held it to his ear.

'Hello?' he said.

He turned down the volume on the radio.

'Durim?' said an unknown voice. 'Where are you?'

'Who's asking?' he asked, aggressively.

'The person who pays your bills.'

Redzepi took his foot off the accelerator and let the car cruise for a while as he tried to work out if he'd heard the man's voice before. It was clear, neither high nor deep, angry or gentle. It was completely neutral.

Hang up now, Redzepi told himself. It might be a policeman.

'What do you want?' he asked. 'Who are you?'

'Daddy Longlegs is dead.'

'I know.'

'He was shot and killed last night,' the man said.

Redzepi started to wind down the window. He was about to throw the phone out when the man said, 'It was me who killed him.'

What the hell was going on? How had this man got hold of his number?

'And I need you to finish the job.'

Redzepi's thoughts were racing.

'Who are you?' he asked, and just then, a memory surfaced. That job he'd done out at the Scandic hotel in Asker one day, on the petrified policeman's laptop. The name he'd deleted from the Indicia report.

It was him.

'You don't need to worry about that,' the man said. 'But what you do need to worry about is doing your job properly. And it's not finished.'

Redzepi shook his head and thought about his girls, what Daddy Longlegs had promised.

'Not now that Daddy Longlegs is dead. You'll have to sort it out yourself, I don't care.'

He was about to hang up.

'You don't care about Doruntina and Svetlana?'

Redzepi said nothing.

'Well?'

Redzepi's grip on the steering wheel tightened.

'I know about your family, Durim.'

He swallowed.

'What are you saying?

There was a moment's silence.

'Henning Juul and Rasmus Bjelland are both still alive,' the man continued. 'Finish the job and I'll tell you what Daddy Longlegs found out about your wife and daughter.'

Redzepi had to swing sharply to the left to stop the car from swerving onto the other side of the road. He ran a hand over his cropped hair. The most sensible thing would be to keep on driving, away from Norway, and let this guy sort out his problems himself.

But he knew their names.

'You have to give me something first,' Redzepi said.

'Hm?'

'How can I be sure that you know anything about my family?'

Another silence.

'Your word's not enough,' Redzepi said. 'You have to give me something first.'

For a second, all he heard was the static fuzz on the line, then the man at the other end sighed.

'Daddy Longlegs got a man to check what your brother had done with all the money you sent,' he said, eventually.

Redzepi felt his heart start to pound.

'Why did he do that?'

'Because knowledge is power, Durim. We always keep an eye on our investments.'

He was thinking hard.

'What did he find out?'

'I'll tell you when you've finished the job.'

Redzepi shook his head.

'That's not enough. You have to tell me something that'll convince me you're telling the truth.'

There was a sharp intake of breath on the other end.

'Your brother's called Jetmir, and his wife is called Justyna and they have a daughter called Mischa. They live next to a big furniture factory in Koljovica Ere, on the outskirts of Pristina. I'm not going to say anymore, because as soon as you know what I know, you'll just carry on driving – you'll have no reason to come back and finish the job. And the clock is ticking, Durim. We're running out of time.'

Redzepi considered this. The information about his family was correct. Maybe this man really did know something about his girls.

Redzepi realised it was a while since he'd accelerated. The semitrailer had passed him again.

'Well, what's it to be, Durim?'

The very thought of turning around and heading back to Norway, to Oslo, where the police were hunting for him night and day, made him feel sick; his body broke out in a sweat. He wiped his forehead and thought about his dead friends. He wanted to avenge them.

He switched on the GPS; it showed a turnoff to the right up ahead, and a bridge where he could cross over to the other side.

'I'll do it,' he said in a feeble voice.

'Good. Do you have any idea about how to get hold of them?'

'I think so. The carpenter, at least. Juul isn't always easy to catch at short notice, but I've got something that might work.'

Redzepi explained what he was thinking. The man at the other end hesitated at first, but then said. 'That doesn't really get us any closer to Juul. It might even make him stay away.'

'It's the best I've got.'

Silence again.

'Get the ball rolling then.'

After he'd been given some more instructions, Redzepi put the phone down and pulled into a layby. He rang his friend in Gothen-burg and asked if he could get hold of Flurim Ahmetaj. Ten minutes later, Redzepi got a call from an unknown number.

'Brother,' Ahmetaj said. 'What is it now?'

Redzepi took a deep breath.

'If I told you that you could stay exactly where you are right now, as long as you had your computer with you, and still earn a heap of money in no time at all … what would you say?'

He didn't answer.

Redzepi knew that Ahmetaj seldom said no to good money.

'You'll get 10,000,' he added.

'If you're talking euros, you've got a deal.'

Redzepi thought about it for a while, then he said, 'OK.'

He heard a burst of laughter at the other end.

'Now you're talking my language, brother. What d'you need?'

'I need you to send an email.'

'An email? Should be able to manage that.'

'And I need to know the carpenter's exact position,' Redzepi said. 'You haven't turned the trackers off, have you?'

48

It had become even colder, Henning thought, when he stepped outside. He tried to pull his fleece jacket tighter over the sling and around his body, but it didn't provide much extra warmth.

It felt strange to be on his feet again, like he was on his way home after a long night on the town. So he took a taxi back to Seilduks-gaten, as he was fairly certain that Durim Redzepi or any of the others in that gang wouldn't bother to stake out his flat now – not after all that had happened.

But he couldn't be 100 per cent sure, so he got off the street as quickly as possible, and prayed that he wouldn't meet anyone on the stairs on the way up to his flat.

His postbox was stuffed full, but it would have to wait. He limped up the stairs and let himself in.

It felt odd to be there again. He hadn't spent a night in his own flat for as long as he could remember. The last time he stood here in the hall, he had narrowly averted a gas explosion. One of the windows was still open. It was as cold inside as it was outside.

He could very quickly see that there was no one there; all was quiet, there were no lights on, and everything was as he remembered, down to the position of the shoes by the door and the number of bottles in the plastic bag by the green cupboard.

Henning went through the flat quickly, picking up what he needed – an extra jacket, a pair of gloves, some more money – and the car keys. He couldn't remember where he'd parked the yellow car that he'd bought only a few weeks ago, but he eventually found it in Fossveien, just by the entrance to the old sailcloth factory.

Henning had just got in when his phone vibrated in his jacket pocket. A text message from Bjarne.

Thought you would want to know: Charlie Høisæther has been
reported missing by his girlfriend in Natal. Didn't come home last
night. BB

::·

Henning sat there and wondered what it might mean. Had Charlie's
past caught up with him? Had the truth about his game in Natal got
out? Had someone taken revenge?

OK, Henning wrote in reply and started the car. There was a beep
before he even managed to manoeuvre out of the tight parking space.

Where are you?

Henning didn't answer, started to drive instead.

It wasn't easy with only one working arm, but somehow he
managed. Twenty minutes later he left the car in the big parking
place by Huk.

Huk was where they'd met, Henning and Bjelland, in autumn
2007. They'd sat by the white restaurant that had originally been
built as a bathing house for Vidkun Quisling, the Norwegian Nazi
who seized power during the Second World War. The seagulls had
screeched and boats had glided silently past further out on the water.
Airplanes had left white trails in the otherwise perfect sky.

In many ways, it seemed fitting to meet in the same place, Henning
thought. Where it all started. Hopefully now, the final pieces would
fall into place.

Henning was there early, primarily because he hated being late, but
also because he wanted to make sure that they were alone. In summer,
Huk was possibly the most popular beach in Oslo, with throngs of
people visiting from morning to night. They came with disposable bar-
becues, Frisbees and guitars, not to mention alcohol and other highs.
But there was no one there now, no one other than a man walking along
the asphalt path towards him, about 100 metres away – a man who
looked as though he was keeping a cautious eye on his surroundings.

It had to be Bjelland, Henning thought. The last time they met,

Charlie Høisæther's joiner had been chubby with a receding hairline and thin hair. All that was gone now, the extra kilos, the wispy hair, but the man on the path moved with the same wariness as before, the same guarded expression and searching eyes. The same quick step.

About 30 seconds later, he stopped, a little hesitant, in front of Henning, as though he wasn't quite sure he'd come to the right place. He held out a similarly hesitant hand.

'That bad, huh,' Bjelland said, looking Henning up and down. And Henning realised that he didn't look the same as he had two years ago either.

'Yep, afraid so,' he said.

Bjelland let go of his hand and turned around. A man in a dark jacket had appeared but was walking in the opposite direction. And soon enough they were alone again.

Bjelland turned back to Henning.

'I wasn't sure if you'd … want to meet me again,' he said.

'Why?'

'Because…'

He looked out over the water. A small wave broke on the rocky shore.

'Because of your scars,' he said.

Henning knew what he was thinking. The last time they met marked the start of the events that would eventually lead to Jonas's death. And he might very well have blamed Rasmus Bjalland for it, he could have hated him, but what good would that do? It wouldn't bring Jonas back, and the decision to delve deeper into the Tore Pulli story had been his own. If anyone was to blame for Jonas's death, other than the people who got Durim Redzepi to start the fire, it was Henning himself.

He pointed to some smooth rocks by the water. 'Shall we sit over there?'

Bjelland glanced at Henning before nodding, then looked around. A ferry was moving slowly round the point. They sat staring out over the fjord.

'You're a difficult man to find,' Henning said.

'With good reason,' Bjelland said.

Henning looked at him, waited for him to talk.

'After we met last time,' Bjelland started, with a sigh, 'and especially after I'd seen what had happened to you and … your son, I realised that I had to lie low if I wanted to live. Not that I had much to live for, but … well, you want to stay alive, don't you? You get scared, so you try to protect yourself.'

Henning nodded.

'I found out about your wife,' he said.

Bjelland looked away for a few seconds. Henning waited for him to say something. He had to wait a while.

'It was my car she was driving,' he eventually said, almost in tears. 'I didn't think they'd come after us so quickly, but … they did.'

He shook his head.

'My only comfort is that she probably didn't even know or feel anything before it was over.'

Bjelland picked up a small stone from the ground and rolled it between his fingers. Henning studied the man who looked as tired as he felt. Bjelland had great circles under his eyes.

'And that's why you wanted to talk to me two years ago,' Henning said. 'You wanted revenge?'

Bjelland glanced over at him.

'Something like that.'

'And now you've contacted me again. What's happened in the meantime?'

Bjelland sighed.

'Two guys came to my door last night,' he said, and lowered his eyes. 'They tried to kill me. I…'

Henning looked over at his hands. The scabs on his knuckles.

'I'm so tired of it all,' Bjelland said. 'Tired of being on the run. Tired of having to look over my shoulder all the time. And I'm pretty sure you and I have the same people after us.'

Henning was sure of it too, but wanted to hear Bjelland's theories, to see if they echoed his own.

'Especially after what happened to your colleague.'

Bjelland threw the stone out into the water.

'Iver Gundersen phoned my mother,' Bjelland continued. 'He was trying to get in touch with me. My mother and I, we…'

He looked away again.

Took a few deep breaths.

'Mum had a secret email address that she never used anywhere other than at work,' he said. 'And I, well, I've been living under another identity for the past two years, so whenever something popped up to do with me, she let me know.'

'So your mother told you that Iver wanted to get in touch?'

Bjelland nodded.

'And even though I've been lying low, I've tried to keep up to date – especially after Tore Pulli was killed. I saw that you were on the case again, and that you were working closely with Gundersen. According to my mum, he wanted to talk to me about Charlie Høisæther and my bankruptcy in 1996, what kind of collaboration we'd had after that, and I realised you'd got someone to help you dig around, to investigate anything to do with Tore – just like you did two years ago.'

Bjelland paused.

Henning took the opportunity: 'So you contacted Iver?'

Bjelland nodded.

'I sent him an email, yes.'

'Why did you do that?'

'Because I'd started to think about it.'

Bjelland sighed deeply, leaned forward and tugged at some grass that was growing in the cracks between the stones.

'At first I was pleased that Tore was dead. Until he was killed, I was sure he was the one who started all the rumours about me in Brazil.'

'Before you go on,' Henning interrupted. 'Tell me about that. Tell me what Tore had to gain from doing that. As far as I know, he was busy with his own things in Oslo at the time.'

'Yes, but he was doing a lot more,' Bjelland said. 'He'd had a long list of clients as an enforcer and still knew lots of people who were involved in criminal activities and needed to do something with their dirty money. They went to Tore, and he sent the money to Charlie in Brazil – where it was then poured into various property projects.'

'Money laundering, in other words.'

'Right. Tore made a bit from it himself, but after a while, the same clients didn't see the need to go via Tore – they now had their own route, direct to Charlie, and several of them even started up for themselves down there in Natal. So Tore was getting less and less money, and I don't know if you know, but he was in a lot of debt by the end. From gambling and the like.'

Henning looked up at a seagull that swooped overhead.

'Yes, I had heard that.'

'Whatever, towards the end of my time with them, Tore and Charlie were arguing a lot about money. Tore thought it was unfair that he didn't get any compensation for the business he'd generated for Charlie. I know that he wanted a flat, among other things, as payment or thanks for all his help. But I didn't have much to do with them the last six months I was down there. Mariana and I had started our own business.'

'And that wasn't so popular, perhaps?'

Bjelland shook his head.

'No, everything changed between us then. I actually think that Charlie fancied my wife even before we got married, but he wouldn't admit it. That's basically why I didn't think Charlie had anything to do with the rumours about me; he would never had done anything to put her life in danger.'

Maybe that's at the bottom of it, Henning thought, the real reason why Charlie and Tore fell out. Charlie loved the woman that Tore was partly responsible for killing.

'So Tore wanted more money,' Henning reasoned out loud, to himself and Bjelland. 'He wanted fewer players in Natal, so that potential clients would come to him, and everything would be like before.'

'That's what I thought, as well.'

Bjelland stood up and looked around. Then he slowly sat down again.

'Like I said, for a long time I thought it was Tore who pulled the strings, as had always been the case when Tore and Charlie did business.'

Bjelland let the blades of grass slide between his fingers and then he clapped his hands lightly to brush off any dirt.

'But then when Tore was killed, and in such a sophisticated way, I started to wonder.'

He moved a little closer, so that he was sitting directly opposite Henning.

'I don't know if you found out which murder Tore was involved in, but…'

'I think so,' Henning interrupted. 'Bodil Svenkerud, 1996.'

Bjelland smiled momentarily, and nodded.

'I saw it all,' he said. 'From a window on the third floor. I'd just started to do up a flat in the building where she lived. It was a hit-and-run, poor woman, she was literally run over.'

He shook his head.

'Killing her was Tore's idea. Charlie told me a few years later, when he'd had a bit to drink. But if you think about it – it wasn't a particularly smart thing to do – to run over an old lady like that, on the street. Anyone could have seen them.'

'But you saw them, and you … didn't tell the police?' Henning said.

'No, I did, it was me who called them and spoke to them. At that point I didn't know it was Charlie and Tore's work. Anyway, they got away with it, and afterwards they had the sense not to do business together for a while – at least, not in Norway. Charlie moved to Brazil and that was where they started the little joint venture that made them rich, Charlie, in particular. And it was actually quite a smart game. It certainly worked.'

Henning moved a little. The rock they were sitting on was starting to feel cold and hard.

'And they did really well for years. Then in 2007, there was a police operation and almost everyone who dealt in property was hauled in by the police. Only a few got away with it. And Charlie was one of them. Then suddenly there were all these rumours that *I* was the informant, because I was one of the ones the police didn't charge. Which was also a pretty smart move, if you look at it objectively. With a bit of luck, I would be killed, the people down there in Natal would have their scapegoat, and that would be the end of it – plus, there would be less competition as a result.'

'But then your wife was killed instead, and you came back here.'

Bjelland nodded.

'My point is: Tore and Charlie could behave like complete idiots sometimes, and be super sophisticated at other times. And, of course, people get smarter as they get older, but still, there was something that didn't fit. I found it hard to believe that they could think up such a refined plan on their own.'

Henning thought about what Trine had told him, about the threats she got on the phone. Someone had been smart enough to record the phone call they'd made to her that day, a recording that would later link her to an unsolved murder which, if it fell into the hands of a newspaper, could ruin her career. A smart move, at short notice, just after they'd done something that wasn't so smart.

Henning knew where Bjelland was going.

'So then you thought that maybe someone other than Tore was responsible for the rumours about you? Which led to your wife being killed. Someone who might have been part of the whole Natal deal from the beginning in 1996?'

Bjelland nodded.

'Tore might well have spread the rumours, but I think that someone else gave him the idea.'

'So that's why you contacted Iver. You wanted him to find out who was behind it all.'

Bjelland nodded again.

'You don't have any theories yourself? Not even after all those years in Brazil?'

This time Bjelland shook his head.

In which case there must have been someone invisible pulling all the strings, Henning thought. It could have been Daddy Longlegs, only Henning had always seen Daddy Longlegs as a middleman, and he was dead now.

And Charlie was missing…

Henning wondered if Iver had managed to sniff out this person.

'So you and Iver corresponded by email?'

Bjelland nodded.

'He asked questions, and poked around, but I couldn't tell him much more than what I've told you now. I don't know who was behind it.'

Which is why they took Iver's laptop and mobile phone, Henning thought. They were scared that someone else would get hold of this, either in the form of a document or an email – even though the main player was unknown.

'OK,' Henning said. 'So we're sitting here again, my colleague is dead and someone is after both of us.'

'Yes,' Bjelland said. 'And I thought that we could maybe join forces in some way or another.'

'And how do you see that working?'

Bjelland shrugged.

'I don't know,' he said. 'But I did think that you could maybe tell my story, either in your paper or to someone you trust in the police. I'm not going to risk talking to them; I killed a man last night. I would never survive more than a week in a Norwegian prison, because of the gangs that are in there, who still think I was the informer in Natal.'

'So you want to use me as your microphone stand again.'

Bjelland sighed.

'Call it what you like. I didn't know what else to do. I'm scared, and I can't face living in hiding any longer.'

He rubbed his fingers against his thighs, as though he needed to generate some warmth.

'We don't have any evidence,' Henning said. 'And right now, people around me have a tendency to end up dead.'

Bjelland picked up another stone, studied it briefly and then threw it into the water. They watched the rings widen on the surface of the water, before they too disappeared.

Henning got out his phone and saw that Bjarne had tried to call him again. He'd also received an email. As there was a natural pause in the conversation, he opened his email account. The sharp light and reflection from the water made it difficult to read, so he held the phone closer and squinted.

The subject was NORA.

Nothing else.

The email had been sent from an address that was made up of lots of numbers and an email server Henning had never heard of. There was only one line of text in capital letters:

FINAL WARNING

The reference was clear.

On the evening that someone had broken into his flat, a similar message had been left on the inside of his front door – a message that Henning had only discovered as he jumped through the wall of flames into Jonas's room.

The message was from Durim Redzepi.

The man who had set fire to his flat.

There was a picture file attached. Henning opened it, held the phone even closer to his face so he could see what it was.

It was a photograph of a photograph.

An ultrasound picture.

It had been placed on a kitchen table and he immediately knew where the photograph had been taken.

In Nora's flat.

And beside the ultrasound image of Nora's unborn child was a box of matches.

'What is it?' Bjelland asked.

But Henning didn't answer. He was thinking about Nora, about what he should do. There was absolutely no doubt what the picture meant: if Henning didn't let things lie, Durim Redzepi would kill Nora and her unborn child, in a fire, just as he'd done with Jonas.

'What is it?' Bjelland asked again.

There was also a link in the email. Henning clicked on it.

The photographs were unclear and jumpy, but again, he had no doubt about what he was seeing. Live pictures from Nora's flat, from a camera somewhere on the ceiling, in the lampshade, perhaps. He saw her wandering around the flat, and some big boxes on the floor. There were piles of clothes lying around. Small clothes.

Henning closed the feed and dialled her number straightaway, got up and walked back and forth in front of Bjelland while he waited for an answer. Luckily it didn't take long.

'Hi, Henning,' she said.

'Nora.' He took a few steps away from Bjelland, 'Are you alone?'

'Yes.'

'Have you locked the door?'

Nora hesitated for a beat.

'Yes,' she said. 'I always do. Why do you ask?'

'Has anyone been round to the flat recently?'

There was silence on the other end for a moment.

'No one apart from Mum and Bjarne,' she said. 'What is it, Henning? Why are you asking?'

Bjarne, Henning thought. Bjarne was going to make sure she was protected.

'Nothing,' he said quietly. 'I just wanted … to check. What are you up to?' He changed tack, steering her thoughts elsewhere. 'How are you?'

'I'm tidying a bit,' she said. 'Going through all the baby's clothes I've got. I haven't been able to face it until now. Jonas had so many lovely things.'

Henning closed his eyes. He hadn't been able to look at the things he'd kept after Jonas died either. It was impressive that Nora could now, after everything that had happened.

'Do you remember his little sailor outfit?' she said.

Henning nodded, could hear her smiling at the memory.

'Oh, he was so sweet in that outfit,' Nora continued.

Then she was quiet again, and he heard her sniff.

'It was Iver who prompted me to do it actually. To go through Jonas's clothes.'

'How's that?'

'He'd bought a baby hat just before he died.'

Henning nodded, but wasn't really listening; he was too busy thinking about what he should do about the threat he'd just received.

He swore silently.

'But really, I'm just trying to get time to pass,' Nora said. 'How are you? Where are you? Sounds like you're by the sea.'

'Yes, I…'

He tried to get the right words out.

'Could you do me a favour, Nora?' And then, before she had time to answer: 'Can you go somewhere and lie low for a few days? Without letting anyone know, especially the officers keeping an eye on you?'

Again, there was silence.

'What's going on, Henning?'

'I … don't know,' he said. 'Yet. I don't know.'

He turned around in a full circle. There was something lurking at the back of his mind that he couldn't quite catch.

'You're not making sense, Henning, what's wrong?'

'I haven't got time to explain right now,' he said. 'But can you do it, please? Can you go somewhere else?'

Nora didn't say anything.

'I'm not sure where I could go,' she said. 'It scares me when you say things like that.'

'I can't tell you any more right now,' he said.

'Do you want me to talk to Bjarne?'

'No,' Henning said quickly. 'Don't do that. Just sneak out and go somewhere where no one can find you. If you know of somewhere like that.'

Nora sighed.

'You can't expect me to do that without knowing why, Henning.'

'It's just to be on the safe side,' he said.

'But something must have happened, Henning, I can hear it in your voice. Why can't you just tell me?'

He shook his head, unsure as to whether he should continue or not. He knew how stubborn Nora could be.

'Has someone threatened you?'

He didn't answer.

'Are they threatening you by threatening me?'

Nora, Henning thought and closed his eyes. He should have guessed she'd put two and two together.

'It would seem so,' he said, quietly.

'But … why don't you want me to talk to Bj—' She stopped herself and Henning knew that she'd understood.

'Do you think … he's got something to do with this?'

Henning exhaled heavily.

'I don't know,' he replied. 'I just don't think it's worth taking any chances.'

Neither of them said anything for some time. A gust of wind made the line crackle.

'So, can you do that?' he asked again. 'Can you go somewhere without anyone knowing?'

She sighed.

'I don't know,' she said. 'But I can try.'

The same ferry that had gone out to the islands a little earlier was now on its way back. Bjelland stood up and looked out over the fjord, then at their surroundings. Henning did the same. Saw a woman pushing a buggy along the path, still some way off. She stopped to straighten the baby's hat.

Henning stood there with his phone in his hand and then it struck him. Everything at once, like a torrent in his mind.

'The hat,' he said quietly, to himself.

'What did you say?'

It was Nora who asked.

'You said that Iver bought a baby hat,' he said, 'just before he died. Do you know where he bought it?'

Nora didn't answer straightaway.

'Why are you asking about that, Henning?'

'Please, Nora, just tell me.'

She took a deep breath and then exhaled loudly.

'I've got the receipt here,' she said. 'The shop's called Little and Light, and it's in Tønsberg.'

In Tønsberg.

'He bought it there on Saturday.'

Henning didn't realise that his mouth had fallen open.

Holy shit.

'OK,' he said. 'I've got to go. Can you do what I asked?' he repeated. 'Please go somewhere, so no one knows where you are.'

Nora hesitated before answering: 'I'll do my best.'

Thoughts were bombarding him from every direction.

'But what are you going to do, Henning? If someone is threatening you?'

'I don't know,' he said. 'Just get somewhere safe. I'll call you later.'

Henning ended the call and hurried back to Bjelland.

'I have to run, sorry,' he said. 'Straightaway, I have to check something.'

'But...'

'I'm not quite sure what you and I should do after today,' he interrupted. 'But you kept out of the way last night. Can you do that a little longer? And I'll contact you by email as soon as I've ... I have to check this out *now*.'

Bjelland looked at him, wide-eyed.

'Yes, well ... I guess so,' he said.

'Great. Sorry to rush off like this, but ... I just have to.'

Then he turned and walked as fast as he could back to the car. He wondered what day it was. Thursday, wasn't it?

He got into the car and sped off. He was so deep in his own thoughts that he didn't notice the Lexus that was parked in a side street off the car park, its engine running. Nor did he see the silver grey van that drove into the car park just as he left.

49

Trine stopped in front of the entrance to a building she'd not set foot in since 11 September 2007. She hadn't once thought that she would come back, had never thought there would be a need for her to do so, and certainly not of her own free will.

Well, it wasn't exactly of her own free will.

She didn't have much choice now, it was simply necessary. And it was something she should have done a long time ago.

The keys on her key ring jangled. She couldn't understand why on earth she'd kept her mother's keys there. Perhaps to remind her about what had happened, she thought, as some kind of punishment. It didn't really matter, she was here now and about to go in.

She put the key in the lock and turned it. Opened the door, and as soon as she stepped into the hall, the smell hit her: stale air, cigarette smoke, food and meals that had long since been eaten. Trine took a deep breath and headed towards the stairs, even though her feet were reluctant. She forced herself up the first few steps, and then the rest followed, as though on autopilot. Soon she was at her mother's door.

What will happen when I open the door? she wondered and studied one part of her surname on the nameplate. Trine didn't know how she'd react when faced with the spineless old bat again. What she would think and feel. Fortunately, it was still quite early, so there was less chance of her mother having drowned her sorrows in drink.

Trine rapped on the front door at the same time that she put the key in the lock. Opened it. Went in. Saw the shoes in the hallway, all higgledy-piggledy. The doormat was crooked. The cupboard nearest the door was ajar, full of coats and jackets, an umbrella, more shoes, most of them worn and well used.

'Hello?'

She tried to call, but her voice somehow didn't carry, not properly. So she closed the door behind her and called again, louder this time. A noise from the kitchen made her prick up her ears. The rustling sound of clothes moving. Trine popped her head round the door.

And there she was.

Christine Juul.

She sat there and stared at Trine, her eyes wide and her mouth open. Both her hands on the table in front of her, as though she needed the flats of both of her hands to support her. Before she could say anything, she sobbed and started to cry. Christine Juul rose from the table and stumbled over towards Trine, tears streaming from her eyes.

'Trine,' she said. 'Trine, Trine, darling.'

Again, Trine had no choice; she had to stand there, and accept the full weight of her mother, who weighed little more than fifty kilos, accept the arms that were thrown around her in a tight embrace, hugging, stroking. But Trine couldn't bring herself to reciprocate.

Her mother pushed her away, as if to make sure it was true. Trine watched her face, her wet, searching eyes. She felt a happy sigh on her skin. The smell of the morning after and not enough food.

'Is it really you?'

Trine didn't answer, just felt slightly sick. It was exactly like the last time she'd been there to get Henning's spare key. She'd wandered around the living room, listened to her mother go on and on about her neighbour, the people on the other side of the street, the cars that started too early in the morning, the haulage driver down on the ground floor who always came home late when he had a week off. And then all the questions about her job, how well she knew the prime minister, such a handsome man.

The kitchen was just as she remembered. A small, cramped sofa that no one ever sat on, a corner counter where the radio was playing, newspapers and magazines spread out over the table, empty bottles lined up on the floor, and the washing-up piled high by the sink.

'But sit yourself down, sit down,' her mother said, and pushed passed her, hurried over to the kitchen area and opened the fridge, rummaging for something to eat. But didn't find anything. She opened one of the cupboards instead.

'You don't need to magic something up, Mum. I don't want anything.'

'Of course you'll have something!'

'I'm not going to stay long.'

Christine Juul didn't seem to hear; she opened another cupboard, moved things around.

'Would you like tea or coffee, Trine?'

'Neither, Mum. I…'

'Well, a glass of water, then?'

She turned to look at Trine.

'I don't have any juice, otherwise you could have had some.'

She beamed, revealing her nicotine-stained teeth. The repulsion that Trine felt for her mother rose up with renewed strength.

'Why don't you just sit down, Mum?'

But the woman refused to listen, she opened a drawer, moved a packet of crispbread, some jars of sauce, tins.

'Argh, I can't find it,' she muttered to herself, filling the kettle with water and switching it on. She pulled out her own cup and quickly rinsed it out.

'How lovely,' she said, with her back turned.

Trine said nothing.

'How are you, anyway?' her mother twittered.

'I'm fine, Mum. Thanks. But your son's not doing so well.'

Trine's mother turned round. Her smile looked as though it had frozen on her face. Then slowly it disintegrated.

'And how is that handsome husband of yours?'

Trine sighed. Didn't answer, just waited until her mother had sat down. Which didn't happen until the water had boiled, the tea had been made and two cups had been placed on the table. Christine Juul pushed one of the cups over towards Trine.

'Mum,' Trine started, without taking the cup – she knew she had to swallow the rage that flared up. 'This is the last time we'll see each other.'

Christine Juul's jaw dropped slowly.

'But before I go,' Trine continued. 'I have a couple of questions for you. And you're going to answer them, whether you like it or not.'

50

Pia Nøkleby was reading the preliminary autopsy report for Vanja Kvalheim when Arild Gjerstad, the head of investigations, came into her office.

'Did they find anything in particular?' he asked.

He stood behind her and read over her shoulder.

'She had an abnormal lesion on her neck,' she said. 'A tiny prick on the hairline.'

She turned to him. Gjerstad seemed to know what she was thinking. Tore Pulli had been killed with a piercing needle that had been dipped in a deadly nerve agent, a poison that Ørjan Mjønes had bought in Columbia. It was not unlikely that he'd taken home more than one lethal dose. It was an incredibly quick and efficient way to kill someone, especially if you wanted to avoid any immediate suspicion.

'We'll ask the lab to look for batrachotoxin specifically,' Pia Nøkleby said.

Gjerstad nodded.

'I'll call them straightaway,' he said, and disappeared back into his office.

Pia Nøkleby leaned back in her chair.

Gjerstad had reminded her of something Henning Juul had asked just after Tore Pulli had been killed. If she could find out who Pulli had rung while he was in Oslo Prison. At the time, she hadn't given much thought to Henning's request, in fact, she'd been a little irritated that he was telling her how to do her job.

But Henning thought that Pulli had called someone from the prison, someone he had tried to blackmail into helping him. And the fact that, in the end, Pulli had chosen to ring Henning – a journalist who had been on his back trying to uncover how he earned all his money – showed how desperate he was and that he'd tried every alternative.

So who had Pulli spoken to from prison, other than Henning, his lawyer and his wife?

Nøkleby turned around and pulled out a file that said NORWE-GIAN CORRECTIONAL SERVICE from the shelf behind the desk. Opened it and leafed through the pages, until she came to one that gave contact information. She ran her finger down the page until it stopped at the name Knut Olav Nordbø.

She dialled his number.

'Nordbø, can I help you?'

'Hi, this is Assistant Chief of Police Pia Nøkleby from Oslo Police.'

'Hello.'

'I was just wondering about something. Prisoners' phone logs ... I know that the prison service has access to the logs on an internal computer system, and that the logs are deleted when a prisoner either dies or is released. But do the deleted logs disappear altogether, or would it be possible to access them again if necessary?'

Nordbø's chair creaked.

'Yes, it's possible,' he said. 'But not if it's longer than six months.'

Pia Nøkleby straightened up.

'Is that something *you* could do?'

'No, you'd have to ask the administrator.'

'Could you find out who that is?'

'Yes, it's ... I can do that. But I can't just ask him to call up the files you need. You'll have to...'

'Get a court order, I know, that's not a problem. If you can get the administrator to come to your office, or wherever they can get hold of the data, I'll meet you there.'

There was silence for a moment.

'Time is of the essence, Nordbø, so I'd be grateful if you could prioritise it.'

The chair creaked again.
'There's not a lot going on here today, so…'
'Good,' Pia Nøkleby said. 'See you shortly.'

51

Rasmus Bjelland. Roger Blystad.

He'd got so used to calling himself Roger that it was hard not to, even in his head. But there was no doubt about who he was going to be in the new life he was going to lead, when he was free.

Bjelland waited for ten minutes after Juul had gone, then he walked back. His shoulders felt more relaxed, his step lighter. It had done him good to tell his story, to share the thoughts he'd carried alone for so long. His hope and belief that he could live a normal life again had been renewed.

Juul might be able to help him; perhaps he would manage to expose whoever it was behind all this, and make the accepted truth that Bjelland was an informer disappear forever. The police might also accept that he killed in self-defence. It wasn't a given that he'd end up in jail again, even if he admitted what he'd done.

This normal life would be without Mariana, without his mother, maybe even without Helene, but at least it would be on his own terms. He could try to set up another business, start with small jobs, then slowly build it up, see how things went. In Brandbu or some-where else.

He turned away from the sea and walked along the asphalt path, kicking a fir cone that had fallen from a nearby tree. A man came jogging towards him with white earpieces in his ears. Bjelland kept a keen eye on him as he got closer, but then he ran past, leaving behind a trail of muffled drums, guitars and angry voices.

Bjelland longed to run too, without always feeling that his fate hung heavy on his head, or the knowledge that the next day would be just like the last. He considered taking a little wander around the highly desirable streets of Bygdøy, now that he was out here, but then told himself that it was probably best to keep his movements to a minimum.

Then he heard footsteps behind him and a voice saying 'don't move' in broken Swedish. Bjelland couldn't help himself; he spun round. The man who had spoken was standing there with a gun in his hand, partially hidden inside his jacket.

'Walk towards the car park,' the man in front of him said, but Bjelland's feet had become glued to the ground.

'Who are you?' Bjelland stammered. 'What do you want?'

The man didn't answer.

Bjelland tried to process what was happening. The man in front of him had a similar face to the two who had tried to kill him the day before.

He swallowed.

'I can just as easily shoot you here and now,' the man said. 'Not a problem for me.'

Bjelland looked around for help, but there was no one, no one running, no one walking their dog, no cars.

He took the first steps, heard the man following behind him.

Soon they were at the car park.

'Stop here,' the man said.

Bjelland stopped, continued to look around to see if there was anyone who could help him, anyone he could alert. But he saw no one.

'Hands behind your back.'

Again, Bjelland obeyed. Wrist to wrist. Something hard and sharp was wound around them. Then the man opened the side door of a silver van and indicated with his head that Bjelland should get in. He did as he was told, and sat down on the back seat. The door slammed beside him. The man got into the front.

'Where are we going?' Bjelland asked. 'Who are you?'

'Don't you worry about that,' the man said, catching his eye in the rear-view mirror.

And that was when Bjelland recognised him. He'd seen his face all over the papers in the past few days.

Durim Redzepi.

The man the police thought had killed Iver Gundersen.

The man who had also tried to kill Henning Juul.

Bjelland swallowed and scanned the back of the van to see if there was anything he could use as a weapon. Something to help him cut through the cable ties around his hands. He had to find something, he had to do something. If not, he would die.

∵

Durim Redzepi waited until he was out on the motorway, then dialled the number. It rang for a long time before there was an answer.

'I've got him,' Redzepi said. 'And I've sent the email to Juul, but I don't know if it's enough.'

There was silence for a moment.

'OK,' the man said. 'Take care of Bjelland, and we'll talk again later.'

Redzepi shook his head.

'How do I know you'll keep your word when I've done what you need me to do?' And then he added, before the man could answer: 'I want to meet you. I want to look you in the eye when you tell me what you know about my girls. I'm doing nothing with the carpenter until you promise you'll meet me. And I want my money. What we agreed on the phone earlier today.'

The man at the other end sighed.

'And I want it in euros. Cash.'

This time, the silence lasted for some time.

'OK,' the man said. 'Take Bjelland with you to the cabin. I'll meet you there.'

Redzepi cocked his head. How did the man know about the cabin?

Who cares, he thought, and pulled in behind a taxi in the inside lane.

'And Durim?'

'Yes?'

'Deal with Bjelland before I get there.'

52

Henning knew he was driving faster than he should, but the adrenaline haring round his body made it hard not to.

It all added up.

It all fitted.

And now that he'd warned Nora and seen, via the link that was sent in the email, that she was no longer at home, and had hopefully gone somewhere safe, it was impossible not to follow through the thoughts he'd had when he spoke to her on the phone.

Henning wondered if he should call someone, but the only person he'd had any real contact with in the police was Bjarne, and he didn't know if he could trust him or anyone else in the main station. He could perhaps talk to Pia Nøkleby, but he still needed evidence. And as yet he had no idea how he was going to get it.

Including a stop for petrol, it took Henning just over an hour to drive to Tønsberg. He discovered that Little & Light, the baby clothes shop where Anne Cecilie Hellberg worked, was in the shopping centre next to the Hellberg Property offices. That's handy, he thought, and prayed that no one from the offices would spot him as he drove past and parked.

There was nothing to indicate that anyone had, when he walked into the shopping centre and found Little & Light up on the first floor, beside a flower shop. The shop wasn't big, maybe fifty square metres or so, but it was packed full of clothes for children. Henning felt his stomach knot, knowing what would happen to Nora if he wasn't extremely careful in the next few hours.

Henning couldn't see the woman he'd come to talk to, so he wandered around the shop until another assistant came over and asked if she could help.

'I was looking for a baby hat,' Henning said.

'Yes, they're over here, let me show you.'

He followed her without paying much attention to where they were going, instead looking around. And thinking.

'Was there anything in particular you were after?' asked the blonde woman, who looked like she was in her early twenties.

'Not really,' Henning said. 'But maybe you can help me. A man came in here and bought one on Saturday. Quite tall with shoulder-length messy hair, dark, old corduroy jacket.'

A smile twitched on her lips.

'Oh yes, I remember him.'

Henning could just imagine Iver looking around the shop, smiling at the customers and assistants.

'He was one of Anne Cecilie's customers. They talked for quite some time.'

Henning nodded.

'Is she working today?' he asked. 'She normally works on Thursdays and Saturdays, doesn't she? Would be great if I could talk to her.'

The woman looked at him, then turned and walked towards the till.

'I'll just go and see if she's finished her lunch,' she said.

'Thank you,' Henning replied. 'I'll wait here.'

The woman disappeared into the back room, and after no more than thirty seconds came back. Anne Cecilie Hellberg was right behind her.

She stopped as soon as she saw Henning.

Like the last time, the colour drained from her face, and the friendly saleswoman smile suddenly disappeared.

'Hello again,' Henning said.

He'd picked up a pink baby hat.

'Have you got a couple of minutes?'

Anne Cecilie Hellberg looked at her colleague, who shrugged – he was the only one in the shop, apart from a young couple who were wandering around between the shelves, dreaming of their future.

She came over towards him.

'What are you doing here?' she asked.

Henning scrutinised her hands, her face, her eyes. She was, if possible, even thinner than the last time they'd met.

'Did he buy one like this?'

Henning held up the baby hat.

'Who?'

'Iver Gundersen. My colleague who came here last Saturday. Who was killed the following day.'

She put on a bewildered face.

'Your colleague just told me that he was here,' Henning told her.

Anne Cecilie Hellberg tried to catch the other assistant's eye, but she was busy with the young couple. They were guessing whether it was going to be a boy or a girl; it was easy to see the bulge under the woman's jacket.

'What did he ask you, Anne Cecilie? What did you talk about?'

Again, she avoided his eyes. In fact, she looked as though she might burst into tears. Henning remembered how she'd behaved when he was at their house. At first he'd thought she was ill, because her hands were shaking so badly and she didn't seem to know what to do or say.

Now he understood.

She was afraid.

Nervous.

But why? Because Iver had been there?

'I'd like you to leave,' she said.

Henning shook his head.

'Not before you tell me what you spoke about.'

Once again, she looked over to her colleague for help. Henning positioned himself in front of her, filled her view.

'Why did he come here to talk to you?'

She clutched her own arm, held tight.

'I'm happy to go elsewhere and talk, if that's easier for you.'

Henning tried to look her in the eye, but she kept turning away.

'We could go to the back room, for example.'

He motioned in that direction. Anne Cecilie Hellberg nodded briefly. He let her lead the way. Her legs seemed to be struggling to keep her body upright. She was bent forwards, as though something was pushing her down towards the floor. From behind the counter, they went into a small, cramped room that smelled of old coffee. On the table was a coffee cup, emblazoned with the Hellberg Property logo, and a plastic container with the remains of some salad in it. Anne Cecilie Hellberg sat down on one side of the table, and Henning on the other. He leaned towards her, adjusted his arm in the sling. He looked at her hard, waited for her to start talking.

She folded her hands. Stared at the table.

'Your colleague bought a small white hat,' she said. 'That was how he opened the conversation. He put the hat down on the counter and said, "I'd like this one, please." And then he smiled.'

Henning could picture it clearly. Iver had an easy charm.

'And then he asked if I'd been down to Natal recently.'

She didn't raise her eyes as she spoke.

'At first, I wasn't sure what he meant, so I asked. He said he knew about our flat down there and that it was in my name. Then he asked about a number of other things that were also in my name.'

'What other things?'

She hesitated before saying, 'A luxury boat in France. A foundation in Singapore. Another one in Switzerland. He showed me some printouts he had with him, which confirmed it. I was confused. I knew nothing about it. And told him so.'

'What do you mean?'

'Well, William has always looked after our finances, so I told your colleague that he'd have to talk to my husband.'

Henning watched her while he waited for her to continue.

'Then he looked at me and smiled. And that was it, he thanked me for my help and left.'

Henning studied her; she was sincere, but incredibly nervous. As though she was frightened that he might do something to her.

Anne Cecilie's colleague stuck her head round the door.

'Oh, there you are. Can you mind the till for a while? There's quite a few customers in here now.'

She glanced quickly over at Henning, who nodded curtly. Hellberg hurried out, and Henning sat there alone in silence. He could see it all now; Iver getting straight to the point, as he always did, with the unsuspecting person. He wanted to see her reaction. Wanted to gauge how much she knew.

And he'd got his answer. She'd said he should ask William Hellberg. And Iver already knew that Tore and Charlie had been given help over the years by someone with brains. Someone who knew them and knew the property business. Who knew Daddy Longlegs.

And that was why Iver had gone to Preben Mørck, Henning reasoned. He wanted to confront him, perhaps, to find out if he'd drawn the right conclusions. Get a statement for the article he wanted to write. Make Mørck nervous. Try to get a source that could help him build a comprehensive and detailed case against William Hellberg.

But of course that didn't work; Mørck had just as much to hide as Hellberg. So they made sure that Iver was killed.

A few minutes later Anne Cecilie Hellberg was back. She sat down again. Seemed even more subdued and anaemic than before.

'What did you do after Iver had been here?' Henning asked. 'Did you talk to your husband?'

She fidgeted with her fingertips before she answered.

'He said he'd done it so that he, or rather *we*, wouldn't have to pay so much tax.'

'And no more than a day later, my colleague was dead.'

Henning didn't ask any questions this time, just looked at her. It seemed she was battling hard not to break down.

'What did you think then?'

She didn't answer.

'That it was a coincidence?'

She still didn't react, just twisted her fingers more and more, then started to pick at a splinter on the surface of the table, which she eventually pulled off.

'Let me ask you another question: was your husband at home yesterday evening?'

Anne Cecilie immediately looked up at him. She was about to answer, but then stopped herself. Henning wondered if she knew what he was alluding to, and had decided not to answer in order to protect her husband.

'Preben Mørck was killed last night,' he said.

She lowered her eyes. For a moment, Henning was scared that her colleague would come in and interrupt the conversation, but that didn't happen. Instead, a tear trickled down from the corner of Anne Cecilie's eye.

She looked up at the clock that was hanging on the wall. Dried the tear.

Just then, Henning heard some movement out in the shop. He guessed it was the other assistant coming to ask for more help – after all, it was the middle of the working day – but it wasn't.

It was William Hellberg.

Henning's eyes widened. He turned towards Hellberg's wife. Her eyes were now glued to the floor. And he realised what had happened when Anne Cecilie was out in the shop for a few minutes.

She'd let Hellberg know.

William strode into the cramped room.

'Hello, Henning,' he said, with a great sigh. 'You don't give up, do you?'

Henning couldn't get a word out. He looked at Anne Cecilie Hellberg.

He thought about Nora.

'You were sent an email earlier on today,' William Hellberg said. 'Did you manage to read it before you came here?'

Henning nodded, then lowered his head.

'Please,' he asked in a quiet voice. 'Please don't do anything to her.'

'I have no plans to,' Hellberg said. 'Certainly not right now. But that could easily change.'

'Please,' Henning repeated. 'Don't…'

'You know what has to happen now?' Hellberg asked.

Henning nodded.

Hellberg turned to his wife.

'There's a back exit, isn't there? To save us going through the shop?'

She nodded, almost imperceptibly.

'There's a door further in,' she stammered and pointed towards the back of the room. 'It takes you out the back of the shopping centre.'

Henning didn't follow her finger, he just thought about what might happen now. That this was the end, that there was no escape. He couldn't ring anyone. He couldn't do anything, because then it would affect Nora. Maybe not today, maybe not tomorrow.

But one day.

'So what happens now?' he asked, and looked up.

'Now,' William Hellberg said, 'you and I are going for a drive.'

53

It was a short walk from police headquarters to Oslo Prison. Assistant Chief of Police Pia Nøkleby walked quickly, as she was keen to know what would happen in the next few minutes. Knut Olav Nordbø, who was responsible for communications in the Norwegian Correctional Service, had managed to get hold of an administrator, who was now sitting waiting for her in Nordbø's office, ready to access Tore Pulli's deleted telephone log.

Nordbø met her by the entrance, and they shook hands quickly before rushing in.

'Thank you for managing to do this so fast,' she said.

'My pleasure.'

Nordbø, a man in his mid-forties, stroked his salt-and-pepper beard as they walked down the corridor and tried to find out from Pia Nøkleby what it was all about, but she was evasive and general, giving him the same standard phrases she usually saved for the press.

They got to Nordbø's office, which smelled of a mixture of sweat and burnt coffee. The administrator, a man called Reidar Linnerud, stood up, making his belly quiver under the crumpled polo shirt that was open at the neck. He had a round red face and a sparse amount of hair on his head. Nøkleby guessed he must weigh at least 120 kilos.

They shook hands.

'I recognise you from TV,' Linnerud said. 'Only you're more attractive in real life.'

He grinned.

Nøkleby tried to smile, but didn't quite manage it. Flirting and compliments seldom worked when she was in uniform. It looked as though this had dawned on Linnerud, as he sat down again rather sheepishly. Nordbø's chair creaked.

'So, let's have a look,' he said, and tapped away on the keyboard in front of him. 'It's a good thing you're doing this now. In a couple of months, it will all be gone. Wolf Communications…'

He looked up at her.

'They run the system,' he explained. 'Not exactly the best name in the world, but…'

'Reidar,' Pia Nøkleby said.

'Hm?'

'Tore Pulli. I need to know who he called before he was killed.'

'Ah, yes.'

He slapped his thigh.

'Of course,' he said. 'But what I was going to say is that the way the system works is that the prisoner is given a number so that outsiders, employees at Wolf Communications, for example, can't go in and identify the prisoners. So, everyone gets an account.'

'I see,' Nøkleby said. 'Nordbø, you've given him Pulli's number, haven't you?'

She looked over at him.

'I've found it, yes. You said that getting a court order was just a formality?'

Nøkleby handed him the envelope she had with her. Once Nordbø had inspected the contents, he nodded to Linnerud and passed him a piece of paper.

He took it and immediately started to type the numbers into the computer in front of him. Pia Nøkleby followed intently on the screen, telephone numbers, columns. Just numbers, no names, but she was prepared. She had a list of the telephone numbers of the most relevant people in Tore Pulli's contacts.

She soon recognised Veronica Nansen's number, Pulli's wife. She saw phone numbers belonging to Pulli's lawyer and Henning, but other than those three, there was only one mobile phone number that came up repeatedly in the fortnight before Pulli died. He had called it four times.

Pia Nøkleby got out her own phone and punched the number

into a search engine. The answer made her wrinkle her nose, but at the same time wonder if she'd discovered something crucial.

She turned to Nordbø and Linnerud and said, 'Thank you, boys. You really were a huge help.'

∴

William Hellberg led the way, with Henning just a few steps behind. And Anne Cecilie Hellberg was just behind Henning. The sound of her high heels on the pavement was sharp and hard, and uneven. As though she was on her way home from a long night on the town.

Henning turned briefly towards her. But even now she wouldn't meet his eyes and he had a fairly good idea of what was going on in her head.

He reckoned that deep down, she may well have suspected what her husband had done, but had repressed it, perhaps because she didn't want to face reality. Or didn't dare. Perhaps she was simply trying to protect herself, or her family. They had a son together. How to carry on living with a man she knew had killed other people was perhaps not something she could contemplate right now. Right now, it was simply a matter of dealing with the most immediate problem. In other words, Henning.

Soon they were in the car park by William Hellberg's SUV, which looked like it had come straight from the car wash.

'You're driving, Henning,' Hellberg said.

'Me?'

'Yes. It would be too hard to keep an eye on you if I was driving. I don't think you're stupid enough to try anything, but … you never know.'

Henning saw a bump in his inside pocket. A gun, no doubt. Maybe the one he'd used to kill Preben Mørck.

Henning took the car keys.

'Wh-where are you going?' Anne Cecilie Hellberg asked.

William turned to look at her.

'It's best you don't know,' he said.

She started to cry again.

'Are you…?'

She looked over at Henning.

'Are you…?'

William Hellberg embraced her. 'Go home,' he said. 'Make a nice meal for Oscar, and we'll speak later this evening.'

Then he pushed her away. Smiled tamely and kissed her on the forehead. Before she turned and walked back, she glanced briefly at Henning.

He saw what was in her eyes.

She was asking for forgiveness.

Henning looked up at the sky and filled his lungs, thought he caught a whiff from the canal down by the quay, as though something was rotting. He was absolutely certain that this would be his last day alive.

54

Henning drove as slowly as he could, and registered everything they passed. Dogs on leads on the pavement, children on bikes on their way home from school. A tractor in a field. A cat, back arched, as it snuck up on its prey. An old man who took off his glasses and rubbed his eyes. A young woman out for a walk on her own, who looked like she was singing.

He saw a flock of birds swoop and chase each other to their next meal. There were thin dark streaks across the grey sky, as though someone had painted over it with a coarse brush.

All his senses were sharpened.

He noticed the slightest variation in the car's air conditioning. The smell from an old packet of lozenges. A trace of cigarette smoke. Aftershave. The smell of the fabric of Hellberg's expensive suit.

'Where are we going?' Henning asked, as they drove out of Tønsberg.

'Stick to the main road. I'll tell you when to turn off,' Hellberg said. 'But it's some way yet.'

They drove in silence for a while. The buildings gave way to open fields, empty and sad after the harvest. A Norwegian flag was billowing in the wind outside a farm set back from the road. It made him long to be here. To be allowed to stay here. The feeling took him by surprise.

Hellberg got out his mobile phone and checked for any missed calls and messages. He slipped it back into his pocket and pointed towards the road sign for Oslo. Henning indicated to the right and turned onto the E18 in the direction of the capital.

As he drove, he thought about the man sitting beside him, who for years had helped Tore and Charlie whenever they ran into problems.

And who no doubt had been richly rewarded for his advice and services, money he had invested in boats and foundations around the world. Who preferred to stay out of the limelight, safe behind his family facade.

No doubt it spiced up his life a little, Henning thought, to know that his mind was well-suited to criminal activities, but equally confident that he would never be caught.

'Why did you meet Tore that day?' Henning asked.

Hellberg looked over at him.

'Which day?'

'The day my son died.'

Hellberg turned in his seat, so he was half facing Henning.

'It was you sitting in his car, wasn't it?' Henning continued. 'It was your name in the Indicia report?'

Hellberg didn't respond.

'Come on,' Henning said. 'What does it matter now? I won't be able to tell anyone.'

Hellberg brushed off some dust that had caught on his trouser leg.

'At first I thought it was Preben Mørck who met Tore,' Henning said, when Hellberg remained silent. 'That he was the one who was keen to have his name removed from the report, especially as it was Mørck who hired Ørjan Mjønes to get rid of Tore.'

Henning looked over Hellberg, who was now staring out of the passenger window.

'But Mørck was never anything other than a middleman. Someone who acted on behalf of others.'

Hellberg removed something that had got stuck between his lips.

'Please, Hellberg,' Henning asked. 'You said yourself, we've got a way to drive. It wouldn't hurt to talk a little in the meantime.'

Hellberg looked over at him again. Henning could tell that he was on the right track. Hellberg took a packet of cigarettes out from the inner pocket of his jacket and lit up. Henning tried not to cough.

'I tried to get them to make up again,' Hellberg said.

'Tore and Charlie?'

Hellberg took a drag and nodded.

'The fact they weren't talking wasn't good for any of us. They knew too much about each other. And not least, they knew too much about Preben and myself.'

'So … you took on a kind of mediator role?'

'You could call it that. But they were both stubborn fools. Loose cannons. The number of ridiculous situations they got themselves into, you've no idea.'

He shook his head.

'But then a patrol car was sent out to talk to you and Tore, so your name ended up in an Indicia report.

Henning saw out of the corner of his eye that he nodded.

'And it couldn't stay there. Not after you'd arranged for him to be killed.'

Hellberg suddenly turned and looked at Henning.

'He threatened you, didn't him? From prison?' asked Henning.

Hellberg didn't answer.

'Tore became a desperate man after serving a year and a half for a murder he didn't commit. And apart from Preben Mørck and Charlie Høisæther, there was only one man who knew about your role in what went on in Natal, and everything that happened here in the wake of Bodil Svenkerud's death. And how you threatened my sister.'

Henning could see his conclusions were right.

'Not only that, Tore also knew something crucial about your family. He had, after all, killed someone for your mother. And he knew why she wanted her sister-in-law out of the way.'

Henning thought about the envelope that Tore had kept in his safe, the letter that went a long way to prove that Hellberg Property – of which William was the director – was established with blood money. He might manage to wangle his way out of that, the sins of the father and all that, and maybe even pay a symbolic sum in order to morally redeem himself and the other living members of the Hellberg family. But it might also implicate his mother in an unsolved murder. And Tore knew about Preben's role as middleman.

He knew too much.

So he had to die.

Hellberg took a long drag on his cigarette and then shook his head before blowing out the smoke.

'Tore wanted me to pay for a private investigation into his case,' he said. 'But of course I couldn't do that. It would only lead to a lot of questions.'

He snorted, then sighed, put the cigarette in his mouth while he got out his mobile phone again, checked the screen, then put it back.

'And when Tore got in touch with you – you, who might get him to tell you everything, so you could write about it in your paper – well, there was no going back.'

He took another deep drag on the cigarette.

'But most of all, I was frightened that he would say something about what happened in Natal,' he said, and slowly exhaled. 'That it was my idea to blame Bjelland when the police carried out the major operation against the property sector down there in 2007. Tore's word was still worth a good deal in those circles and there was a risk that any revenge on their part might harm my family. And I couldn't allow that to happen.'

Henning thought about Bjelland and the information he'd given Iver, which led to Iver's murder. Bjelland was still a potential danger for Hellberg, which meant it would be wise not to mention that they'd been in touch.

Had it not been for the display on the dashboard, Henning wouldn't have believed the engine was running, it was so quiet in the car. Like sitting in a machine that hovered over the ground.

Hellberg looked out of the window, cigarette between his fingers, leaning on his elbow against the door.

'So now you've got rid of everyone who might cause you problems,' Henning said. 'Tore, Preben, Charlie. And by this evening, you'll have killed me too. What then?'

Hellberg shrugged.

'You thought you'd just go back to being the good citizen for the rest of your life?'

Hellberg shrugged again.

'Who knows,' he said.

'I don't think you can,' Henning said. 'It's not in your blood. You'll miss solving problems for people, proving to yourself that you've still got the brains. People like you don't change.'

Hellberg laughed, but didn't say anything.

They slipped into silence again. Henning would have preferred to take the back roads where time didn't go so fast, where the lower speed limit would allow him to admire the trees and autumn, where the stones and rock faces would be close enough for him to see the cracks. Jonas always used to point at everything when they were driving and comment on the colours, the cars, the ones that looked like they could go fast.

The thought of Jonas brought him back down to earth.

'Was it your idea to set fire to my flat, too?'

Hellberg turned towards him again, took a last drag on his cigarette, then stumped it out in the ashtray. He opened the window a little, so the sound of the wind filled the car. He closed it again, and immediately there was silence.

'Charlie asked if I had any suggestions,' Hellberg said, but didn't explain. He didn't need to either, Henning understood the rest: Hellberg had come up with a plan, Mørck had hired people who could do the job – as he always had done – while Hellberg himself kept a low profile. Which was why he didn't know the details of what would happen on the street where Henning lived on 11 September 2007. The night Jonas died.

A car sped past to Henning's left. The woman sitting in the passenger seat sent him a long look. She had the same short brown hair as Nora. Henning wondered where she might have gone. What would happen to her after all this?

'There's just one more thing I wonder about,' Henning said.

Hellberg turned his head.

'The day I was shot. It was you who told them, wasn't it? That I was on my way back to Oslo?'

He didn't answer straightaway.

'I'd been to your house, after all,' Henning said. 'You could quite easily have noted what kind of car I was driving, the registration number.'

Hellberg gave a fleeting smile.

'Did you just tell them that I was going to police headquarters?' Henning finished.

Hellberg said, 'I wouldn't have got this far if I didn't have a degree of intuition. You told me that you hadn't shared your theories about Preben with the police yet, so it was only a matter of time before you did.'

Henning nodded, reflected on what lay ahead. A thought struck him: he could drive off the road, into a rock face or an oncoming lorry, then it would be over and done with straightaway. And he'd kill Hellberg, in the bargain. He would get his revenge.

He'd thought about it so many times, about what he would do when confronted with the person responsible for Jonas's death. But now that he was actually here, when he could actually do something to this person, he realised he didn't have it in him. To kill someone. That he wanted to live for as long as possible. He hoped for a miracle.

But he also hoped that death, when it came, would be painless.

That it wouldn't be drawn out.

He didn't know exactly how long they'd been driving, but it had to be close to two hours. They'd driven straight through Oslo and on, east. Hellberg had dialled a number and said they were on their way. There was more and more forest, and fewer and fewer cars. Then Hellberg instructed him to turn onto a forest track.

Immediately, the tyres crunched and Henning drove slowly, as though to delay the inevitable for as long as possible. The sky above them was increasingly drab. It would soon be dark, and the evening would be chilly in the forest.

55

Bjarne was waiting for a phone call when Pia Nøkleby knocked on his office door and came straight in.

'Have you got time for a quick meeting?' she asked.

'Eh ... not really,' Bjarne replied.

Nøkleby took another step into the room, and looked at him expectantly, thinking he would give an explanation. And when he didn't, she said, 'OK, I'll tell you very quickly then, before I brief the others. Tore Pulli was in frequent contact with William Hellberg in the weeks before he was killed. You know who that is, don't you?'

Bjarne nodded and straightened up, ever so slightly.

'Of course, it doesn't need to mean anything, but I think he's someone we should look at more closely,' Pia Nøkleby said. 'Preben Mørck was his lawyer. There must be a connection somewhere.'

There had to be, Bjarne thought.

Nøkleby waited for him to say something, and when he didn't, she added, 'Well, OK, come as soon as you can then.'

Bjarne could see that she was agitated. She always got a flush on her throat when she was tense. She turned on her heel and closed the door behind her.

Bjarne sat there, looking at his phone.

Come on, he thought.

Ring!

∴

The forest made Henning think about another murder case he'd worked on many years ago. A man had been found on a bonfire, killed by his brother-in-law. It was the result of a family feud about who owned what and where. The case had fascinated him, seeing just how little it took for so much to go wrong in a family. A boundary here, a limit there. The man, who eventually confessed to the murder, didn't even like the forest.

Cases, Henning thought.

Crime cases had been his life for so long. He enjoyed meeting people, passing through their lives, winning their trust and their stories, then going back to the office, his fingertips itching with words and sentences. To see the result in the next day's paper or the weekend supplement, spread over five, maybe even six columns, certain that he had touched someone's life, changed something, put the focus on something.

It had been important.

It felt like an eternity since he'd been that person. And it had been a long and painful journey. He was exhausted. Damaged. Tired of the constant pain, tired of the hunt. But he finally found a peace, inside.

There was a time when he'd cultivated that stillness, he'd sought it out. And had only sporadically found it, on the terraces at the Dælenenga football ground or in his own flat. He'd wallowed in the melancholy, stared at the walls, had scarcely put a foot out the door. He hadn't even listened to music.

But he would give anything to be able to do that one more time.

And to see the sea one more time as well. Experience the peace that always filled him when he saw its vast expanse. He would have loved to go out on the water, to fish, watch the sun go down over the horizon, to see the moon rise over the rocks and cast a greenish-white shimmer on the black eternity. He would love to see the stars in the sky, never clearer than at the cottage in Stavern. He would have talked to people, try to get to know them. Would have looked for things that made him laugh. He would have read more books. Drunk ridiculously expensive wines. He would have smoked a cigar, moist and full of flavour. And he would have stared into the flames and seen his own son there, without crying.

'Over there,' Hellberg said, pointing to a red cabin.

Henning was roused from his thoughts. There was a silver-grey van outside.

He accelerated a little; the road was narrow and bumpy, but William Hellberg's big car was easy to steer, even with only one arm. Soon they were in front of the cabin. Henning turned off the engine. Hellberg opened the door as soon as he stopped the engine, and got out. Slammed the door shut. The whole car shuddered.

Henning sat still in the silence for a few seconds.

He wondered if he would fight death when it approached, when the pain started and the seconds ticked by towards that one final destination.

He wondered if he'd be frightened.

If he would cry.

He got out, and breathed in the smell of the forest and the evening, raw and chill. The door to the cabin opened and Redzepi came out. He had a gun in his hand. Henning caught his eye for a moment, but then found his own eyes drawn to the red splashes on his t-shirt. They looked like blood. And his hand was also covered in small red dots – as though something had sprayed him at close quarters. But now he was heading straight for Henning with a determined step.

56

Pia Nøkleby was pleased with the meeting. It had been efficient and quick, and they were already taking action. But it was important not to get William Hellberg in too soon. First they had to understand why Tore Pulli had spoken to him so often on the phone, and what kind of connection they had in the past.

The head of investigations, Arild Gjerstad, had been instructed to ring Tønsberg Police immediately to get all the information they had on Hellberg. They would also check Hellberg's phone log to see who else he'd been in touch with around that time, and who he had been in touch with more recently. But, most of all, they needed to know where Hellberg had been the evening that Preben Mørck was killed, and where he was now.

There was a lot to do all at once, and at the same time the search for Durim Redzepi had intensified. They needed all the hands they could get, so Pia Nøkleby knocked on Bjarne Brogeland's door again and walked in without waiting.

But he wasn't there.

Nøkleby turned and went out into the corridor, spotted Ella Sandland going into her office and called to her, then hurried to catch up.

'What is it?' Sandland asked.

'Have you seen Bjarne?'

Sandland shook her head.

'Have you tried calling him?' she asked.

'No, but he was in his office not long ago, busy with something, and he was supposed to come to a meeting when he was done.'

Sandland shrugged.

'I've no idea what he's up to.'

∴

Henning half expected Durim Redzepi to aim and shoot him down, but it didn't happen. Instead, he stopped in front of them.

'Hello Durim,' Henning said. 'Nice to see you again.'

Redzepi didn't answer. He looked over at Hellberg and said: 'Have you got the money?'

'It's in the car,' Hellberg said.

'Get it.'

Hellberg hesitated a moment. Redzepi made a movement with the gun, in the direction of the car.

'OK, relax,' Hellberg said. 'I'll get it.'

Hellberg turned and went back to the car. Henning quickly understood the relationship between Hellberg and Redzepi. Non-existent, until Preben Mørck – Daddy Longlegs – had to die. Henning wondered if he could exploit that in some way. Draw out the time he had before the inevitable.

Hellberg opened the boot and got out a small, black sports bag. It wasn't long before he was back.

'Do you want to count it?'

Redzepi seemed to consider it.

'I don't think you're dumb enough to try it on,' he said. 'Not now that I've seen your face. But I was starting to wonder; it took you so long to get here.'

Hellberg pointed to Henning.

'This man here suddenly showed up out of the blue. Handy for us, as we don't need to keep looking for him or wonder if he's finally called it a day.'

Hellberg threw the bag down at Redzepi's feet.

'You should be grateful. You don't need to hang around here any longer than necessary now.'

Redzepi glared at him.

'Where's Bjelland?' Hellberg asked.

Henning turned quickly towards him.

Bjelland?

Hellberg made an 'I didn't have any choice' movement with his hands.

'He's lying in the boat,' Redzepi said.

Henning turned and peered through the trees. Saw there was a lake nearby. He studied Redzepi's hand again. The red spots. The splashes on his t-shirt.

He closed his eyes, recalling what he'd said to Bjelland not long ago. 'Right now, people around me have a tendency to end up dead'.

'There was quite a mess,' Redzepi said. 'And I'd already cleaned the whole cabin. There's no way I'm doing that again.'

'So what are you thinking? To kill him out here?'

Hellberg nodded towards Henning.

'No,' Redzepi said. 'He can come out in the boat. Less to wash. I've been here too long, I want to leave as soon as I can.'

Henning opened his eyes.

'You know it'll be you next,' he said to Redzepi.

Redzepi squinted at him.

'Afterwards, when you're done here. You're the only one who's seen Hellberg's face and knows that he's behind it all. You've worked for Ørjan Mjønes; you've worked for Preben Mørck, or rather, Daddy Longlegs, as you probably knew him. You know a lot about most of them. But this guy,' Henning said, and nodded in Hellberg's direction, 'he's made sure that anyone who can identify him is killed. So why would he suddenly spare *you*?'

Redzepi glanced over at Hellberg.

'And do you think he'll just let you go with all that money?'

Henning pointed at the sports bag.

'He lives for his money,' Henning said. 'And he'll do everything he can to protect his family.'

'I have no interest whatsoever in harming you, Redzepi.' Hellberg had adopted his salesman face and calm reassuring voice. 'He's just trying to make you uncertain,' he continued. 'But there's no need to worry. As soon as we're done here, I'm going home. Then it's all over, and you can leave … go wherever you want.'

He threw open his arms.

'He's got a gun in his inner pocket,' Henning said to Redzepi. 'Why do you think he's got that with him?'

'That was for you,' Hellberg said to Henning. 'In case you didn't want to come of your own free will.'

'Do you dare take the chance that he's a man of his word?' Henning said to Redzepi. 'Do you dare take the chance that he's not going to turn his gun on you?'

Henning shook his head.

'I certainly wouldn't.'

Henning could see that he'd made Redzepi doubt. But he was still the one holding a gun.

'You mentioned a boat,' Henning carried on. 'Is it big enough for all four of us? Is Hellberg coming with us, too?'

He could see Redzepi's mind working overtime.

'I'll wait here until you're back,' Hellberg assured him. 'You don't need to worry.'

'There's no reason for him to wait once you've rowed us out onto the lake.'

Redzepi looked at Hellberg.

'I don't know you,' the Kosovo-Albanian said. 'I don't have any guarantee that you'll wait.'

Hellberg sighed.

'I realise it might all seem a bit suspect, but...'

'Give me your gun,' Redzepi said, aggressively. 'Come on, give it to me. *Now.*'

Hellberg gave him an exasperated look, before he reluctantly did as he'd been told. He made quite a show of putting it down on the ground and then standing up slowly with his hands raised, Redzepi moved over and picked up the gun. Put it in the sports bag.

'You're coming with us down to the lake,' Redzepi said, glaring at Hellberg. 'There's not enough room on the boat, but you'll wait down there.'

'You decide. But could we step on it, please? It's starting to get dark and I'd like to get home while there's some of the evening left.'

Redzepi looked at Henning, indicating that he should move.

'Where?' Henning said, playing stupid.

'There,' Redzepi said, and pointed to the lake. 'And fast.'

Henning nearly stumbled on a root that had grown over the path. Hellberg was behind him, with Redzepi bringing up the rear. In front of them, the black water glittered. He heard an owl. Was it an eagle owl?

It was colder now.

It didn't take long for them to reach the edge of the lake. A boat had been pulled up on the shore. There was a big, black oblong package already in it.

'Sit there,' Redzepi said to Hellberg, and pointed at a tree nearby.

'Honestly, Redz, I…'

'I don't give a shit what you say. It'll take ten minutes to row out to the middle of the lake and back. And ten minutes is more than enough time for you to get away from here. So sit next to that tree over there.'

Redzepi went over to the boat, picked up a knife that was lying there, and cut a two-metre length of rope. He was on his way back to Hellberg when he stopped in his tracks.

'What is it?' Hellberg asked.

'I thought I heard something,' Redzepi said.

None of them moved. They all listened. There was silence.

'What did you hear?' Hellberg asked.

'Don't know,' Redzepi said, but Henning could see that he was unsettled, on his guard. He listened again. Heard nothing.

For a brief moment, Henning hoped it was Bjarne, that he had somehow managed to find them, but he immediately dismissed the thought as ridiculous. He wondered if any of this could have been different if he'd let Bjarne know, told him en route that he was on his way to talk to Anne Cecilie Hellberg.

Maybe.

Maybe not.

Nora would still be under threat and William Hellberg would still be Durim Redzepi's employer. If Hellberg had been caught earlier, and if he'd been sentenced, he might still have been able to get to Nora from prison, through Redzepi. He could have made his threat good from there, as some kind of revenge or punishment. But now there was no reason for Hellberg to go after Nora. She could no longer be used as leverage to get to Henning. She was safe. The child was safe. That's all that mattered to him.

Redzepi grabbed Hellberg's arm and pulled him over to the tree. Forced him to sit down.

'Is this really necessary, Redzepi?'

Hellberg was breathing fast and hard, and seemed to hate the fact that his suit was becoming damp and dirty.

'Yes. Hands behind your back.'

Hellberg rolled his eyes.

Redzepi tied him to the tree, then straightened up. Looked around, in among the trees. Listened.

He looked at Henning and nodded towards the boat. Henning took the first hesitant step. A good thing Bjelland's body hadn't started to smell yet, he thought.

The boat rocked when Henning got in. He turned towards Hellberg, kept an eye on him all the time, even when Redzepi put one foot in the boat and used the other to push off from the shore.

They slid out onto the lake. The water rippled along the bow, making a sucking, lapping sound.

My last journey, Henning thought, and noticed a mist drifting in over the silent, dark water.

Redzepi sat down in the middle of the boat and grabbed the oars. Then he started to row.

57

Bjarne drove as fast as he could, out of town, unsure if the car would take the strain. It was a while since it had been serviced, and he'd noticed that the engine had been making some funny noises recently. Luckily, the worst of the rush hour was over, and the cars pulled obediently onto the hard shoulder when he flashed his lights and tooted the horn. And if there was a queue, the siren always came in handy.

His phone rang. It was Pia Nøkleby.

'Hi Bjarne,' she said. 'Where are you? What are you up to?'

Bjarne explained the situation and why he'd had to make such a hasty exit.

'OK,' she said. 'Just don't do anything stupid before we get there.'

A tractor appeared on the road in front of him. Because there were other cars around, he had to slow down and weave between the vehicles that were trying to get out of his way. The loss of those few minutes frustrated him.

'I don't think there's time to wait for you,' he said.

'Do what you think is best,' Nøkleby said. 'Where are you?'

'Just turned off at Grønmo.'

'OK. Good luck.'

'Thank you.'

Bjarned accelerated again as he zoomed the GPS down to five hundred metres, and saw on the map there were small roads and lakes everywhere. Ideal if you wanted to get rid of someone.

He was on Highway 155. Trees in every direction. Because he was driving so quickly, it felt like he was encapsulated, as though the forest around him was a narrow tunnel with high walls.

Ten minutes later he studied the map again and saw a small side road a few hundred metres in front of him. He slowed down and turned off. The car was immediately swallowed by the trees, and the headlamps shone between the trunks and branches. He turned them off. Drove a little further. Stopped. Saw a cabin about two hundred metres away on his right. There were two cars outside. One was a silver van, the other a black SUV. The lights were on in the cabin.

Bjarne took some binoculars from the glove compartment, adjusted the focus and looked at the cars. He turned off the engine, hurried round to the back of his car and opened his gun case. He ran down the gravel without closing the case or the boot. He didn't notice that he passed another car, a Lexus, hidden behind some trees nearby.

∵

Durim Redzepi watched Henning Juul sink down into the water.

He waited for about thirty seconds, then he put the oars back in the locks, backed away, then turned the boat round and headed towards the shore. The mist lay thick on the surface now, so he couldn't see further than ten metres ahead. The only sound he could hear was the oars in the water, the water dripping off, interwoven with his own breathing, which was fast, but easy.

He stopped rowing, sure that he'd heard something. From the water. He peered into thick mist, but saw nothing. He couldn't hear anything but the sound of the boat gliding through the dark, cold water.

Death cramps, he thought. Air bubbles.

He carried on towards the shore and before long he could see William Hellberg.

'I see that went OK,' Hellberg shouted, with a satisfied nod.

Redzepi didn't answer, but steered the boat into the spot where he'd left it before, let the speed of the boat carry it the final stretch. There was a scraping under the hull. He pushed one of the oars to the bottom and felt the mud give way, but it was still firm enough to get the boat up onto land. Suddenly the boat came to a halt and he could get out. He didn't bother to pull it up any further.

He stumbled up the path to Hellberg and loosened the rope.

'Now I've kept my side of the deal,' he said. 'Where are my wife and daughter? Where are Svetlana and Doruntina?'

Hellberg stood up and assessed the damage to his suit, brushed off some leaves and grass, and smoothed the trouser legs.

'Shall we go back to the cabin?' he suggested.

'No,' Redzepi said. 'Here and now. I've waited long enough. Done more than enough shit for you to tell me what you know about my girls.'

He pulled out the gun and aimed at Hellberg.

'Take it easy,' Hellberg said, with a sigh. 'I'll tell you what you want to know. But I'm not actually sure that you really want to know the truth.'

Redzepi squinted at him. Hellberg got the packet of cigarettes from his inner pocket and lit one. He offered one to Redzepi, but he just shook his head.

'Your brother,' Hellberg said, drawing the nicotine down into his lungs, 'he's not a good person.'

Redzepi frowned.

'As I said to you on the phone, we checked what he had actually done with the money you'd sent him. And do you know what Daddy Longlegs found out?'

Redzepi just stared at him and waited for the answer.

'Do you know what your brother's been doing?'

Hellberg took another drag.

'Nothing, Durim. Absolutely nothing.'

Redzepi didn't know what to say.

'There are two possible explanations,' Hellberg said, and started to walk towards the cars and the cabin. 'Either he can't be bothered to look for them but is quite happy for you to send him money all the time – after all, he knows that you can't go back because you're wanted for double murder.'

He gesticulated as he walked. Redzepi followed behind him.

'Or it could be that he's found them, but doesn't think there's any point in telling you – for the same reason. He likes you sending him money. But, Daddy Longlegs's man never established whether he'd found them or not.'

Redzepi blinked furiously as he considered what he'd just heard. For so many years he'd prepared himself to hear that they were dead. That was the conclusion he'd come to himself. But he hadn't been prepared for this.

Not at all.

The next moment a branch cracked right beside them.

'Stay where you are, both of you,' a loud voice shouted.

Redzepi turned his head towards the trees and saw a dark shape step out on the right, just ahead of them. Redzepi could only see the outline of his body and that he was holding something in his hands.

'Put down the gun.'

The voice was clear.

Redzepi's instincts screamed: do something, before it's too late. Shoot – it was two against one, it might work. But the man in front of him was a policeman, and he had a gun in his hands that was pointing straight at Redzepi's chest. He wouldn't have time to do anything. And presumably the policeman had let others know where he was. So more were on their way.

Redzepi thought about his brother. If he was ever to see him again, if he was ever finally to find out what happened to Svetlana and Doruntina, he couldn't chance a shoot-out. He had to play the long game. He was still in his forties, would have plenty of time when he got out of prison. Years that he could dedicate to making his brother's life hell.

Redzepi sank to his knees and dropped the gun. The policeman was quick to move and kicked it away from him.

'Where's Henning?' he asked.

Redzepi felt the handcuffs close around his wrists. The policeman looked around.

Neither Hellberg nor Redzepi answered.

'Where's Henning Juul?'

The policeman stood up.

'Henning?'

The frantic cry disappeared over the water and was soon swallowed by the mist. The man shaded his eyes with both hands and looked from side to side.

Redzepi turned towards the blue flashing light that looked like it was dancing among the trees. It was only a matter of minutes before the place would be crawling with cars, and men and women in uniform.

'Where's Henning?' the policeman shouted again, looking at Redzepi, then Hellberg.

Neither of them answered.

A film seemed to fall over Hellberg's face, like a mask. The policeman bent down over Redzepi and shook him.

'Where is he? Where is Henning Juul?'

Redzepi took a deep breath.

Then he turned his head towards the lake.

'He's out there,' he said. 'He died about ten minutes ago.'

Epilogue
Eight days later

Ullensaker Church was a little over half full.

Trine had perhaps expected there to be a bit more fuss, maybe some media, but it suited her fine; she couldn't face any more than was necessary. She didn't know how long she would need to come to terms with everything that had happened. Perhaps she never would.

Pål Fredrik took her arm and tucked it in his, pulled her closer. They were sitting at the front on the left bank of pews. The coffin was in front of them, up by the altar, covered in beautiful flowers. Every now and then she turned to see who had come in. Recognised some faces she'd known when she was a girl. Some were crying. Others talking quietly, as the organist played a slow tune.

Henning would have liked that tune, Trine thought, and a memory from their childhood popped up: the funeral of Leonid Brezhnev, president of the USSR, which was shown on Norwegian television in the eighties. Henning was lying on his stomach under the coffee table listening to the music, and afterwards he said that the intense, sad melodies had filled his body with stillness, in a good way.

Trine saw Katarina Hatlem come up the aisle. She pushed back her long, curly red locks and looked at Trine with a small sympathetic smile. Trine stood up, waved to her former communications director to come to the front. Hatlem hesitated before saying something quickly to the man she'd come with, and then came forward. Trine stepped into the aisle with open arms.

'My condolences,' Katarina whispered.

'Thank you,' Trine said, and smiled. 'And thank you for coming. Let's talk again afterwards?'

Katarina smiled.

Then she turned and went back.

Trine spotted Nora Klemetsen, who had come alone. Trine wanted to go over and hug her as well, but had to make do with a nod as the organ stopped playing. She caught a glimpse of Bjarne Brogeland too, who had been so in love with her when they were younger. She'd spoken to him a lot over the last few days.

The church bells rang. Trine sat down again and folded her hands, something she never usually did. The bells clanged in her head and then a compact silence sank over the congregation.

The priest came in, and walked straight to her and Pål Fredrik. Shook her hand first. He said nothing, but his hands and his eyes expressed his sympathy.

He was a good man, a fine priest. He had talked with such warmth when he came to see them, all the way out to Ullern, even though it was well outside his parish. He drank his coffee and listened with interested eyes. Hadn't asked any sensitive questions. And he'd quietly taken notes.

The priest stood in the pulpit and looked out at the congregation. Trine knew she would block out everything he said. She would sing the songs, as best she could, she would listen to the man playing 'Clair de Lune' on the piano, and would nod and say thank you, and accept the hugs and words of comfort offered outside the church afterwards.

The funeral service lasted for forty-five minutes, but it felt like hours. On the way out, she walked behind Pål Fredrik and the other coffin bearers. Fortunately, it was a beautiful autumn day. On the horizon, a plane was coming in to land on the runway at Gardermoen. The hills were full of colour and blazed in a way they only did in autumn. Red and green and yellow, all mixed together.

Trine put on her sunglasses, grateful to be able to hide her eyes. But still she kept them on the ground and concentrated on not stepping on heels in front of her.

Soon they stopped. People gathered around the grave. The white coffin was lowered onto a platform that would then be lowered further into the ground. The priest stood beside it and finished the service with a final hymn, then threw on the earth. Some people went forward and laid red roses on the coffin. Then it was lowered into the ground, after which people started to murmur and crowd around Trine and Pål Fredrik.

It was while she was embracing someone she'd never met before that she saw him up on the path between the gravestones. He was standing with his hands in his pockets beside Bjarne Brogeland, looking down at them. It felt as though he was looking straight at her, and maybe he was.

Trine let go of the woman, who was replaced by a man with a scratchy beard, but she didn't hear what he said, just said thank you and kind of you to come.

Henning stood on the path, in a dark suit and sunglasses, and then he started to walk towards them, slowly, as though with dread, his arm in a sling. Some people made their way to him and shook his hand. He nodded, and she heard him say thank you.

It took another fifteen minutes, perhaps, until people started to drift way, relieved to be able to return to their lives. Trine stood by the grave, which would be covered in earth by the end of the day. She turned towards Henning, who was standing a few metres away, beside Nora Klemetsen.

There was no trace of grief in his eyes; they were just dull, as if he had no energy left. She felt sad, not because both their parents were now dead, but because neither of them had a family of their own. Not a whole one. She had denied Pål Henrik a family, and was in part responsible for Henning losing his.

She went over to him.

'Hello Henning,' she said.

'Hi Trine,' he replied.

'How…'

She couldn't say the rest.

'I'm fine,' he said. 'How are you?'

Trine opened her hands in a kind of shrug and tried to smile.

'I don't quite know what to say.'

She turned towards the grave.

'I didn't see you in the church,' Trine said, turning back to him.

Henning said, 'No, I don't cope very well with that kind of thing after…'

He glanced over at Nora, before lowering his eyes.

Trine hadn't gone to Iver Gundersen's funeral, which she knew had been held a few days earlier. She presumed that Henning had been there, but possibly in much the same way as today; that he'd stayed in the background.

The policeman who found Christine Juul said that she was lying on the floor beside the oxygen therapy stand, with the mask in her hands. It seemed likely that she hadn't been able to turn it on. She was drunk. She had died the same day that Trine had been there, and so she felt she was to blame, given what they'd discussed.

'Henning, I have to talk to you,' she said.

'It was you,' he said.

'Sorry?'

'Who paid the people to follow me,' he continued. 'To protect me. The ones in the Lexus.'

Trine lowered her head and found a patch of ground to focus on.

'Bjarne told me,' he said. 'That you both agreed on it. Before he helped me leave the hospital the evening after I'd been shot.'

Trine could feel his eyes; it was as though they were boring straight into her head.

'They were following me when I passed out outside Ann-Mari Sara's house that evening. It was them who drove me to hospital.'

Trine felt a tear falling.

'So Bjarne told you everything then?' she asked.

He nodded.

They had kept an eye on him since he discharged himself from hospital. They'd followed him to Huk, where he met Rasmus Bjelland. Followed him to Tønsberg, where they saw Henning getting into a black SUV, which they followed to the holiday cabin not far from Ytre Enebakk. And they'd let Bjarne know en route.

Trine had read the interviews with Henning afterwards, knew that he had at first accepted his fate, that he had sunk deeper and deeper into the dark water, waiting to die. But even people who have decided to commit suicide often end up fighting with the rope they've tied round their neck, and something similar had happened to Henning, far under the water.

As his oxygen ran out, his survival instinct kicked in, and he'd tried to push himself up towards the surface.

He wasn't able to, so instead he thought about getting to the shore. It was some way off, thirty metres or so, but it would be easier to pull the weight along behind him than up. He'd kicked and struggled, even though he knew that Durim Redzepi would probably kill him if he managed to get there. But then, at least, it would be a different death.

Then suddenly there was light all around him, beams moving across the murky water, and he had seen shapes, waving arms, and he hadn't understood until some strong hands grabbed hold of him and pulled him up. Towards the surface.

Trine's former bodyguards did not have guns, but they had kept themselves out of sight, and on a couple of occasions had been certain that Durim Redzepi had either seen or heard them. They had moved stealthily through the woods and had seen what was about to happen, so they'd entered the water as quietly as they could. Under the cover of the thickening mist, they swam towards the boat, slowly and largely underwater, and then, when Durim Redzepi was on his way back towards the shore, they dove under and found Henning.

One of the bodyguards who was interviewed later said that it wasn't a particularly deep lake and Henning had been underwater for less than a minute and half before they managed to get him to the surface.

They were frightened of making too much noise, but Redzepi hadn't been able to see them through the mist. He'd heard something, he said, when he was being questioned by Bjarne later, but hadn't turned to check; his main concern was to get away.

Henning took a step closer to Trine.

'You saved my life,' he said.

Trine stood silently, just looking at him.

Then she sobbed.

'It wasn't m…'

'Yes, it was,' he said. 'It was you who saved me. Thank you.'

Trine's eyes filled up, and she struggled to regain her composure.

'But that wasn't what I wanted to tell you,' she said with a sniff.

Henning looked at her, puzzled.

'And I could probably have found a better time to tell you,' she said, 'but in many ways, it seems right to do it here. In front of them.'

She pointed to the open grave and the gravestone alongside it, then gave a sign to Pål Fredrik, who immediately suggested to Nora that they should leave and let brother and sister speak in private.

'Will you wait for me up there?' Henning asked, and looked at Nora.

She nodded.

And then there was only Henning and Trine. She took a few steps towards the grave. Stopped in front of the hole where her mother's coffin lay, beside their father.

Jakob.

Died at the age of 44, eternally loved and worshipped by his wife, who, after his death, never stopped hating the realities of life, the fact that she was a widow and that, in her eyes, it was Henning's fault.

Trine hadn't managed to talk or think the morning after their father had committed suicide. It didn't help that their mother just screamed and screamed and screamed, and in the days and weeks that followed, seemed to take up all the space.

But even she, deep down, must have known what her husband had done with Henning. Fortunately not *to* Henning, which explained why Henning himself didn't seem to know anything. His father had just sat there in Henning's room, looking at him, when he thought that everyone else in the house was asleep. Sometimes with the duvet on, sometimes with it off.

Trine had been woken up one night by the sounds coming from Henning's room. She'd tiptoed out into the hall, towards the light and sounds. She'd peeked round the door and seen her father sitting there, eyes closed, with his trousers off.

Trine had stood there, transfixed by the fast hand movements, the half-open mouth, the closed eyes.

But then the floor creaked underneath her.

She hadn't been able to stand still, hadn't been about to tiptoe back either, and when her father snapped out of his trance, he'd pulled on his trousers and run after her. Trine had managed to get into her room and lock the door before he reached her.

She'd sunk to the floor with her back to the door and cried, while her father had begged her, as loudly as he dared, in order not to wake the rest of the house, to open up. But Trine hadn't opened the door until late the next day, long after he'd gone to work.

In the afternoon, when she got home from school, she'd made sure she was never alone with him. And Jakob was silent; he hadn't spoken to Henning, or to his wife. It was like being in a dead house.

Then one day, Jakob ambushed her. He hadn't gone to work. Instead he was waiting for her in the garage where she kept her bike.

'Trine,' he said. 'We have to talk.'

Trine didn't answer.

'I've never laid a hand on Henning. I've never done anything to him.'

Still she didn't answer.

'Please, Trine, you have to believe me.'

And then he had tried to make light of what he'd done. He knew that it was wrong, that he should never had done it, but in his eyes, it hadn't hurt Henning in any way, because he didn't know.

Jakob Juul had stood there with tears streaming down his cheeks; he'd shaken his head and mumbled that their mother didn't understand, that she'd always been so jealous of Henning because Jakob loved him more than he loved her. She'd told him, many times, but she didn't know the ways in which it had manifested itself. It would devastate her, he said, if she discovered what he'd done. And he would be a social pariah, everywhere, if the truth were to get out.

Trine had just stood there, looking at him. He'd realised that she would never let him get away with it, and that no doubt was why he'd taken an overdose of insulin one evening, after everyone else had gone to bed.

Trine believed that her mother knew, deep down. And that was what she had confronted her with on the last day she was alive.

∵

Henning looked as his father's gravestone as he tried to process what Trine had just told him. It should, perhaps, have hurt; he should, perhaps, have been disgusted, but he was neither.

He felt ... nothing.

It was as though it was all part of someone else's life, perhaps because it happened so long ago, and because he had so few memories of his father.

He looked at the open grave. The coffin, beautiful and white, was covered by a thin layer of earth. A few roses had fallen off the coffin and now lay on the ground by the grave. He wondered which way she was lying.

He thought about the way his mother had always looked at him, accusingly. Her breathing, always strained. Hard as he tried, he couldn't remember what she looked like when she smiled. They should really raise a glass of St Hallvard liqueur, he thought, in honour of the poor soul who had been their mother, but it was hardly appropriate in a graveyard. Perhaps Trine had bought a few bottles for the reception.

He offered her his good arm, as they started to walk up towards the car park. She took it, and they walked in silence between the gravestones.

Nora and Pål Fredrik were waiting for them by the cars.

'I won't be coming to the reception,' Henning said to Trine.

'No, I guessed that you wouldn't,' she said, with a careful smile.

They stood there looking at each other. An airplane thundered overhead as it ascended into the sky. Trine took a step towards him and opened her arms. Henning let her in.

It felt so strange to hug his own sister again. It must have been at least twenty years since they last hugged. But she had protected him for so many years, held the truth inside. The fact that they hadn't had much contact was perhaps Trine's way of protecting herself as well, so she wouldn't be reminded of what had happened.

Trine pulled away from him and dried a tear. Took a step back, and then another. Then she lifted her hand in a brief wave.

'Goodbye,' she said.

He lifted his hand, too.

'Bye.'

Henning and Nora stayed by the cars and watched Trine and Pål Fredrik drive off.

'Was it OK?' Nora asked.

Henning turned to her.

'Hm?'

'Your little chat?'

She nodded down to towards the grave.

'Oh yes,' Henning said. 'Yes, that … fine. In a way.'

Nora pulled her dark-grey coat tighter around her. As always, her cheeks were rosy after being out in the autumn air. And her lips were dry.

They stood there and listened to the silence.

'So, what happens now?' she asked.

Henning took a deep breath.

'Durim Redzepi's behaviour during questioning has been exemplary,' he said. 'I think he's doing everything he can to get a good deal. Which of course has made it harder for William Hellberg and Ørjan Mjønes. Redzepi's got a lot of key information on them all.'

He shrugged, and winced at the pain in his shoulder.

'I meant with you,' Nora said. 'What happens with you?'

Henning looked at her for a long time.

'I don't know, Nora.'

The sun went behind a cloud and it got colder straightaway. Nora put a hand on her stomach, and tried hard not to pull a face.

'Is it…?'

Henning pointed to her stomach.

'I just feel a bit sick,' she said.

He nodded.

'Would you like a lift home?'

She shook her head and pointed to a car that was parked a bit further along. They stood looking at each other for some time. Both thinking about that other grave, back in Oslo.

'OK,' he said, eventually. 'Well, see you around then. And thank you for coming.'

∴

Henning had spent the first few days after he'd been fished out of the water at home in his own bed. He'd slept. Eaten. Slept again. He'd had a cup of tea with his old neighbour, Gunnar Goma, who'd recently had a heart operation. And Gunnar had told him about the war, about all the ladies he'd known, about all the cafés he still frequented in Grünerløkka, always with nitroglycerin in one pocket and a tooth guard in the other – ready to defend a damsel in distress. Henning had smiled and wondered what he would be like when he was old.

He'd bought himself a wok and finally started to use the gas cooker that had stood unused for as long as he'd lived in the flat. For a long time, he'd had an issue with flames. He'd stir-fried meat, chicken and vegetables – he'd even used his wok for fish.

He'd gone for walks.

He thought. About Iver and about Jonas. About Trine.

About what he would do now.

But there was one thing he still hadn't done, something that he both looked forward to and dreaded. Which was why he decided to do it as soon as he got home from the funeral.

First he went and bought a bottle of cognac – the kind that he'd been drinking on the evening Jonas died. When he got home, he opened the bottle and poured himself a generous glass, and put it down on top of the piano. He lit a candle and sat down.

Before he opened the lid and looked at his old friends, black and white, 88 in total, he closed his eyes and sang the tune in his head, the song he'd written for Jonas the night that Nora had told him she was pregnant.

The night when his whole world changed and nothing would ever be the same again.

Henning looked at the glass, the light, the wall the piano stood against. He savoured a mouthful, swallowed, felt it burn down his throat, into his chest, forced himself to put his lips to the glass again. Swallowed. Thought. Closed his eyes and contemplated some more. Everything that lay behind him, ahead of him.

In front of him.

He put down the glass and looked at the places on his hands where the flames had got him and melted his skin like plastic. The scars had started to fade.

He wondered what he was going to do with those hands. They were scarred now. Damaged.

But they still worked, he thought.

They could still play a melody.

'Lullaby',

an original piece for piano, composed and performed by Thomas Enger for Henning's son, Jonas, is available to listen to here: https://soundcloud.com/thomasenger/lullaby.

Acknowledgements

I have spent six years of my life writing the Henning Juul series. Six years that, in many ways, have changed my life, not just my hair (yep, it's got greyer and thinner). It has been a long and strenuous journey, and I would never have reached my destination without help. A huge thanks to Kari Marstein and Trude Rønnestad for all the meetings, emails, thoughts and input, not to mention support. This is also true of my Norwegian publisher, Gyldendal. Thanks for everything. Thank you for giving my dreams wings.

Thanks also to everyone who, over the course of these five books, has answered the questions I have had, big or small. I am so grateful for your help.

A special thank-you to all you lovely translators and publishers out there, around the world who have helped the Henning Juul series reach even more readers. It has been, and still is, a joy, a privilege and an honour to represent you, and to be represented by you.

As this is an English edition I would like to pay special tribute to Kari Dickson for doing such an excellent translation, to West Camel, for taking such good care of the end product, and to Mark Swan for designing one of the most gorgeous cover jackets. I'm going to frame it and put it up on my wall.

This book would not have seen the English light of day had it not been for Karen Sullivan. Karen, you truly are one of a kind. Not only are you every author's dream publisher, you're also a brilliant editor, amazingly kind and generous, and you're super-duper company as well. Thanks for making me part of Team Orenda. I love all you lovely people.

Anyone who subjects themselves to the mental rigour required to write a book (try five, which all have to correspond) is dependent on the people who cheer them on. I am fortunate enough to have had many, many people along the way. Thank you for all the emails with kind words and smileys. Thank you for asking when the next book will be published. Thank you for all your good wishes.

My greatest thanks go to my family – Benedicte, Theodor and Henny – for putting up with me throughout these years.

Thomas Enger
Oslo, December 2017

THOMAS
ENGER

What secret
would you kill
to protect?

'One of the most unusual and
intense talents in the field'
Barry Forshaw,
Independent

'Outstanding'
Ragnar Jónasson

CURSED

A **HENNING JUUL** NOVEL